THE DRAGON LEGION

Book One Of The Sunborn Series

Isaac Hill

CONTENTS

DEDICATION

For EE Hill

PROLOGUE

"**S**hip to port, Captain!" the lookout above them shouted from the crow's nest.

"Aye! First mate, lower lines!" El Alera called out.

The wind howled across the deck of the ship, the cold cutting through clothes and chilling the men of the *Ralaria*. El Alera looked out across the deck of the small cutter. It was sleek and fast, made for darting between islands, a small fish designed to be faster than the prey she would outrun.

The Ralarians had been on the sea as long as their history was recorded. They were one with the sea. El Alera could remember the first time he'd set his feet on deck—he'd felt like he belonged. A lowly deck boy, now a captain of the fleet.

He took a deep breath as he watched the small rowboat, a distant speck of light at first, growing larger as it grew closer in the darkness. The light bobbed up and down as it moved across the shallow bay the Ralarians had moored in.

Men scurried across the deck; El Alera watched as ropes flew down to the rowboat, the men below tying her up as it drew close to them.

The ropes creaked, the rowboat clattering against the side of the *Ralaria*.

"Ease the lines!" El Alera called out before his first mate could.

His first mate gave him a look of apology, to which El Alera shook his head.

These newcomers were obviously flat-footers with no sense of the sea. They didn't know how much slack to give the lines. El Alera knew The *Ralaria* could take it. The little row boat on the other hand? Their boat would take a beating against his cutter without slack in the lines. He didn't want to rescue them when their boat began to sink.

The Ralarians pulled on lines to help the passengers make the deck.

The first two up were barrel-chested and broad-shouldered, with long dark beards and hair braided in the Eastern fashion. El Alera spotted the bulge of daggers hidden beneath their leather vests with empty sheaths at their sides.

He smiled. They underestimated him. The deal had been brokered, no weapons to be brought aboard. This slight was forgivable, but now he knew that they did not respect him and didn't think he was smart enough to spot it.

The third man, much smaller than the first two, was hauled up and over the rail. He was covered in a dark cloak, black, and heavy. He sported a cane, slight but well-crafted.

El Alera walked towards the three, swaying with the boat.

The three looked to be fish out of water, hanging onto the deck, bucking the swells.

"Sirs, welcome aboard the *Ralaria*!" El Alera welcomed them with a bow on the deck.

"Captain," the third man greeted him, impatient and without a bow.

"What brings you here tonight?" El Alera asked.

The third man sneered, moving forward with his cane.

Click, click, click.

The man approached El Alera, coming within arm's distance of him, almost falling as the ship tilted to the port side.

He steadied himself with his cane. "Captain, what say you to our proposal?"

El Alera met the man's gaze. "I took this meeting out of respect for Kassar. He has served me well as a broker in the past."

"You took this meeting because you are a pirate and I offer gold for your ships."

El Alera said nothing.

The third man narrowed his eyes and looked around. "You know the terms?"

El Alera nodded.

"I offer you gold. I need twenty ships, and I need them for a voyage across the Eastern Sea and back."

"What is the cargo?" El Alera asked.

The smaller man fixed him with a stare. "Kassar agreed that the terms were no questions."

El Alera nodded. "You come to me because you need ships to move men, no? Kassar says cargo, but no one needs twenty ships to move cargo. They need twenty ships to move an army."

El Alera's first mate took a step forward.

The two Easterners did the same, their hands buried in their vests.

El Alera put his hand up. "Enough."

"We had a deal," the little man spit out.

"No, we agreed to meet. To hear you out. But the Ralarians do not interfere with the business of flatlanders."

The little man took another step forward, towards El Alera. "No questions. That was the deal. What do you care what you take across the seas?"

"The blood you are going to spill will color the seas. We will have no part in chumming the waters."

"Bloody pirate!" the slight man brandished his cane as if it was a sword.

El Alera spit on the deck of his ship. "You insult me and bring weapons aboard my ship. We will not work with those who do not honor the terms of a deal."

"I offer you more gold than you could carry in your hold. And you *spit* on our deal?"

El Alera put his hand up to stay his men. The Ralarians had circled the two Easterners and now were forming a ring around El Alera and the slight man in the black coat. "Leave. We will have nothing to do with you."

The man's eyes bulged, his face turning red. "You'll regret this. *Pirate.*"

El Alera said nothing, motioning for the man to leave, to get off his ship.

The three men returned to the port side of the ship and lowered themselves over its side. The two larger men helped the slight man over and down to the rowboat and followed behind.

None of the Ralarians moved to help them.

"Cast off!" could be heard from below.

The Ralarians pulled their lines back up onto deck, coiling the ropes at the deck rail.

El Alera nodded to his first mate, and walked away from the main deck.

El Alera was not a man of the land, he was of the sea, of the wind and the salt spray, a man of the Ralarian Islands. But he knew full well that what this dark man had proposed would rock the world of men and the lands from one sea to another.

"What of it, Captain?" his first mate said quietly, as they walked to the bow of the ship.

El Alera let out a long breath, one he hadn't known he was holding.

"We are men of the seas. We do not concern ourselves with what happens on land," El Alera said to him.

The first mate nodded. "Aye, Captain."

They watched the small rowboat push off their bow and make for the dark cove to the west. Its small torch flickered in the night, a beacon in the inky blackness. The waves rocked it to and fro, The Ralaria a mirror in the swells.

El Alera cursed.

"What is it, Captain?"

El Alera turned and made for the wheel of the ship. He put his hand to his mouth. "Raise anchor, make ready the mainsail!"

He turned to his first mate and cursed again. "We should have killed that man. He will bring the Pit down on all of us."

"It is for the flatlanders to decide, it does not concern us," the first mate said, referring to the men on land.

"Ah, but war, she spills to the seas, and they turn red with the blood that soaks the earth," El Alera said, quoting his own father. "You tell the men, no one speaks of this. Not in the ports, not in their lover's arms. Not a word."

El Alera gave his first mate a look. He needed him to understand that they were playing with fire.

"Zufier save us," the first mate whispered to himself.

The cutter began to move in the night, the anchor pulled out of her prison at the sea's floor. The ship rolling as she cut through the surf provided comfort to El Alera. The sea's winds blew in his face, breathing life into his sails.

CHAPTER I

"D ragh!" the jailer called down the damp stone hall.

Dragh stood with his arms resting on the bars of the cell door, hands hanging into the prison hallway. His jailer liked to bat at Dragh's arms, trying to catch them with his club as he made his rounds.

It was a game they played. Dragh's head bowed down as he tried to stop the world from spinning.

The cell's iron bars were the only place that Dragh could rest to keep from puking. He kept his eyes closed to keep the world straight, from painting the floors with his guts.

The rest of the cell was the hard granite stone of the mountains around them. Cold. Unforgiving.

'Mhh," Dragh grunted, his mouth dried of saliva. His stomach turned over as he grunted.

The jailer was whistling, the tune not quite carrying down the stone hallway; its sound mixed with the sputtering of torches in the early dawn light.

Sunlight hit his back, warming him from the one window high in his cell. The heat made his nausea all the worse.

Footsteps echoed down the hall, and their cadence told Dragh he'd screwed up royally. He could hear the cane tapping along with each footfall.

Click, click, click.

Every step conveyed annoyance. He'd hear about this. No hiding his long night out.

Dragh shook his head as if it would banish the hangover he felt.

"Dragh," the voice dripped with frustration, contempt.

"Ellis. I should have known they'd send you," Dragh almost barked the words, his mouth dry.

Ellis scoffed. "They? No, *HE* sent me."

"He sent his errand boy, did he?" Dragh's knuckles turned white as he gripped the bars of the cell.

"I'm your father's advisor. Not an errand boy. Your Highness," Ellis said loudly.

Dragh grunted, his head was already splitting from his headache. 'shut up, leave me be."

Ellis paced back and forth in front of Dragh's cell.

"You shouldn't be in here. All you have to do is tell them who you are."

"I am Dragh, a man of the Second Legion."

Ellis walked the length of his cell, his cane tapping on each bar, the noise reverberating in Dragh's skull.

"He's not going to be happy. First you spur his requests, then you go and join the Legion."

Dragh considered him, rubbing at his temples. "I know what I am, and so does *he*. I joined the Second, they are my family now."

"Boy. You are royal by blood. A fight outside of a pub is no reason for you to be in here." Ellis looked around the prison cells as if they might absorb him.

Dragh laughed. "I'm in the Second because they only take criminals. I am what I am."

Ellis sighed, shaking his head. "You've been summoned to the Palace."

Dragh peered at Ellis, shaking his head. "Well, *he* can go to the Pit. I won't be there; the last time I went to the Palace, I almost killed him."

The corner of Ellis's mouth raised in what Dragh thought was a smile.

"I told him as much. But nonetheless, you owe him your fealty," Ellis's eyes narrowed, appraising Dragh. "It's about your little bastard, the one you seem to have forgotten to mention," Ellis wagged his cane back and forth. 'tisk, tisk."

"What the Pit are you talking about?"

Ellis laughed. "Oh, this is perfect. You didn't know?"

Dragh sighed again. His head was a mess. The anger rose in him like a bile, his meaty fists gripping the bars as a lifeline. He could feel blood rising in his face. He wanted to strike out at Ellis, to rip his throat out. He settled for less.

"Fuck off, Ellis."

He watched with some satisfaction as Ellis took a sharp breath at the anger radiating off of Dragh.

Ellis said nothing as he walked away, his mouth a tight line.

Dragh knew what he'd have to do now. He'd made it worse for himself, he knew that as the words left his mouth. Ellis didn't speak for himself. He spoke for others, and he'd be relaying the message.

He knew he'd have to go to see her, if what Ellis said was true. He hoped to Zufier that it wasn't.

——

"See you again soon," the jailer said, shoving Dragh out of the prison gates and into the dawn's sunlight.

Dragh righted himself, almost falling over. He swung around, his fists bunched, but the jailer had closed the iron gates to the prison.

The jailer gave a wave with each finger.

Dragh took a step forward, then thought better of it, as he had to close his eyes. The world spun.

All the jailer knew was that he'd been given a pass. Not who he was. Just a man of the Second who had been freed after a fight with the guards.

"Pit." Dragh rubbed his face again. His mouth felt like dry smoke.

Dragh squinted at the sunlight peeking over the Car Lauch Mountains. The stone that built many of the buildings around him, the walls of the city he was in, and the palace of the nation of Landor.

The jagged white peaks still made him shiver, even years after his training in the army. The troops of Landor's army trained in the mountains, fighting each other in imaginary wars.

Sometimes men died, but mostly they got hurt, fell from peaks or just lost toes and fingers to the frostbite.

Dragh squeezed his right hand. It still tingled where it had turned a waxy white in the early morning of his last day up there. His beard had been a sheet of icicles hanging from his face, his breath steaming as it issued from his mouth.

His squad had hidden in the drifts in the night, waiting for dawn, to ambush the last enemy squad. He'd known the pain was going to be bad, but not how bad until they found one of his men, dead from the evening in the snow.

He'd known regret then. Then anger. Anger for the generals that made them play their stupid games.

The jailer had known Ellis was someone. Or that he was working for someone who was above his station. What Dragh had to do with it, he was sure to wonder.

Dragh was on the main road of Landor's main city now. He could see the palace in the distance, its walls and towers seeming to rise out of the base of the Car Lauch Mountains. The stones cut from the granite walls were not far from the mountains, blending in with the peaks.

Flags of Landor and her king snapped in the wind. Even from a distance, Dragh recognized the white peaks on the gray background and a sun between them.

"Look who's alive!" a lazy voice called out from behind him.

Dragh turned on the cobblestones, narrowly missing a passing cart. The driver gave him a rude gesture and grunt.

"Pit, it is good to see you, Hemmelle. I thought you were a goner after that big lad from the Pass took a swing at you!" Dragh clapped his friend on the back.

They began to walk. The route from the prison to home was one they both knew.

Hemmelle laughed and returned the gesture. He looked around, his eyes taking in the people around them. He said lower, so that only they could hear it. "Ellis was back, looking for you this morning."

Dragh nodded to him. "Aye, he found his way to me."

Hemmelle chuckled. "I had guessed you were... ahem... held up by pressing matters after your little show last night with the guard."

"You know I hate them. They have been at the Second Legion for years. I just wanted to show the captain of the guard the error of his ways." Dragh gave his friend a dark smile.

"I know they must hate how they put us into the dungeon only to salute us now." Hemmelle laughed out loud, the laugh echoing on the empty streets.

"I just decided he needed a little reminder of who the Second are." Dragh put his hands on his knees, breathing in the cool air. "Gods, I shouldn't have drunk that much ale."

"You didn't have to piss on him after you taught him that lesson." Hemmelle gave his friend a look. "Come on, we're almost there."

Dragh pushed off his knees, sucked in air, and kept walking.

"Well. It was worth it." Dragh spit blood onto the cobbles and pulled back his lip to show Hemmelle his mouth.

"They got one from you there, huh?"

"Well." Dragh winced as he ran his tongue over the missing tooth. "They decided my face could use some time with a boot in it."

"You'll never learn will you." Hemmelle shook his head. "What did Ellis want?"

Dragh looked at his friend.

"Fine, fine." Hemmelle put his hands up in mock surrender.

The pair made their way through the city and into the heart of the tenements that held the majority of the population.

Landor was once a small village outside the walls of the Palace. Landor spread slowly as more people ventured closer to the Palace for its protection. Its walls grew outward as its population grew.

As time went on, the citizens of Landor made their way to the Palace in larger groups. Masons followed the people, building up houses, then churches. The churches brought people from all around, and small villages moved their population closer for the churches, the markets. Many picked up trades that were needed in the cities. All needs were met, and the town grew. People needed places to stay, then they needed the goods of everyday life.

The pinging of the blacksmith's hammer and the braying of donkeys and horses could be heard in the merchant district. Goods were hauled into the markets from outlying farmers and the nations around them. Clothes and rugs were shown in the streets where the weavers lived and plied their trade.

And of course, soldiers and tradespeople drank together in the pubs and drinking houses. It mattered not where you came from or who you were in the pubs and inns. It was all the same: ale, spirits, and entertainment.

Some places took more than a coin from its patrons, as was evident by the gap in Dragh's teeth.

Hemmelle and Dragh lived together in a squat house squeezed between two tenements. The house was a cheap rent while they waited for their next campaign out of Landor.

Hemmelle pushed open the door, not waiting for Dragh behind him. "Oye, Relish, up you get," he said, kicking a dark pile on the ground beside the fireplace.

Dragh found the mug of water he'd left out. With shaking hands, he drank deeply. The water spilled down the sides of his beard.

Hemmelle knelt by the fireplace, pushing the coals around from the night before to light some fresh kindling.

"Any chance you'd make us some oats? My head feels like it's been kicked by a mule." Dragh squinted as he drank more water.

"You drank me under the table. I'll tell you that." The pile beside Hemmelle rumbled as a pair of arms emerged from it.

"Ah, Relish. Did you decide to start paying rent?" Hemmelle asked as Relish emerged from under the pile of clothes he'd slept under.

Dragh winced and laughed at the same time. Relish shot up from the ground and swung at Hemmelle, missing widely.

"You bastard, some of us have *headaches*," he said, rubbing at his temples like Dragh.

"Well, I see that you're avoiding the question." Hemmelle raised his eyebrow at Relish.

"Well, when the Royal Highness King Kallen decides to up the wage that pays his loyal soldiers, I will let you know about the *rent.*" Relish gave an exaggerated bow to Hemmelle.

A smile played on Dragh's lips as Hemmelle laughed at Relish. Dragh thought back to Ellis and the summons that Ellis delivered.

Dragh was expected at the Palace , and although he'd rejected it, the sinking feeling in his stomach had nothing to do with his hangover. He knew he had to attend the king.

"I hear we are shipping out tomorrow. Orders came from on high," Relish said casually.

Dragh closed his eyes, feeling the wave of anger and frustration of not being in control of his own life.

"The Council has decided to send us away again? Where to now?" Dragh asked.

The Council was made up by the real rulers of the nations. They installed kings and queens. They instituted order and control. They even put the Skellen Pass Legions in place, bringing men of all nations together to serve in the defense of their realms against the Horde in the West.

The Council gave orders and kings followed them. They dressed their orders in fancy terminology, things like "peace keeping missions" and 'defense patrols." But really, the Council commanded armies.

"I'm told this is from the palace. The North is stirring up trouble again."

"Zufier above, why do the tribes always rebel?" Hemmelle asked.

Dragh shook his head. "They are raised in war. It is all they know."

Relish and Hemmelle started to prepare oats, filling a pot with water and setting it to boil.

The noise of the spoon scraping the pot's bottom hurt Dragh's ears.

"I'll be back," he said to them both, getting up from the chair.

"Don't do anything stupid!" Hemmelle called after him.

"Aye, like he'd ever needed help out of a pickle before," Relish snorted, taking Dragh's seat behind him.

Chapter 2

Dragh let the cool air soothe his headache. The water helped, but he needed to move.

Dragh walked down the cobblestone, pushing himself through the headache. The clattering of carts, the clip clop of the horses and mules, pounded his head.

He cut across streets and down alleyways. He knew how to get to her house as if it were his own.

Dragh recognised when he was getting close because of the smell. The perfume of roses wafted in the summer air across the street. They named the street the Street of Roses. The white cobblestones and white houses were all built in the first age of Landor. The street was named after the very plants that the first families settled here with.

His headache was replaced by a feeling of dread. Could it be true? Could she really be pregnant? Ellis's spies were rarely wrong, and the palace was always well informed.

Dragh cursed them again.

He made his way to the heavy oak door of her house, his feet taking him down a path he'd walked many times. His chest was heavy with worry, and he knew what he had to do.

Dragh braced himself for the conversation he was about to have. It wouldn't be easy.

He knocked on the door of the home, taking a deep breath.

"Coming!" a voice came from an upstairs window.

"Please, let it not be true," Dragh said to himself. He rooted his feet, not letting himself run as his mind told him he should.

He could hear footsteps down a set of stairs, coming closer to him. He felt nerves returning to him. He knew she'd be angry. But he needed to see her. He squared his shoulders, readying himself for the door to open.

The door flew open, its hinges creaking as it hit the wall. Dragh watched her eyes as they took him in. A smile was on her face, and he saw recognition in her eyes. He watched them narrow, and a scowl replaced her smile.

"Dragh."

Dragh was surprised by the venom. Yes, he expected her to be angry, he'd not seen her in weeks. He had been out on the town for weeks, not concerned with anything but the next pint in the next inn, the next drink of spirits with the men. He'd been in and out of Landor, to the lowest of places they could find.

"Lucille, I thought..." Dragh started.

Lucille pushed him, catching him by surprise. "You didn't think, did you!" she yelled at him, stepping after him into the street.

Dragh caught himself with his back foot, almost falling as he was pushed backwards down her steps.

He put his hands up to defend himself from blows.

She'd never been this angry with him before. He'd been out drinking before. Gone for months with the army. This time was different.

Lucille followed him down and onto the road, her arms up as if to hit him.

"What did I do?" Dragh asked, pleading with her.

"What did you do! What did you DO!" Lucille yelled at him, following him into the middle of the street.

Dragh watched her cheeks fill with color, her face turning red.

Dragh glanced around the Street of Roses. Even in the early morning, there were people out tending to the gardens out front of each house, watering and weeding. Most likely those people were servants. But Dragh knew that these were the people you had to fear the most. The talk of Landor was spread through the mouths of servants.

"Lucille, let's go inside and talk. I didn't come here to fight with you," Dragh pleaded.

Lucille looked at Dragh, her face red with fury. She was a head shorter than Dragh and had a shock of auburn hair. It was short and straight, the bangs falling into her face as her eyes narrowed.

Her eyes were full of rage as she took a deep breath, readying another tirade for Dragh.

Dragh put his hands up in defeat. "We need to talk. I'm sorry!" He offered peace.

Lucille peered at him with furrowed brows. He watched as the anger leached from her body and she unclenched the balled-up fists by her side. "Get inside before the street wakes from your foolishness."

Lucille stormed into the house.

"I think that ship has sailed," Dragh muttered.

"What did you say?" Lucille turned mid stride.

"Nothing!" Dragh said, shaking his head.

She always heard him. He should have learned by now. She gave him a withering look and then kept going into the house.

Dragh swallowed; the pit in his stomach was back. He wasn't ready for this.

The house was beautiful, white stone on the outside, wood on the inside. Light streamed through windows inside the house. Windows spanned the entire front of the house. Inside, twin stairways flanked the open floors up to the third floor. Railings made of ornate woods from across the oceans spoke to the wealth of Lucille's father. He was a ship's captain who'd started off as a deckhand and beggar.

He now owned the largest shipping business outside the Council's holdings. He was a merchant of the highest order in Landor.

"Is your father back?" Dragh asked.

"No, he... I haven't had word from him in some time," Lucille said, her face breaking around her eyes as she turned to look back at him from the stairs.

Dragh nodded. "I'll ask my father where the Council sent him, if you want me to."

She gave Dragh a look. She knew who he was, who his father was. And what it meant to swallow his pride and ask for his help.

She turned back up the stairs.

He'd take that as a no.

Dragh followed Lucille up into her room on the second floor. The entire floor had been gutted and turned into her quarters. The place was full of gilded furniture, hand-crafted tapestries, and richly carved wood.

Even his father didn't have such finery in his chambers.

"Well?" Lucille turned to him as he closed the doors.

"Well, what? Why are you so angry with me, Lucille?" Dragh asked.

"Why am I angry with you? He asks why I'm angry!" She threw up her hands and shook her head.

"Aye, why wouldn't I ask? You yell, push, and shout. All because I went off for a couple of weeks with Relish and Hemmelle." Dragh fell into one of the armchairs beside the fireplace.

Lucille walked over to Dragh, her face set.

"THIS is why I'm angry." Lucille flattened her white dress against her stomach, a bump extended from between her bosom and navel.

Dragh stared at her for a moment before he truly understood what Lucille was telling him. What she was showing him.

She was pregnant. Ellis was right.

He shook his head in disbelief. It wasn't possible. He started to do the math in his head, counting the weeks since he'd seen her last.

"But...it can't be. You can't be," Dragh exhaled, his shoulder slumping into the chair.

Lucille shook her head in exhaustion. She walked over to her bed and fell into it.

"AHHHHGGG," she shouted into the pillows.

Dragh got up, unsure if he should go to her, unsure what was right.

He didn't want her to be pregnant, but he didn't want to leave her either.

Dragh watched, not sure what was happening. He ran from responsibility. He did not seek it out, look for it.

"Is it mine?" Dragh asked, his face cold, his palms sweaty.

"IS IT YOURS!" Lucille screamed at him, getting up from the bed and stalking towards him.

Dragh almost fell over the chair he'd sat in, trying to escape her wrath. He scrambled away from her, but to no avail. She cornered him against the closed door.

"How dare you even ask." Lucille had her finger pointed in Dragh's face. "Get out!" she said to him, pushing open the door.

"Lucille, no stop," Dragh said to her as she pushed him out of her room towards the stairs.

"Get out and don't come back, Dragh!" Lucille gave him a shove.

Dragh could have stopped her, pushed back, but he was defeated.

Before he knew what to say to her, she'd ushered him out the door. He couldn't believe what had happened. He didn't understand how he'd been so careless.

The doors slammed in his face, their ornate carvings just a hand's width from his nose. He felt the wind of the doors as he glimpsed the last of Lucille, flustered and angry.

Dragh, a father-to-be. It was impossible. He couldn't be.

He watched the doors slam, hoping she would open them back up, so they could make up like they always did.

The building was quiet behind him, the servants surely there but hidden.

He could hear Lucille's sobs beyond the door.

He reached for the door handle, then paused, midway to the handle. He took a deep breath and turned, walking away and out of the house.

He'd sworn he wouldn't have a child. Not in this life or the next.

Chapter 3

"Another?" a high-pitched voice cut through Dragh's muddled mind.

Dragh looked around, pulling his mind into the present. He was at the Duck's Beak Inn. The inn doubled as a tavern at night, the bottom floor full of tables and a bar where locals liked to drink their hard work into memories.

"Huh? Yeah, thanks Anne," Dragh said.

Once, he would have worried that he might be outed. A prince in a place like this. But after he'd joined the Second, that wasn't an issue. Men of the Second left the mountain looking more animal than man. Beards and hair, long and wild.

He and his Squad had kept the look since.

He looked at Anne and couldn't help but smile. She was a portly inn owner, her husband dead a decade before, at Skellen Pass. The years had been kind to Anne, her full figure helping with tips. She was a favorite of the local soldiers. Her husband had originally been in the Eighth Legion, before he died fighting at the Pass.

Dragh hated the General of the Eighth Legion, General Serras. Anne's husband had been long before the General.

"Hard go, huh? I heard you are shipping out soon?" Anne asked, trying to make conversation with Dragh.

Dragh tweaked an eyebrow in a question to Anne.

"Aye, you know how they talk. They say ol" Nestor is marching. Soldiers never stop tongue waggin." Anne laughed at herself.

"I didn't know. My thanks Annie," Dragh said, giving a half smile.

Dragh knew that before he left, he had a summons to answer. Yet, he sat at the table, hiding in the corner of the inn, drowning himself in ale.

Anne took a step closer and gave Dragh's shoulder a squeeze. Her face had a knowing look on it. "Stay as long as you need," Anne said, moving off to the bar.

The hum of conversation, the scraping of chairs and the clinking of mugs let him forget his own thoughts. His mind caught bits of conversation from the people around him. He was hunched over his drink at the back of the room, his preferred table.

The table was stained with spilled drinks, splotches of food, and other strange marks. Dragh ran his hands over the table marks, where he and Hemmelle had dared each other to race knives. They both stabbed daggers between their fingers, back and forth, as fast as they could. Daring each other to go faster.

"Drinks for the Second!" a loud voice shouted in the crowd.

A cheer went up.

Dragh felt like smiling, but his face wouldn't cooperate.

The smell of stale ale filled his nose as he drew a deep breath in.

Another mug of ale was placed on his table. A round paid by a rich patron.

Dragh tried to let the ale soothe his mind, but the more he drank, the less he wanted to. He had to talk to Lucille again, to deal with this... problem.

"Pit," he said into his mug.

"Thought we'd find you here," Hemmelle said, plopping into a chair opposite Dragh.

Dragh sighed, waiting for the rest of them. "How'd you know?"

"Well, it's like this: we drink here too," Relish said, sitting on the bench beside Dragh.

"You know," Dragh said to Hemmelle and Relish. "The Second saved my life. I was... I was going to end up dead if Nestor hadn't given me a second chance."

Relish and Hemmelle listened. Nursing their ales.

"I wanted to serve Landor. Just not the way they wanted."

"What—."

Relish was about to ask a question when Hemmelle interrupted.

"The boys should be with us soon," Hemmelle said.

"Where are they?" Dragah asked, looking around the inn.

Dragh shook his head. He'd almost slipped up. He was getting too comfortable. He nodded his thanks to Hemmelle.

"Pello and Zeffo? Who knows... they will be here," Hemmelle chuckled, taking a sip from his mug.

"I think I heard them fighting a street back," Relish said, gulping his ale.

Dragh shook his head. He knew what the brothers were like. "Making their mum proud."

"Aye, guess that's going around today, ain't it?" Hemmelle said to Dragh. "Never raised right, them two."

Dragh glared at Hemmelle, feeling the rage bubble up beneath the surface. Hemmelle knew who his father was, who his family was. Dragh glanced at Relish, who was in his usual drunken stupor.

"Watch your words," Dragh said with some venom.

Relish piped up from his sagging stature. "Wass the matter ol" Dragh? My mum was a whore in the Ralarian Islands before me dad met her." He belched. "Ooof, felt that in me nuts."

Hemmelle looked at Dragh, the corners of his mouth playing up into a smile. He raised one eyebrow and shrugged.

Dragh laughed at his friend, a momentary reprieve from what his night was to become.

"You heard? Nestor called his bastards to him?" Hemmelle asked.

"The Second goes into the maw of Death again," Dragh said.

The Second was a legion made up of criminals. Some reformed, some perfecting their criminal arts under the cover of the Landorian Army.

"Anything is better than the Car Lauch," Relish murmured.

They all had served time in prison; many of the prisoners were killers or worse. Dragh and his friends had been given a choice: prison or the mountains. Those who survived the training of the Car Lauch mountains could survive anything.

"Aye, I've heard," Dragh said, his voice dropping to a whisper. He finished his drink in a long gulp.

"I heard we are marching up north," Hemmelle said, not bothering to keep his voice down. He knew as well as the others that the Duck's Beak knew all. It knew all before the king sometimes.

"Shit," Hemmelle said.

Dragh followed his gaze to the door.

"The Praetorians," Dragh cursed.

"The third one. Is he from last night?" Hemmelle asked.

"Zufier. I think that might be the one I pissed on," Dragh said, sinking back into the corner. Hoping they hadn't seen him.

"You what?" Relish said.

Dragh ignored him, his heart was pounding. He didn't want a fight tonight. He already had his fill with Lucille. He was about to have his fill with his father.

"You need to go. Get out of here before they see you," Hemmelle said.

Dragh looked around; the crowd was thick. It would be some time before the Praetorians could make their rounds. He could see them asking Anne questions and looking around the place.

"I've got something to take care of before we shove off," Dragh said, steeling himself for what came next. He knew that the Praetorians were an excuse. They couldn't be looking for him. But he had to go to the Palace . He had royal business.

"Just be sure to be back tonight. I don't want to find you in another cell come morning. There will be hell to pay from General Nestor." Hemmelle nodded to Dragh.

Relish let out a loud belch that shocked the next table over. "I'll save you a drink!" he laughed.

"Of course, my friend." Dragh gave him an empty smile and threw a couple of coins onto the table for Anne.

Chapter 4

Dragh's feet scraped across the cobblestone, his senses dulled by the mugs of ale he'd ingested at the Duck's Beak Inn.

The night air he breathed in seemed to sharpen him; the cool breeze pushed him along. It was always warmer here than his days in the mountains.

He felt his way along the stone fences and walls, down alleys and paths between buildings. The way was familiar. He'd spent most of his life sneaking out from the palace, and then back in.

He heard the racket of the guards before he got to the gate. Their breastplates clanged as they moved in the night. He slowed himself, ready for the beating he would take if these were the same men from the night before at the Duck's Beaks Inn.

"Who goes there?" a voice came from the gate house above.

Dragh could see the tips of spears lower in front of him: two men in the front with weapons in hand, two men behind them with swords drawn. They had shining breastplates and helms. He could see that one of them had a black eye. They all looked angry to have their night disrupted.

They stood guard in front of the gates of the Landor Palace, a palace where his father and mother sat upon their cold thrones of marble.

It was an oddity to have a visitor to the palace in the middle of the night. Especially a drunk one.

He laughed.

"State your name and business or you'll be thrown into the Pit," the head guard called from the top of the gate.

"Oye, I recognize this one. The Duck's Beaks, eh?" One of the guardsmen with the black eye pulled up his spear and stood up straight.

"Tell Ellis that I'm here," Dragh barked at them, trying to hide his drunken slurring.

Dragh could hear shuffling and steps in the guardhouse, some talking, too low for him to make out any specific words.

The guard eyed him, hitting his partner's shoulder. "I told you 'bout this one. We made him pay for it. We did."

The guard behind him scoffed. "I heard he pissed all over yah, Pars." He and the other swordsman sheathed their swords. "Let's go, this one is looking for another beating."

"I'm looking for Ellis, tell him I'm here," Dragh said.

He knew that time was short, and he might be run through before Ellis could get to him. Words might not save him soon.

"Aye, yes master. What's that we can do for you? Would you like to put your feet up while you wait?" the guard named Pars asked. "Callen, fetch the rug for our friend. His feet are cold."

The other guard with the spear gave Pars a phlegmy chuckle and nodded his head up and down. They were both short and out of shape.

The Praetorian Legion had let themselves go. They didn't have the sense to stay fit. Dragh knew that killing took some effort, if you wanted to stay alive.

The two Praetorians moved around him, one on either side, a common flanking move. Dragh sighed, frustrated that it came to another fight. He was tired. And the worst fight was still ahead of him once he dealt with these fools.

"Now boys, don't make me remind you of what happened last night, eh?" Dragh looked from side to side, noting the grips on spears loosening, hands on hilts. They were fools, but they were trained fools.

"We'll see who shows who," Pars snarled.

Dragh set his back foot, giving his feet width, feeling the warmth of the fight. His blood pumped, his senses reached out, letting his body ready itself for a fight.

His training, years of it, took control of him. He set one hand on the hilt of his sword, the other across the dagger at his belt. The alcohol in his veins disappeared.

He was ready. A coiled snake ready to strike.

Dragh pulled his sword and dagger with speed, brandishing them at the men on either side. He kept his centre of gravity low, letting his feet keep loose.

"Let's go, you scum!" Dragh shouted at them. He could see they were unused to such a foe.

Palace Praetorians. Pah.

"HOLD!" a voice called from the open gate.

Dragh glanced over quickly, his eyes drinking in detail in the low light of the torches around them. A figure with the Pratorian's armor bellowed the call. From the look of the swordsmen behind the guard, he was the head man.

And then there was Ellis.

He knew that slimy shape everywhere. He was a shadow of his childhood. A shadow of his adult life. Every shit thing that Dragh had been through, Ellis was there, in the background, at the palace, training grounds, and now even prison.

Dragh kept eyeing the two Praetorians on either side of him. Would they back off?

"I said HOLD, Pars, Callen," the man said again. "You know who this is?"

Dragh grimaced.

"This little pisseater? He ain't nobody, Primus," Pars said to his commander.

"He's Dragh *Sunborn*," Ellis hissed from behind them. He pulled his sword from his cane.

Dragh chuckled at Ellis, always playing the soldier. Ellis pulled out his little sword and threatened people that were below him in the social order. He'd never pull such a move on Dragh. A man who knew the blade.

Ellis also let people think that he'd been wounded in battle or in some duel. Hence the slight limp when he walked and the reason for the cane.

But the gossip of the palace knew better. Dragh had been told in quiet corners that Ellis had been stabbed by a woman he'd been in bed with. A lover's quarrel. It just so happened that they were both married to other people.

They all laughed at Ellis behind his back, and in Dragh's case, to his face.

The Praetorians stiffened at the name Sunborn. They knew what it meant to strike a member of the royal family. They were the protectors of the royal line. The line of the Sunborn. They had beaten him, kicked him and worse, taken a tooth last night in a fight at the Duck's Beak.

"Highness." The two came to attention, their faces gone white with fear for their lives.

A Praetorian was put to death for harming a Sunborn.

Dragh sheathed his sword and dagger, his posture still defensive. He was sure these fools would try something. They knew he had the power of life and death over them. They might try to go out with some glory.

He looked between the two, noting their sweaty white faces. Glory was on their minds as they looked from Dragh to their Primus and back.

He walked by the Primus. "My thanks," he said stiffly. He ducked through the door and passed the other two Praetorians, who averted their eyes from him.

Click, click, click.

Dragh knew Ellis had followed from the sound of his cane sword, the sound bouncing off the stone walls.

"Let's get on with it, Dragh. He has been expecting you," Ellis said, walking ahead without glancing back at Dragh.

"Of course he knows," Dragh muttered to himself. He mounted the steps in the flickering light, sure of his feet. He'd been up and down these steps for much of his life.

He knew each step, each crack in the stone, each groove worn in over generations.

They walked into the courtyard, an expansive stone courtyard surrounded by walls and stairways leading to various wings of the palace. The walls were manned by Praetorians, ready to defend the palace from the inside. The courtyard was a major funnel, Dragh realized after his youth of playing there. It would be a bloodbath if anyone made it through the main gate.

He and Ellis took the stairs to the throne room, taking the steps two at a time, their long legs making short work of the journey.

"Keep your mouth shut," Ellis said, pushing a large set of oak and iron doors open.

Dragh shook his head. What a piece of work this man was. The head of the king's court. They walked across the threshold to the quiet sound of arguing.

Dragh could tell by the punctuated angry statements.

"You said you'd take care of the problem in the North." A short fat man pointed at the king. He wore the robes of the faith, and his eyes were dark and beady.

King Kallen leaned forward. "You mean, *Sire.*"

"Of course—Sire." The fat man shrunk back from the hard look that Kallen gave him.

"My lord, Kallen," Ellis said as he crossed the room to bow in front of the throne.

Dragh stayed in the shadows, letting the men in front of him talk. He watched. He knew what came next.

"You're welcome to leave, Father Malek," Ellis said to the fat man.

Malek began to complain to the king but was brushed off by a wave of his hand.

The king had other things on his mind. He watched the shadows, his eyes boring into Dragh.

"Trust me, you've got it better," Dragh said to the priest as he fled the chambers in anger. The fat man gave Dragh a disgruntled grunt, looking down his nose at him as he passed.

"Boy," the words came from the throne, a tired drawl to them.

Dragh took a breath, his calm escaping him. He hated Malek, and the way his father treated Dragh with contempt.

Like he was unworthy.

"I see you're keeping good company as usual, Father," Dragh said to Kallen as he walked towards the throne. Dragh raised his brow at Ellis. Dragh knew his father would understand it was an insult.

Dragh gave a mock bow to the king as he reached Ellis's side.

Kallen laughed out loud. "You only call me that when it suits you." He got up from the throne and stretched, and walked down the stone steps to pour himself a drink from a pitcher.

"I'd offer you a drink, but I can smell the ale on you from here," Kallen said to Dragh, rubbing his forehead.

Dragh watched as his father lifted the gray metal crown with four points on it off his brow and placed it on the table with the pitcher of water.

"Why am I here?" Dragh asked.

Ellis snorted. "You are the one who decided to come in the middle of the night. You had your invitation this morning."

"You're here because I am the king, and I ordered it," Kallen said to Dragh as he drank from his cup.

"Of course, *sire*," Dragh said.

"You petulant shit," Ellis said, his usual calm facade slipping for a moment.

Dragh smiled at him, happy his game still worked.

He knew how to piss off Ellis better than most. He'd been practicing since he was born. As far as he was concerned, it was a win. And they both knew it. He turned to his father. Waiting for what was to come.

Kallen sat at a small table set to the side of the throne's pedestal and motioned Dragh to sit across from him.

Kallen massaged the bridge of his nose.

"I've called you here because you know what's happening tomorrow," Kallen said to Dragh. He was a mirror of Dragh, with a gray shot through his beard and hair. They were both broad shouldered. Hours of training with weapons each day did that. Both of them had faces made for war helms. Noses that had been broken, and brows with criss-crossed scars from being split in fights.

"I ship out tomorrow with the Second," Dragh said, leaning back in his seat and stretching.

He still had not recovered from his beating from the Praetorians. He still had not decided if he'd make them suffer. Or if holding their lives in his hands was suffering enough. They'd struck him; he could have them killed.

He wanted them to keep their mouths shut. He didn't need people knowing he was a Sunborn.

"You will not ship out with the Second," Kallen said to Dragh, his finger pointing at Dragh.

"I'll do as I please," Dragh spit back at him.

"I said you will not ship out, and that is final, boy," Kallen said, his eyes wide and his face reddening.

"I'll do what I damn well want to and to the Pit with what you think," Dragh said back in retort. His anger was getting the best of him. "I told you when I left, I wasn't going to be king. Damn you for trying to force me."

"That was before you had an HEIR!" Kallen yelled at Dragh.

Dragh looked to Ellis, seeing the smug look on his face told him what he needed to know.

"You told him, eh?" Dragh said, getting up from his chair.

"Sit down. Do not disrespect your king," Ellis said, his voice wavering in anger.

"I'll do what I damn well please, Ellis. You would do well to watch yourself. Mark my words," Dragh said, his voice dripping with venom.

"Sit down. Now," Kallen said to Dragh, his manner collected from his outburst. "Leave us," Kallen said to Ellis.

"Sire, I just…" Ellis started, trying to regain his position.

"Get out. I will talk with my son now," Kallen said to Ellis and waved him away.

Dragh watched Ellis, his face going through anger, frustration, and then a calm steeled look. He narrowed his eyes at Dragh before bowing to Kallen and retreating.

"Heel, dog," Dragh said, just loud enough for Ellis to hear as he walked away.

Ellis's pace slowed and his shoulders stiffened. He looked about to turn around, but then continued to walk away.

"Why must you aggravate him so, Dragh?" Kallen wiped his face with his hand.

"Because he is a leech on you and Mother," Dragh said quietly.

Kallen looked over to Dragh at the mention of Dragh's mother. He took a deep breath and carried on.

"You have a child on the way, you know this now, don't you?" Kallen asked.

"Aye, I do. Your spies have made you aware of that. There seems to be nowhere in this city that I can go to escape you," Dragh complained.

"Indeed, no place in the king's capitol where you can go that I do not hear. I also hear that a man of the Second Legion was beaten after pissing on a Praetorian. What do you know of this?" Kallen asked, his eyes accusing Dragh.

"You should ask General Nestor of the Second. He would have an accounting of the men under his command," Dragh replied.

"Aye, and I bet the rest of the criminals and degenerates of the Second would cover for you, the same as you for them," Kallen said in disgust.

"It's a brotherhood, you wouldn't understand the bonds that we have together. I will not give them up to come and play prince at the palace with you and Mother," Dragh said, his eyes defying the king.

"You know nothing of obligation and sacrifice, boy. Nothing," Kallen said with some anger in his voice.

"I'm done," Dragh said, getting up and walking away from his father.

"You're done with the Second. I want you out. You will raise your child here at the Palace. You are a prince. I want you to start acting like it," Kallen said to Dragh.

Dragh stopped, his hands clenched into fists.

"I've told you before, I'll not be a prince, I will rise on my own. Keep your gold and silver, keep your palace, I don't want any of it," Dragh said to his father.

"It's time for you to grow up. Think of what your child might want some day. Is it too much for you? Too bad. You are of the Sunborn line. I will not have you out there traipsing around like a coward, spilling my BLOOD because you don't have the honour to step up," Kallen said to Dragh, his voice raising to a shout.

Dragh stared at him, his voice cold. "You know nothing of honour. I'll not leave my brothers behind. I'll not betray my brothers for your stupid crown." He turned his head and walked from the room.

Chapter 5

"Sunborn!"

"Wait, Sire!"

Dragh pushed past the guards, ignoring their shouts as he left the castle and let himself be swallowed up by the dark. Hot tears were on his face, salty as they tracked down his face and across his beard and mouth.

Dragh's mind was full of rage and anger at his father and at himself. He knew what he was getting himself into when he went to the palace. He knew his father, and he knew what his father had wanted of him.

But then there was Ellis.

That bastard.

Ellis somehow knew that Lucille was pregnant before Dragh did. He knew it when he had Dragh released from his cell this morning. The smug look was on Ellis's face not because Dragh was being called to his father nor because he'd been summoned to see the king.

No. It was on his face because he knew something Dragh didn't. Ellis knew, and he'd told the king.

That dung heap.

He'd pay for this. Dragh swore to himself. He'd been embarrassed by Ellis for the last time. He would not go through this suffering again.

He'd find a way to make Ellis pay. To knock him off his high perch in the High Court of Landor.

The smell of roses hit him, the smell sweet on the warm evening breeze. The moon was bright in the sky, almost glinting off the cobblestones of the Street of Roses.

He looked up at the old familiar house. Its windows were dark, the flickering of torches leapt at the stone, reflecting on the glass like stars on a lake. He took a breath and thought about what he would do.

He needed to see her. He needed to know she was okay.

He loved her. He had to tell her.

He scolded himself. He'd become attached, attached in a way that he swore he never would be. His mother and father were in a loveless marriage. He'd not seen them hold hands, hug each other, or show any affection his whole life. His mother Sherris was cold even to him.

He'd been half-raised by nannies, the other half by his uncle Nestor, now his commanding general in the Second.

His uncle Nestor had taken him everywhere when Dragh was a child. He'd spent more time in the camps of the Second than in the palace. He'd never worked out what his uncle had done to gain entry to the Second. There were rumors, of course. There were always rumors. That was one thing that was for certain in a military camp. They knew how to talk.

He took a breath and knocked on Lucille's door. It echoed down the street. The quiet of the night made it sound like the hammering of a mason on stone. Each blow reverberated from house to house. He cringed.

"Lucille," he said quietly, but not a whisper. He hoped she could hear him.

He listened, straining to hear anything from the house. A sign that she was up, that she'd heard the door. He dared not knock again.

He sat on the step, not sure what to do. He wanted to see her before he shipped off, to tell her. To tell her what? Dragh thought to himself. To tell her that he would be there for her? He laughed at the idea.

Shipping off with the Second, Dragh didn't know if he'd even make it on a ship back. He might die out there.

That's what he wanted to tell her. That he'd be back for her. Back for the baby. Damn his father, damn Ellis. They were nothing— he'd marry Lucille.

They'd have this child. He wouldn't let Ellis and his father ruin it. Ruin them.

He would provide for them. He would be there for them. He wouldn't abandon them like his parents abandoned him. To be raised by another.

He began to talk to Lucille, telling her what he'd do. The house was dark, no sign of life. But he told her anyway, speaking into the dark, knowing she was asleep in her own bed.

He'd be the man that she needed.

CHAPTER 6

Dragh leaned against the side of the vessel, the *Maren*. A fat ship meant for troop transport. Sleep still pulled at his eyelids despite the early morning sunshine.

He'd woken at Lucille's door at daybreak. No sign of life on the street or inside the house. He had woken with a renewed purpose: make it back.

He looked out over the dock. Men of the Second milled around the sailors of the Landor Navy. The navy was made up of a mix of vessels that were repurposed.

The Landor Navy had a sheltered harbour leading to the sea at Landor, and it served Landor well for fishing and for merchants shipping goods to other nations. The vessels were pulled together from the fishermen and the merchants. The shipyards, built up around the docks and around the bay, carried cloth, grains, goods and supplies for seafaring folk.

Gulls called in the air, and a slight swell rocked the boats. Dragh could feel the slight movement, even in the large ship *Maren* he leaned against.

"Where to?" Dragh asked a passing sailor.

The man stopped, a cap on his bald head, his legs slightly bowed, as if still on the rolling deck of a boat. "North," he said, turning and walking away before Dragh could ask another question.

Dragh looked around him. It made sense now. North. Relish had been right.

Landor and the Northern Tribes were always fighting small skirmishes. The Tribes were far from Kallen's seat of power. But still they were subject to Landor.

Those were small skirmishes. Landor mobilized troops many leagues across the mountains of Car Lauch. It took weeks to move north. Moving Legions through the mountains had the extra burden of troops watching out for ambushes. The steep mountain passes served as a funnel for much of the journey.

Moving troops over water could take longer, but it cut down the risk. They would choose a port town, or a landing beach, and create their beachhead. A fortified position allowed for ferrying troops and supplies from the sea.

No one liked the mountain passes. No one felt at home in the cold and unforgiving terrain. Except the Second Legion.

The true sea power in the land was the Ralarians.

Dragh scanned the mouth of the harbour. Its defenses were weak because it was a simple set of docks and warehouses for goods. The mouth of the harbour led out into the sea.

The watch were always on the lookout for the Ralarians. A fleet of Ralarians were a death warrant. They were the best sailors in the land, and they could tack and move across the water like no others.

The Ralarians inhabited a set of islands to the south, and their business was trading and seafaring. Even the Council used the Ralarians.

Dragh moved up the plank of the ship. Its narrow rungs, set a foot apart from each other, helped sailors climb its steep angle. Dragh set his bag down on deck and looked out across their fleet.

Dragh and his lot knew the truth. The Ralarians were pirates. They preyed on the high seas. Their ships were wolves of the ocean.

"My good man, you look like you drank the bottom of the bottles last night!" a voice cut through Dragh's inner monologue.

Geral, Hemmelle, Pello, Zeffo, and Relish walked up the plank of the boat and onto the deck. They dropped their belongings along the rail as they made their way up to Dragh's position at the front of the vessel.

"What's on your mind, my good man?" Pello asked.

Dragh laughed. "I was thinking that we'd be fucked if the Ralarians decided to meet us at the mouth of the Landor Harbour."

"Gods, he's in a foul mood today, man." Zeffo, Pello's younger brother, laughed aloud.

Dragh looked at the two of them; they were not quite identical twins. They were broad and strong, both with blonde hair and easy smiles. Two well-built men from the docks of Landor. Zeffo had killed a man in a fight after a night of drinking. Pello had stood in to defend him. They had both made it to prison.

"Poor bastard didn't even have a proper sleep last night," Relish slurred, still under the influence of drink.

"Where did you rest your head last night, poor Dragh?" Hemmelle asked in mock concern. He leaned beside Dragh on the rail of the ship.

Dragh shook his head, looking over to the quiet one in the group, Geral.

Geral had come to the Second shrouded in mystery. He hardly spoke. He was always watching others, but never participated in conversation. He was tall and lithe, his skin tanned from hard years in the sun. When he was on a boat, he was alive. Dragh and his friends had dragged the truth out of Geral on their last voyage: Geral had been a fisherman's son.

Only put in the Second after he'd stolen a boat.

Geral gave him a raised eyebrow. No words of wisdom.

Dragh sighed.

"I was with your missus. Had to see her off before we left on our merry adventure," Dragh spit back at Hemmelle.

They laughed at him. They knew they'd gotten under his skin.

"I'd like to see how you snuck into my bed last night with us. Mind you, I had so much to drink I might not have remembered, myself." Hemmelle punched Dragh on the shoulder.

Dragh pretended it hurt, mocking Hemmelle.

"Aye, you had so much to drink she may not have remembered it," Relish said. Dragh could smell the alcohol on his breath from the other side of Hemmelle.

They all laughed at the joke, Relish being the notorious drinker that he was.

"Enough bullshitting. Anyone know what we are getting into?" Zeffo asked, with a snarl of frustration.

"What's wrong? You miss your mother already?" Relish poked at Zeffo.

"Easy, she's mine too." Pello put his hand in front of Zeffo, pushing him back. His face was turning red with anger at Relish's joke.

"Down boy, down." Hemmelle slapped his leg, egging Zeffo on.

"What's this now, a little pissing match between my dogs?" a tired voice asked.

The group of them turned to the walkway, where their primus walked onto the ship.

"Primus Cello," they all chimed.

Primus Cello had been a thief in his former life. He was a fat and short man who'd given his life over to the Legion. No matter how much time the Legion spent on the campaign, Cello never seemed to lose weight. He was a taskmaster, and a hard primus to serve under.

"One of you shit-eaters sleep with Hemmelle's whore again?" Cello barked at them.

Dragh tried to choke back a laugh, and he heard grunts from the others who were not as successful. They saluted Cello, an arm over the chest with a clenched fist.

"Aye, Primus," Relish said, his voice even and calm.

Dragh raised an eyebrow at the sobering of Relish. He'd been sluggish and drunk just moments before.

"Must have been you, eh? Can't help yourself when you get to drinking." Cello laughed at Relish.

"You know, sir, it may have been. Funny that, I don't remember anything from last night," Relish replied.

"I bet. I was with you at the Duck's Beak, pulling you out of a fight." Cello gave Relish a shake of his head.

"Dragh, the general's asked for you," Cello said, the bark back in his voice.

"Aye sir. Where is the general?" Dragh asked.

Cello jutted his chin out, an eyebrow raised. "On the *Ajan*," he said, referring to the floating troop carrier beside them at the dock.

Dragh looked over to the monster beside them. The *Ajan* was triple the size of the tub that they were on. It could carry five squads to the *Maren's* two. It had supplies for months and a crew of sailors who were misfits from all over the nation, including some Ralarians who'd been exiled from their islands.

"I'll be back before we launch, Primus Cello." Dragh nodded to his primus.

"See that you are. I won't be waiting for you to get your head out of the general's ass. Can't figure what he'd want from you," Cello said, walking away from them to shout at the sailors preparing the *Maren*.

Dragh looked to his friends. Hemmelle gave him a knowing look.

"What's all this?" Zeffo asked, still sour about the personal jabs they made at him.

"Mind your fuckin' business is what it's about." Hemmelle cuffed Zeffo on the back of the head.

"Okay, easy!" Zeffo rubbed at his head, his eyes filled with rage.

"I ran into the general when I left the Beak. I'm guessing he wants some reason for how drunk I was. Might be in for it," Dragh muttered to them.

None of them accepted the answer, and Relish gave him a blank stare.

Dragh walked away; worried that his friends were growing suspicious of his real identity. He'd kept it a secret for a long time. His friends would eventually work it out— his life was too odd to leave unquestioned.

He was a criminal like the rest of them, and they had no reason to suspect he had royal blood in his veins. The general had never requested him outright before now, sneaking in a word in passing here and there.

The last time he'd seen the general alone had been when the general had saved Dragh from a small granite cell with bars across the door and window.

On occasion, he'd run into Nestor on the training grounds in a troop review. He'd always acted the general. Never the uncle.

What had changed?

Dragh made his way down the gangway and over to the entrance to the *Arjun*. It was a three-masted monster. The beautiful teak wood was scrubbed clean of the ocean, its masts sparkling in the sun. The bow had an easy line that melded with the short rail surrounding the boat.

He came to the gangplank for *Arjun* and was stopped by two guards of the Second.

He scoffed at them like he'd scoff at a Praetorian. They were just as bad, thinking everyone in the Second were out to get General Nestor.

"What's your business here?" the first guard, a thick necked guard, asked, his hand on Dragh's chest.

"My business is mine. I've been requested by the General," Dragh responded, his anger showing in his face.

"Get out of my face or you won't be making it on this ship," the second guard, narrow-faced guard squealed.

Dragh looked at the second guard. The guard's face reminded him of a rat's face, narrow with a pointed nose.

The guards both squinted at him, their hands on their swords.

"Let him through!" A voice cut through the tension between the guards and Dragh. Dragh relaxed his hand on the sword he'd half drawn.

The two guards looked up at the deck of the ship. Nestor was at the rail, pointing at Dragh.

"You heard the man, get out of my way," Dragh said to the pair, pushing past them and shouldering the big guard on the right.

"We'll be seeing you," the second guard squeaked, getting out of Dragh's way.

Dragh ignored the comment and marched up the boardwalk.

The *Ajan* was much different than the last ship he'd traveled on. There was a wooden crane rigged and pulling supplies off the dock, moving barrels and crates into the hold of the ship; men were hardly involved. The sailors were at their stations, many of them standing at attention and not busying themselves getting ready.

The deck was long and wide. Three masts jutted out of the deck, and two companion ways led to the lower levels of the vessel. In between them was a large hatch-style opening where supplies were being lowered for the journey north.

The general's cabin was at the end of the vessel, its large oak doors opened. General Nestor stood in front of them. He motioned for Dragh to come to him.

Dragh saluted him, his arm to his chest and fist closed. "General, you wanted to see me?" he asked, his face a mix of frustration and surprise.

"Aye, Dragh, come with me." Nestor motioned with his hand towards his cabin. Dragh followed.

Dragh closed the doors behind him, letting the natural light from the back of the cabin, a window, light the room. He looked around. His uncle's room was sparse: a war chest in front of a small cot, a table set up with maps and weights on them to keep them from moving. All of the furniture was secured to the floor to stop it from moving with the sea.

A small metal brazier threw heat off, pushing back on the damp air.

Nestor pointed to the chair by the window and dragged another over from behind his desk.

Dragh sat heavily, not sure what to say to his uncle. His general. "What are we today? Soldiers or blood?" he asked finally.

Nestor chuckled. "Always a way with words, my little nephew."

Dragh took a deep breath and released it. The tension he felt from meeting with his father, the news of his new fatherhood, Lucille. It all melted as his uncle slapped his shoulder and grinned.

"Congrats, boy. I knew you had it in you!" he laughed aloud.

"Of course you know. I should have guessed. You never call me up." Dragh felt the weight of his fatherhood settling back down on his shoulders.

"Well of course I wanted to see you; it's not every day that you find out you are going to be a great uncle. This is good news." Nestor got up and poured two glasses of spirits from a jug in his war chest.

"How much of that do you have in there?" Dragh asked.

"It's full. Best grog you can get, this side of Skellen Pass." Nestor handed a glass to Dragh.

"Did you ever serve there, Uncle?" Dragh asked, taking a sip of the fiery liquid.

"At the Pass?" Nestor asked. "Gods, no. That was not my calling. I gambled too much to be sent to the Pass," Nestor replied.

"Is that how you ended up in the Second?" Dragh asked again, probing, trying to avoid talking about Lucille and his expected child.

Nestor gave Dragh a smile, a knowing one. He'd never told Dragh how he ended up in the Second. Like Dragh, he'd been imprisoned for a crime. That was his penance. Rumors were all around the Second; men talked in dark corners about what the general had done. He was a disgraced king, a rapist, a murder—Dragh had heard it all.

"You know, I've never been outright asked that since I became a general." Nestor smiled.

Dragh toyed with the idea of pushing his uncle. He'd win a fair amount of coin if he could drag it out of him. Men of the Second had been betting on what Nestor was in for, long before Dragh was in the Legion.

Dragh sighed. "What do you want me for, Uncle? You never call me to your cabin."

Nestor's face dropped its jovial look and the general came out. "I've spoken with your father, Dragh."

He never referred to Kallen as the king with Dragh. It was always his father or Kallen.

"And what, you want me out of the Second too?" Dragh shot back, his anger up.

"I want what's best for you, boy, you always know that," Nestor said.

"You know, this is the only family I have. I can't leave my squad behind, and I can't leave you. I have nothing in Landor…" Dragh started.

"Nothing but Lucille," Nestor said softly. "And your child, it seems."

Dragh let the words hang in the air. He did not know what to say to Nestor; the truth still had not set in. Him, a father.

"I need to go on this mission, Uncle. I can't stay here now. I need the money," Dragh said.

Nestor gave Dragh a questioning look. A prince of Landor needed nothing by way of money, and they both knew it. The royal treasury would help him with any money he needed.

"I'm guessing what you mean is that if you stay in Landor, you may find yourself killing Ellis?" Nestor joked.

"Aye, that is what I mean." Dragh accepted the falsehood. His uncle gave him an easy out.

"I need this," Dragh said again to Nestor. "What are we doing in the North, anyhow?"

"Don't tell your squad." Nestor paused, gathering his thoughts.

Dragh waited, knowing that Nestor liked to create suspense.

"The Northern Tribes have started a rebellion." Nestor ran his hands through his long hair. Dragh watched Nestor; his heavily-muscled frame moved easily as he got up and poured himself another drink. He looked like King Kallen, without the slight paunch that inactivity had given the king.

"What have they done this time?" Dragh asked. It was not odd for the tribes to act up, but a rebellion sounded a little more serious than usual. A whole Legion moving north signified the force Kallen thought was needed.

"They've raided a number of villages on the coast, some on the borders in the south. A little too close to Landor for your father's taste," Nestor replied.

"Nothing new. What's different this time?" Dragh asked, not sure why the whole Second was moving north.

"Because they killed every man, woman, and child in every village they'd been to. They burned the villages to the ground and left the bodies mutilated and strung up for all to see," Nestor replied darkly, his voice colored by hate.

Dragh shook his head. "They've never done that before," he muttered, more to himself than for Nestor.

"Our border scouts say that they've seen babies with their heads bashed out on walls, women cut from belly to neck, split like... like nothing more than animals." Nestor strained to describe the hateful crimes.

"Need to bring them to heel. Those bastards are killing Landorians like they are no better than livestock." Dragh was horrified by what Nestor described. Crimes against a village for food, for horses, for some spoils of war, were one thing. You left the village where it lay. Occasionally, a man would die, and the tribes would declare a blood feud between the offenders, only settled when more blood was spilt.

This was different. This was killing for killing's sake. The tribes did not usually kill for sport. They knew that blood was precious, and that they were neighbors. They even married into many of the border villages.

This was an act of war against his people. This would only be answered by more blood.

"I will do what I must. We have to stop them," Dragh said to Nestor, his mouth dry, his teeth grinding against what he knew he had to do.

He might not have wanted to be king, but Landor was his country, and he would defend it with his blood. He would make sure Lucille and the baby were safe.

CHAPTER 7

Dragh walked from the general's quarters to the port side of the ship, making his way down the gangplank. The guards looked up at him, lopsided grins on their faces.

"See the poor sod making his way back to his ship? Must have given the general all he wanted. Fast, eh?" one of the guards quipped.

Dragh didn't think, his body moving on its own. Years of training let loose in a moment of anger.

His fist lashed out, catching the guard in the chin and dropping him to the ground. He pulled his sword out and held it to the second guard's neck, pressing it into the skin.

"Test me again, and you'll not live to regret it," Dragh said with venom, his breathing heavy.

The other guard nodded as best he could with the sword jabbing into his neck.

Dragh could see a trickle of blood form and roll down the guard's neck. He pulled his sword back and walked away to his ship, leaving the guards.

He knew he'd pay for that again; another enemy to add to his list.

They pulled the gang plank of the *Arjuin* in as soon as he'd made it onto the deck. Dragh could hear shouting from the deck as the ship moved into the deep water of the harbor.

Dragh passed by the deck of the oarsman. Small windows allowed their oars to stick out like quills on a porcupine from the belly of the ship. Sweat rolled down their unclothed backs. There were rows of two men per bench on either side of the ship's midsection. Rivulets of sweat poured off them as they heaved together: pull, up, pause, forward, pull, up, pause, forward.

The rhythm stopped him for a moment, a shiver going down his own back.

This ship had its own men at the oars. He remembered his time on the benches. The ache, the blisters. He could feel it in his hands. The smell of sweat, blood, and piss washed over him. This deck of the ship never truly came clean.

Dragh made his way back to the *Mauren*. His mood was dark, unsettled after talking to his uncle. He found the ladder to the lower decks and made his way down, finding his friends in the belly of the ship as it left the harbour.

The bottom deck was for the men. Water ran down both sides of the keel, its frames meeting up, the center filled with ballast for the journey. There was a rough floor, not fully covering it all. The running water and stone glinted in the lamplight.

It was dark and gloomy in the ship. Men's shapes were cast by shadows further down. The lamps silhouetting them.

Dragh loved the smell of the sea, the salt in the air itself. Little salt water seeped through the joints, but the little that did kept the stink of men at bay.

Some were in their hammocks, hung across the ship's frames, others sitting and talking on the side planks, their backs curved to match the profile of the ship.

"What was all that about, eh?" Zeffo asked, looking up from his game of dice.

"Shove off, I'm sure it was the general's business and Dragh's. None of ours to ask," Hemelle said to Zeffo.

Pello made a snide comment, too low for Dragh to hear. Geral gave him a shot to the side in response. Pello's sneer told Dragh it was something awful.

Relish was drinking from a bottle, passing it back and forth between two Ralarian sailors he was betting with.

Zeffo held the dice and shook them. "I'm just taking these poor sods' money before they go on a row." Zeffo chuckled as he threw the dice onto the small sea table they ate on.

"Fuck," Zeffo cursed. His dice was a four and a seven.

"Looking for snake eyes shouldn't be so hard for a guy like you," Relish blurted. He and the Ralarian sailors laughed.

Dragh watched in amusement as one of the Ralarians with a long black braid rolled snake eyes. He felt some satisfaction as Zeffo swore.

"You cheats!" Zeffo exclaimed, his hand down at his knife.

"Don't start something that'll get us gutted in our sleep, Zeffo," Hemmelle spoke up from his hammock a few frames from where they played dice.

Dragh gave Zeffo a raised eyebrow; the man's anger was getting the better of him.

Zeffo threw two slivers on the board and stormed away, muttering in anger at the Ralarians. He swept past Hemmelle and towards the bow of the boat.

"Dragh," Hemmelle called out, nodding to Dragh as he dropped from his hammock to the floor.

Dragh followed Hemmelle back out the hatch and up onto the open deck. Men were running around the deck at the call of the captain of the ship. Dragh spotted Cello, their primus. Both he and Hemmelle saluted.

"What was all that about?" Hemmelle asked, leaning on the gunnels of the ship.

Dragh spit into the sea, looking back at the small mouth of the harbour. He could see the mouth, but not the building beyond it. The creak of the tack was loud as the ship's sail caught the wind. He could hear the call for oars to be hauled in.

"The general wanted to see me," Dragh said defensively. He looked away at the coastline, trying to pick out villages he'd been to, looking for landmarks. He could feel Hemmelle's eyes on him.

"What did the general, *your* uncle, want from you, Dragh?" he asked.

Dragh took a sharp breath in. Hemmelle knew of his family, who he was, and where he was from. Hemmelle rarely used the word uncle; he loved the general. Dragh had confided in him years ago when he'd joined the Second Legion. In fact, it was Hemmelle who told him that it was best kept a secret. No one needed to know who his family was, lest they take advantage of him.

They were all brothers in the Legion, they were all in the Second for the same reason. If they found out that he was a welp of the king, if they found out why he was in the Second, he wouldn't last long in her ranks.

"Dragh, I know you need to talk. Something is off with you. What happened with Lucille? What happened with your father?" Hemmelle pushed at Dragh.

Dragh rubbed salt spray from his face and down his beard. He needed to talk; he needed to let out the rage and frustration.

"Lucille is pregnant, Hemmelle. She's having my child. And they know," Dragh said, looking at his friend.

Hemmelle stood at the gunnel, blinking. His eyes narrowed, and he watched Dragh.

"What?" Hemmelle said, his voice unsteady.

"It's true. I found out yesterday at the prison, from Ellis." Dragh laughed out loud, the insanity of the turn of events in his life catching up to him, how much had changed in such a short time. His father, Ellis, Nestor. The North.

Hemmelle was speechless for a few more moments before laughing with Dragh. The tension of the moment was released as they howled with laughter.

"You bastard, you are in some pile of shit now, aren't you?" Hemmelle said, slapping his back.

"Aye, I am in for it. My father and uncle know. That fucking Ellis would have found out somehow. Could have bribed Lucille's servants, something. He's always had it out for me."

"And I'm guessing that your father wants you back in the family now, eh?" Hemmelle asked, guessing at the conversation he had with his father.

"Even Nestor wants me to leave the Second. He wanted me to stay back and stay out of this campaign," Dragh told Hemmelle.

"The general said that?" Hemmelle asked, surprise written on his face.

"Aye." Dragh shook his head. "I don't get it either, Hemmelle. The man was happy to have me when I joined the Second, happy that I wasn't following in my father's footsteps."

Dragh sighed. He was disappointed in his uncle, a man that he thought highly of. He thought Nestor would understand his commitment to the Second. To defending Landor. Joining the Legion had straightened him out, kept him from death. He owed the Second. The Legion was his home.

"He must have his reasons," Hemmelle replied.

Dragh scoffed. "My father is the reason. He can't stand the idea that I might die out here, and he'd be down an heir."

"You're his only child, Dragh, I'm sure he doesn't think of you as only his heir. He's your father first."

Dragh had heard this drivel before. Hemmelle wanted to think the best of the king. Dragh knew better than he did.

"My father thinks of the throne and the kingdom first. Always. I don't pretend that I'm anything more than a bloodline to him. My uncle wants me to quit because his king commanded it." Dragh spit into the ocean off the rail.

"And why are you not gone then? Has Nestor refused his king's command?" Hemmelle asked.

"I'm not gone because a king cannot command a general to dispel one of his men without his consent. Landor passed those laws after the Cleansing," Dragh recited to Hemmelle. They were words from his last life, the life of tutors and education.

"Why?" Hemmelle asked.

Dragh knew that Hemmelle grew up less fortunate than Dragh. Hemmelle's family taught him that hard work might one day let Hemmelle live and earn enough food for a family and shelter. But that was all he'd been taught to hope for. He loved to talk to Dragh for hours about history and the times before the kingdom.

"Because a king must have his limits. The empire was split up under the kings. The Council saw to it that no man would control everything. They insisted that each nation be led by their king, but that the king had to be chained to the law. Unlike the emperor. They made sure that the generals, the leaders of the armies of the nation, had sway."

"And to make sure they did not take the countries from the kings?" Hemmelle asked, taking the bait as Dragh had done many times before him.

Dragh smiled as he realized he was telling stories the same way his tutors had, leading Hemmelle into questions he didn't know he had.

"Indeed, my friend. The Council also brought together the nations at the Skellen Pass. They had each nation give them men, a squad, sometimes more, to be the standing army of the Council."

Hemmelle nodded, his mind working. "Could they send us there some day?"

"Why would they want criminals like us?" Dragh asked.

They both laughed, their serious tones forgotten again as they slapped each other on the back.

"So, you are staying with us?" Hemmelle asked after they got their breathing back under control.

"Aye," Dragh grunted.

"And what will you do about Lucille when you return?" Hemmelle poked at Dragh.

Dragh looked at Hemmelle to gauge him. He was serious. "First, let us survive this war, my friend. For I truly do not know."

They both looked back out over the ocean. The waves were lapping at the prow of the boat, cutting through the sea. The sun shone on them, warming the deck. A light breeze came from the east.

They were both lost in thought.

"Let's go see if we can get some money out of those Ralarians," Dragh suggested.

"Aye, let's make sure that Zeffo hasn't stabbed one of them," Hemmelle said grimly.

Chapter 8

Dragh watched a rat scurry across the dim slice of light the lantern cast on the floor of the ship. Its scurrying was loud in the quiet night.

"Kiever below. I hate those little bastards," Dragh said.

A laugh came from Zeffo's hammock. "Better than those rat-faced Ralarians."

"Oi, shut up down there," a shout came from further up the bow.

The lanterns, turned down low, casted a dull light, orange and flickering.

Dragh stifled a laugh as Relish held up the crux towards the bow.

"Did he tell you what he was in for?" Pello asked in the darkness beyond the lantern light.

Dragh waited, not realizing the question was for him. He fought off sleep.

"Nah, he just fixed me with that look. You know, the one they teach generals," Dragh said.

Hemmelle laughed. "I'm still trying to sort out why Cello is in. That fat bastard couldn't be a thief. He's too slow."

"He'd never commit adultery. Not good-looking enough," Zeffo added.

They laughed.

Another jibe came from up towards the bow.

The men around him talked, each of them half listening as they always did when they were together in the evenings. Long days made for long nights when you could only get a ship's length away from your squamates.

Dragh could feel the boat moving through the water, though he felt like he was floating in his hammock. The odd sensation of being on solid flooring, yet being unsteady. The rocking of the boat was putting him to sleep after a long couple of days.

Dragh listened on with amusement. He had asked, but Nestor never said a word. He thought that he should ask Ellis, then thought better of it. That nosey bastard knew everything.

Zeffo complained about the money he'd lost to the Ralarians. They made an inspiring comeback in their game of dice to win Zeffo's purse. The Ralarian men had taken leave of their oar duties and come back to humiliate Zeffo.

Zeffo's theory of the general's crime was the grandest of all, that General Nestor tried to kill the king. He argued into the dark night that because the Royal Family couldn't execute Nestor, they gave him the Second as punishment to protect the king he'd tried to kill. Dragh had laughed at that— his uncle trying to kill his father.

"I've got to take a piss." Dragh rolled lazily off his hammock.

"Mhhm, Relish said, joining him at the ladder.

Dragh and Relish made their way up the steps to the deck of the ship. Calling them steps was generous; they more resembled a ladder. Sailors had a particular way. They had names for their ship, and its pieces made sense only to them.

Relish was quiet, still a little drunk, Dragh suspected. But then again, it was hard to tell if Relish was sober or drunk most of the time.

Raised voices caught both Dragh and Relish's attention. They looked to find where it was coming from in the darkness.

"What's all that, eh?" Relish asked, his voice slightly dry. He licked his lips.

Dragh looked over at the crowd gathered on deck by the mast. "Not sure, they seem to be looking over something."

Dragh and Relish made their way over to the crowd of sailors and soldiers.

"What happened?" Dragh asked, moving to get a better angle to see between the men milling about.

A commotion had broken out. Dragh could see shouting and shoving.

Dragh's friends came up from behind them. Dragh nodded to Hemmelle, who had his sword strapped to his waist.

He stopped. A body was on the deck: its neck slit, blood down its front, and clothes dark and red. Dragh looked up to Hemmelle, meeting his eye.

It was one of the Ralarians they'd all been playing dice with.

"Looks like someone came from behind and sliced him. He died quickly," Hemmelle related to Dragh.

Dragh nodded, looking around at the crowd of men. The sailors among them were angry, he could see it on their faces. The soldiers were confused, looking at each other with questioning looks. He spotted Primus Cello in conversation with a lithe older man, his legs bowed from a life at sea.

The stars and moon gave a little light, and everyone was visible thanks to the clear sky.

"The captain?" Dragh said, nodding to the pair. They were animated. Cello shook his head, throwing his hands up. The captain raised his chin and crossed his arms.

"Looks like Cello is being told where to go," Hemmelle said grimly.

Dragh and Hemmelle both knew that if the primus was being told what to do, he and Hemmelle would be next. Shit rolled down the hill in the Legions.

"Here he comes," Dragh muttered as Cello turned to the crowd.

"Men of the Second, I want you all on deck and at attention!" Cello boomed, his primus voice carrying. "Go." Cello nodded to a young man who had just joined their squad.

Dragh thought his name was Verras, a dark-haired youth from Landor. He ran below deck to gather the squad.

Dragh and the men on deck moved to arrange themselves shoulder to shoulder. The mast and rigging were in the way of a perfect formation, but they made do and spaced themselves out around it.

They waited, and Cello paced as the men from below deck made their way up to the top deck. Cello clasped his hands behind his back.

Cello's face was red. His teeth clenched beneath his cheeks.

"This is not good," Dragh said, looking at the looks of hatred from the Ralarians.

"No. The Ralarians think it was us," Hemmelle replied under his breath.

"Odds are that it was one of us," Dragh said quietly to Hemmelle.

Dragh felt the nerves then, the ones you felt before battle, before your fate was decided. In this moment, a man's fate was going to be decided.

He wondered whose.

The rest of the squad filled out from below and stood at attention beside their squadmates. Cello stopped and looked them over.

"Men of the Second, we have a problem," Cello began, looking down at the deck and then back up at them. "One of us has spilled the blood of our brother-in-arms," He let the statement hang in the air.

"Ralarians ain't our brothers," someone behind Dragh said, low so that Cello couldn't hear him.

"What was that?" Cello bellowed, his rage letting loose. "Does anyone have any idea what happened here?"

The squad straightened up. None replied. Dragh did his best not to glance at Zeffo. He'd complained about the Ralarians all night. Did Zeffo have it in him to kill one of them?

"One of our own is dead. And it was someone on this ship. You are all accounted for." Cello pointed to the captain.

"The captain has allowed us to dispense our own justice. He is in command of the ship, and I am in command of you. The Ralarians will search the ship for the weapon. Once it is found, I will pass judgment." Cello looked over the men in his squad. "The guilty party will be found. Justice will be dealt out. Anyone with any reason to harm our brother-in-arms will be questioned. If you have any information, I expect you to come forward."

The men stood at attention, and the moonlight cast a glow over them. Dragh began to sweat in the cool evening. He could hear the Ralarians rooting through the bunks they'd been given. Packs were being thrown up onto the deck, contents spilling out.

"We're the Second. There are more swords and knives down there than in an armoury," Hemmelle said.

Dragh knew that many of the men would be angry—their worldly possessions were being ransacked. Many, like him, only owned what they carried. He had his weapons and his clothes. Not much else. He could feel the anger running through them all.

"You'll all be called for," Cello said to the squad. He nodded to the captain. "Hemmelle!"

"Yes, Primus?" Hemmelle answered.

"With me," Cello said and walked to the stern of the ship, past the group of Ralarians.

Dragh watched the Ralarians on the deck. Their eyes were full of bloodlust. Avenging their kin was on their mind; Dragh could see it behind their looks.

Dragh understood. If it had been Hemmelle dead on the deck, he would have burned the boat down.

"Do we just stand here?" Zeffo asked, his eyes darting back and forth.

"Shut up and stand at attention. You know what happened last time," Jal, one of their squadmates, muttered to Zeffo.

Dragh could still feel the lashes on his back. He'd stepped out of line, and Cello had responded kindly.

Jal was a bald, lithe man in his later years. He'd been caught up as a pickpocket in Landor whose luck had run out after stealing from a visiting dignitary. He was their connection to the black market. Anything you needed, he could get you. Or he knew someone who knew someone.

Dragh had bet Hemmelle once that Jal could get them the king's throne. They laughed, but thought it best not to ask Jal. Dragh would have loved to see the look on his father's face.

One by one, the men were called. The Ralarians grew tired of glaring at the Landorians, and they went about their business. As one man was called away, the other filed back into his spot.

Dragh waited, but his time never came.

The night turned to morning as the sun crept over the edge of the open sea.

"Enemy sails!" A call came from the bow.

All of them looked to the coast. A set of sails were furled, then two, then three. All of them raggedy-looking boats, but the ships sailed for the head of the Landorian fleet.

The Ralarians threw themselves into action, not waiting for the calls of the captain or first mate.

"To your station, men, ready for boarding!" Cello's voice boomed above the din of the busy ship.

Dragh and Hemmelle ran first to the hold. They dove for their weapons and then had to fight their way back through the squad to the deck.

"It was him, wasn't it?" Dragh muttered, catching his breath and trying to calm his heart rate.

They stood now at the rail of the ship, watching the enemy sails grow larger as their fleet grew closer.

Hemmelle ran his hand over his face, wiping the sweat on his tunic. "Might be. We will beat it out of him once we are ashore."

Dragh grimaced. He hated Zeffo. He'd known he was a worm the minute they'd met. He'd never seen Zeffo commit any crimes, not against his own brothers. But he knew it was Zeffo. Even if he couldn't prove it. Dragh would make him talk.

The enemy's boat crept forward, straight towards them.

The Landorian fleet was spread out. There were lengths between the ships so that they would not run into each other. Their sails filled the horizon behind Dragh's squad's vessel.

The enemy fleet was coming within range.

"Get ready," Dragh said, watching projectiles fly from the lead Landorian ships.

They were midway in the fleet. The first boats used arrows to engage the ships. They'd be in range of boarders soon.

"If they make it to us, let's swing on their decks. I've got an itch," Relish said, taking his spot beside Dragh.

"A little sword like that might not scratch it," Pello joked with Relish.

"I'll see it through your side and out the other," Relish challenged Pello.

Typical banter before facing pirates, Dragh thought.

"Keep them off my lines! Ain't no more boatyards up north!" the captain shouted to the men of the Second.

As the enemy boats passed the second line of ships of the Landorian fleet, Dragh could see flaming arrows fly from the first Landorian boats. The arrows streaked bright against the clouds, a trail of smoke issuing behind them. They cut through the sails and onto the decks. Their wrappings were coated in oil, which on impact, would hit the deck, stick, and set fire to the deck timbers.

Dragh shuddered, remembering the first time that the Second was attacked with fire arrows. He could still smell the smoke, still taste the acrid taste in his mouth. He watched with dark interest. He couldn't hear any calls for a fire or a general alarm from the enemy vessels.

"The pit is going on?" Hemmelle murmured.

Dragh watched on. The boats were veering away from the Landorian's formation on the sea. They moved on their original line, never wavering from it.

The enemy ships crossed in front of the path of oncoming boats and then sailed out into the ocean.

He could see no one at the helm of the vessels as the enemy vessels began to burn. Dragh watched as the fire consumed the boats. The orange flames licked up the sails, building off the decks of the boats. The ropes snapped and whipped in the heat of the fire. Smoke billowed like a blacksmith's forge as Dragh's boat passed them off the port side of their ship.

They all stood at the rails of the *Maren*, their boat. It felt like a funeral. Watching the death of the great wooden beasts of the sea.

Dragh stood at the rail with his squad for the rest of the voyage. Some took turns to relieve themselves and to get water and rations. The Legion knew that one attack was usually the beginning. Landor had been lulled into a false sense of security before. Never again.

The Second prided themselves on being the best; they would not be caught flat-footed in enemy territory.

"Dragh!" Cello called out. It was time to answer the primus. Dragh looked at Hemmelle, who nodded to Dragh. They'd handle this themselves.

Legion justice. Men of the sqauds dolled it out, not the primus.

"Yes, Primus!" Dragh replied. He gave Zeffo a withering look.

The Ralarians around them were still on edge, murder in their eyes, as they watched Dragh go to the primus.

——

The Legion made landfall in a bay just south of the main port of the north, Wurth Cliffs. The large port was sheltered by cliffs on either side for many leagues. No army could land close to the port, because its beaches were protected.

The town itself was situated in a natural harbour, the first large one north of Landor and above the Car Lauch Mountains.

The General chose the last bay before the cliffs, electing to make the journey over land where the Legion was most comfortable. Landing at an enemy's port did not seem to be the best idea. Many grumbled in Dragh's squad. They did not know yet why they were in the North, that rebellion was fomenting.

The Ralarians were animated. They'd not found any weapons to match the wounds of their slain comrade, and no proof that one of the squad members was the killer.

The captain was arguing feverishly that the Landorians would not leave the ship without a payment of justice. Cello's face was blood red with frustration. The Legion dealt with its own. Cello would kill the ship of Ralarians if he had to. Dragh knew he was loyal to the core.

Eventually they disembarked, the ship making landfall behind the bulk of the fleet. They'd been delayed by the captain's argument. No Ralarians were in sight, electing to stay under the deck and allowing the Second to unload their own supplies.

Dragh dropped over the side of *Maren*, hoping to never see her again. The best rowers took the Squads supplies and men into shore on the two boats that they were given. The Landorians were slow on the sea, without the expertise of the Ralarians.

Relish elected to take both boats back and swim to shore. He'd grown up on the water.

Dragh and his Squad were at the back of the beachhead. A string of supplies was being moved further inland. The Legion had already chosen a sight for their camp when a wet and dripping Relish showed back up from the ocean.

With their squad complete, Cello ordered them to march to camp.

They hauled their own supplies, tents, weapons, packs. None of them spoke as they settled into the cadence of marching, onward towards the camp site.

"Cello, what the fuck happened to you all?" a voice called out from on top of a mound of dirt that had already been thrown up.

They made their way over the grass plains, a small forest off in the distance inland. The earthworks were the first thing Dragh saw of camp, recognizing it from the number of times they'd dug the trenches of the camp themselves.

The squad stopped, all looking up to the large man atop the pile. Legate Calahan. Men worked all around him. His arms were as thick as Dragh's legs, his chest bulging at his armor.

As one of the five legates of the Legion, Calahan was responsible for Cello and four other squads under his command. He reported to General Nestor.

"Aye, Legate Calahan, there was an incident on the ship. A dead Ralarian. We were delayed by the captain. He demanded justice," Cello said, his face drenched in sweat from the short march towards the tree line where they were setting up camp.

"You told those bastards that the Legion handles their own?" Calahan asked.

"Aye, Legate. You will have a report by morning," Cello replied.

"Make it tonight, before the sun goes down," the legate replied.

Dragh nodded to himself. They'd have to handle this quickly. Hemmelle bumped his shoulder. They knew they were short on time. Dragh shrugged off his pack and nodded to Hemmelle. They were there to dig. The camp was made up the same way every night. It was meant to protect the Legion. They could fight from it, or they could attack from it. It was their strength.

He grabbed his shovel from his pack with white knuckles, the frustration with Zeffo hard to shake.

They had a job to do.

The camp was built by throwing up walls of earth and wood. Sharp stakes in the ditches helped thwart any attackers. Guard towers at each corner helped lookouts to call out any advancing parties. The gates on each of the four walls allowed for escape or attack. They would never be trapped unless an enemy could surround them completely.

Each squad was given a task. It rotated on occasion, but some tasks were punishments. Latrine duty, once the camp was made up, was a task that Dragh's squad knew well. They more often than not deserved it.

They were digging the trenches that would make up the perimeter of the camp. Other squads were cutting the trees that would make up the gates, the walls, and the sharpened stakes. Some squads were set out in the perimeter, guarding the camp in the event of an attack.

The Legions all made camps wherever they went outside of Landor.

Dragh looked around. The general and the legates had chosen a slightly elevated hill, not beside the forest, but close enough to cut wood from it. The camp would take up the entire hilltop. Around the newly-erected camp were rolling hills, gullies, and valleys. The place gave them a good viewpoint.

Dragh set about digging with his squad, their shovels dipping and tossing the earth up with an even, practiced pace.

"I think we need to take a walk." Hemmelle said to Dragh after an hour had passed. They'd stripped down to their tunics, the armor beside them in the event of an attack. The perimeter squads would give them enough notice to don it.

"Primus, we need a piss!" Dragh said to Cello, who was digging down the line.

"Make it quick, you lot. And bring back some water from the baggage train!" Cello replied.

"Let's go," Hemmelle said to Dragh.

Dragh and Hemmelle pulled themselves out of the trench they had been digging; it was nearly complete. The rest of the squad was working in rhythm. Dig in, toss up. Dig in, toss up.

"Zef," Hemmelle signaled Zeffo.

Zeffo looked up at them, his torso grimy with dirt and streaked with sweat. "What?" he asked, his eyes narrowed.

"Help us with a barrel," Dragh suggested, nodding to Zeffo.

"Give me a hand." Zeffo replied, holding his hand up.

They both grabbed him and pulled him out of the trench.

The baggage train was behind the camp towards the shore, protected by the whole camp beside the gates. They walked past squads working on the walls, sharpening stakes, and building the gates. The whole exercise would take them hours, no more. They were a practiced machine. New squad mates quickly adapted to the work each night, knowing it would save their lives.

They made it to the baggage train without issue. The wagons were arrayed in a group to keep the supplies protected. The perimeter squad was far from them. Dragh pulled down his breaches and relieved himself, followed by Hemmelle and Zeffo.

They quickly finished and went to the water wagon piled with barrels, big and small, for water. Hemmelle pointed to a midsized barrel that the three of them could grab. Zeffo stepped in front of them to get a better grip.

Dragh drove his elbow into Zeffo's side, letting him collapse into the barrel in front of him.

"Oof!" Zeffo cried out as he lost his breath.

He tried to turn, but Hemmelle and Dragh both grabbed an arm and shoved Zeffo against the cart's wheel. Dragh let his forearm ride up and cut off Zeffo's shout by jamming his neck against the wheel.

"What the fuck was that on the *Maren*?" Hemmelle hissed.

Zeffo's face had turned red, his limbs flailing as he fought against the larger men that had him pinned. He gagged, trying to breathe. Dragh let him have a breath by allowing a little pressure off his neck. Zeffo coughed, trying to get his wind.

"Why did you do it, you little fucking weasel?" Dragh accused Zeffo.

"I didn't!" Zeffo defended himself, his voice strained with Dragh's forearm at his neck.

Dragh flicked his elbow up, making contact with Zeffo's chin and snapping his head back.

"Try again," Dragh said through gritted teeth.

"It was self-defense! He attacked me!" Zeffo cried, spitting blood and shaking his head from disorientation.

"Like Pit it was self-defense. You could have gotten us all killed!" Hemmelle hissed at him.

"I swear," Zeffo said, gulping air. "He came after me at night. I was taking a piss off the deck and he came at me in the dark."

"Why would he do that? He had all your money, Zeffo," Dragh asked, still holding him against the wheel with Hemmelle.

"He must have been angered by what I'd said to him. I hate Ralarians, but I was defending myself, I swear!" Zeffo said in earnest. His voice was desperate.

Dragh gave Hemmelle a look. They let him go.

Zeffo collapsed to the ground, his hands going to his neck.

"What the fuck," Zeffo said, his voice hoarse.

"I don't believe you, and I don't trust you," Hemmelle said to Zeffo.

Dragh looked over the man. Zeffo was a worm. He'd shanked a man in a bar fight in Landor. That had gotten him life in prison. He'd been given to the Second because he'd made more trouble in prison than he was worth.

Should Dragh believe that Zeffo had defended himself? He wasn't sure.

"If it happens again, you are over," Dragh said. Zeffo was scum.

"What gives you the...." Zeffo started.

Dragh and Zeffo shared a look, and Zeffo stopped talking. Dragh was ready to kill him here and now. His hand was on his sword at his side.

"Leave," Hemmelle said to Zeffo.

Dragh and Hemmelle watched as Zeffo got off the ground and scampered away. He looked back with hate in his eyes.

"That's going to be a problem," Dragh commented.

"I know. I need to talk to Pello," Hemmelle said to Dragh.

Pello was the calm brother, the reasonable one. They both knew that Pello kept Zeffo on a tight leash. He was the reason Dragh hadn't killed Zeffo already.

"Let's get this barrel back to Cello before he passes out in that trench," Dragh said without humour.

They hoisted the barrel off the cart and carried it between them back to the trench.

CHAPTER 9

"Gods, this is good," Hemmelle said, stuffing more pork into his mouth.

Dragh mumbled in agreement, letting the juices fall down his face as he chewed. The charred skin and salt gave the pork a tangy taste. Wild.

Their plates were full of pork. A wild pack had wandered too close to the patrols from the beachhead. The scouts were always looking to spend a few arrows.

The camp was set up as a standard camp—men on all sides of the centre and the general's quarters in the centre, flanked by his own guard. The cook and cook fires were to the side of the general. Two things that the army had to protect: its general and its cook. All others were expendable.

Dragh shrugged, letting the mist that had collected on his cloak roll off the back.

"What of the plan? Why are we up here, Dragh?" Hemmelle asked.

They sat around their own fire, the rest of the squad out among the other soliders.

Dragh looked out among the tents. "Where is Relish? We need to keep him sober."

"So, he did tell you, eh?" Hemmelle pressed, shifting forward on his log seat.

Dragh shrugged.

"Fine," Hemmelle sighed, pushing more food into his mouth.

Dragh was happy for the reprieve. Hemmelle might know that the general told Dragh of the plans, but Dragh didn't know what to make of them yet. He hadn't yet sorted out what the tribes were getting out of this. Freedom? Did they want out from under the control of the Landorians?

His father rarely exerted any pressure on the tribes.

A horn sounded in the parade ground of the camp. Three blasts called them all together.

Dragh and Hemmelle both made their way forward, through the tents and into the press of bodies in the crowd.

Excitement ran through the crowd, infectious, as the men spread rumors of what Nestor had in store for them.

Dragh waited, far from excited. He knew what was to come. The killing of Tribesmen, the death of men of the Second.

War took no sides. Death visited all men, and the Second would not be spared in the fighting to come.

They were all gathered to await the general. He was planning to address the Legion, as was his habit on the night of their first encampment. They were to leave Landor without question, a test of their loyalty. Only finding out what their mission was once they were in enemy territory.

"They should have had more men." Hemmelle took a drink of his ale that he'd brought from beside the campfire.

The general liked to throw a feast on the first night. Food and drink. The easiest way to a soldier's heart.

"Which?" Dragh mumbled through a full mouth of pork.

"The boats that attacked us today, they should have had more men. Does it seem odd to you that it was only a skeleton crew, with one or two men aboard?" Hemmelle asked Dragh.

"They attacked us. Who gives a shit how many men were involved?" Dragh dismissed the issue.

The men around were roused, full of ale and food, content, and now hungry for information.

"Aye, who gives a shit. We burned them up like it was nothing. Have you ever seen a small group attack a *fleet*, Dragh?" Hemmelle pushed it.

"So what? The Northerners are stupid," Dragh commented, annoyed with Hemmelle.

"Stupid enough that they didn't have enough men to fire arrows back at us?"

"I can't account for who they put on their ships—neither can you. Why are you so concerned about it?" Dragh asked.

"Suppose they are doing it on purpose? What if they are tricking us? We think they are weak, and we will get pulled into a battle of their choosing."

Dragh scoffed. "And you think they have the numbers to come over these walls?" Dragh motioned around him to the fortification surrounding the camp.

The camp was a small fortress. The walls were high, with towers and gates lit by fires on all sides. Torches on the walls and moonlight pushed through the mist.

"No. But we should treat them with respect. An underestimated enemy is a dangerous one." Hemmelle went back to his ale.

"Aye, let's go tell the general that he should be careful," Dragh said with a raised eyebrow.

They lapsed into silence. The wait was on.

Dragh loved the feeling of eating in a camp; it felt like family. Men talked at their fires, telling stories of the day, becoming brave, or stretching the truth. All of them were passing time into tomorrow, to the next day.

A long horn sounded in the night from the general's tent, which was set up at the edge of the parade ground. The men all rose to look at the general. They saluted, a closed fist to their chest.

"Men of the Second!" General Nestor's voice boomed out as he exited his tent and leapt onto a nearby wagon.

Dragh was always impressed by his uncle. He could fight and drink with the men of the Legion, his strength that of men half his age.

A cheer went up from the Second.

"I suppose you want to know why I've pulled you from your soft beds in Landor?" Nestor asked.

The men laughed in an answer.

"You are getting soft and fat, that's why!" he laughed aloud.

Nestor pulled out his sword, digging its point into the wooden floor of the wagon he stood on. He looked down at it, and a silence fell over the Second.

"It's time to use these again," Nestor said so quietly that Dragh had to strain to hear him.

The men of the Second strained as well. They were caught in Nestor's web and the General knew it. They wanted to know, wanted to hear what their mission was.

Trust. They trusted that their general would not lead them astray.

Tension filled the Second, anticipation.

Dragh could see it in the men around him, leaning forward and listening.

"Men of the Second! They call you the Damned!" Nestor roared, his voice loud and strong. His neck bulged with the effort of projecting over the crowd.

"Arrooo!" the Second replied; a deep pride burned in them. Dragh could feel it.

"They call me the General of the Damned!" Nestor called out.

"ARRROOO!" the Second replied again, the sound reverberating off the walls of the camp.

Dragh felt the wave of excitement building now.

"We are here to put down the North! We are here because there is a so-called KING of the tribes." Nestor paused, letting that sink in.

The North had no king. They were a tribal people who warred and killed each other. They had no love for one another, and no camaraderie like the men of Landor.

"This so-called KING Saravas has declared that he is done with Landor, done with their TRUE KING, Kallen Sunborn."

Cries of the Second were scattered. Some booed, some yelled obscenities. Dragh could feel the energy of the men building. Nestor wound them up slowly now. A master of oration.

The Legion was buzzing. The build-up slowed, anger forming in its place.

"I say this will not stand. Saravas had killed our men and women of the Car Lauch. Murdering and pillaging, raping our lands and our people," Nestor held his sword up, pointing to men in the crowd, making eye contact with them. "What say you, men?"

"Kill them all!" a nameless voice cried out of the mass.

"ARRR!" shouts came from behind Dragh and Hemmelle.

Some men spit on the ground, cursing the tribes with colourful Legion language.

Dragh watched his uncle, entranced.

Nestor nodded, his eyes looking off into the distance. "We are here to remind this *Saravas* of his place. To remind the North that we rule this land. That LANDOR is the power in these lands. The king calls you, what do you say?"

"Arroo!" the men cried out.

The build—Dragh felt it start again.

"Are you ready, men of Landor!" Nestor asked the men of the Second.

"We are ready to die for Landor!" The call was answered by the Second.

The shouting pushed back, echoing off the walls of the camp. Even the men in the towers shouted to their general's call.

Dragh raised his hand in a fist.

"I AM THE GENERAL OF THE DAMNED, AND WE WILL HAVE OUR BLOOD!" Nestor cried out, his face red with effort and anger.

"AROOO, ARROOOO, ARRROOOO!" the Second replied with anger and bloodlust.

Dragh and Hemmelle let themselves get caught up in the chant, faces red with spittle flying all around them, the intoxication of an army moved by its general. Dragh could feel it in his bones as they chanted.

The tribes were in trouble.

The men of the Second knew they were the Damned, they would have their blood from these northern heathens.

"Now, drink up and get to sleep. We march north in the morn!" Nestor said to his men, hopping off the barrel and clapping the Legates who had flanked him on their backs.

Dragh raised his mug of ale in the air, saluting the general. He felt the rush of blood and battle lust. He drank his ale and shouted with the others, liberated from the bonds he felt in Landor and the chains he felt to his old life.

He was alive in the Second. He was built for war.

Chapter 10

Dragh woke to a loud clanging, his mind foggy from the ale he'd drunk. He shook his head and slapped himself, trying to get alert.

"Get up, you lazy whoresons! We are under attack; get to the wall!" a voice cut through the fog.

"Arg," grunted Hemmelle, who was bedded in the same tent.

Dragh rolled to his side and grabbed at his sword belt beside his bed. He grabbed in the darkness from memory, fumbling to get the belt wrapped around his midsection.

"Up!" he shouted, to get Hemmelle moving.

He pushed his way out of the tent and into the night. He could hear Hemmelle pushing open the tent not far behind him. He checked his sword and dagger, patting the belt to feel the pommels on either side while he looked around.

He tried to get his bearings, remembering that he was in the North, in camp. The ale slowed his mind.

"North wall!" a shout rang through the clamor of the camp.

Dragh took in the chaos of the night attack: men running from their tents, grabbing gear and trying to push the sleep from their minds. Metal clanged, feet scoffed the ground, and men shouted to their squad mates and primus. Legates shouted orders.

Gone was the excitement from the general's speech. Men were running like fools, trying to find their squads. Jumpy, like it was their first time under attack.

Dragh calmed himself, thinking through the fog of his own mind.

"Let's find Cello and form the squad," Dragh said as a breathless Hemmelle reached his side.

"Aye," Hemmelle said as they broke into a sprint towards the north wall.

Darkness pushed in on the camp, the earlier reprieve from the fog losing its battle. The fog made their dash to the wall slow as they weaved around tents and men.

They reached the north wall, finding Relish, Zeffo, and Pello already there. They all had the look of dazed men, roused from a dead sleep. No matter how many times it happened to them, it never got easier.

Dragh felt the familiar nerves. His mind raced. He worked to calm it. He could smell the smoke of the fires burning down low, hear the yells of the men around him, sharper, louder.

"Men, form up!" Dragh yelled to his squad as he spied more of his fellow soldiers around him.

He looked for Cello, but was not able to find him. He shouted to the watch commander, instead. "Legate, Cello's squad is here!"

Legate Jaze of the Fifth Legion looked over the squad and over from the top of the wall.

Jaze shouted over the din of battle to Dragh. "You're in charge of your squad until Cello is here. Don't fuck this up." He kept Dragh's eye for a moment longer before Dragh understood the implication.

"Yes, Legate Jaze!" Dragh saluted.

"Form up at the centre of the gate. They are coming with horses." He pointed to the gate beneath his feet. Jaze turned abruptly, his cape whirling around with him as he stalked off across the wall, giving orders and ducking as projectiles were thrown up against the wall.

"You heard him, men! Form up on Dragh!" Hemmelle echoed Jaze's orders. His voice strained with the nerves of combat.

"Prepare for anything, men," Dragh said, watching the gate. He could hear the yells of the Northerners, although Dragh could not see them. The screams of men came from the walls of the camp as arrows rained down on them from above on the wall.

He glanced to his left and right. The men were nervous, some still rubbed sleep from their faces.

"Remember, you are the Second!" Dragh shouted.

"Aroo!" the call was answered by his men.

To the south, he could hear another call from a battle horn. The south gate had attackers as well. For a moment, Dragh considered if they should move to the south.

He looked up at the walls and towers. Jaze was nowhere in sight. Cello nowhere to be found.

"They are at the gate!" a call from above came.

Moments later, Dragh could hear the sound of axes at the gate. Then, the thud of logs fashioned into a ram. Dragh looked to the squads beside him. They were scarred and hard men of the Second.

They were the rock that stopped the tide.

They were ready.

"Shields and spears to the front!" Dragh commanded his men.

He thought he heard his voice falter, and Dragh prayed for the strength to get through the fight. He had never commanded before. After his time in the Eighth, he'd been a nameless soldier of the Second.

Men formed up on either side of his squad, filling in from behind them.

Dragh smiled. His squad held the place of honour. First to the gate, first to form.

Other primuses called their shields forward. Three squads abreast now faced the gate in a semicircle, with Dragh's squad at the centre.

"Gods be with us," Hemmelle whispered to himself.

Cracks began to take form in the logs of the gate in front of them.

Dragh shook his head, gripping his sword tightly behind the first wall of shields. He breathed in and out, letting his mind enter the battle without the stress of hope from the gods.

He was trained for this, honed for battle. Forged in the mountains of his homeland, scrapping with the Praetorians, training from the cradle to hold a sword. His father had made him a soldier, whether he liked what he did or not.

A new fear bubbled up in his chest. He needed to make it back to Lucille. To their child. His breath caught in his chest. He needed to live for them.

"Ready, lads!" Dragh called. "Archers, ready your volley," he called to the men in the back line of the squad.

Each squad had their mix of weaponry. The primus's job was to know how to use it.

The other two primus did not question his command. The archers in each squad prepared just the same.

Axes chewed through the wooded gate, its green wood no match for the hard biting axes of the enemy. Dragh could see small glimpses of men and weapons. The dull thud of the battering ram had the gates starting to sag with each hit.

"It's coming," Hemmelle said, his voice tense.

A loud creaking began as the battering ram hit home one more time.

"Fire!" Dragh called out as the north gate collapsed inward on the right side.

The gate fell in and downward, revealing a large mass of angry Northerners dressed in furs and leathers. Some had war paint down their faces and some were bare-chested, screaming war cries at the Landorians.

Dragh could taste the rage rolling off of them.

"Protect the camp!" Legate Jeze yelled to the squads below.

Dragh locked eyes with Jeze, whose face was red with exertion. An arrow was protruding from his left arm. It hung uselessly, and blood streamed down it.

"Forward!" Dragh shouted, focusing on the enemy now. His squad surged forward as one, a practiced move from many battles they had fought together. Dragh was swept up in the surge, no longer in control of the fate of the men, no longer in command of a squad, but a moving spectacle of blood and death.

They would deal out death to the Northerners, who would try and take their camp and their lives. The press of bodies pushed Dragh forward. In moments, they clashed with their enemy.

They cut down the Northerners like a scythe through wheat. The front of the squad was locked together, shield on shield, spears at the front. The lockstep pace and the wall of steel could not be stopped by so few.

The front slowed as they surged over the dead and dying. Dragh was a line behind the front, stabbing between the spearmen, taking shoulders and eyes, anyone who might make it past the steel of the spears. He stumbled on a body and was righted by the man beside him. Dragh kept going with the squad.

All that was left was to keep killing. Dragh looked around, trying to find the squad next to them. He could only see the press of Northerners on either side.

They were a squad's length from the gate. They just had to keep pushing.

"To the gate! Push, you bastards!" Dragh yelled at his men.

The squad pushed hard, shields pushing as one, the middlemen of the wall setting the pace. They pushed and stabbed with their spears. Dragh's line stabbed at any men that came between them. Dragh could sense it before he could see it— the right side of his squad buckled.

Dragh glanced to his sides. He could feel the other squads struggling.

He held panic at bay. If he let his squad move forward too fast, if they couldn't keep up, the enemy would start to cut at his flanks.

He slowed his mind. *Trust the squads beside you.*

Verras, the dark-haired youth who Dragh and Hemmelle had found fighting with Zeffo one night, went down, a sword to his chest. When he dropped, his squad mate beside him took his place, holding back the oncoming Northerner.

Dragh yelled at Hemmelle to fill in beside the new youth, Baratan. Baratan was defending Verras, fighting on top of him. The Second didn't abandoned their wounded.

The youth, Baratan, had been picked up for stabbing a merchant in a game of dice. The way Baratan told the tale, the merchant had been cheating. Dragh pushed it from his mind.

"They are giving way!" Relish called from the left flank of the squad.

Dragh looked over; his squad was pushing into the gap that the Northerners left behind.

"Hold the line!" Dragh shouted to Relish and the squad.

The worst thing they could do was to let the Northerners fold on one side, allowing their squad to lose their footing. Many squads were undone by this tactic, a feint, designed to pull the squad's front lines in and to buckle the enemy lines once they were caught off-guard. Lucky for Dragh, Relish was no fool, and he held his end of the squad.

The other squads made ground and pushed forward, surging into the tribesmen.

Suddenly, the pressure was off. Men were falling to the left and right of the squad. Some men now had no one to kill, doubling up on whoever was in front of them. Dragh slowed the squad, allowing himself time to look around.

Battle horns could be heard outside the walls, echoing from the forests. A sharp shout from beyond the gate stopped Dragh and his men in their tracks.

Dragh looked over the battle, over the heads of his men and the Northerners. They were retreating.

"Second, HOLD!" Jaze called from the wall.

Dragh looked up, catching the legate's eyes. Dragh held up his sword in acknowledgment.

Jaze gave him a curt nod.

Dragh looked over to the south wall's gate, directly across from them. The gates still stood, with some holes in them.

"Let's get some axes and lumber and get the gate back up," a sharp voice barked out from behind Dragh.

Dragh looked over to see a clean and proper Cello walking towards the squad. His sword was still sheathed.

Dragh looked him over with disgust.

"What are you all looking at?" Cello said with a sneer as he reached Dragh.

Dragh lurched forward, but before he could get his hands on Cello, he felt an iron grip on his shoulder.

He looked over to find Jaze, covered in blood, his eyes alight with fury. Dragh looked away, unable to match his stare.

"Cello?" Jaze asked aloud. Loud enough for the squad to hear.

"Legate Jaze, the men have done well, haven't they?" Cello said, straightening up under Jaze's gaze.

"I would say so, under the command of their new primus." Jaze clapped Dragh on the shoulder.

Dragh nodded to Jaze. "Thank you, Legate."

"New primus?" Cello sputtered, looking around to the men he'd lost command of. "I was in charge the whole time, just at the back line!" Cello said to Jaze by way of explanation.

"And you think me blind?" Jaze asked, his temper showing through his words. He grimaced, looking at his shoulder, the arrow still embedded in it.

"Sir, you should get that looked at," Hemmelle said from beside Dragh, to the legate.

Jaze glanced at Hemmelle, then back to Cello. "You answer to Dragh or you answer to the general for your incompetence. Your choice, Cello. Petar!" Jaze yelled for the primus who'd attacked beside Dragh's squad.

"Yes, Legate!" Petar replied, running to attend to the legate. He was a stocky man, a head shorter than Dragh.

"Post a guard outside the gate until Dragh's squad can clean up this mess!" Jaze commanded.

"Yes, Legate!" Petar replied, turning. He issued commands to his own squad to guard the gate.

"Squads, support Petar's squad outside the camp!" Jeze shouted to the remaining two squads on either side of Dragh's new squad.

Jaze walked away, flanked by two hard-looking men covered in blood that was not their own.

Cello looked blankly at Dragh and Hemmelle, then around at the men of his squad. He turned and walked away and back into the camp.

Dragh shook it off. Not the time.

"Huh, a promotion and an angry squadmate. What a good day." Hemmelle laughed. "Congratulations, my friend. I knew you had it in you, primus."

"Aye, what will you do about the angry ex-primus?" Relish asked, picking at his teeth with his bloody dagger.

"Zufier above, Relish, clean that thing off," Pelllo said from behind them.

Dragh looked around; all of them were staring at him. "What are you waiting for?"

They looked at him blankly.

Pello grunted a laugh. "Your leave, Primus Dragh."

The squad laughed with him.

"Get the pit out of here and get some lumber for the gate." Dragh clapped Pello on the back.

The squad moved off, leaving Dragh and Hemmelle at the ruined gate.

"What are you going to do with Cello?" Hemmelle said gravely.

Dragh knew what he was asking. Cello was not one to forgive this. He would consider this a personal slight. They all knew his history. He'd tried to kill a man who had accused him of theft.

"I'll work him just like the others. I have no words that will heal this wound," Dragh said to Hemmelle. He gave Hemmelle no chance to reply and allowed himself a moment before walking to gather supplies with his men.

CHAPTER II

D ragh washed his hands in water warmed by the cooks. It was a large cauldron, lukewarm, no longer hot by the time he'd gotten to it.

He scrubbed at the blood caked on his hands. The blood was pressed into the lines and creases on his hands. Splinters peppered his skin. Tough as they were, they stung with the warm water he rubbed into his hands.

He chewed at the splinters and was rewarded by the relaxation that came afterwards.

Dragh could smell the burning flesh as they hewed new boards for the gate, fitting them with cross beams and pegs. He splashed his face, trying to wash the smoke from it, the smell from his nose.

Dead bodies did not mix well with the living. Every man in the army knew that a pyre was in their future if they fell in battle.

He looked up into the sky—a rosy sky kissed the mountains to the south and hills around them. Blood had been spilled. The earth knew of the foul deeds of men.

Dragh wandered over to the cooks's line, where men were waiting for their morning meal. None had slept, and many of them swayed back and forth, fighting off the lack of sleep from the evening battle.

Dragh walked forward and shuffled one step at a time until he made it to the front of the line.

The cook, a fat man like Cello, handed him a piece of bread and a bowl of oats. A strange reminder that it was just past dawn.

Dragh nodded his thanks, too tired to waste words.

He wandered over to where his men sat and picked a seat by Hemmelle.

The camp was quiet, the lull after a battle. The men were weary. They knew that a long day was ahead of them, no rest after a night of fighting. Dragh could see men sleeping where they sat. Hands with bread and oats gripped in them.

The men grumbled a welcome to their new primus. Dragh waved it off.

He sat, focused on his chewing. The morning sun warmed his face as it rose.

"Eat up, the legate wants to see you." A voice shook Dragh out of his thoughts.

Dragh looked around to find one of the guardsmen who had flanked the legate Jaze earlier. A veteran of the Second, by the look of his gray hair. His arms were scarred over from fighting.

"Aye." Dragh nodded back. The veteran turned on his heel and stalked off.

"Shit, but that man scares the life out of me," Hemmelle said to Dragh.

"Me too,. He must be one of the legate's men. He never seems too far from Jaze," Dragh replied.

"Jaze has always got two monsters with him. A legate must be careful, like the general. I heard he's had a couple of men try and kill him in the camp," Hemmelle mused.

Dragh had heard the same. "In a camp of killers and cutthroats, who's safe?"

"The general is safe. He walks among us all the time," Dragh retorted.

"You don't see the watchers, then." Hemmelle had a sly smile on his lips.

Dragh shook his head. "That's hogwash."

"An army is, at its core, a bunch of criminals. Killers. Every one of us Dragh. Don't ever forget that. Even General Nestor."

Hemmelle paused and leaned in so that only Dragh could hear him. "Your father. All leaders wind up their men until they are ready to break. The mountain breaks us, but the Generals set us upon the world with sword, ax, spear and bow to shed blood. Each and every one of us is here to kill his fellow man." Hemmelle took a bite of his meal and wiped his face on his tunic.

Drag considered Hemmelle and what he had said. Did his own father know what he was letting loose each time he commanded the Second to leave Landor?

Did the general know that he was really letting death out into the world? Of course—that's what Dragh was here for.

"Aye, for a man that was not brought up by tutors, you are wise beyond your years, my friend," Dragh said to Hemmelle. As much as he wanted Hemmelle to be wrong, his father and uncle knew what they were doing. Perhaps they wanted Dragh out of the Second because they knew he'd find his place. His place among the killers of the world.

That was what they feared. That he wouldn't come back to them a man, but a killer.

If that was true, what would he come back to Lucille as?

"Go, don't let the legate whip you for being late on your first summons!" Hemmelle laughed. "Don't worry, it can't be worse than taking Argyle."

Dragh gave him a rude gesture and left the fires and his men. Nothing could be worse than the winter months they had spent at Argyle. A cold hell that Dragh would never forget. Their first battles after the Car Lauch.

Dragh shook his head. Hemmelle and Pello would make sure they were packing. They'd be marching with orders soon. Two attacks: one at sea, now at night. They would move to strike the tribes, to go on the attack themselves soon.

He walked through the camp to the legate's tent, one of the six in the centre of the camp. There was a tent for each legate and a tent for the general. Dragh spied Jaze's tent by its sigil. He presented himself to the men in front of it.

"State your business," the guard on the left said.

Dragh cleared his throat. "Uhh... Primus Dragh reporting for Legate Jaze."

The two guards exchanged a look and then turned to Dragh. "Go on, he's waiting." The tall one nodded to the tent door.

Dragh entered, pushing into the tent.

He stood at attention, looking around the tent, at the men assembled. They were focused on a map laid across a table.

"Dragh, about time. I called for you, you come. That is your job." Jaze's voice cut through any kind of notion that he was going to be treated better as a primus than as a soldier of the Second Legion.

"Legate Jaze, sorry. I had—" Dragh stumbled in.

Jaze cut him off. "I didn't ask for an excuse, Dragh."

His sharp tone cut at Dragh's confidence. Dragh looked to the legate, his mouth shut. He didn't know what to say. As he looked around, he found the four other primuses under Jaze's command. Kaffer, Mallen, Faras and Petar. Dragh knew Petar from the attack at the gate and only knew the other three from afar.

"Already chewing on the new pup, eh, Jaze," a booming voice came from the tent flap.

All eyes turned to the entrance of the tent. They all knew the voice, Dragh most of all: General Nestor.

"General!" Jaze welcomed the general with a salute.

Dragh noticed Jaze's wound was bound. His shoulder had fresh bandages with a hint of blood underneath.

"Jaze, continue. I wanted to see you and your new primus," Nestor said to Jaze, giving him a knowing look.

Jaze gave the general a nod, his mouth and eyebrows a firm line.

Draghs gripped his sword so hard his knuckles were white as he watched Jaze.

He looked around. The rest of the primus were still as statues. Their eyes followed their legate, then the general. Dragh was confused by them. Why were they afraid of the general?

Dragh listened as Jaze outlined their mission. They were to face the Northerners as fast as possible. The king and the general wanted to stop the bloodletting on the borders of the Car Lauch Mountains. Enough villages had been razed.

The king wanted to show the people that there was no one beyond his rule.

Dragh waited, knowing that at some point, his time in front of the legate was coming. The new man in a squad always got the shit kicked out of them. Dragh remembered his first day. He pissed blood for a week when he joined.

"Dragh!" Jaze shouted, making Dragh jump.

"Yes, Legate?" Dragh asked.

"Did you hear any of that?" Jaze asked.

"Yes, Legate. My squad is to patrol the forward east flank and protect the Legion from the low hills," Dragh replied.

"And what are we worried about in the mountains?" Jaze's eyes narrowed.

Dragh looked around at the men. The primuses had smirks under their severe looks.

"The mountains, sir?" Dragh glanced at the general, whose face remained impassive. He swirled a cup, apparently bored.

"Are you an idiot, Dragh? Of course, the mountains. We are worried about the Northerners hiding their men in the rolling hills where we don't have any way to see them. There is no line of sight out there, with all of the valleys and gullies. I could hide an idiot as big as you out there," Jaze snapped at Dragh.

"Yes, Legate, sorry, Legate." Dragh's face turned red. He could feel the heat move up his face.

"Now that you have your orders... " Jaze looked over the rest of the men. "Any questions?"

The rest of them looked back to Jaze and then to the general.

"General?" Jaze asked Nestor.

Nestor was seated, watching his legate command the army for him.

Dragh knew a test when he saw one. Even a legate had to prove themselves.

"No, Legate, we march within the hour. See to it, men." Nestor tipped his cup back, draining it.

Dragh let a breath out. His head hurt. He was tired and still hungry from last night. He wanted to be back with his men. Listening to the brief from Jaze was tiring.

He started to leave behind the other primuses, who had been led out by Jaze.

"Primus Dragh," the general said aloud.

Dragh turned back, surprised by Nestor. "Yes, General?" Dragh replied, not hiding the tiredness in his voice.

"I'll excuse the rudeness. I know you were at the north gate last night, Primus Dragh," Nestor said. His eyes bored into Dragh.

"Yes, General, sorry, General." Dragh stood up straight. His uncle was in no mood, apparently.

Nestor set aside the cup he was drinking from. He got up from his seat and then ducked at the tent door, looking outside.

"What I will not excuse is stupidity," Nestor said to Dragh.

"Pardon, General?" Dragh asked, confused.

"Considering it was your grandfather who beat the Ralarian army using the same tactic, I say you are either stupid or lazy. You couldn't figure out what Legate Jaze was asking just now?" Nestor gave Dragh a knowing look.

Dragh smiled. "Yes, General. Everyone has to pay the price of being new."

"Smart boy. I see he was right to promote you." Nestor nodded, smiling widely.

"You had nothing to do with it, General?" Dragh asked, suddenly self-conscious.

What if Nestor had made his promotion?

"Cello fucked up. You were in the right place at the right time. It was yours to lose, Dragh." Nestor sat back down in a camp chair, running his hand through his hair. The gray stood out among the black.

Dragh thought on that for a moment. "What happens to Cello now?"

Nestor chuckled. "He's your problem. I'd say you'll have your hands full with him soon."

"I figured as much."

"Remember, your men will follow strength. Cello will seek to cut you down behind your back in any way he can." Nestor raised an eyebrow. "Ever the teacher. I think my time is up."

Dragh was surprised by Nestor. He was not usually so sullen. "I'm grateful, Uncle."

Nestor had a sad look in his eyes. "You have a leak in your ship. That's how Ellis knows so much about you, Dragh."

Dragh felt anger in his belly. *Ellis.*

He gripped his sword; his hand hurt from it.

Of course Ellis had someone spying on Dragh. He'd not realized it before. He wanted to yell, to break something. He hated the man.

Nestor watched Dragh.

"That fucking worm." Dragh closed his eyes and took a breath.

Nestor got up, smoothing the front of his tunic with his hands.

"Watch them. Cello most of all. He needs to be dealt with." Nestor paused, his face changing from concern to something else. "Your father would be proud of you... so am I."

He dipped his head to Dragh before walking from the tent.

Dragh stood there for a moment before he realized he had to go. The legate would not take kindly to Dragh standing around the legate's tent alone, no matter if the general had invited him to stay there.

He left the tent and made his way back to his men. They were in the sea of tents set up to house the men of the Second. Each man had one or more bunkmates, depending on his station in the squad, and they all shared a tent.

"Primus, what news from the legate?" Relish called out.

Dragh stopped himself from firing back an insult, realizing that Relish was being serious, and there was no jest in his question. He watched the men around him, all in the process of taking down their tents and packing their belongings into the squad's wagon.

"Men, we march to meet the Northerners. Our squad is going to push ahead to the eastern flank, between the army and the sea. There are hills and valleys that need to be probed," Dragh addressed his men.

"We've been demoted to scouting?" a sniveling voice piped up from the crowd.

Dragh took a second to find the face.

Cello.

His anger flared. Was Cello the one who was selling him out? Was he the leak in the bucket? He'd known of men who had loose lips in the past. They had doled out justice before, the Second Legion's own brand of justice. Like they had with Zeffo.

"Yes, Cello, is that a problem?" Dragh said through gritted teeth.

Cello pretended to be considering what Dragh had said, putting on a show for the rest of the squad. Dragh watched as a couple of the men went along with it and some chuckled.

Hemmelle and Reilsh had stood up from their work, watching Cello with fists at their sides.

"Fine," Cello replied after his false consideration.

Hemmelle moved forward, fast.

"Fine, what?" Hemmelle said, slapping Cello across the back of his head.

Cello turned red, enraged by Hemmelle. He started to raise his hand to strike Hemmelle, to yell at him, but thought better of it when he looked around to Relish, Geral, and Pello. They were all gathered around him.

"Fine... *Primus,*" Cello conceded through barred teeth, and walked away.

Hemmelle locked eyes with Dragh, asking if he should stop him.

Dragh waved Hemmelle off. He didn't need to put his foot on Cello's neck. The fat man's first attempt to beat him had been thwarted.

Hemmelle nodded to the men around him, telling them to go back to work, then made his way back over to stand beside Dragh. Dragh's tent that he shared with Hemmelle was already packed up and ready for transport.

"Thank you, Hemmelle," Dragh said quietly. Hemmelle had saved Dragh from having to take Cello on alone.

"We've hated that man since Car Lauch. It was my pleasure, *Primus.*" Hemmelle smiled. "You know, if he is ever made primus again, he will come for you."

Dragh grabbed a water skin and drank deeply, still thirsty from a hard night's work.

"If he is ever made primus again, that will be the least of the worries my friend," Hemmelle said to Dragh, clapping him on the back.

Dragh thought on it. What was he going to do about Cello? Was there anything to do right now?

"Hell, I might skin you for an extra ration, if we really have to fight our way through the whole of the North," Hemmelle said in passing.

"What do you mean?" Dragh asked Hemmelle.

Hemmelle looked around, making sure no one was in earshot of them. "Have you considered what this is really about, Dragh?" He looked deeply concerned, his face a mix of emotions.

Dragh waved to the army around them. "Do you think the North has anything that can stop us? We are the Second," Dragh said with more confidence than his face told.

"My friend. The North is three times the size of the Nation of Landor. Three times the size, Dragh." Hemmelle wiped at a bead of sweat on his brow. "The Fifth disappeared up here, Dragh. They *disappeared*. That has never happened before, a whole Legion of men, a whole baggage train, gone."

Dragh scoffed. "General Theas was a fool. They might very well have gotten lost in the mountains. The Fifth would never have trained like us, in the peaks of Car Lauch."

The Fifth had disappeared in Dragh's grandfather's time. Tales of the Fifth's fate were kept quiet, but as with every secret, it makes its way into the world. The word in the army was a cautionary tale told in hushed tones: a legion was sent to kill a rebellion in a show of force. The Fifth left through the mountains, never to be seen again. Not a bone or sword.

As if the Fifth never existed at all.

"You know yourself, your family does not elect fools for generals. Theas was killed in the mountains and swallowed up into history. We are fighting a similar battle, putting down a rebellion. What do you think the population of the North is going to do when they turn against us?" Hemmelle took a breath, waiting for Dragh to answer.

Dragh didn't take the bait.

"My father was smart enough to send us by sea. We learn. We will not let this be some protracted war, my friend. We will end this quickly and be gone before the population turns. The Tribes know their king. They know they owe him fealty." Dragh spit on the ground, wiping his mouth on his sleeve.

"You think the Tribes know the king? He's never stepped foot in the North, Dragh. He is an idea. One we are enforcing at the tip of a spear. We are here because a few villages took issue? Why? Who convinced your father, the king, that this was the only answer?" Hemmelle raised his eyebrows, his mouth set in a line.

"You'll see. We have a whole Legion. The best Legion. Sometimes you must show force, let the rabble know that you will not be prodded. They crossed the line when they killed our people." Dragh slapped Hemmelle on the back.

Hemmelle said nothing, walking with Dragh to the main thoroughfare leading out of camp.

Relish waited at the front of the squad, the baggage deposited for their journey to the next camp site.

Dragh took in his new position, the leader of the squad. A primus. The men looked at him, waiting for orders.

"Let's move, men," Dragh said to his squad.

——

Dragh and Hemmelle sat in a cold camp on the eastern flank of the Legion. They sat in a small gulley, with hills of green grass surrounding them, moving and flowing with the wind.

He'd been contacted by a runner midafternoon that he was to hold the position for the camp to be built. They were to wait until the sun was leaving the sky before going back to the camp.

"Weird, isn't it?" Hemmelle mused to Dragh, both of them scanning the plains of grass in front of them.

They had stopped on a set of hills. They could still see the mountains to the south.

"What's that, eh?" Dragh spit out the blade of grass he'd been chewing between his teeth.

"Not holding a shovel. Odd. It's been years of shoveling before camp. I always worked up an appetite before camp was set."

Dragh elbowed Hemmelle in the ribs.

"What!" Hemmelle grabbed at his side.

"What the pit are you on about? You want to shovel tonight? You fool." Dragh shook his head at Hemmelle.

"It beats sitting out here on my ass waiting to see if the tribes want to take my head off," Hemmelle protested.

"We are a screening party, to make sure the camp is warned. If you ask me, it beats digging out shit holes." Dragh wrinkled his nose. "They don't even wait for them to be finished before they use them."

"Ugh," Hemmelle half-retched and covered his mouth with one hand.

"Remember when Cello..." Dragh burst out in laughter.

"You bastard. He bloody knew I was in there." Hemmelle shuddered and threatened to hit Dragh.

Dragh laughed uncontrollably, his sides aching, tears forming. "It was ALL over." Dragh squeezed out between gasps for air. His laughter increased as he saw the anger in Hemmelle's face.

"You bastard, you said you wouldn't tell a soul!" Hemmelle protested.

Dragh laughed hard, his face turning red. He slapped his own knee, his breath hard to control through the laughter. He watched Hemmelle's expression change from frustration to anger to laughter. Hemmelle cracked a smile, his teeth showing, although Dragh could tell he was trying hard to hide it.

"Primus!" Relish called out.

Dragh and Hemmelle stood, looking to the north.

"Looks like a single man!" Relish called.

The squad was armored and ready, their weapons now in their hands. Dragh held his sword and his shield. A small knife was strapped to his hip. His sword was the length of his torso, his shield about equal size. The pommel of his sword was wrapped in leather; his hand fitted snugly on it. His hand had sweated and bled on the pommel for years.

Hemmelle, beside Dragh, carried a battle axe, double bit, with a large spike on its head. He never carried a shield.

The rest of the squad held various weapons— spears, swords, bows, and axes. Anything that could kill. They had a mix of long and short-range weapons for their foes. Anyone with a bow had a secondary weapon, ready to kill up close and personal.

They all trained in the use of each weapon. Weeks of their time on Car Lauch in the cold was training in weapons. Your hands cold and icy, unused to a bow handle. Dragh shivered with the memory before bringing himself back to the present.

Who was this? A lone man walking towards them had him on edge. "Watch for an ambush, he may have friends," Dragh said to Relish, who he'd moved beside.

"Aye, Primus, "Relish responded, sending two members of the squad out to scan their flanks.

Dragh recognised the dark-haired youth from the attack at the camp, Verras. The youth had been arrested for stealing food for his younger siblings. The other was the balding, older man, Jal. A pickpocket from Landor.

Dragh was glad to see Verras hadn't died of his wounds. He scolded himself for not checking on his wounded. There was no one else that would, now that he was primus.

"Who goes there?" Dragh called out to the hooded figure as he drew closer.

Dragh watched, his sword held at the ready in the mid-guard.

Old, wispy arms snaked out of long sleeves as the man pulled back his hood. The old man with steel grey hair ran his hand over his face as he stopped in front of the squad.

"I am Azal," Piercing blue eyes scanned the squad and landed on Dragh.

Dragh watched the old man with a strange feeling of familiarity. As if he'd met this man before.

"What do you want, old man?" Dragh asked, his sword still at the ready. He looked to Relish and Hemmelle, who both shrugged. No attack from the flanks; this man appeared to be alone. Brave, in a country at war.

"First, he holds a blade to us, asks what we want, and offers not a seat or refreshments? And they call us barbarians," the old man named Azal seemed to mutter to himself.

"What was that?" Dragh asked. He looked with a raised eyebrow to Hemmelle.

"Invite me to sit with you, offer me a drink, as is our way, as is the code," Azal said louder, to the squad.

"He does seem to be alone, Primus," Relish said to Dragh.

"Stay alert. Hemmelle and I will talk with him, see what he knows." Dragh nodded to Relish.

Relish gave the soldier's salute to Dragh, his arm across his chest.

"Come with me, old man, let us talk." Dragh nodded to Hemmelle, who held his axe at the ready.

"He invites us, finally some princely behavior," the old man muttered.

Dragh spun around, his heart taking a leap in his chest. "What did you just say?" he asked, a little too loudly.

Azal put his hands up in mock surrender. "So they don't know," he said loudly.

Dragh was trying to recover from the shock of it. Did this old man know who he was? How could someone this far north, whom he'd never met, know that he was a prince? A Sunborn. Dragh eyed the old man suspiciously.

Dragh looked around at his men, none met his eye.

The three of them moved away into the gulley and sat in a circle.

Hemmelle and Dragh sat on the ground, just far enough from the rest of the squad to have a private conversation. But not far enough that a shout wouldn't get their attention. Dragh indicated that Azal should sit, offering him a waterskin and some bread.

The old man chewed hungrily on the bread, finishing the entire provision. He then drank the water skin dry. Dragh and Hemmelle watched without commenting.

"Who the pit are you?" Hemmelle asked the strange man.

Dragh watched Azal's reaction. His features were like Dragh's own, not like a Northerner with pale skin, more Landorian than anything else. Not an islander, Ralarian, either.

"Thank you for the water and the food." Azal tossed the empty skin to Dragh. "It's been weeks."

"I said..." Hemmelle started.

"Yes, I heard you, Hemmelle." Azal looked over to Hemmelle with a smirk on his face.

Hemmelle cocked his head to the side, surprised by Azal.

"I know you all. You've been in my visions for many moons. Many years," Azal said to them both. "I know that you are a prince, more royal than these men with you now. Than even you know."

"What does that mean, many moons and years?" Dragh asked, confused by the old man.

"It means that you are a man of destiny, young Sunborn," Azal replied, smacking his lips and wiping at his face with his sleeve.

"How do you know all this?" Dragh repeated himself.

"Take your hand off your sword, you aren't going to use it." Azal laughed out loud. "Trust that I know that much. Our paths are going to cross again, that is written in the stars."

"You're drunk. You talk nonsense, old man," Hemmelle spit out, angry with Azal.

Dragh looked around, making sure the men were not too close.

Azal fixed Hemmelle with a look. Hemmelle held his gaze with anger. "Is that so, young man? Were you wrong when you were arrested and thrown into this Legion?" Azal asked.

Hemmelle looked uncomfortable as his face turned red.

"That's what I thought. They don't know you beat that guard for hurting a child, do they? You told them that it was a drunk brawl. You didn't want them to know you have a beating heart under the armor of your mind." Azal looked back to Dragh as Hemmelle looked away, unable to hold Azal's look after all.

"What do you want with us? Speak plainly. You know some of the stars, that is nothing that an informant couldn't tell you," Dragh retorted.

"Like an informant your uncle told you of? That kind?" Azal asked Dragh.

Dragh shut up. No one was there when his uncle told him of the leak among his friends.

How could he know what his uncle told him?

"I'm here because I wanted to meet you before our time. Remember, the tribes do not forget, they do not forgive," Azal said, sighing. "You will need to repay blood with blood, young man. This will become apparent when you take the mantle from your father."

Dragh laughed out loud. "If you really knew me, you'd know that I will never take the crown, you fool."

"There is more than one way to serve. Just remember. To avert the war, you must pay the blood debt," Azal said, his gaze fierce.

Dragh's breath caught. Azal's eyes alight with mischief. Dragh's mentor and keeper, Praetorian Donn, had always reminded Dragh that he was to serve, to be of service.

Did this Azal really *know*?

"If you haven't noticed, Azal, we are at war," Hemmelle said, his voice faltering as if he'd just found it.

"Yes, young Hemmelle. It will be worse," Azal said, his eyes closed.

"Worse? How?" Dragh asked, not sure if the old man was a spy, an enemy.

"Tribal law says that you must grant me hospitality, and you must keep your honour, young Dragh. I came because I wanted to see what destiny looked like. I wanted to keep you on the path."

"And you think I need to pay a blood debt to do that?" Dragh said with sarcasm.

"I tell you because I cannot tip the scales. But I can nudge them." Azal scoffed at himself. "Perhaps I am growing too old for this. The emperor always taunted me for my age."

Dragh looked to Hemmelle. There hadn't been an emperor in these lands for hundreds of years. Generations. This man was certainly crazy.

Azal got up, quicker than Dragh thought he could for his aged look. "I must be off." Azal started walking away from the pair with speed.

Hemmelle and Dragh exchanged another look.

"Hey! Where are you going?" Hemmelle said to the old man's back.

"Beating the messenger. Time for you to return!" Azal said, waving his hand, and walked quickly to the east.

Hemmelle and Dragh watched as the old man went up and down hills, disappearing in between them.

"Primus!" Relish shouted.

"Aye, Relish!" Dragh replied, tearing his eyes off the spot where Azal had disappeared.

Relish waved to the south. A mounted scout of the Landorians rode for the squad. A messenger.

Dragh looked back to the east, seeing nothing but grass and earth. Dragh rubbed his eyes and gave a look to Hemmelle, who shrugged in response.

"What do you make of that?" Hemmelle asked.

Dragh ran his hand through his hair, watching the spot where the old man had vanished from sight. "I think it's a problem for another day, Hemmelle."

CHAPTER 12

"What a fuckin' pit this place is," Zeffo complained as the squad moved through the range of mountains and hills of the North.

"Shut up, you lazy prick," Pello said to his brother.

"I'm just saying, so many hills. My legs are killing me from our patrols this week," Zeffo whined.

"Not to mention the bloody fog," Hemmelle complained.

'Shut up, the lot of you," Dragh said.

He felt the fog and the mist that settled across the hills and gullies. Just like the rest of his men, he just had to keep going. He knew that if he complained, all would.

Hemmelle chuckled beside Relish and Dragh at the front of the squad. They were aligned in a three-wide column marching through the hills.

The green grass became boring after a time. Like the sea, the waves of the hills and grass were hard to watch and to remain vigilant day after day. Each rise looked the same. Each hill and rock formation had little to differentiate from one day to the next.

"Funny, isn't it?" Relish said to Dragh.

"You've got to admit that they couldn't be more different." Hemmelle shook his head and said louder to the whole squad, "You'd think they came from a different mother. Perhaps a different father."

Dragh stifled back a laugh at them all bickering.

"By the Pit, I think you are from a different mother, swine!" Zeffo shouted to Pello.

Pello answered by smacking Zeffo across the back of the head. Dragh could hear the hit from the front. The squad burst out laughing at the pair, their arguments making their days on patrol enjoyable.

They'd been bored since their run-in with the odd man Azal.

Dragh was still suspicious of the old man. He was odd for certain, but he'd talked to Hemmelle late into the night: he'd known things he couldn't. Things that he'd have to be a spy to know.

Dragh considered telling his legate. He knew that they should have kept Azal prisoner. A potential spy in their midst. But letting him go had sealed his mouth. Along with the fact that he'd have to explain his relation to the general. To the king.

None in the Second knew of his royal blood, with exception of Hemmelle and Nestor. That was the deal he'd struck with his uncle to join the Second.

In the end, they decided it best to keep it between themselves.

After that, the days had filled with boredom. The Squad went out on patrol; they set up a perimeter close to the sun falling from the sky, and then back to the camp anew each night.

———

"Funny they haven't attacked us again, innit"?" Relish said to them.

Hemmelle grunted in agreement. "Not our usual, is it?"

"Not like Argyle, not like our last mission into the plains out west," Relish commented.

"Them were hard bastards out in Argyle. I remember when Cello was transferred, when our primus caught an arrow in his chest," Hemmelle commented.

Dragh looked back at Cello. The fat man had lost some of his width in the last weeks on patrol. Marching through the countryside had given them all a new level of fitness. Dragh had had no run-ins with Cello or the others, no challenges to his command.

He'd fit right into the role of primus. The men walked easy around him with a respect that Cello had never had.

"Aye, I'm glad it's you now, Dragh. I think Cello is too, though he won't admit it." Relish gripped Dragh's shoulder in a show of admiration.

"He did good while he was in charge. I will give him that," Dragh said.

"Is that admiration for our old primus I hear? From Dragh? Gods strike me, it's a miracle," Hemmelle said, laughing.

Dragh smiled. "Knock it off, the title is heavy. Keeping this many dark souls on the path of the Gods is a weighty burden."

"Ohhh, now that Landor has her infestation of *priests*, our leader Dragh is one of the converts. Next, he'll be telling us that the Council and the faith are what keep our nation free," Hemmelle jested.

"Oh, Lords, bless my evil soul. I didn't mean to kill them bastards." Relish put both of his hands up in a mock prayer.

Dragh screwed his face up, trying not to laugh at the two fools. "Fuck off, you little pricks, I'll have Cello whip you."

Hemmelle and Relish exchanged a look.

"Oh, Lord Dragh, let not the whip fall on our pious back, we will pray to you!" Relish mocked.

"Must we wipe your ass, Lord?" Hemmelle heckled.

"Oh yes, Lord, let me donate my money to the faith, don't let me be whipped," Relish pressed his act further.

Dragh lifted up his hands in the sign of the pious. "I will now bless you, you evil killing bastards."

"Our swords keep the nation, not the faith, you rotten bastards." Hemmelle threw up an obscenity at the clouds.

"Funny that. They think their prayer keeps them safe. Let them fuckers come out here and face some heavy horses. I'll show them the spears, guts, and screaming that lets them pray. Landor's been so long without a war on the home front. Come with me, that'll keep 'em praying."

"The Council's coffers are full whenever the faithful sell prayer," Dragh commented. He thought about the "priest" he'd run into at the palace who had pushed his father to spread even more lies. What kind of person was bold enough to push a king?

"Village!" Relish called out to the squad, pointing to the northeast.

Dragh halted the squad, making his way forward. He could see a clump of huts, and smoke issuing from a couple of them. He estimated that the Legion would be facing a village of less than fifty people. The village was set on a rise, from what Dragh could see. Some houses were built further down into a gully, as roofs disappeared beyond his sight.

"Shields up!" Dragh gave the command, letting his men know that they'd not be caught unawares if this was a trap, or the villagers were unfriendly.

As the squad made their way closer, Dragh could see the village was centered around a communal square.

Chickens, pigs, and cows were throughout the different fields. Some of them in paddocks, some wandering around the outskirts of the village.

The squad prepared themselves, drawing weapons, swords, axes, bows. Relish pulled out a wicked-looking war hammer.

Dragh gave Relish a look.

"Won her in a game of dice with the Ralarians." Relish shrugged.

Dragh nodded his appreciation for the weapon. Its back was an evil-looking hook, ready to tear and rend by the look of it.

"Remember men, we are here to fight the army of the Northern Tribes. Not the people," Dragh said so that all could hear.

"Aye, sir," Cello said, his voice dripping with sarcasm.

Dragh bit back a retort, trying to calm his anger at Cello's attitude.

They made their way into the village and to the main square. Dragh could see men and women stirring from their dwellings, some in the main square that all the buildings funneled to.

He watched as the villagers collected around them in the square.

"Who's the leader here?" Dragh called out as they set up a defensive position at the north end of the square. Dragh looked around at the buildings, many of them stone and thatched roof construction.

The village was many decades behind the cities surrounding Landor. Dragh had his men move to the north end of the square to ensure that they had multiple exits; through the crowd was their last resort.

Dragh had seen the king's Praetorians train. He knew the power of the crowd. Not even a full army could stop its people. Revolt was power. An army only had intimidation to count on, like his squad did now.

The square was clearly the village's central gathering point. Booths were set up, and vendors sold goods. Food, trinkets, blankets, tools, and weapons.

"Watch that," Dragh said to Pello and Zeffo on his right.

"Aye, Primus," Zeffo said, giving a curt nod to Dragh before moving to the weapon vendor's stall.

"Who's in charge here?" Dragh asked the gathering crowd again.

A smallish white-haired man with a slight hunchback came forward.

The man favoured his right leg; the left dragged a little behind as he walked. His eyes were sharp, the look of eagles about him. The old man tilted his head to the side, looking Dragh up and down. Recognition dawned on his face.

"That would be me, young pup." A look of mirth in the old man's eyes sparkled.

Dragh was shocked to see the old man. At first, he could not understand what he was doing here, the old Praetorian Legate Yarrin. The man who'd been at his father's side for most of Dragh's young life. The man who'd protected his father from countless attempts on his life, in battle, and in his own cities around Landor.

"Legate..." Dragh began.

"Ahhhh, it's just Yarrs now, my young prince." Yarrin strode towards Dragh.

Dragh embraced the old man, a reminder of his old life. Yarrs felt fragile and old compared to the old days. Dragh remembered him as a giant the last time he saw Yarrin.

Dragh looked around his squad. The men around him looked on with a mix of emotions. Some looked at him in confusion.

Did they now know? Did they take the old man seriously? Relish and Geral looked on without shock.

Hemmelle smirked. The secret was out. Now it would be time to face it. All of it. This would spread through the Second Legion like a wildfire through a dry thicket. Dragh sighed.

"What are you doing here, my old friend?" Dragh asked the old Legate. The legate was given a Landorian feast when he retired. He'd reached the age of retirement, and his father had wanted him honored.

"Ahhh, a long story. Come, come, let me show you the hospitality of the North." Yarrs waved towards the south of the square.

Dragh looked back to his men. Yarrs stopped limping and looked back.

"Let your second-in-charge come, the rest can stay. I will have refreshments brought to them. As long as they can behave themselves." Yarrs gave Dragh a stern look as if he was still speaking to Dragh as a child in the Landor Palace.

"Relish, you are in command while Hemmelle and I visit the village *elder*." Dragh emphasized the word.

Relish nodded to Dragh, his face splitting with a smile.

"Elder, pah," Yarrs said, turning around and speaking to the villagers who had gathered, sending men and women out for food and water.

"Let us be quick, Your Majesty." Hemmelle gave a tight bow.

"Fuck off with all of that." Dragh growled.

He turned to the rest of the squad. "That goes for all of you. I owe you an explanation. I know. For now, you can call me Primus or Dragh. Anything else, and you will feel my boot."

Dragh could see the squad squirm, some with pursed lips.

Pello opened his mouth to say something.

"You heard the primus," Hemmelle cut them all off, saving Dragh from dolling out some punishment.

Hemmelle gave Dragh a nod towards Yarrs, who was walking away from them.

Dragh sheathed his sword and with Hemmelle behind him, they headed towards the old man across the square. Dragh was greeted by an altogether different village. Now, the men and women around them were happy they were not going to be attacked, happy that the squad was not here to dole out violence.

Dragh wondered at that. Why would you have a village out here in the hills? Why build it in a place that cannot be defended?

Dragh ducked his head under the low door that Yarrs led them to.

He looked inwards to the hall that Yarrs led them to. A set of tables were set in rows, two across and four deep. He estimated eighty or more seats. A lead table was set up, higher than the rest. The hall was built with hewn lumber, rough-cut, with markers peppering each beam. The lumber beams were rough, but they joined in beautiful hand-carved arches, like the ribs of a great beast making up the hall's roof.

Dragh must have been off on his initial estimates. There were much more than fifty in this village. He scolded himself. Never underestimate. They were hiding, unsure of his squad.

"What do we call you now, Legate Yarrs?" Dragh asked aloud. They appeared to be the only ones in the hall.

Firelight flickered, smoke issuing through beams of light from the upper windows.

"You can call me, Yarrs!" Yarrs boomed. His humour evident. His joy at a familiar face lifted Dragh's spirit.

"This is my second, my friend, Hemmelle," Dragh introduced Yarrs and Hemmelle.

"Welcome to our village, men. Thank you for approaching in peace. We are not a warlike village up here." Yarrs sat at the head table, motioning for them to join across from him at chairs set out.

"What gave you the idea to live out here, Yarrs? This unprotected land in the middle of a war." Dragh asked.

"What Legion are you with, Dragh?" Yarrs asked his own question, ignoring Dragh's.

Dragh grimaced. He knew this would be asked. He knew Yarrs would want to know of his life.

"The Second," Dragh said, preparing for a tongue lashing.

"Hmmh," Yarrs grunted and laughed. "I figured that you would end up there. You were a rebellious little shit when you were young."

Hemmelle laughed with Yarrs. He'd not been exposed to anyone in Dragh's old life before. Not like this. Occasional run-ins with that little prick Ellis aside, Dragh thought.

"Who's general now?" Yarrs asked, always a martial man first.

Know your enemy. Always. Dragh remembered his lessons, even from a young man at Yarrs's knee.

"Uncle Nestor is the general now," Dragh said.

Yarrs scoffed. His statement spoke more than words. "What did you mean by, why am I in the middle of a war?" Yarrs pressed the question to Dragh and Hemmelle. His demeanor changed to that of a man in charge. The power shifted under Dragh and Hemmelle's feet.

"The Second marches north. We march to press the North back into submission," Hemmelle spouted what Nestor had sold them.

"Men. Listen to me. I am the headman of this village. I can tell you that I am not at war with Landor. Pit, I served the king for a lifetime. Thirty years. I bled, and I gave my leg to the nation." Yarrs gave Hemmelle a stern look.

"Your army has butchered and pillaged our villages along the Car Lauch. They killed and raped and burned. We march to right the wrong done to us," Hemmelle said with force.

Dragh put his hand on Hemmelle's shoulder, trying to calm his friend.

"I speak with many other villages. I tell you now that the king would say the same: there is no war here. We have not attacked Landor. Why would we?" Yarrs asked them both.

Dragh felt the tension in Hemmelle through his shoulder. He was rigid. Dragh squeezed his shoulder. Looking across at Yarrs, he could tell the old man was angry. He shifted forward in his seat and set his shoulders, his Praetorian demeanor shining through despite his old body. Dragh watched him become the legate that he remembered, commanding attention and respect.

Dragh shook his head, giving Hemmelle a look to quiet him before looking back to Yarrs.

"We mean no offense, Yarrs. It is what we have been told. It's what's been reported to the king," Dragh explained. "We are but weapons of the realm, you know this."

Yarrs deflated, and the hard look in his eyes softened. "I know, lad, I know. A soldier's job is to kill, not to question." Yarrs motioned to someone behind

Dragh and Hemmelle. A village woman came forward and refilled their cups, returning to the shadows once she was done.

Dragh wondered how many others were in the hall that he could not see. He scolded himself for not paying more attention, letting his guard down around Yarrs.

"How would you know you are at war?" Hemmelle said through gritted teeth.

Yarrs looked between the two men, picking up his cup of ale. He toasted them both before taking a long drink. "Because, young Hemmelle, I know the value of politics. I am a man who makes it his business to know." Yarrs put his cup down, motioning for it to be refilled.

"You ask me why I live in a place that cannot be defended? I have no need—we have no need of high walls and defenses like Landor's Palace and city walls. The North is a hard place to survive at the best of times, and the weather is harsh. Wind and snow and ice are here always, the summer is short to grow, and the animals must be hardy to survive. Like the Tribes. We have not time for petty squabbles and war. We fight to survive."

"And you keep your ear to the ground with all this business?" Dragh asked, listening to the old man spin his tales.

Yarrs smiled. "Of course, what else is an old man to do but gossip and listen?"

"Who is killing my people, then?" Dragh asked.

"Your people? I guess they are, eh?" Yarrs rubbed at the stubble on his chin, eyeing Dragh. "Raiders, mercenaries, I don't rightly know, Dragh."

"What proof do you have?" Hemmelle asked, his voice betraying his stress.

Dragh gave Hemmelle a kick under the table. He needed his friend to stop pushing the old man. He might not tell them what they need to know if Hemmelle crossed the tribesmen. The Northeners might not be attacking Landorians.

"I have no proof but my own wits, young man. I tell you now that the Northern Chieftain is not one to upset the balance of power. What would it benefit him? What would the Chieftain Saravas gain from going to war with Kallen and Landor?" Yarrs asked.

"He's a vassal to Landor. He would gain his independence." Dragh threw back at Yarrs, trying to defend his honour and his Legion. He was fighting this war, after all.

"And what of the men that have attacked us? The men that attacked the camp when we landed?" Hemmelle piled on.

"What of the men that attacked a foreign legion who invaded the North?" Yarrs spit on the ground. "Pah, that could have been any of the tribes. Do you blame them? Do you blame them for coming to the defense of the nation they live in? Not all tribes owe allegiance to Saravas."

"Why do the tribes not owe allegiance to their supposed king?" Dragh asked, taking a drink of his ale. It was refilled without comment by another of the servants from the dark.

"The tribes are not like Landor's people, more like the people of the west, the hordes." Yarrs began to explain. "They believe in honour, justice, blood feuds, and hospitality."

"They are just like any other tribal people. You want us to have mercy on your village," Hemmelle blurted out.

Yarrs gave Hemmelle a hard look, ignoring his comments. "The tribes are all their own. They do not pay homage to a chieftain in the way that the citizens do the king in Landor. I grew up here, boy. I know these people better than most. I tell you now, we, the North, are not at war. Some of the tribes may be rebelling, but not the alliance collected by Saravas."

"What alliance?" Dragh asked. He shot Hemmelle a withering look over his ale, hoping Hemmelle would keep his mouth shut.

"Smart lad, you know what to ask," Yarrs commented on Dragh's question.

Yarrs cleared his throat. "He is a chieftain, a tribal leader. But for you folk in Landor, just think of it like a king. He was elected by the Council of the Tribes. They gathered, they voted, and Saravas was elected after the trials."

"What are the—" Hemmelle began, but was cut off by Yarrs.

"The trials are faced by all elected by their tribes. There are over twenty tribes in the North that I know of. They each put forward their champions. Each champion went through trials. Saravas was the only one to complete them. He was elected leader. Before you ask, I don't know what the trials are. The shamans of the tribes are the only ones allowed to be there. The ones who govern the tribes between leaders."

"Shamans... like Azal," Dragh muttered.

"Azal, is that what you said?" Yarrs asked, interrupting Dragh. His voice held concern. "How do you know that name?"

Dragh exchanged a look with Hemmelle.

"He found us, on patrol some leagues to the south. We were on patrol while the Legion built the camp, he came to us... He had some interesting things to say," Hemmelle told Yarrs.

"And what did he have to say about you two? What did he tell you?" Yarrs asked, his keen eyes alight with interest.

"He said... well, he said that I was a man of destiny, that he wanted to meet me. He knew I was a Sunborn," Dragh told Yarrs. He was curious about Yarrs's sudden piqued interest.

"Interesting," Yarrs said quietly to himself.

"And he knew much of my life. Too much..." Hemmelle lapsed into silence.

"Aye... he is a shaman of Saravas. He wonders through our nation... through the tribes. He's always looking..."

"Looking for what?" Dragh asked. He sensed that Yarrs knew more than he was letting on.

Yarrs shook his head. "Lads, I'll tell you this, the North is not at war with Landor. We are allied with King Kallen, with the Sunborn line."

"There is nothing we can do Yarrs, you know this. Nestor leads the Legion. He is convinced that the North has instigated a war, and we are here to put the North down," Dragh told the old man.

"It is the soldier's job to lead up. His job is more than just to kill, to be the blade of the nation. His job is to be its heart and soul," Yarrs said to them both, looking between them. "I need you to bring this message to Nestor. Tell him that we are not at war, that he must sue for peace with whatever tribe is fighting him. If it even is a tribe. It may well be mercenaries. The north is vast, we are not the only ones up here." Yarrs clapped his hands.

A banging on the door of the hall echoed. Dragh looked from Yarrs to Hemmelle, who shrugged.

"Let them in," Yarrs spoke to the shadows.

The door opened, and a breathless Zeffo ran to their table. "Primus, horsemen are here."

"Ours? These people are not a threat to the Second," Dragh said, draining his mug of ale.

"No, Primus, a squad of them are here, on the hill outside the village," Zeffo gasped. "They are mounted for war."

"NOO!" Yarrs leapt up from his seat with anger.

"We must go, stop them before they charge the village." Hemmelle and Dragh were up and moving behind Yarrs, who was running through the hall as fast as his old legs would take him.

Dragh moved with fear and anger. The Cavalry of the Second was known for their resolve; they were a strong set of hardened men. They would charge any army they were faced with, against any odds.

Dragh knew that the Second, all men of war were killers. The worst of them were sent to the cavalry. Their legate, Dara, was rumored to have skinned a man. General Nestor sent the men who belonged on the chopping block to Dara. He was hard enough to bring the others into line.

When the Cavalry were away from the main host of the Second, they were out of control. The rumors in the Legion were that the Cavalry killed entire villages, trampling them, cutting them down, worse.

Reports always surfaced that the villages they destroyed were full of enemy soldiers.

Any desperate villager would pick up a sword to defend themselves from an attack, Landor's enemies or not.

All of this ran through Dragh's head as he sprinted back into the square. Yarrs shouted commands to his men and to the rest of the villagers. They scattered like flies.

"To me, men of the Second!" Dragh bellowed.

"Move, you fuckers! The cavalry is upon us!" Hemmelle called.

Dragh and Hemmelle ran through the crowd, who parted for them. They saw that the squad was up and running towards them from the north of the village. Dragh and Hemmelle pushed their way through the square back to the south, to get out of the village and hopefully intercept the cavalry before they attacked Yarrs and his people.

Dragh hoped he could beat Yarrs and the men of the village to the cavalry's line of sight. If not, he'd be trying to stop horseflesh, blood, and guts from flying. Dara and his men would charge at the simplest provocation.

Dragh moved swiftly, his arms pumping, his sword slapping his leg in its sheath. He trusted the men at his back. They would be there when he arrived at battle. They had his back. He didn't need to turn around. He could hear Hemmelle's laboured breathing, Relish shouting at the men to hurry up.

In front of him, the cavalry spanned the rim-like hill around the village that Dragh had crested not hours ago. They lined up across the rim, a wall of horse flesh.

"That fuckin' Venor," Relish grunted to Dragh.

Dragh remembered that Relish had run-ins with Venor, the Primus of the Cavalry Squad under Dara.

Venor had earned a nickname, one that was hard to earn in a Legion of criminals and killers. The Butcher. The nickname was never said to his face and never in public. Always whispered, quiet.

Relish was almost run over by Venor's squad during a battle at Argyle. Relish had been furious, fighting with the primus afterwards. Dragh marked the man as one to watch.

Dragh had been one of the men to pull the two apart. What he remembered of Venor was the glint in his eyes—Venor had been excited to fight even one of his own men. Dragh knew the mark of the killers who killed for the pleasure of it.

"I can see him now," Hemmelle said, his eyes almost as sharp as Relish's.

"Wave the flag of peace," Dragh told Zeffo.

"That won't work. We need to line up for battle," a voice came from behind them.

Dragh looked around, surprised to see Cello behind the group.

"Cello, what was that?" Hemmelle asked.

Cello grunted; not being addressed as a primus had to bite.

"I said, the flag will do nothing. You all know that those cavalry bastards will not stop until they have blood on their lances."

Dragh looked around at the men and then back to Cello. He was not sure what to do. Listen to the old primus? He was talking sense. Would that be a show of weakness?

"Dragh, you know I'm right. They are crazy. We need to set our line of defense, then send a messenger up, and be prepared for them to attack the village first," Cello addressed Dragh with desperation in his eyes.

He realized Cello just wanted to be heard.

Dragh looked to the men. They were his responsibility. He nodded to Cello. "I need your help."

Cello nodded back, his jaw set. "Primus."

Dragh roared to the men. "Set a line of defense! I want it six wide with spears at the front, bows in the back."

The men began to move into line, their movements practiced and precise, as they'd been in many battles together. Dragh could hear muttering about the horse's asses in front of them.

"Cello, I need you to go to Venor. Explain that these people are not our enemy. They are led by an old legate of the Praetorians," Dragh paused. "He served my father. Tell him."

Cello paused, and his eyes narrowed. "Yes, Primus."

Cello took off on a jog, his frame much narrowed since losing the primus position.

"Hemmelle, I need you to go to Yarrs. Try and convince him to pull his men back to the village. I don't want to antagonize Venor. Don't give him an excuse to charge. If the villagers come out to face the horsemen, Venor will burn it to the ground."

"Aye, Primus." Hemmelle took off to the villagers amassing behind the squad.

"What of it, Primus? Do you think they will attack?" Geral asked beside him.

Dragh glanced over. Verras and Jal were lined up beside Geral. "Aye, I think we need to be ready. Hope that Cello can talk us out of this mess."

"What will the village elder do?" Verras asked, his voice full of fear.

Dragh thought about Yarrs, even with his limping leg. A warrior through and through. "He'll fight to the very end. They all will. The North does not give up."

They were quiet, the words instilling more fear than comfort.

Dragh watched as Cello crested the rise, his hands without weapons to show he was not a threat. The cavalry might wear the same clothes of the Second, but even Cello knew the cavalry was not to be trusted. Some soldiers killed first and looked later. Sometimes not at all.

Dragh held onto hope that they would listen. He could hear a ruckus behind him. Hemmelle with Yarrs and the villagers. He didn't glance back, trusting his second in command to do his job.

"Sir," Pello commented quietly.

"I see it," Dragh acknowledged.

Three of the horsemen broke off from the rim, riding hard for the squad.

"HOLD, MEN," Dragh called out to his squad. He knew that Venor was the type to piss off a squad of foot soldiers by riding too close to them and by knocking men to the ground.

Cello started back to the squad behind the horsemen. Dragh could see him walking. Not running. That was a good sign at least.

"They are going to give us a run for our coin, ain't they?" Jal said aloud. "To the pit with them," he said loud enough for the rest of the men to laugh at.

Dragh smirked. His men would hold.

They cantered down the slopes in perfect unison, their gaits matched as each horse was given its head. They were trained for war, these horses. Dragh had spent many years in the saddle in the army. He knew the feel of power when you sat atop the horses of war. It was ironic now, watching them, him on the ground, a wall of horse flesh rolling down the hill at him.

The group of three reigned in mere feet from the squad. An involuntary "pit" slipped out behind Dragh, as their spears were within a hair of him.

"Primus!" The call went out from the centre horsemen as he looked out over the whole squad and to the villagers behind them.

"Aye, Vanor," Dragh said to the man. He could see a flicker of disappointment in his face. The man was squat, as many horsemen were, dark-haired and dark-skinned from days in the sun. His beady eyes gave away his intent.

"Sorry, Primus Dragh. I was confused when Primus Cello approached us," Vanor smirked, looking down his hooked nose at Dragh.

Dragh tried to bite back his retort. "Aye, some of us can trust our men."

Dragh looked at the two thugs on either side of Vanor. Two killers from the docks of Landor, if he remembered correctly. They bristled at the insult. Their horses snorted and pawed, feeling their riders' energy.

Vanor glared at Dragh with naked hostility. "Your legate *commands* you back to the Legion."

"Is camp built?" Dragh asked.

Vanor sneered at Dragh's question.

Dragh considered Vanor and the thugs with him. He looked back at the villagers behind them, massed. "These villagers are not a threat. Their headman is a former Praetorian of Landor."

Vanor smiled with too many teeth. "Aye, why don't you go along and we will watch them, just in case."

The two thugs on either side of Vanor smiled, wicked things full of teeth.

"You go, I have business to take care of," Dragh said, waving a dismissive hand at Vanor. He turned and walked away.

"Dragh!" Vanor called to him.

Dragh turned around. "What, Vanor?" His guts clenched.

"Watch yourself. The north is a dangerous place. One might get—lost," Vanor sneered again and wheeled his horse around. His thugs wheeled in behind them.

Dragh watched as they cantered up the hill, almost hitting Cello, riding on either side of him, splitting at the last moment.

"They can ride," Hemmelle said, coming up beside Dragh.

"Aye, they can ride." Dragh gave them that concession.

"What next, Primus? What news?" Hemmelle asked.

"They tell me that Legate Jaze calls us back to the Legion. I suspect they are pissed off that they won't be able to soak the ground in blood."

"I'm thinking that they will have their chance, if Jaze is calling you back. The only reason he would do that on the march is if he has new orders for us," Hemmelle commented.

"I have something to do before we go," Dragh said, setting his mind up before walking on to the village.

CHAPTER 13

Dragh stood at attention. His back was sore from the marching, and his mind was sore from thoughts running through his head on the march back to the camp. He made it by the end of the sun's light.

Just.

He stood in his legate's tent. Jaze shouted at Dragh for being late, for having to repeat himself.

Jaze stalked the room, his shoulder set back, his face a mask that made Dragh more nervous.

He stopped in front of Dragh and, with his full hand and all of his fingers extended, hit Dragh in the chest.

Hard enough that Dragh had to grunt.

"And what's your piss poor excuse for this now?" Jaze asked Dragh.

"He is, sir," Dragh pointed back to Yarrs, who stood behind them both in the tent. Yarrs's back steeled as he stood straight.

"Who in Zufier's balls is that?" Jaze asked, pointing to the old man.

Yarrs chuckled at the comment. His humour much the same as when Dragh knew him in his previous life.

"Why, Legate Jaze, I remember asking you the same question many moons ago," Yarrs responded as he walked into the firelight in the tent.

"The pit is this..." Jaze looked on as the crippled man limped forward, his back straight and proud in the military camp.

"Now don't tell me you don't remember the fun that the Second used to have with us at the palace?" Yarrs smiled at Jaze.

"Legate Yarrs," Jaze said, shock on his face. "What are you doing in the North?"

"Aye, it's good to see you too, young pup." Yarrs clapped Jaze on the back.

Jaze smiled like he was greeting an old friend. Dragh was confused, not sure how these two men knew each other. Something else Yarrs forgot to mention. "Good to see you, sir."

"None of that shit between us. I trained you, and I'm proud that you made legate. I'm just Yarrs now."

"Sir, you honour me. You'll always be my legate." Jaze dipped his head to Yarrs.

Yarrs pointed to a chair beside the fire. "Do you mind, Legate? I'm getting to be an old man."

"Of course. Can I get you drink or food?" Jaze offered, snapping his fingers to the guard at the door, who moved off quickly.

"My thanks," Yarrs replied, sitting in the camp chair.

"Think nothing of it." Jaze looked back to Dragh. "What are you doing with this shit-eater?"

Yarrs stretched out his back and leg, clearly sore from the march back to the camp.

Dragh had to work hard to convince Yarrs to talk to the general. Dragh had insisted that Yarrs go with Dragh to see his legate, that they follow the chain of command and not use his relationship with his uncle, Nestor.

"This young pup had a run-in with the Butcher's men. Vanor. I think that was his name. A young primus. He wanted to blood his men, I think," Yarrs started his explanation. "I'm glad that Dragh was there. He headed off Vanor and those damn cavalry."

Jaze gave Dragh a look. Something resembling respect, Dragh thought.

Dragh said nothing, giving a curt nod to his legate. He'd learned long ago from his arguments with Cello that it was best not to interrupt the conversation that was happening with Yarrs and Jaze. Even Jaze was listening intently.

Yarrs launched into a story of his interactions with Dragh, how he knew him, and what had transpired at his village. The meeting with the Second, Dragh's squad, and then eventually the horsemen.

Dragh was happy that Yarrs skipped over the comments about Azal the Shaman. That was the last thing he needed to explain to Jaze. The Legate had enough on his plate as it stood.

Jaze leveled a hard look on Dragh when Yarrs let slip that Dragh was indeed a Sunborn, a nephew of the General of the Second and a prince of Landor.

Dragh cringed and reminded himself that his men and now the Legate knew. You could trust certain things to men. Certain things to an even smaller group of men.

This would never remain a secret.

He was a royal. A Sunborn.

He was screwed, and he knew it.

At the end of the story, Yarrs lapsed into silence. He looked like a weight was off his shoulders. The North was not at war with Landor. The Second didn't have to attack the North, and the king was certainly not interested in an all-out war with the tribes.

Jaze nodded. "Well, I need to talk to the general about this, you know this, Yarrs." Jaze looked at Dragh, his face pinched tight with anger. "You and I will talk soon."

With that, Jaze turned on a heel and left the tent, his guardsman leaving with him.

Dragh let out a breath. His shoulders were sore from a long day and a long time standing at attention.

"Thank the Gods you came, Yarrs," Dragh sighed.

Yarrs had a small smile on his lips. "Lad, that was a start." Yarrs wiped his face, rubbing at his eyes.

"What do you mean? Nestor can call off the Second. We have no need to attack the North now," Dragh asked, confused by Yarrs's reaction.

"It's not all as it seems, my young prince. Not all men will listen to the truth, and not all will believe the truth when they hear it," Yarrs sighed. "I've seen it many times."

"No, you'll see. Nestor is a good man. He'll see reason," Dragh said, not so certain himself, anymore.

"Well, look at it from their side, Dragh," Yarrs smiled at Dragh. "He sailed his entire Legion here to the North on reports of the King of the North. Some false king killed his people on the border of the Car Lauch."

"And?" Dragh asked.

"And how well do you think a general, the one who led his men here, and King Kallen would take news that they were wrong? Nestor can't just pack up and leave. He can't take the word of an old man, even if I was once a legate. I am... less than I once was," Yarrs said with an eyebrow raised.

Dragh was pacing now, back and forth, thinking. Dragh felt the blood rush to his face. The embarrassment at not seeing the obvious. The embarrassment at dragging Yarrs here. "Gods. What can we do?"

"Nothing. We are not kings. We are not generals," Yarrs said to Dragh.

Their conversation was interrupted by a rustle at the flap of Jaze's tent. Dragh tensed in anticipation of his uncle and Jaze.

Jaze walked into the tent, dipping his head to Yarrs.

No one else came with him.

"The general commands you both to his tent," Jaze said to them.

Dragh and Yarrs left the legate's tent. Jaze eyed Dragh as they did. They made their way to the general's tent. The guards outside the tent let them in without question, showing some deference to Dragh.

He knew the signs. They knew who he was. It had begun.

As they ducked into the command tent, Dragh could feel tension in the air. It was a thick feeling, the air itself clung to them.

"General Nestor," Dragh said in greeting to his uncle.

"Salute your general," one of the guards said to Dragh, having followed them into the tent.

Dragh was surprised by the request and looked from his uncle, who stood leaning over his maps table, to the guard.

Nestor had a sour look on his face.

Dragh saluted, bringing his arm to his chest with a clenched fist. "General," he said through gritted teeth. "Yarrs has news from the…" Dragh started.

"Your general has not addressed you. Keep your mouth shut," the guard said, his voice cracking slightly.

Dragh looked the guard in the eyes. He knew, and yet he was treating Dragh like a common welp on the street. "What is—?"

"Yarrs. Tell me your news," Nestor said to the old man.

His tone of voice told Dragh that Nestor already knew the news, and he was not impressed. Dragh knew where this was going.

Yarrs told his story to the general, short and to the point. The report of a soldier who was used to giving short reports on complex problems to his superiors.

Dragh watched. His uncle Nestor looked irritated, waiting for the report to be done so that he could speak. He was not really listening.

"That's it?" Nestor asked Yarrs.

Yarrs's jaw worked and his mouth closed. He blinked hard. "Yes, General Nestor. I beg you, please give up this folly and treat with the leader of our tribes. He claims no kingship."

"Explain to me. Why do I have letters from King Kallen that tell me there have been more atrocities by your so-called *king* in the passes south of us?" Nestor held up folded letters on parchment and waved them at Yarrs.

"The king has not been informed properly," Yarrs defended himself, trying to hold himself tall. His unsteady leg betrayed him, making him grasp the back of a chair he was never offered.

Nestor waved at Yarrs. "I'm tired of lies from a tribal headman trying to save his little village." Nestor looked to the guard behind them. "Take these men out of my tent. The old man can leave the camp." He looked back at his maps, never having moved away from them.

"Uncle, he was a Landorian Praetorian, a legate!" Dragh broke rank to plead with his uncle.

"That's GENERAL to you, boy," Nestor roared.

"I didn't..." Dragh stuttered.

"Of course you didn't. You didn't think when you brought this man into our camp. For all you know, he is a traitor, a spy sent to report back to our enemy!" Nestor turned red with frustration.

"We have to listen to him. We are here on false pretenses," Dragh sputtered.

Nestor strode forward, eating the space between them with his stride.

"WE are here because we have it on good authority that this upstart is killing our people. I will not be told by a soldier how to use my Legion. I am a General of the Second," Nestor shouted, spittle flying from his mouth.

Dragh could feel the general's breath on his face.

Dragh was angry. Blood flowed to his face, and his arms vibrated. How could Nestor be so stubborn? What was his problem? He took a step forward towards Nestor.

"I am a Sunborn. I am the son of a king." Dragh lifted his chin up, defying Nestor.

Nestor took a deep breath. "You are nothing but a soldier in the Second, like every man under my command. And now you are not a primus. You are a man with a sword, like everyone else in your squad. You can go and tell Legate Jaze. Get out of my sight."

Dragh's face fell slack.

He was no longer a primus? Nestor was taking that from him?

The guard pushed him out of the tent, hesitant, yet firmly.

Dragh left the tent in a daze. His own uncle. Why? Why did he dismiss Yarrs. Was it really pride, or was it something else?

Dragh tried to stop the guards, but they hauled Yarrs away quickly, barring Dragh from following.

"Gods," Dragh said to himself, still shocked by his uncle.

He walked to Jaze's tent, and then somehow found his way back to his own.

"What happened?" Hemmelle asked as Dragh sat on his bed, stunned.

Chapter 14

"You shit eaters think I want to be transferred over to this squad?" the new primus berated them.

Dragh bit his tongue, not wanting to say anything that would get his men in trouble. He shook his head—they were not his men anymore.

"What's that, Dragh? Do you have something you'd like to say?" Primus Ols asked.

They stood in the evening sun, having patrolled the eastern flank of the marching legion again. Before they were ready to return to camp, Ols had decided to chew them out. Give them a once over.

They had passed through the Gallas Forest earlier in the week, spending days in it.

They were now in a valley a couple of leagues from the camp, having finished their patrols.

In the baking sun, they stood at attention. Sweat formed on Dragh's neck, rolling down his back and itching the whole way. He did his best to stay still, but his legs were spent and his head ached for a drink of water.

Dragh could hear his companions' stomachs grumble. He resisted the urge to think about food.

"I hope he wasn't good friends with Vanor," Dragh said quietly.

"What was that, you little stain?" Primus Ols snarled in Dragh's face.

The primus stood a head shorter than most of them, making up for his height in his anger. He screamed at them day in and day out.

"Nothing, Primus Ols!" Dragh responded with too much enthusiasm.

"I know your kind. I've been in the Second for longer than you've been alive. You give me any more shit and I'll make you cup your hands every time I take a piss. Do you hear me?" Ols shouted in Dragh's ear.

Dragh closed his eyes, trying to remain calm. "Aye, Primus."

Hemmelle took a sharp breath.

Ols noticed. "And you?"

"Aye, Primus." Hemmelle replied.

"You are all sad excuses for soldiers. Back when I joined the Second, you had to cut a finger off to prove your loyalty. Do you know what kind of guts that took? No, of course you don't. You just tell your little stories of crime and laugh." Ols held up his hand that was missing a finger. "We were fuckin' killers. Now you little shits are all soft." Ols covered a nostril, blew snot out of his nose, and walked away.

The primus crested the hill, looking off into the distance. Relish no longer headed the patrols.

"No wonder Dara has problems. They are crazy bastards," Hemmelle said, looking to make sure Ols was out of earshot.

The new primus was from the cavalry. Dragh and the men knew it was to punish them. To put them in their place.

"Good thing they are on our side, eh?" Dragh said.

"I don't know if they are, some days," Hemmelle commented.

Dragh sat down with the rest of the squad, happy that Ols was scouting ahead for a moment. It was a reprieve.

"What was that for?" Relish asked, passing them both water skins.

"I think he's sweet on Dragh," Hemmelle jibed.

"What do you think is going on here?" Dragh asked them both, ignoring the jibe.

Relish looked around, making sure the rest of the squad was far enough away from them. "I think that Nestor doesn't like playing second fiddle to you, Dragh. You are a Sunborn, and he is too."

Hemmelle finished the thought. "He doesn't like that you are in line for the throne and technically outrank him. That's why he busted you down. He had to be seen to be in charge of his Legion. He can't have the rest of the Legion thinking you're in charge."

"And he put someone here to punish us. To make us think twice about stepping out of line," Relish tossed in.

"After this, I think I'm going to have a lot of explaining to do to Lucille," Dragh commented, his mind wandering back to home.

Hemmelle and Relish exchanged a look. Dragh shook his head.

"Up, you bastards!"

They all looked to Ols, at the top of the hill. He shouted and waved for them to join him.

Relish groaned.

"Let's go before this one shits himself," Cello commented, making his way towards Ols.

Dragh laughed at the joke, slapping Cello on the back. They exchanged a smile. "He looks the type, doesn't he?"

Cello smirked as they walked. "You good, Dragh?" Cello asked.

Dragh knew this was as close to cordial as they would ever get. Cello was offering an olive branch to him. "Aye, I'm good. Thank you." He nodded to Cello.

"The general is a man of moods. It'll pass," Cello said.

"I don't think so, this time," Dragh replied, snorting.

"Well, you could always pull rank." Cello gave Dragh a slap on the back and let himself move backwards. The moment was over.

Dragh thought of that wisdom. Pulling rank was what he tried to do. It didn't work. He was demoted from primus. He was a prince, but in this legion, he was just another soldier, punishment for what he'd done. That would have to change when he got home.

The squad moved through the set of foothills that seemed to stretch on into the horizon. As far as they could see, a sea of grass and rock. Dragh thought he might be able to see mountain peaks in the distance, but he'd need Relish's eyes for that.

"Do you hear that?" Hemmelle asked.

Relish nodded. "South."

Dragh slowed his march, closing his eyes to listen. "Is that... hooves?" Dragh thought he could hear the faint thunder of horses moving in a pack.

"I know they have wild horses up here. This is where Landor's stock originally came from. I think they call this place Cymru," Hemmelle commented.

"Must be the cavalry. Their stain of a friend has been demoted to leading us lot," Dragh replied, referring to Primus Ols.

"Horses to the south!" the call came from Ols.

Relish had been moved from his usual position of leading the squad. He was back in the trenches with Dragh and Hemmelle. Pello and Zeffo were also there, but they endured the insult without comment.

"Aye, we knew that," Relish muttered.

"Form up!" Hemmelle called out to the squad.

Dragh cringed. Ols would not take kindly to that. An ex-second-in-command issuing commands to his squad.

"Belay that order," Ols shouted loudly from the front of the squad as he marched down the hill.

Dragh shook his head. Hemmelle cursed loudly.

"They must be ours, coming from the south, Hemmelle. Stop being a coward," Ols shouted out.

Hemmelle looked as if he was going to explode in rage. Dragh grabbed his arm, hard. His attempt to stop Hemmelle was a shout in the wind. It went nowhere.

Hemmelle broke Dragh's grip with a swift shot in his wrist and was stalking towards the new primus.

"Don't!" Dragh tried to stop Hemmelle once more.

"Go to the pit" Hemmelle said through gritted teeth, rolling away from Dragh's grip. He was almost on top of Ols with his last stride.

Dragh stepped up beside Hemmelle. He was always taught that if you can't stop them, defend your friends. He figured out the truth of it after.

"The fucking cavalry might be the enemy. We have to form up!" Hemmelle shouted at Ols.

Dragh could see men around them nodding in agreement. The noise of the hooves was louder now. He could hear them in the distance. Dragh risked a quick glance to the south. Dust was rising like a lazy cloud above the mouth of the valley they were in. No horsemen in sight yet.

"I said, they are our men. Now get out of my sight. In case you've forgotten, you both *report* to me now." Ols motioned to Hemmelle and Dragh both.

Dragh stepped forward. "If you don't issue the command, I will."

Ols glared at Dragh for a moment, then looked around the group of men that had collected around them. The whole squad. "You wouldn't dare. You'd be charged and executed for mutiny."

"Not if the commanding officer was derelict in duty, and the commands were for the safety of the squad." Hemmelle replied, citing the laws of the Legion, of the Landorian Army.

"You have moments. They will be on us soon," Dragh said, pressing the issue.

Ols gave them both another look of hatred. His face is a deep shade of purple.

"Get in line, men!" Ols shouted, his voice cracking with rage. "You two get the pit out of my sight."

"Aye, Primus," Hemmelle replied curtly.

Dragh and Hemmelle moved to the back of the squad as the horsemen crested the hill in front of them. The squad moved into a block of men, five wide and ten deep.

They were hemmed in by a cliff on their left, the hill on the right. A funnel for the horsemen to come down on them like a sledgehammer.

The men moved with practiced ease. The only man out of formation was Ols. His pride stopped him from moving into the protection of the squad, behind the spears and shields. He was six paces in front of the squad after they formed, standing as if greeting his friends.

"Who are they?" Hemmelle asked. The dark horsemen were wearing what appeared to be Landorian uniforms, colors of gold and red.

Dragh didn't have a chance to respond. Ols stood without his weapons raised, welcoming the horsemen who appeared to be from Landor.

"Something is off. Those aren't our horses." Dragh said, noticing the large beasts.

The arrows thumped, and the sound of the bowstrings twang followed.

Ols turned to them, mouth opened, arrow jutting from his right eye and chest. His body crumpled to the ground.

"DEATHHHH," came a war cry from the horsemen streaming down the hill towards the squad.

Dragh braced behind the man in front of him.

"SHIELDS!" Dragh shouted, bracing his with his shoulder, kneeling on the ground with one knee.

The heavy horses streamed towards them.

Fear gripped them. The only thing keeping them together, Dragh knew, was a loyalty to one another. Nothing else could hold you in line during the charge. Loyalty was owed to your brother-in-arms.

The shockwave of the horse hitting the squad almost threw Dragh on his back. The horses moved down the hill in a pack; the canter tore them through the squad like a knife through cloth.

The first three cavalrymen collapsed forward with spears embedded in their chests. Two of the horses on the flanks reared, the spears hitting them and their riders.

Archers on either side of Dragh fired their arrows, nocking and firing at will.

Dragh tried to catch his breath, and the squad started punching forward. The first three lines of men were dead or down. The fourth and fifth line swung swords and axes at the horses. The beasts and riders were leaping their dead and fallen comrades.

"Swing right!" Hemmelle called from Dragh's right.

Dragh immediately understood. They hugged the left hand cliff, the right flank was open for horsemen to cut open the soft underbelly of the squad's flank. No squad could withstand that.

"Wheel! WHEEL!" Dragh called out to the men.

The archers dropped their bows as they had drilled, pulling swords as the last three lines of the squad ran to the right to defend their flank.

The line was thinner now, a gamble to save their lives. To buy more time.

Dragh didn't know how many were in the enemy attack party, but he knew if they wanted any chance of survival, they would need to kill their way out of it.

The horsemen made another pass at them, charging again and cutting more men of the Second down.

"TO ME, MEN!" Dragh called as he hefted his sword and shield. Hemmelle hefted his axe, moving at Dragh's side.

The squad moved quickly, but not quickly enough.

A horsemen cut down two men as they raced in front of Dragh.

"Hemmelle!" Dragh called.

Hemmelle grunted something to Dragh, pivoting mid-stride to face the rear. He yelled for Zeffo in the rush.

Dragh looked forward, trusting his friend to protect him. One man against a horseman was bad news. But Hemmelle and his axe were a terrible foe to face. A killer among killers. The blade was wicked.

"DRAGH!" a shout came from beside him.

Dragh looked over as Cello tossed him a spear, running towards Dragh from the main line of the squad.

Dragh caught the spear, dropping his shield, and dropped to one knee in the new front line.

Two horsemen were breaking from the back of the attacking party. They were gray beasts with frothing months and nostrils, close enough that Dragh could see the whites in the rider's eyes.

Dragh set the spear in the ground, praying to the Gods that it was firm enough to take on the impact. He thought of Lucille. He thought of his unborn baby.

"HOLDDD!" he called out to his men.

His men.

"ARRHHHHHH!!!" the collective shout came from them all as the horses slammed into them.

Dragh felt the weight of the horse on his spear, then it was torn from his grip as he was tossed into the air.

He landed in the mud, face down. The last thing he heard was the screaming of horses and men. The smell of mud and blood overwhelmed him.

He closed his eyes, and darkness wrapped around him like a warm blanket.

—

"Wake up, you bastard!" Dragh heard as he came to.

"What?" Dragh asked, his head splitting.

"He's alive!" a voice coated with excitement came from somewhere in front of him.

Dragh couldn't see, his eyes stung. He tested his limbs. There was a sharp pain in his arm, and his legs were stiff and cold. His chest felt as if a horse had stomped on him.

The last couple of minutes came to him. Perhaps a horse had stomped on him? He remembered seeing hooves flying in front of him, and then he was in the mud.

"Dragh, get up you bastard," a gruff voice came from somewhere in front of him.

Dragh flailed, not able to see what was in front of him. His mind tried to catch up with his reality.

"I can't... I can't see!" he mumbled. Dirt and blood mixed in his mouth.

"Hold still!" the strained voice came to him again.

Dragh felt hands on his shoulders, holding him to the ground. Then on his face. He started to panic, not able to breathe. The water enveloped him, in his mouth, his nostrils, and then his eyes.

His eyes! He could see again, blurry, but then the world slid into focus as he blinked. Hemmelle and Relish were on either side of him. Hemmelle had a gash across his forehead above his eyes. Blood had coated his face but clumped up at the wound.

Relish looked like a demon from hell. His face covered in mud and blood. The whites of his eyes were the only thing that looked human.

"What happened?" Dragh asked them both.

Relish and Hemmelle laughed without humor. "I told you, Relish. He's in another fuckin" world."

Relish grinned. His white teeth sharp against the muddy skin. "Aye, he's stupid since he lost the primus promotion."

Dragh laughed, his head splitting from the noise. "Arrh," he winced.

"Get up, you'll need to walk that one off. You musta flew like a bird," Relish said, helping Dragh to his feet.

Dragh swayed, unsteady on his feet. He put his hand out and gripped Hemmelle's shoulder to try and steady himself.

"Easy," Hemmelle said quietly.

Dragh looked around, wiping at his face to try and clear the mud and debris. "Give me some water." He held his hand out to Relish.

Relish handed him a water skin without comment.

"Who did we lose?" Dragh asked, looking around at more bodies than he'd expected. He could hear screams all over. The valley they fought in was littered with bodies, some still moving. Most of the bodies were still, the kind of stillness only the dead possessed.

Hemmelle looked away from Dragh and took a deep breath.

"Tell me, who's left?" Dragh said with some more authority in his voice.

He tried not to let his voice waver as he looked around at his squad. It was his squad, no matter what Nestor said to him.

These were his men.

He knew he wasn't made for a crown. He was made for war. He knew that. He should never have let Nestor take the squad from him.

"It's... it's easier to count the living," Hemmelle said, tears in his eyes.

Dragh patted Hemmelle on the back.

"Relish, Zeffo, Geral, Pello, Verras, and Cello are with us."

Dragh felt his stomach drop, and he keeled over to release the contents of his stomach.

"Gods," Dragh said aloud, wiping at his mouth.

"Aye, I think they were with us, my friend. It is a miracle that we killed as many as we did. They sent heavy horse for us. Men such as us fall to heavy horse like tinder to a fire," Hemmelle responded.

"Who sent them? What are you talking about?" Dragh asked, confused.

"Come with me." Hemmelle walked away, towards Relish and the rest of the survivors.

Dragh walked to them. They were huddled around a fire, bodies all around them. The sky was dark with cloud cover. He could see his squad mates wrapped up, some with wounds that made him feel like heaving up the contents of his stomach again. The enemy laid where they fell.

A scream came from the body beside the fire. A mess of limbs and blood.

Dragh didn't say a word; the enemy lived. And the fallen man was in pain. The animal side of him wanted nothing more than to find his sword and run the bleeding soldier through, sending him to the pit.

Or, to skin him alive.

The darkness in him wanted revenge for his brothers.

Dragh could see sealing irons, knives heated in fire to seal up wounds, strewn around the ground. Battlefield medicine. None of them were proficient, but they knew how to stop themselves from bleeding out.

They knew they'd need their strength this day.

"Tell him what you told us," Relish said to the man.

Dragh watched as Relish gave the man a drink of water. He could smell the stink of a gut wound from where he stood. The smoke from the little fire did nothing to mask it. He watched as water and blood came out of the man's wounds.

"I told you already, I will make it," the man said to Relish.

"I know, I know. Where are they sending you?" Relish asked, taking a patient, but firm tone with the man.

Dragh assessed the man from being somewhere in the south. Not a northman at all. His skin was that of an islander, a Ralarian. Yet, the face was almost like horsemen from the west.

The clothing he wore was indeed old Landorian red and gold colours. Dragh could tell that it was old, cut, patched, and stained. Good enough to fool them at a distance, but not good enough for an up-close inspection.

"He thinks he's somewhere else, talking to who knows," Cello said, surprising Dragh by offering him his seat at the fire.

Dragh nodded to the ex-Primus.

Dragh watched as the strange man's eyes rolled in his head, the whites of his eyes visible under his fluttering eyelids. "They are sending us north, past Landor. We go to the mountains."

"And who are you fighting?" Relish prompted the man.

A spasm hit the dying man, his face screwed up and his body jolted. Tears streamed down his face. His eyes focused on Relish. "I don't want to die. I don't, please, please help me!" he cried out.

"I know, I know. What is your name?" Relish asked, his voice quiet.

The man seized up again. Blood foamed at his mouth, and some dribbled out as he screamed. His gut wound oozed black liquid. He gave a final scream, and then his body came to a sudden stop.

"What did he tell you?" Dragh looked around the fire, at the men gathered there. All of them sported some wounds. Relish had a bandage on his shoulder soaked in blood, Geral had a cut across his arm. Pello and Zeffo both looked like they had been in fist fights. Cello had a nasty gouge across his leg wrapped with a red tinged cloth.

"He told us that he was a mercenary from the south," Cello coughed, spitting some blood onto the ground. "He came to raid and pillage. His masters, from the east, promised towns and villages with much gold. They planned on taking gold and slaves." Cello chuckled darkly. "He was disappointed..."

"That there was just us to kill," Dragh finished.

"Aye. The rest you heard. He was in and out with the pain," Cello agreed.

Dragh rubbed at his aching head. He was not the only one being lied to. He was not the only one confused about what was going on here. Mercenaries from the south? Masters from the east? What the pit was happening. Why did these mercenaries come to kill them?

"We need to move," Hemmelle said.

They all grunted their agreement. Most of them looked around at the bodies of their friends, their brothers in arms.

"Let us commit them to the fire," Relish said, looking to Dragh for approval.

"We don't have time. It's been too long already. We need to inform the Second. They are in danger," Dragh said, looking to his second, Hemmelle, who blanched.

Respect for the dead was everything to a soldier. Even an enemy soldier.

"Dragh," Relish said, letting the silence speak for itself.

"The Legion need us. More than the dead," Dragh said, looking around at his men that remained. They stared at him with dead eyes, exhaustion on all of their faces.

"We must make for the Legion as fast as we can. We do not know the numbers of these mercenaries. We must warn them," Dragh paused. "You all know who I am, who my family is. I have to; it is my duty."

Dragh waited. For the first time with the men, he said it aloud. He was a Sunborn.

They all nodded to him.

"I must warn my uncle. Whatever this is, whoever these mercenaries are, I need to warn my uncle of the danger the Second is facing." He held each of their gazes for a moment.

"I'll go," Cello said abruptly. "Take care of the men, Dragh. I will take one of the horses and ride for the Second."

Dragh locked eyes with Cello, giving him a silent thanks. "Go."

Cello nodded, looking around at the men. "Get yourselves south as fast as you can." He walked away from them without waiting for a response and grabbed at the reins of one of the mercenaries' mounts that remained on its feet. Its owner was dead on the ground.

"Gods protect you," Zeffo said as Cello left.

"Gather wood for the men," Relish told the rest of them. "I will say the words."

Dragh didn't see the need to add anything to what Relish had requested. The men deserved the time, they deserved a good burial. He set about gathering wood with what was left of his squad.

They didn't have to work hard to gather wood for the dead. They were surrounded by deadfall. The valley had been hit by storms blowing off the ocean over the years. The trees could only withstand so much. They worked at cutting and dragging the deadfall for a couple of hours. They piled it, crisscrossing the deadfall to make a pyre.

It took longer than Dragh had wanted. The men moved slowly after battle. They had used all their energy surviving, and now the labour was almost too much for them.

The fog descended late in the day, relieving them of the heat of the sun.

Finally, they moved their dead to the pyre. Many of them were mutilated from battle. Arms, legs, and parts missing or destroyed. It was a sickening thing to do, moving their dead. Dragh grimaced and bore the pain of it, tears streaming down his face silently.

Their dead deserved it. If you didn't care for your dead, how would a man fight beside you, knowing you'd been food for the scavengers if you fell?

Relish stood at the pyre as Zeffo and Pello took logs alight with fire and spread them over the pyre. Flames licked at the dry deadfall as quickly as dried tinder.

"We give you to earth and sky,

We pray you are with the gods,

From the earth we come,

To the earth and sky, you go."

Relish bowed his head, saying goodbye to his brothers.

Dragh watched the men, all of them in silent commune with the dead.

He let more tears streak down his face. He would find the men that sent these mercenaries north. He would find them and he would kill them.

He swore it to Zufier above. To Kiever below. The Old Gods understood vengeance.

"We kill whoever did this," Dragh said to the men around him, their eyes catching the glint of the funeral pyre.

Dragh took out his knife and slid it into the flesh of his hand. He let the blood well up around his palm and then squeezed his hand into a fist. The blood squeezed out between his fingers and dripped onto the ground.

"By my blood, I swear it. They will pay," Dragh grit his teeth in anger.

Hemmelle pulled out his dagger, cut his hand, and dripped blood onto the ground.

The others followed suit; each of them could feel the anger in the air. The hatred. They would avenge their dead.

"Let's hunt, men," Dragh said.

"Mount up, Relish, lead us back to the Second," Hemmelle issued commands to what was left of the squad.

Dragh and Hemmelle each mounted a horse close to them. Dragh moved slowly due to his injuries. His body was beaten up and bruised.

Relish, Pello, Zeffo, Geral and Verras all mounted horses, finding them scattered throughout the valley.

They mounted the horses, enough to go around to the survivors of the squad.

Dragh listened to the groans from his men, trying to hold his own back as he found his seat in the saddle.

"Let's go," Dragh said to the mounted men, spurring his horse out of the valley and towards the Second in the south.

As he rode, his mind wandered, foggy, but working through the problem. Who were these men? Why did they hunt him and his men? It was an oddity to send a large force of men against a single squad. It was odd again that they were dressed in Landor red and gold. Who had given them the colours of the nation?

Who sent these men, these killers, against them? Why Southerners? It was unusual for anyone from the south to raid this far north. It was another thing again to be hired to raid and kill. These men were sent here to kill Dragh and his squad.

Or were they sent to kill Dragh? Did they know who he was?

Dragh overtook Relish as he pushed his mount forward. He had to get to Nestor. To the men of Landor.

The men chewed up the leagues that were between them and the Legion quickly. As they crested a particularly high set of hills, Dragh could see smoke on the horizon, even through the fog hung around them like a cloak.

Something was burning. Something big. The inky blot rose up in a diagonal column and disappeared into the clouds. Dragh could see a glow beneath it, the blaze still going.

Dragh looked back, his men not far behind him riding up the crest.

"Hurry!" he shouted to the men, urging his mount to push harder. He could hear the ragged breath of his mount. He knew he would run this horse to death if he pushed her.

He had no choice. His men, men of Landor, were dying.

"Dragh!" Hemmelle called from behind him.

Dragh could barely hear it in the wind. His mind was focused on what was in front of him. He had to get back.

"Dragh!" tThe call came to him again in the wind.

Dragh looked back quickly. He'd outpaced the men behind him by half a league now. Most of them were struggling to keep up on their borrowed mounts. He knew that many were wounded, them and their horses both.

He reigned in, pulling his horse back to a trot, to let the others catch up.

Hemmelle was the first to make it to him.

"You know what that is, don't you?" Hemmelle asked Dragh, a rhetorical question.

"Aye," Dragh said, trying to catch his own breath. The ride was taking more out of him than he thought. His head was alight with pain from the ride.

"Someone's set fire to the camp," Relish said quietly.

Dragh looked at the thick, black smoke. Something burned, something big. It was a dark smoke from green wood and something else. No seasoned wood would burn with such dark smoke.

"We don't know until we see it for ourselves," Pello commented.

Zeffo's usual sneer was replaced by a somber look. He spoke quietly, "We know they came for us. I think we can assume that they have come for ALL of us."

Geral sighed, "Dragh. We are riding into something we don't know. I think we should use some caution. Cello went ahead, but he may be too late."

Dragh looked around at his men. He knew Geral was right, and the look Hemmelle gave him let Dragh know Hemmelle agreed, too. The horses they rode and the men that rode them were all hurt.

Dragh knew his men sported wounds, some bandaged, some still open. The horses had bloody froth at the corners of their mouths. They'd be lucky to make it to the camp that the Second might have retreated to. Or started building.

"Verras?" he asked the young man who had said nothing.

Verras looked around, uncomfortable speaking up in front of the seasoned soldiers around him.

"We speak our minds here. Tell me what you think, boy," Dragh said. He needed to know what his men thought, he needed to temper his anger. If it were only him, he would dive head first into killing if he could. But he needed his men with him for that.

Verras cleared his throat. "I think... I think Geral is right, sir," he replied, looking down at the ground.

Dragh took a deep breath and ignored Zeffo's snort at Verras's comment.

"I was never perfect, but I won't drive us into a trap," Dragh said to his men, letting the frustration bleed out of him. "I won't lose more of you," he admitted to them.

Looking around, Dragh met all their eyes. A pride was there. They were his men, and they were proud of it. He was responsible for them.

"Relish, lead us. We need to see what's in front of us. I want to move quickly, but I don't want anyone to know we are here," Dragh said.

"We need to ditch the horses before we get too close, sir," Relish said, recognising that Dragh was in charge again. "If the Second are under attack, we do not want to hit the flank of an enemy with so few."

"Aye, we do. Good idea, Relish." Dragh nodded his thanks to Relish. Relishs's use of "Sir" did not go unnoticed among the group. "I'm Dragh, until further notice. Not sir. Not anything. I'm of the Second, just like you all," Dragh told them.

"Well, not quite like the rest of us," Hemmelle commented.

The rest of the men broke up in laughter. The joke and laughter broke the tension they were all feeling. It was a welcome change.

"Let's go. Daylight is going to start fading," Hemmelle told them all.

Dragh looked to the murky sun through the fog, nodding. It was half past its peak. It was soon to be evening. Darkness was coming. And they had hunting to do.

"Lead on, Relish," Dragh commanded again.

Relish kicked his horse into action, and the rest of them followed. They were into a canter again, the horses straining to keep up with their riders.

They rode in silence. The only sounds were the snorting of the horses, the hooves on the ground, and the creak of leather tack and saddle. Dragh could taste blood in his mouth and smell the copper.

He prayed to the Gods for the second time in the day. Let his uncle live. Let Nestor, the rock of his life, live.

The Second was his family. The last weeks did nothing to his love for his uncle. Nestor had always been there for him when his family hadn't. He understood that Dragh didn't want the crown.

Nestor was always there to listen.

They could see the dark smoke more clearly after another couple leagues. The wind had died, and Dragh could smell the green wood burning. The camp was alight, he knew it in his bones.

They came to the sparse forested area that had shielded the camp's build site. Dragh and the squad had left it this morning, ranging far ahead of the main army, scouting ahead. He knew it would be a good campsite. There was some natural protection from a ring of trees that bubbled out from the main wooded area they'd already passed.

This time, Dragh didn't have his squad. He only had Verras, Pello, Zeffo, Relish, and Hemmelle.

The smoke shot up into a column in the air, a pyre to the gods. The smell hung in the air, in the fog itself.

Dragh knew that the camp could not have been complete before the second was attacked.

He knew what it meant. The Second had been attacked on the move.

While ranging in enemy territory, the Second moved from camp to camp. If they were attacked early enough on the march, they could retreat to the first camp they had left.

They all dismounted on the inner edge of the forest ring. Between them and the camp were some hills and craigs, but mostly open ground. There was little cover to help them now. It was time to take revenge for his men.

"Where is Cello?" Hemmelle said quietly.

Dragh squatted down on the forest's edge, looking towards the burning camp in the distance. He could see Landorian bodies of red and gold strewn across the earth before them. But could not make out any details.

The camp was fired, and the main gate facing north was destroyed. It hung on a single hinge from the top, having been broken inward.

"Who could do such damage?" Dragh said to himself.

Fear touched him. If the enemy was brazen enough to attack a fortified camp, how could he do anything against them?

"We need to move, Dragh," Relish told him, touching his shoulder.

Dragh jerked back to the present, his mind lost in what he was about to face. "Move fast, we will follow."

They ran low and fast.

Dragh gripped his sword, trying to reduce the rattle between it and the shield on his back. Hemmelle ran in front of him, trying to keep up with Relish. The little bastard could move like the wind.

They ran at the edge of the trees, down and around to the east side of the camp.

By the time they were parallel with the camp, they turned inward.

Relish picked up the pace, moving faster across the open ground. Dragh felt as if his legs would fail him. His lungs burned. Blood was flowing from the wound on his forehead, one he didn't know he had.

All he could hear was the crackling of the fire and his own wheezing gasps for air as they ran.

Dragh could see light starting to fade. The sun burned through the fog, hitting the tips of the trees in the west. He would have chuckled at the genius of Relish, but he was afraid to collapse. Relish made sure they were running in the woods until he was sure they would have some advantage; the sunlight being blocked gave them some cover in the dusk of day.

The camp was still alight, not the intense inferno that it might have been earlier, but a steady burn. The closer they got, the more intense the acrid smell of burning flesh became.

They were at the east gate now—no enemies in sight. They pushed inside, slowly, through the partially-opened gate.

Dragh gave them a hand signal, no talking. He wanted to keep the element of surprise.

Blood and gore greeted them; bodies of men and horses were strewn everywhere. Arrow shafts and spears jutted out from the ground. The mud was slick with waste, with blood and shit. The smell was all the worse, knowing it was their Legion.

Dragh and the others scanned for the enemy, but the enemy was gone. Some of their dead, in old red and gold, were here and there. But it seemed it was a mostly mounted attack. None were left alive.

Their uniforms were Landorian like the Seconds, but old enough that a practiced eye could tell the difference.

"How did we... how did we miss this?" Relish asked, his voice breaking.

Dragh let tears drop down his face. "The Gods punish us."

Hemmelle shook his head. "The Pit is what we see in front of us."

Dragh's anger returned. "We will visit this evil on our enemies. I will skin them alive," he said with venom. "Where the fuck is Cello?"

"Dragh!" a call came from the front of the camp.

Dragh turned, his pretense of stealth gone with his anger. Verras stood in the front of the camp, looking at what was once the north gates.

Dragh and the rest jogged to him. "What is it?"

Verras gaped upward at the towers on either side of the north gate. The rest of them followed his line of sight.

Dragh heard Hemmelle and someone else vomit. He wasn't paying attention anymore.

Up on the half-burnt towers, on either side of the burning gate, were bodies.

One was Cello. His head was cut from his body, hanging by the spine. The spine was white and crooked.

The other was Jaze. His arms were cut off, blood staining the wood behind his body.

"What in the Gods," a weak-voiced Hemmelle asked aloud.

"Monsters," Relish whispered.

The crackling of the fire was all that they could hear now. No one spoke.

Verras still hadn't recovered, joining some of the others and spewing what food he had left in his stomach on the ground.

"Gather what supplies you can. We need to move. Zeffo, Pello, we need the horses," Dragh spoke to them softly, knowing the pain they all felt for their ex-primus and legate.

Zeffo and Pello took off to the north at a jog to where they'd tethered the horses in the forest.

"Let's get them down..." Hemmelle pleaded with Dragh.

"My friend, the camp burns. We can no more reach them now than forge iron with bare hands." Dragh put his hand on Hemmelle's shoulder.

"I... I don't know if I can do this, Dragh," Hemmelle whispered, tears in his eyes.

Dragh took a breath. "I know. I know," he tried to comfort Hemmelle.

They'd seen death before, but never had they seen their own men strung up and brutally murdered. War was one thing, this was another.

"I need your help," Dragh said, pulling Hemmelle's head to his and clasping the back of his neck. "Brother, I need to make it back to Landor. We need to move. Nestor could be alive. Others too." Dragh clapped his friend on the back, leaving him to be with his own thoughts.

Dragh set about collecting supplies with his men. He knew the best leader was always right beside his men, doing what needed to be done. His father had taught him that a leader leads from the front.

He also needed to keep his mind moving. Lest it stay here, in this place of carnage and death. It was more than his mind was prepared for.

"Stay on their trail, Relish," Dragh looked around at the rest of them. "We are going to go after these mercenaries."

Zeffo and Pello trotted back to them, horses in tow behind each of them.

"There has to be thousands of them, Dragh. What the pit are we going to do against thousands?" Zeffo confronted Dragh, dismounting his horse. "I'm telling you all, this is a death wish."

Dragh fought off the exhaustion he was feeling. After a day from the Pit, now this. He didn't know if he had the strength to go on.

"I know, Zeffo. We are the rock in their boots. We need to be quiet and quick, in and out before they know we are there. This is a rescue mission now. They may have taken men of the Second with them. We cannot kill thousands, but we might be able to save men of the Second. They couldn't have killed them all."

Dragh said the last part not only for the men but for himself. He had to believe some from the Second were alive. Part of him held out hope that it was his uncle.

Zeffo glared openly at Dragh. "We. Will. Die," he said through gritted teeth.

"Then stay here," Dragh said fiercely, taking a step towards Zeffo.

Hemmelle shifted his great war axe on his shoulder. "Zeffo, get in line."

Zeffo sneered at both Dragh and Hemmelle before shaking his head and turning back towards his brother, behind Geral.

Geral stepped to Dragh and Hemmelle. "Where are they going?" he asked, looking to Relish.

"South, it seems, through the Gallas Forest" Relish said tightly.

Geral and Relish exchanged a look.

"What?" Dragh asked them.

"Yarrs is south, isn't he? What will mercenaries do to a village on their war path?" Geral put to Dragh.

"Gods." Dragh rubbed at his throbbing temple. "Let's move."

They threw packs on their horses, tying what supplies they needed to their saddles. Mounting, they rode off to the south, towards Yarrs's village.

Dragh knew he had to get back to Landor. He needed to tell his father what was happening. The king would know what this was and what it was all about.

He felt a pang, his heart heavy. He might never meet his child, and he might never make it back to Lucille.

Chapter 15

"Feels eerie, doesn't it?" Hemmelle said, walking his horse beside Dragh.

The Gallas Forest had a natural path to it, its geography the same as the plains, hills, and gullies. The forest was thick with vegetation, but the valleys and path through the forest wound their way like a snake from north to south. They followed it now. That was the only real option in such a dense forest. They'd argued, but taking a route to the east or west of the main valley would take an extra week.

Dragh furrowed his brow. "What's that?" he asked.

Dragh pretended he didn't feel it too, that strange creeping sensation tingling in his spine. The forest felt alive. As if it were watching them.

"Well, this has to be it, doesn't it?" Hemmelle grunted. "The Fifth, and General Theas."

Dragh looked around, The forest through the valley was a perfect place for an attack. They were able to ride two abreast for much of the journey, but like any natural rock formations, there were choke points that would lead to a trap for any strategist.

"I never thought of it, Hemmelle." Dragh shook his head. "Nestor will be next."

"How's that?" Hemmelle asked, confused.

"Well, he's the second general to lose a legion to the North. I just hope that he's alive, but..." Dragh left the rest unsaid.

"They will sully his name if we don't find him," Hemmelle finished it for him.

"I need to find him or, at least, his body. You know how some historians talk of General Theas. Gods, even the public spit on the ground at the mention of his name."

"Aye, I understand. He's family," Hemmelle replied.

"He's a father to me, Hemmelle. He was there when Kallen was not," Dragh sighed.

Dragh had been battling his feelings since they left the camp. He was afraid for his uncle. Afraid that he was dead. He didn't care that Nestor had chewed him out and busted him down in rank. He still loved his uncle.

"We will find him. If he was not at the camp, he must be to the south," Hemmelle told Dragh, trying to reassure him.

"And if we know that, the enemy knows that." Dragh exchanged a look with his friend.

"Let us be swift," Hemmelle said.

"Aye," Dragh said.

They were all tense as they rode.

They made a cold camp that night in the woods, off the travelled path in the forest. A small clearing with a rock outcropping to hide them from anyone who might be passing by.

"I want a man on guard all night. We will take shifts," he told them all. "I'll take the first," Dragh told them, taking a swig of water from a skin and passing it on.

Some of the men grumbled. There were the usual complaints of cold, and damp in the mist had settled on them that evening.

"I'll have none of that shit," Hemmelle barked.

Dragh and Hemmelle walked to the top of the small rise that led back to the path. They set themselves off the tracks from their horses, watching, waiting to see who might come.

Dragh offered Hemmelle smoked meat from his bag. He chewed on a piece himself, savoring the salt and juices.

"Easy on them Hemmelle, they are tired. We all are," Dragh said to Hemmelle. "What's got you upset?"

"It's the general, Dragh. We should have found him by now."

"Explain," Dragh asked his friend.

"If he's alive, if they have him, they would be travelling slow. He would not go willingly. We have to be travelling faster than them." Hemmelle looked back, making sure they were alone. "Dragh, have you considered that... that he might be gone."

Dragh looked at his friend. "Of course. I need to believe he's alive. I need him to be. They must have taken some prisoners."

"I understand, Dragh, but we may never find him." Hemmelle paused. Dragh waited for his friend to continue. "If we do not find the enemy in the next few days, we will know he's gone."

"Aye, we will," Dragh said, thinking about what he'd say to his father. He'd lost his uncle, he knew it. Nestor would never have abandoned his men. He would have stayed to the end. He might have sent one of his legates south, to warn Landor, but he'd never flee battle.

Dragh thought back to Landor, to his father, to Lucille. It was all he could hope for, to make it back alive.

———

The next day was the same as before, travelling slowly, but as fast as they could in the forest. They watched the lips of the valley they were in, hoping not to be ambushed. The Gallas felt eerie, its vegetation so dense that even the air didn't move inside of it, under the canopy of trees.

"I've got sign here, Dragh," Relish commented, kneeling in the mud at his horse's feet.

"How many?" Dragh asked.

"Hard to tell. It's a group, a big one. They have many horses and are traveling fast," Relish commented, licking a fleck of stone he picked out of the mud.

"Is it them?" Hemmelle asked, glancing at Relish.

"I can't make out who it is from a hoof print." Relish spit out whatever he'd licked. "But I'd hazard a guess it is them. Don't make no sense that it's our men."

"Could Venor and his squad have made it out alive?" Hemmelle asked the question they were all thinking.

"If they are, they abandoned the Second and ran like cowards," Dragh spit on the ground.

"Let's have our wits about us. If it's the enemy, they are close," Relish said, mounting his horse again.

They'd fed the horses the last of the grain they had taken from the camp. It was not much for war horses. Luckily, they had mountain steeds, hardy creatures who would eat moss and grass and anything green. They'd let them graze in the evenings, giving them plenty of water.

The men moved forward. Dragh kept back, falling in with Pello and Zeffo, who brought up the rear of the column they travelled in.

"Men, how are you?" Dragh asked them both.

Zeffo smiled wearily. "I can smell the bakery down on the Street of Roses."

Dragh watched the brothers, not sure if it was some jest about Lucille.

Pello laughed. "That shop mum used to take us to after church?" he asked his brother.

Dragh was surprised by Zeffo. His usual prickly demeanor worn away by the mess they'd been dealt over the last week.

"Aye, that one that made the sweetcakes. You know, the pink ones that she loved," Zeffo said.

"I remember you stealing them and mum walking you back to that shop to give them the money you'd saved," Pello chuckled.

"Aye, she never caught you, yah bastard," Zeffo accused Pello with a grin.

"Don't blame me now. You were shite at stealing then. Surprised you even made it into the Second." Pello grinned.

"I know it well," Dragh said of the bakery, thinking of the times he'd gone there with Lucille and the times he'd stopped by and picked up a treat for her. "Her favorite are the pink ones too, eh?" he asked the brothers about their mother.

Zeffo smiled. "Aye, she loves them. When I get back, I'm going to buy her two boxes of 'em."

"You'll what?" Pello asked, giving his brother a weird look.

"Well, you and I are going to eat the first one." He laughed aloud.

They joined him, a hearty laugh filled Dragh's dark heart.

"What about you? You must be getting something for your mum when you get out of this mess," Pello asked Dragh.

He looked at the two men, brothers. They'd never asked of his family.

"I don't know what she likes," Dragh said to the surprised brothers.

They both looked at Dragh with wide eyes and quirked eyebrows.

"What now?" Pello asked Dragh.

"I never saw her much. Nestor took care of me after my tutors left me. My mother and father were not around much at all," Dragh told them both honestly.

Pello shook his head. "Since I heard, I figured you'd been born with a gold spoon up your ass."

Zeffo watched his brother with concern written across his face.

"It's okay, Zeff." Dragh waved at Zeffo. "I was born with one in my hand, you shit heels. But Nestor was the one who looked after me. It's why I need to find him. He helped raise me," he explained.

"Understood, Dragh." Zeffo nodded to Dragh.

"What kind of pastries does the general like?" Pello asked.

They laughed again. This time, Verras, who was in front of them, let out a snort as well.

A whistle cut through the conversation from up front. Dragh's eyes shot up to the cliffs on either side of them, scanning for enemies. He'd pulled his sword out of his scabbard.

Two more sharp whistles came from the front. A signal from Relish that he'd found something, something he needed Dragh to see.

Dragh made eye contact with the men around him. They knew the signal, they knew to keep quiet. He nodded to them, kicking his horse into a trot towards the front of the short column.

He made it to Hemmelle and Geral, handing his reins to Geral as he dismounted. The land rose up and crested, cutting off his line of sight to the south.

Relish was on his belly on the rise of land in front of them. Hemmelle and Dragh both knelt on the ground, crawling forward to make it to Relish.

Dragh tapped on Relish's foot as he crawled beside him. Relish gave him the signal to come up to where he was.

Dragh kept his mouth shut, keeping discipline. He wanted to ask Relish what it was, what stopped them dead in their tracks.

Dragh's blood ran cold as he looked ahead of them. The valley in front of him opened up into a bowl of land. Cliffs on either side were ringed with horsemen. Many of them are archers. The bowl was full of men, dressed in the red and gold colours of the Landorians. Fires dotted the bowl, and there were horses in picket lines on either side of the war camp.

In the centre of the camp, seated at the head of the group of men, was his uncle Nestor. General of the Second Legion.

Chapter 16

Dragh pushed himself up, trying to scramble up and over the lip of the bowl. Relish grabbed onto Dragh, putting his leg over Dragh, his hand over Dragh's mouth. They struggled there, Dragh trying to escape, Relish holding onto him. They grunted and rolled.

Dragh gave up. The small man trapped him with his body as he tried to get to his uncle.

"Enough!" Hemmelle hissed to them both.

Dragh let his body relax against Relish, who let his legs and arms relax, letting Dragh roll out from beside him. They looked at each other before Dragh squeezed Relish's arm.

He knew Relish was trying to save his life. Running down into an enemy camp was suicide. He froze.

Guards. Where were the guards? On the path? The enemy had to set a rearguard on the path after the fight they just had with the Second.

Dragh questioned his own thoughts, someone had already killed the only army in the North, would they set a rearguard?

Relish let Dragh go, nodding to them both to retreat backward.

After they'd made it a few lengths back, They stopped, still on their bellies.

"Where are the guards?" Hemmelle whispered, thinking the same as Dragh.

Relish shook his head. "There are none here. Some are on the east and west of the bowl, some on the south."

"They can't be that arrogant," Hemmelle said.

"They are not worried about the tribesmen, and they think the Second is gone," Relish said.

Dragh didn't answer, he was thinking. "We need to get Nestor. I need to sneak down there and save him."

Relish and Hemmelle both looked at Dragh mournfully.

"What?" Dragh asked. Relish blew a breath out of his nose. "Dragh. Look at who he's sitting with." He glanced at Hemmelle who nodded. "He doesn't need rescuing."

"What the fuck is that supposed to mean Relish?" Dragh said with venom.

"Just look, Dragh. I'm sorry," Hemmelle whispered.

Dragh bit back an ugly retort, ready to yell at Hemmelle. He rubbed at his face and turned back towards the lip. He crawled up to it, keeping low as to not be seen. He looked back at Relish and Hemmelle, who were a couple of body lengths down from him now. Their faces were almost ashen.

Dragh peered over the rim to locate his uncle.

The light was fading; torches and fires helped illuminate the war camp now. There were logs rolled out around fires, men sitting about, eating and drinking, laughing at each other's jokes. Dragh could almost hear them from where he was.

His uncle was in the centre of the camp. He could see now that he wasn't tied up, he wasn't retrained.

Nestor was sitting in the middle of the camp surrounded by the enemy. He was eating roast meat and drinking ale from a horn. Dragh could smell the cookfire from where he lay on his front.

Beside him was Vanor, smiling and laughing with Nestor. Around them were men of Vanor's squad, men of the Second's Cavalry.

Dragh felt ice in his veins again. This time it was creeping dread. He crawled back down the lip and back to his horse, where he took a long drink from his water skin. He felt the blood flow out of his face. He felt the cold of the emotions running through him. Geral nodded to Dragh, his face grim.

"It's him," Dragh commented to Hemmelle and Relish who joined him and Geral.

Hemmelle looked over Dragh, then to Geral and Relish. "It's time to go."

Dragh felt his mouth gum up, he couldn't speak. He nodded to Hemmelle.

His heart was broken.

Nestor. A traitor. Eating and drinking, carrying on as if the Second wasn't dead and burning in the North.

He felt tears on his face.

Hemmelle gave the command to leave, and they moved as fast as they could, back north up the path through the forest. Once they'd moved far enough north, they cut into the woods to the east.

The darkness enveloped them, hugging at them until the moon began to illuminate the forest.

Dragh followed them, his mind empty. He felt numb and cold.

———

They sat in the moonlight, looking off into the dark woods. The blades of moonlight dotted the cold camp they sat in. Beams of soft light filtered down between the canopy of leaves above.

The forest was alive with life, animals on the prowl, owls hooting and hunting through the vegetation. The buzz of insects and the chirping of crickets were dense.

Dragh was immune to it all. Numb.

"I'm sorry," Hemmelle whispered to Dragh some time back when they'd set camp.

Dragh hadn't taken part in any of it. His mind was closed to the world. His uncle, with the enemy. With Vanor and the men that had eradicated the Second.

He could not admit it to himself. It couldn't be his uncle. Nestor was a Sunborn. A brother to the king.

"What do we do now?" Dragh asked Hemmelle.

Hemmelle took his time answering Dragh. The sound of the forest stretched between them. "We go to Landor. We get to your father to tell him what's happened."

Dragh wasn't surprised by this; he wasn't surprised by anything, now. "Why?" he asked. "What's the fuckin' point of any of it?"

Hemmelle slapped Dragh across the face. The fire lit up his cheek, and he felt the anger burn up from his belly to his head.

"What the FUCK, Hemmelle!" Dragh half stood up, his hand on his dagger at his side.

Hemmelle stood up. "Get your head out of your arse, Dragh. You're angry? GOOD!" He pushed Dragh.

Dragh pulled at his dagger. Metal started to slide from its sheath.

"You pull that dagger on me and I walk," Hemmelle said, his voice even.

Dragh blinked at that statement. His friend, his closest friend, was threatening to walk away, to leave him. His anger started to bleed away. "Why'd you hit me?" he asked through bared teeth.

"Because I need you to cut out the self-pity." Hemmelle shook his head. "I need Dragh Sunborn. I need you to get your head sorted."

Dragh considered the words, angry at this friend. "You don't understand. Nestor was... He was everything to me."

"And now that's gone. You don't want to admit that Nestor betrayed you. Betrayed the Second and your father."

"There has to be an explanation," Dragh said, desperately grasping for an answer.

"Dragh, it was him. You saw him there, plain as day, with Vanor." Hemmelle let it sink it.

Dragh remained silent, his mind sure that if he were quiet, it might go away. He could accept that Vanor was a traitor, but in the darkness, he struggled to believe that Nestor was too.

"Look at me." Hemmelle shook his shoulders.

Dragh looked at his friend, meeting his eyes. His mouth was dry.

"We live with the fate we've been served." Hemmelle laughed. "You think we wanted to be in the Second? None of us wanted to be caught, all of us did something to make it in. I am glad I did it, though. That kid deserved none of what he got from the guard. Those fuckers deserved it."

Dragh considered his friend. Hemmelle had killed a city guard. The guard and his partner killed a child, a small boy who'd been caught for a crime he didn't remember. The way he'd heard the story, Hemmelle had tried to stop it, but one of the guards caved the kid's head in on a wall before Hemmelle could put them down. He flew into a rage and killed one of them, crippling the other so badly that they couldn't work again.

"I'm glad I met you, Relish, and the rest. Without you, I'd be in prison still. Or dead."

Dragh let the tears come as he thought of his life, of the mistakes he'd made to get into the Second, the people he'd hurt. What he'd squandered. Ellis, that stain was always there to shove it in his face. Nestor was there to listen, always.

Now, Nestor had betrayed his country, his Legion, his own brother, and Dragh.

Dragh was angry now, angry that he'd been betrayed by the one man that had always been there for him.

"I need to make it back to Lucille. To the baby," Dragh said what was gnawing at him. "I'm scared I will die in the North. We need to make it home to Landor. I'm tired. I want to smell the roses, be with her."

Hemmelle's face was painted with relief as Dragh let the truth out. "What will your father do?"

"He'll hear of this soon. His network of spies in the North will bring news of the Legion's demise." Dragh began to think of the implications.

"And then what?" Hemmelle asked.

"He'll invade with his entire army. He will wipe out the North. The Fifth was a stain on Landor. He will not let it go. This Legion will be avenged," Dragh explained to Hemmelle.

"We need to kill him for what he's done," Dragh said, his mind finally accepting what he saw.

"We need to make it back first."

"The fate of Landor hangs on it, Hemmelle. The tribes have been warring in the North for a thousand years. Since the time of the empire. The North is the graveyard of empires. None have conquered them. The Tribes will hold a grudge for a millennium if they think we are their enemy."

Hemmelle stood up. "We move now. We need to make it through Gallas Forest. Going off the path will take us another week. But then we can move fast to the coast, and find ourselves a boat to take us down to Landor."

"We need to go to Yarrs first," Dragh commented, following Hemmelle back to the others. He was moving again, his numbness now a sting in the back of his mind.

"We don't have time, Dragh," Hemmelle pleaded. "We can't save him, he's on his own."

"We need him to take a message to Saravas, their chieftain. We need him to explain that these men of red and gold are not ours. We invaded, and the tribes did too. The Landorians are being dragged into this. This Saravas will not hold back, and the rest of the tribes will demand justice for whatever the pit these men are doing," Dragh said.

"Gods, they are starting a war," Hemmelle said, his eyes widening.

"Who do you think killed our men and women on the border of the Car Lauch?" Dragh asked.

"Fuck." Hemmelle grabbed at his saddle bag that he'd put beside Relish.

Relish gave them a questioning look.

"Men, get up. We need to move now!" Dragh said to them.

They all looked up to Dragh. Their eyes told him they'd been waiting for a command, for a plan. No matter what he dealt with, they relied on him. He couldn't forget that again. To the pit with Nestor. These men were his family now.

"We go to Yarrs, then on to the coast, and Landor," Dragh briefed them.

"We move through The Gallas, off the path," Hemmelle explained.

Dragh expected some pushback. The dense forest was a thing of nightmares. The stories you heard when you were young all told the same tale of missing men and death. No one survived off the path.

Pello chuckled. "First, the general betrays us, now we go to our deaths. What's not to like?" He laughed aloud again.

"Let's ride." Zeffo gave Dragh a nasty smile.

Chapter 17

Dragh could see wafting smoke before he made it to a vantage point where he could see Yarrs's village. He could smell wood smoke for leagues, but had held out hope that it was the smell of any other village's fire pits and cook pits.

He was wrong. He could see a wafting column of smoke, the same as the Second's camp north of The Gallas Forest. This one was fainter, not as thick.

"It's gray, a tight column of fire created this day gone by, no more," Relish commented.

"How can you tell?" Dragh asked his lead scout, not doubting the man's prowess. He'd proven himself for as long as he'd known him.

The mountains had taught them much, but Relish came with all the knowledge he'd needed. Dragh often wondered at it, but Relish never talked of his past.

"The smoke is a different colour. The camp north of The Gallas was a dark black. Billowing. This one is a slow smoke, gray. Most of the fuel has been burned up," Relish commented.

"Let's be careful. They may have left people behind."

Dragh had a sinking feeling in his stomach that he was too slow. It had taken him too long to get through The Gallas Forest; the path had been their only hope.

It was too dangerous, but going through the thick of it had added a week to their journey.

They trotted wide, spread out to ensure they could see as far as possible. The enemy was out there, he knew that.

Where were they? That was the question he asked himself as he scanned the hills and valleys in front of them.

They approached the village with caution, the skeleton of what had been homes stood among the ashes. Dragh could see the burnt husks as they drew closer.

The smell of acrid, burnt flesh hung in the air.

As Dragh saw the skeleton of the village, he held in a groan.

The village was gone.

The squad members rode in silence, slowing their horses down as they made their way to the outskirts of the village. Dragh was repulsed by the destruction.

"The fuck. Did they do this?" Relish cursed.

Hemmelle coughed from the smoke. "They wanted to leave no witnesses."

Dragh nodded along. "They wanted to make sure no one would go to Saravas. The King of the North."

"Let's go." Dragh spurred his mount, turning to go around the village. The rest followed, pushing themselves around.

As they made the crest of the hill, some of them began to retch.

Dragh let a tear roll down his cheek, closing his eyes against the atrocity.

Yarrs and five of the villagers were splayed on logs. Their hands were nailed to the large logs, and their lungs were cut from their bodies, nailed to the logs through their shoulders.

"What in the Gods?" Zeffo muttered, spitting bile to the ground.

"They take pleasure in it," Hemmelle commented.

Dragh felt the coldness still. He hadn't felt anything since learning of his uncle's betrayal. He wanted revenge, oh yes, but looking at the dead villagers, he felt empty.

"What evil was visited upon these people? Yarrs and his men did nothing to deserve this," Relish said.

"There is a story, an old story from the time of the empire. I was told about it by one of my tutors when I studied the histories. There are men that come from the east," Dragh began.

"There is nothing to the east but the ocean," Zeffo commented, more of a question to Dragh than a challenge.

"I said the same. These men, they've come before. They are warring people, men and women both. They are said to do this to their worst enemies. They do it while they still live. It tests the bravery of a man," Dragh explained, remembering his tutors from days gone by.

"Why? Landorians would never commit such a crime against another man," Verras asked, his face red with anger.

"We are all brutes, cutting and hacking each other to death," Hemmelle said dispassionately.

"They are trying to inflame the North. Saravas will hear of this, will see this. He will seek revenge for one of his councilors being killed in such a way," Dragh explained to them all.

"Cut them off. We commit them to the earth," Hemmelle commanded the rest.

Dragh stood guard, watching the horizon for the enemy.

"I damned him," Dragh said to Hemmelle beside him.

"No, what do you speak of?" Hemmelle hissed.

"If I hadn't taken Yarrs to the general, to the camp, he would still be alive today. The general had them kill Yarrs and burn this village. They knew us, knew of us. He is erasing any trace of us."

"He must think we are dead," Hemmelle stated.

"He may, there is no way to know. Nestor is killing his way south. He is going to tell Kallen that it was the Northern Tribes, and he is inflaming Saravas into attacking Landor. There is no way that he would allow this slight to go unanswered," Dragh sighed.

Dragh knew what war with the North would do to his country, his people.

"The tribes will demand blood for what the Second has done. And for what these mercenaries do."

"And they will think it is us," Hemmelle agreed.

Relish spoke the words over the burning of Yarrs and the others.

"We give you to earth and sky,

We pray you are with the gods,

From the earth we come,

To the earth and sky, you go."

In another life, Relish might have been a priest. One of the good ones, Dragh thought. Not like the Council, full of spies and deceivers. Relish would be one of the men committed to bringing the Gods to the people.

"We have a decision to make, men," Dragh told them all, gathered in the smoke of the funeral pyre.

Relish, Verras, Geral, Pello, Zeffo, and Hemmelle all looked to Dragh, gathered in a semicircle.

Dragh felt the weight then, the weight of leadership. These men waited for his plan. He wasn't certain what they should do, but he knew what had to happen.

"We must send an envoy to King Saravas. The tribal leader of the North. I had hoped that Yarrs would go to him, tell him that we'd been tricked into the North. That this death and destruction was not us."

"Do we tell him of the men from the east?" Geral asked Dragh.

His men were on edge. All of them stretched thin over the last days and weeks. He could see it in their weary, bloodshot eyes. He needed more from them, more than he had a right to ask for.

"We must explain that it was not us. And hope that he will see the truth of it." Dragh wondered at it. How could it be? Were they being invaded themselves? Did the Council know?

"I will go," Relish spoke up.

"No, you need to lead them to the ocean. These fools would never find their way there," Hemmelle sighed. "I will go, my friends."

Dragh let out a breath. "I was afraid of that."

His friend was too good to give up to the North, to risk his life. But he had no choice.

"What is it, Dragh?" Pello asked.

"Hemmelle goes to his death. We know how they treat someone from an invading force," Geral explained.

"They wouldn't kill a messenger!" Pello exclaimed.

"I will go with him," Verras said. The youth's voice cracked with stress as he stepped forward.

All of them stepped forward, wanting to take the load, share the burden with Hemmelle. Dragh kept back, watching his friend. He was the glue that had kept them together. He was the voice of reason and the kind words when you needed it most.

What kind of monster was Dragh to ask so much?

Hemmelle favoured Verras with a smile. "No, my friend. You need to get to Landor. That mother of yours will never forgive me if I got you killed."

"May the Gods protect you, my friend," Dragh said to Hemmelle, his heart heavy. He knew that he was sending his friend into the unknown. Alone. There was no other way. He needed to sneak into the North, find his way to Saravas. Find a way to convince the Council of the Tribes that it was not Landor that struck at them, but some ghost, perhaps from across the water to the east.

That ghost struck at them both, fanning the flames of war between the two people.

"I will see you all again. Relish, get them back safe." Hemmelle hugged each of them, trading words with each of them quietly.

Hemmelle gave Dragh a bear hug, wrapping his arms around him. Dragh felt hot tears on his cheeks.

"Survive," Dragh said to his friend, choking on the words.

"Don't fuck this up. I will see you back in Landor." Hemmelle gripped Dragh's shoulder.

They all stood solemnly, a funeral for a living man, as they watched Hemmelle walk away into the North with his horse.

——

"We need to beat Nestor to Landor," Dragh told them all after Hemmelle had left, trotting his horse north, back the way they came.

"We need to survive first," Relish said.

Zeffo spoke up. His face was tired from days in the saddle, little food, and the exhaustion of being hunted. "If Nestor makes it back to Landor first, he will control the history. His side will be what is told, it will take root."

"And I intend to kill the bastard before he spreads more lies about how our brothers died in the North. This whole thing was his game. The world needs to know of this. We move to the ocean. We need to make the coast and find a boat," Dragh told them.

"We need food, Dragh," Verras spoke up.

"We have what we can kill, my friend." Dragh gave a weak smile to Verras.

They all felt the hunger pangs. It had been days since they'd had a hot camp, been able to kill anything to roast over the fire. He knew the hunger that built up in the young man's belly.

The rest of them grumbled, gathering themselves and making ready to leave.

Dragh shook his head. He missed Hemmelle already. He'd have none of this shit. He'd have cut the men's grumbles off at the knees. But Dragh had to walk the line. He needed these men to make it to Landor as they needed him.

His mind wandered back to Landor.

What would he say to his father? How did you tell a man that his only brother had betrayed him? How did you tell a king that his general was attempting to overthrow him?

They traveled with more caution as they moved east, unsure where they were really going. Relish could get them to the sea. The Gods would lead them to a village and to ships if they were feeling kind.

There were times that Dragh had to rub his eyes as he looked back across the rolling hills. Times that he could have sworn he'd seen the movement of men, or horses. Each time, as quickly as he saw it, the movement was gone.

"Thank you, Relish," Dragh said as they moved through the hills to the east.

"For what?" Relish asked Dragh.

"For keeping us going. Without you, I could never have led the men this far," Dragh explained. He knew that Relish was what kept them going, like Hemmelle. He could motivate men in ways that Dragh couldn't.

"You kept us alive. I will lead us to water," Relish said with a smirk.

"Aye, I just wish we could drink it," Dragh said, patting at his water skin.

"We will get back to the drink soon enough, my friend. When we get home, I'll drink myself a tavern of ale."

"Ahh, the Duck's Beak?" Dragh asked, eyeing Relish.

"I'm going to pass out on the bar this time, before Anne can close the doors on me," Relish said with some pride.

"If I had to guess, you might be sweet on her." Dragh poked fun at Relish.

"You know what the Ralarians say, don't you?" Relish said with a grin.

"Huh?"

"Hide your masts when she's dark and windy out," Relish said.

"You wouldn't," Dragh said in mock outrage.

Relish laughed out loud.

"Gods alive." Dragh smiled. "We just might make it, Relish. I thought we were goners in The Gallas. If we can set out to sea, we can make it back to Landor."

"TO THE SOUTH!" a call came from behind them, from Zeffo.

Dragh swerved his horse, pulling on the reins to swing his mount around to face the south. Dread filled him as he saw a squad of horsemen mounted on the horizon.

They were wearing the red and gold of Landor.

"Fuck," he shouted. His anger got the best of him as he considered his options.

"What do we do, Dragh?" Zeffo asked, pulling up beside him.

The horsemen were leagues away, but there were at least fifty of them.

Dragh could see a full squad of strength, at least. After the death of the Second and after Vanor's betrayal, there could be no doubt as to who they were. Men from the east who wished no good will for Dragh or his men.

"You all need to flee. Ride hard for the coast."

Dragh pulled a ring from his hand and shoved it into Relish's.

"I need you to give this to Lucille. Tell her." He paused, considering that this would be the last thing she'd hear of him, from him. "Tell her that I love her, tell her to go to the king and tell him that she bears my heir. She will be taken care of." He gritted his teeth.

He'd never see her, never see his child born.

"No, we can't. Let us fight!" Relish argued.

The others joined him. Geral and Pello pulled their own weapons out.

"Go now. Carry the message to the king of what happened here, men." Dragh paused. "That's an order."

They looked at him with worry on their faces.

And then acceptance.

"GO!" he shouted to them, rage settling in his body and mind.

Dragh kicked his mount's sides, gripping the horse with his thighs. His body ached, his feet, legs and back, from days in the saddle.

He could feel the aches and pains of battle still, cuts on his body, bruises and tweaks from his run-in with a horse and rider that had thrown him through the air. He could feel the bruising up his side and over his back.

Dragh could feel the wind in his hair, the pounding of his heart. The horse's hooves gripped the earth, chewing up the leagues between him and the enemy. He could feel the horse strain, and he let it have its head. Gave it the freedom that it craved from the hands of man. The horse, as wild as she was always, wanted to be back on the plains, in her herd in the mountains.

Dragh let the beast have its way as he sped to his death.

He thought of his life and what he'd have done differently. He was happy that he'd met Lucille. It was the one good thing he'd done in his life. She was good. More than he'd deserved.

He wished he'd mended the vast space between him and his father. His mother.

He could hear the enemy and see them moving in response to his charge.

The charge of one man against many. He laughed aloud like a mad man. Dragh pulled his sword, sitting high in the saddle, feeling the gait of his horse through his feet.

They grew in size, closer and closer.

"ARHHHOOOO!" he shouted as he whirled his sword, pointing it towards the men charging at him.

He was one man against a landslide.

Like a spear thrust, Dragh hit them. He felt the sudden stop and lurched forward over the saddle, his sword held forward, stabbing into the man in front of him. The sword was up to its hilt in the man's chest as Dragh threw himself back.

Dragh lost the sword, but rocked back into his saddle, narrowly escaping the swing of a blade over his head.

Dragh screamed at another man, who charged in with a spear, the butt end flying at Dragh's head. He felt the scrape as he plunged a dagger into the man's leg.

He was rewarded with a shout of pain.

The world tilted as a horse smashed into Dragh's from the side.

Dragh was blindsided, as he'd been flanked. The world turned, and he lost contact with his horse and fell to the mud. He tried to get up, but he slipped and slid in the mud. He could taste the salty tang of blood on his tongue.

Dragh thought of his men, hoping he'd given them enough time to escape. At least he could give them that before his own death.

A horse's hoof put him to the ground, knocking him out cold.

—-–

Dragh came to as he was hoisted out of the mud. He screamed. One of his shoulders had been torn from its socket when he flew from his mount.

"Keep him alive," a thickly accented voice came from beyond Dragh's vision.

Dragh felt the weakness in his legs, the building momentum of sick. He keeled over and vomited onto the ground, splashing the boots in front of him with his sick.

The man exclaimed, his voice rough and thick.

Dragh saw the man move his boots back, and then Dragh felt a quick jab across his face. It didn't knock him out. He landed back in the mud, flipping on his back, with blood streaming from his nose.

He lay there, weeping silently. His face a mess of blood and snot.

"Up!" another boot buried itself in Dragh's side.

"Ooohfff," Dragh gasped at the rush of air out of his body. He gulped at the air.

"Ironside wants him," a large, dark-bearded man said ,as Dragh opened his eyes to see the next attack that was coming.

"I'm going to gut this bastard, he killed Gorin!" a large, bearded blonde man said to the dark-bearded one.

Dragh closed his eyes and focused on not puking. His guts were turning, and his head was splitting. He'd never felt so shitty. Even his time training on Car Lauch had been better than this.

"Ironside wants him whole. He will decide what we do with him," the large man said again.

"Aye, Kaje," the blonde's voice wafted over Dragh.

Dragh half listened, his mind swimming. His eyes were now unfocused when he opened them. His stomach lurched again. He tried to move to his side, but his body wouldn't obey. He threw up in his mouth.

"Get him on his side," Kaje barked out.

Dragh felt himself being pushed over onto his side. He spit out the vomit and coughed hard at the chunks in his airway. He could feel the cold mud on his face as he was pushed onto his side. It almost soothed him.

"Won't get him far like this, tie him up on back." The rough hands dragged him across the ground.

Dragh didn't have the strength to fight back against the rough hands. He felt himself being pushed up and onto a horse. The smell of the beast's flank was sweet and sticky. The sweat heavy in its coat.

Dragh was in and out of consciousness as he bounced on the back of the horse he'd been tied to. His body bounced up and down the whole time he was being transported. Blackness threatened his very vision, drowning him.

He cried, then, weak and broken. He cried for himself, for what he'd lost. There was no surviving this. They had him.

—--

Dragh awoke again, his mind still swimming. He was tossed from the horse he'd been stowed on, the rope attaching him cut. He cried out at the pain of hitting the ground.

They beat him after he'd fallen to the ground. Kicking and stomping on him.

He curled into a ball, trying to keep them from hitting his already beat up face.

They laughed when they kicked him.

He couldn't stand the cruelty of it.

He tried not to beg for death. He knew it would not come. He'd heard the head man tell the horsemen that he was wanted alive. He couldn't hide the tears. The gasps for air as the breath was knocked out of him.

It was dark all around. Some torches were lit, giving the men beating him the visages of demons in the night. He had no idea how long he'd been strapped to the horse, or how long it had taken to get wherever he was now.

All of the Second knew torture. Learning it at the hands of the Legates. On the mountains of the Car Lauch they had beat men until they broke them. Teaching them what pain was.

There, it was all a game. He knew that they would stop. They would never let him die.

Here, it was different. These men enjoyed the punishment.

Dragh's pain turned to rage. Vowing to take revenge on these men. Vowing that if he got the chance, he would visit evil on these men. He prayed to the Gods.

He blacked out from the pain.

——

"Dragh!" a set of hands shook him awake.

Dragh winced back, whipping his head back so that the pain lanced up his neck and into his head.

"Easy, easy now," the voice came again.

Dragh focused his eyes on the voice, his vision still a little blurry. "Relish?" he asked.

"Aye, it's me, Dragh," Relish responded.

Dragh could make his face out in the low light. Looking around, he was confused. They were in some sort of makeshift enclosure. Posts surrounded them with some cross braces between posts. The top posts had ropes dangling down from them.

Dragh felt around his neck. The rope burned into his skin. His hands were bound at the wrist.

Dragh looked to Relish, his mind still dark. "I'm to be a father," Dragh told them, tears rolling down his face.

Dragh felt lost then, no longer a leader, no longer a man with hope in his heart. He was beaten, finished.

Relish took the news without comment. They were trapped in the dark pit.

"I will never meet him, my son," Dragh stated, his heart heavy.

"Dragh," Relish put his hand on Dragh's shoulder.

"What happened?" Dragh asked, desperation in his voice.

Relish paused.

"What is it? What happened, Relish?" Dragh asked with more urgency.

"I'm sorry, Dragh. The kid didn't make it," Relish said.

Dragh shook his head. "Anyone else?"

"No, they rode him down after he fell from his horse. We tried to get back to him, but they surrounded us on all sides." Relish gripped Dragh's shoulder. "I'm sorry, Dragh. I let you down."

"No, my friend, I let you down. I'm sorry we are here," Dragh said, wincing from the pain of Relish's grip.

"What did they do to you?" Relish asked, taking his hand off Dragh's arm.

"They saw how far they could kick my head," Dragh scoffed.

"They told us that we were wanted alive, that if we threw down our weapons, we would live," Relish explained.

"You made the right decision," Dragh said to him.

Dragh's mind rebelled. He wanted revenge, then he was lost. He was exhausted of it all. Tired and angry.

"I wish we would have fought. We should have given them the cold iron for what they did to Verras."

"You made the right decision. Are the rest of the men here?" Dragh peered into the darkness.

"Aye, Primus." Pello said, a body length away in the dark.

Voices echoed in the dark, taking shape in Dragh's vision as the storm his head began to calm.

"Shut up, you scum!" a familiar voice came through the dark.

Dragh turned his head. The rope around his neck allowed some mobility. The guardsman who tied him up and brought him here was walking towards them with a torch, his face lit by the flame.

Relish and Dragh waited for the guard to pass. His torchlight waned as he made his way back to camp. Dragh thought he must be on patrol.

"There must be another guard out there, and some of the guards move with torches," Dragh said to Relish. They spoke in a quiet whisper, not wanting to alert the guard again.

"What are we going to do?" Relish asked, a new excitement in his voice.

Dragh felt the anticipation then. His men were here. He was not alone. Relish's eyes were bright with excitement

Dragh took a deep breath.

"We are going to kill all of these fuckers tonight," Dragh said to Relish. "Are you ready, men of Landor?" Dragh asked the darkness.

Generals and kings had asked of the armies of Landor that same question for as long as they had histories. *Are you ready, men of Landor?*

"We are ready to die for Landor," the answer came from the dark.

Relish grinned, his white teeth glowing in the moonlight.

Darkness bloomed in Dragh's heart. He was going to kill them all. All of them would die tonight. Escape was not enough; he would have their lifeblood.

Chapter 18

Dragh watched the guards through the long hours of the night.

"Another," Relish whispered.

The night camp was lively, not far from where they were kept. An animal roasted over a fire, and men sat around their fires and drank out of skins.

The enemy had set up great tents, large enough for many men to sleep in.

The third guard walked past them in the time it took the moon to move a quarter through the sky.

"Sloppy," Dragh commented to Relish.

His mind was sharp again. The pain was nothing to him, now that he had another mission. He didn't want to escape, he wanted to kill. Hate fueled him. He was no longer tied and no longer hungry or thirsty.

"Have you seen them switch out again?" Dragh whispered down the line of men.

The answer came in a chain: Geral to Pello, Pello to Zeffo, and Zeffo to Relish.

"No switch yet," Relish reported. "When?"

"Wait," Dragh commanded. "If he follows the schedule, he will be switched out shortly, then we wait for him to settle in. With any luck, he will be asleep. They are lazy in their rotation. They should have set out four, but three were set."

Dragh paused. He was about to say that Nestor would have skinned them for such a failure, too much left to chance, too many opportunities for men to slip in between such a staggered guard.

Nestor was dead to him. No longer family.

Twigs could be heard snapping, and the rustling of grass and bushes were all that warned them that the guard was changed. The moon was weak, the night engulfing them almost completely. The guards in the dark had changed out, and one man was relieved.

Dragh could see a man join the fire at the heart of the camp from his vantage point. Tents were set between them and the fire; only a corner of the fire was visible to him from where he was tied.

"Ready, men of Landor. Be brave," Dragh said to his men as much as himself.

A guard rounded the corner with a torch, walking slowly in the night.

"Help!" Relish grunted, slumping down on the ground.

The guard looked over curiously, holding up his torch to shed more light on the figure of Relish.

"What's wrong with him?" the guard asked in a thick accent.

Dragh smiled inwardly. "I think he's tired from sleeping with your mother."

The guard gave Dragh a menacing smile and stalked over to him. He leaned down and punched him in the face. "Funny," he commented.

Dragh spit blood out onto himself. The blow rocked him. "Sorry, must have been your sister."

The guard scoffed. "You really are looking for a beating again, aren't you?" He pulled back his leg, taking aim at Dragh.

"It's your turn," Dragh said to the man, grinning through the blood in his mouth.

Relish kicked out at the man's leg, the one that was left on the ground.

The man warbled, trying to regain his footing with his other leg. He crashed to the ground with a shout of alarm.

Dragh cut off the man's shout by bringing his bound hands down on his neck, striking his windpipe.

The man gasped, his airway cut off.

Dragh looped his legs around the man and pulled him close.

The guard kicked and lashed out as he struggled to breathe. Dragh ignored the blows, wrapping his bound hands around the man's neck.

He was rewarded with weakening blows as the guard brought his elbows back against Dragh. He almost let go twice, but eventually, the guard went limp. Relish landed punches on the guard's sides as Dragh strangled him.

Dragh pulled and twisted, breaking the guard's neck.

Relish spit on the guard after Dragh pushed the body away from him. Dragh dug through the guard's belongings. He tossed the knife from the man's belt to Relish and looked into the night, watching for any movement from the camp.

"Clear," Relish said as he cut free the others.

Dragh put his hands up to let Relish cut him free.

Geral, Zeffo, Pello, and Relish crouched around Dragh.

"We move quickly. Kill the guards on the perimeter first. Pello, Zeffo, you two take the dark. Geral, take the guards on patrol."

Dragh gave them their orders. He handed the sword he took from the body of the guard to Zeffo and handed another blade in the guard's boot to Geral.

He doused the flame from the torch with mud.

"We kill the ones sleeping?" Relish asked with a grimace.

"Is there a problem, Relish?" Dragh asked.

Relish paused before answering Dragh.

Emotions played across his face before he steeled himself. "For Verras, for the Second," he said, his voice low and slow.

Dragh nodded to Relish and the rest.

He moved to the back of the first tent, dragging the body of the guard he and Relish killed. He hoped that dragging it into the shadows might give him the time they needed.

"There are too many, Dragh," Relish whispered after the rest had departed.

"We kill them," Dragh said to Relish. He said it with conviction, not wanting debate.

Relish stood silently beside him, no longer protesting.

Dragh cut the bottom of the tent in a straight line up, stopping the cut at half his height. He moved slowly, trying not to alert the men sleeping inside. He looked back to Relish, handing him the blade, then moved inside slowly, crouched down low.

The men were visible in the tent. Some were in military cots, some on the ground. Dragh could see a partially opened tent flap in the front, leading out to the fire. The noise of the camp made it to him in the tent. The tent walls did little to stop the noise.

Dragh counted the men— six. He and Relish would have to kill three each. Quietly, to stop the others from waking up.

He eyed metal among the furs of the man sleeping closest to him. The glint was a small axe, half the size of Hemmelle's war axe.

He hefted the blade quietly, looking around in the low light for Relish. Relish went to the other side of the tent, leaning over a sleeping man in a cot. They locked eyes and Dragh nodded to him. Relish plunged the small knife into the man's neck, putting his hand over his mouth. Dragh followed Relish's example, clamping his hand down on his target's mouth. The man's eyes opened up in surprise. His mouth worked, but Dragh muffled the sound with one hand and plunged the axe through his neck with the other.

They both moved to the next closest man to them, working to the inside of the tent towards each other. Dragh paused as he heard hooting from outside. It calmed, and Dragh went back to the work of killing his second man.

Dragh turned to continue the job, towards his third man. His foot caught on furs that covered the floor and his other slipped on fresh blood from his kill.

He felt weightlessness, and he fell. Fear gripped him, he held the axe head in front of him as he fell onto a sleeping man.

"ARHHHHHH!" the man screamed as Dragh embedded the axe in his chest. He died as his lifeblood pumped out. Dragh had struck his heart.

Relish quickly killed his third man, the last in the tent, as the alarm sounded outside. Relish helped Dragh up.

Another bearded mercenary dipped his head into the tent to see what the shouting was about.

Dragh threw his axe at the man as Dragh ducked through the back of the tent with Relish.

A scream told him his aim was true.

Dragh cursed himself. They were caught, and at least forty or more men wanted to kill them. He was slow, beaten by his captors. His men were spread in the dark. It was his fault. They should have slipped out when they had the chance in the night. Instead, they were trapped in the camp.

"We need horses," Relish completed Dragh's thought.

Dragh and Relish ran towards the sound of horses. They were met by two more bearded men running in the darkness towards them. Shouts around the camp stirred men from their sleep and drunken stupors alike, like a hive had dropped to the ground from the high branches.

"Stop!" one of them called to Relish and Dragh, both wielding torches and swords.

Relish and Dragh separated, circling the two men, splitting their concentration by moving towards their flanks. The Easterners moved with them, pivoting, not crossing their feet. They held their swords in the high guard, ready to strike down.

Dragh held up his hands with open palms as if to give up.

"NOW!" Relish shouted.

Dragh shot for the guard's feet, moving fast, hoping to get inside the swing of the blade before it came down from the high guard.

The pommel hit Dragh's head as he wrapped his hand around the man's waist, tackling him to the ground.

The man dropped the torch, struggling with Dragh for control of the sword between them. Dragh pushed down with all his weight, moving to get better leverage as they shouted at each other in a contest of strength. Dragh half-rose and then drove down his forearm on the sword, its tip under the easterner's stomach. It moved just enough to pierce the man's guts. Dragh reared up and slammed his forearm down again, the sword going through the man's gut and into the earth.

The man wheezed as he died. His guts spilled into the earth.

Dragh moved to help Relish with his fight, still struggling with the other man. Dragh kicked the man in the head as Relish drew a knife across his throat.

The man stopped fighting Relish and grasped at his neck with both hands. The black blood welled up between his fingers as he gurgled.

Relish got up with the help of Dragh, almost falling over.

"What's wrong?" Dragh asked, steadying his friend.

Relish moaned and grabbed at his stomach. A blade was buried in it.

"Gods, it hurts," Relish said to Dragh.

Dragh's heart sank. A gut wound. A death warrant in the field. He gulped.

"Hurry, let's get to the horses."

Relish's face was pale, even in the night. Dragh put himself under Relish's arm and hoisted him up. "Come on, old friend. We've faced worse," he said, smelling the putrid wound.

No one survived a wound of that smell, he knew. They both did.

Relish chuckled darkly. "We got a few of them bastards, eh, Dragh?" he said, stumbling.

"We did, Relish," he said, focused on the horses rearing on the picket line they were on.

The horses bolted as they got closer. A fire was lit among the tents, spreading from one tent to another. The chaos grew as the flames consumed more and more. The easterners were letting their own horses go before the horses bolted from the fires, or worse, died from them.

Dragh was proud of his men. The darkness multiplied the fear that was sown by a few good men.

The enemy was among them, and the enemy was many. The dark corners you could not see into. Dragh was the evil that hunted them. It felt good to turn the tables on these bastards.

"Dragh!" Two men galloped over to him and Relish, leading two riderless horses.

"Let's go! Geral is with us!" Zeffo panted, blood on his face.

Dragh saw the third man riding hard towards them. He pushed Relish onto Zeffo's saddle without explanation. The two of them exchanged a look.

"I can ride," Relish said, weakly.

"Let's get out of here," Dragh agreed, leaping into the saddle of one of the spare horses. He wheeled around, looking around at the chaos they'd sowed.

He grimaced. His pride, his rage had done this. His hands were slick with his friend's lifeblood.

Was it worth the revenge?

He knew the answer without asking himself the question. They were all that was left of the Second. He spent their lives too easily.

Dragh clucked to his horse, spurring him to canter into the dark. Dragh couldn't see, but his horse could. The darkness drank them in, hiding them from the men pursuing them.

Dragh could see the camp for leagues; it burned bright.

They rode until the horses stopped at a brook. Their night vision improved as they rode in the dark. The partial moon gave shape to the land enough to keep them from falling and breaking their necks.

"How is he?" Dragh asked Zeffo. Dragh slipped from his saddle, taking a break from the nerve-wracking ride in the night.

They stopped in a shallow with a small brook running through it. The stars were out, but the clouds covered most of the moon that evening. The light was dim.

They had ridden for hours, so far that Dragh lost track of time.

Pello and Dragh helped slide Relish off the horse. His body was limp. He mumbled in delirium. They moved him to the brook, wiping away the blood of his wound. The smell was rotten and overpowering.

"I... I should have left. We should have left the camp. I'm sorry," Dragh said to the limp form of Relish.

Pello put his hand on Dragh's shoulder. The move uncharacteristic of him. Dragh closed his eyes.

"I'm sorry, my friends," he said to them all.

"He will not survive the night like that, Sunborn," a gravely old voice said in the dark.

Dragh whipped his head around, pulling on his stolen sword. "Who goes there?" he asked the dark.

A small shape appeared across the brook. "It's me, Azal, young Dragh," the old man said to Dragh.

"What the pit is he doing here?" Zeffo asked, wary of the old man.

"He asks why I'm here. Hahahahah," Azal chuckled to himself.

"The question remains, Azal," Dragh said coldly, raising his sword up and pointing to the old man in the soft moonlight. "Tell us, are you with the enemy?"

Azal looked to his side, shrugging. "I am here because the spirits tell me you needed help, young Sunborn."

"The... spirits? Why do you play games, old man? Are you with the easterners? Is that how you found us?" he pushed back at the old man.

"Pah!" Azal scoffed at Dragh.

"We should kill him. We need to get out of here, get Relish to someone who can help him," Geral pleaded with Dragh.

The two of them were close. Geral spoke to almost no one, Relish being the only exception. He was a man of few words, so Dragh took pause when Geral pleaded for the death of the old man.

Dragh turned back to Azal, expecting a retort, surprised by the placid expression that the old shaman had on his face.

"What of it, old man?" Dragh asked.

"They are young, forgive them," Azal muttered, looking over his shoulder.

"Who are you speaking with?" Zeffo challenged the old man.

Azal's eyes appeared to glow in the dark. He laughed at them, throwing his head back in a cackle. "I speak to the spirits that brought you here. That tell me of the glory." He looked over to Pello. "And the conflict you will face."

Dragh looked to his men, and then back to Azal, confused. "What do you want, Azal?"

Azal waded through the small brook and leaned over Relish, probing the wound.

He looked up to Dragh and the men. "I'm here to save your friend. Your bloodlust has altered the path. He is... important to your future, Sunborn."

Dragh's mouth went dry. He knew that he should have fled the camp and not stayed to fight the men there. He was the reason Relish had a dagger in his guts. "Help us, Azal, please," he said, swallowing his pride.

"Dragh," Zello said to Dragh.

Dragh shook his head to Zeffo. They needed what help they could get.

"Move the horses, let them drink, and then we will go to my camp," Azal said to them.

"Can he be moved?" Geral asked as he knelt with Azal over Relish. His voice thick with concern.

"Yes, Geral, he can be. We must move fast. This one hangs on by a thread." Azal gripped Geral's arm.

Dragh watched without comment. The old man was crazy, but he appeared to be their only hope at saving Relish. Without a miracle, Relish would die tonight. He wanted to ask Azal so many questions. How did he find them? Perhaps the spirits he talked of were real? Dragh shook his head.

They followed the old man, Azal, into the dark. Dragh let his men all go on ahead, following from the rear of the single file line.

He prayed to the Gods then, to save Relish.

———

Dragh sat outside the hut, looking out at the ocean as it swelled and crashed among the rocks. There was the sound of birds calling, and gulls swooped into the froth to pick up crabs and shelled fish. He watched them drop the shelled fish onto the rocks and swoop down before any of their friends could try to steal the catch, eating the meat as fast as they could.

Dragh felt like those shelled fish. His body was beaten and broken. The mending was what hurt the most. His arms, legs, back, and neck were on fire. Hot pokers and needles would be preferable. In fact, he preferred when they closed his wounds with the poker. At least then he could rage against the pain.

This pain was dull and sharp. Constant. Enough to drive a man crazy.

They had put Relish onto a makeshift litter. There were long branches on either side of him, and lashings between the posts connected the branches together. Azal had prepared a cold poultice for his wound; the stink warned them of his chances. They moved through the night to the ocean, making it to Azal's camp by the next morning.

That had been a week ago.

Dragh could see men cresting the hills to the north on horseback.

Zeffo, Geral, and Pello were returning from a hunt. Azal's hut was built into and sheltered by large cliffs to the south. There was a hidden path through the hills that was only obvious once you'd been shown it. The shelter overlooked a small cove to the sea.

Dragh had thought them lost when Azal led them there.

"Looks like I'm not the only one recovering," Relish said, sitting down with a wince.

Dragh looked over to his friend and the bandages around his midriff. Relish's colour was still pale, his face red with effort from the short walk to where Dragh sat.

"The others will be back with some fresh meat soon," Dragh replied.

They both sat in silence. Relish was not healthy enough to travel, and Dragh was still mending from the injuries he'd sustained over their weeks of battling and running. He could move, but just.

"About time, I was getting sick of the deer," Azal muttered, walking past Relish and Dragh and back to the cook pit outside his hut.

Relish and Dragh took the comment in stride. They were never sure if he was talking to his spirits or to them.

"How is it?" Dragh asked Relish.

Relish rolled his shoulders, moving his arms up to test the wound. "Not bad," he said, his eyes telling a story of pain.

"Another day, Sunborn," Azal shouted over to them.

"Thank you, Azal," Dragh fired back, used to the weird, old man. His comments always came when he thought you couldn't hear or weren't paying attention.

A clatter coming down the narrow path of the cove alerted Dragh and the men to riders.

Dragh took his hand off his sword when he saw his friends.

Zeffo, Geral, and Pello dismounted, tying their horses to some scrub to munch on.

"Thank the Gods above. Hare. I was sick of the deer you killed," Azal said to the men as they unloaded their kills from their mounts.

Zeffo raised an eyebrow to Azal's comments.

"Go kill something yourself, you miserable bastard," Pello said to Azal.

Dragh and Relish tried to hold back a laugh. Pello had been battling with Azal since they'd met the evening they escaped the Easterner's camp. Azal told Pello he'd seen his death, which unsettled Pello. Pello had gone about discrediting anything that Azal said, calling the old man crazy and more.

Azal, for his part, seemed to like to fight with Pello. He enjoyed the banter between them, especially when he could get under Pello's skin.

They all avoided discussing the obvious.

Relish was healing. Healing from a wound that would kill a man in a combat hospital. He and Zeffo had exchanged words on it once. Geral had stayed at Relish's side while they traveled and while he lay in Azal's hut.

Zeffo had commented to Dragh that it seemed a miracle for Relish to have lived this long. By rights he should be dead. When Dragh spoke with Azal, the old man laughed and splayed his fingers out, saying he knew of herbs and poultices. He'd sworn that the only thing that kept Relish alive was nature.

They all felt the energy of the old man and the energy of the place they were in.

Dragh watched Azal from across the flames. The light danced in his eyes after they had eaten their meal, a roasted hare from the grass plains. According to Zeffo, his brother missed three shots with the bow before Geral took it from him.

The rest of the men had gone to sleep long after the sun had gone down. Dragh had other plans. As long as Azal was by the fire, he would stay.

The old man owed him answers.

Dragh poked at the fire with a long branch, its tip round and burnt from many fires. He could feel the ironwood under his hand. It was a rare wood in

Landor, coveted for boat sterns, bows, staves, and more. He shook his head and smiled.

This Azal was a mystery.

"Ask, then," Azal growled to Dragh.

Dragh looked up in surprise at Azal.

"I may be old, but I know you've got questions. I will answer as the Gods let me," Azal said with some boredom in his voice.

"You knew we'd be attacked?" Dragh asked, watching Azal.

The old man sighed. "I did, Dragh Sunborn."

"And why in the pit didn't you tell us before, when you came to us on the plains?" Dragh asked in a challenge.

Azal pursed his lips. "The future. It is... something like a lake." Azal paused.

Dragh bit his tongue. He wanted to push the old man, but in the week he'd been in Azal's camp recovering, he knew Azal would speak when he wished to.

"Each of us, we throw rocks. The larger the rock, the larger the ripple." Azal pointed to Dragh. "You are a boulder."

"That doesn't answer my question."

"Must I explain everything to the boy?" Azal looked over his shoulder and then back to Dragh. "The lake is clear. Each of us throws rocks and watches through the ripples. You can see the bottom, but it gets... murky."

"And you're saying that you knew, but not exactly when and what would happen to us?" Dragh pushed him to explain.

"Yes, Sunborn. I knew you'd need me, and I knew my role. But I did not see far enough through the ripples to know what would happen to you and your friends."

"So, everything is set in stone and what happened to us was the will of the Gods?"

Azal scoffed at Dragh.

Dragh felt as if he were at his tutors' tables again, in Landor. A youth who knew nothing. A youth who sat at the table of a master.

"The Gods allow us to do what we must in the moment. But they are the lake. Do you understand?"

Dragh closed his eyes, the concept too much for him. "How can they be the lake? I thought the lake was the future?"

"Boy, if I had to explain the inner workings of the Gods, you'd be dead by the time I finished."

"Then how do you know so much?" Dragh shot back.

"Because I was cursed to live, to know. And to watch," Azal said, his voice weary.

Dragh watched the old man across the fire. He would have guessed him decrepit, but his eyes were strong. His body was that of a soldier, able to move for as long as needed, able to lift and carry weight over a distance.

The scars on his arms told Dragh he'd handled swords, blades. And been cut.

"How long... have you been a shaman for the North, for Saravas?" Dragh asked, cautious.

"That bastard Yarrs should have kept his mouth shut," Azal said to Dragh.

"He's dead," Dragh tensed.

"I know. The blood eagle." Azal rubbed his face. "I've been here for many years, Dragh. Long enough to know the blood that runs in your veins. Long enough to see many come and go. To see an evil rise and overtake the sun."

"And you've always advised the North? Been their spirit guide?" Dragh asked, remembering the term from his tutors in Landor. A description of the tribal religion told Dragh that Azal, if he were a shaman, was much more than just a priest to these people.

"They see my value. Nothing more. I have been here my whole life, and longer than your short life," Azal retorted.

"And how long have you lived, Azal?" Dragh thought he began to catch onto Azal's game. He wasn't deceiving Dragh, but he wasn't being completely honest.

"My Sunborn friend. You are quick, aren't you?" Azal smiled at Dragh.

"How did you heal Relish? He should have died from his wound," Dragh put the question to Azal.

"That is simple herbs," Azal laughed. "The simple mind will see magic where there is none, young Dragh. You and your friends are that of destiny. The Gods have plans for all of you. The Gods tell me that you must live," Azal said through the smoke of the dying fire.

"What of destiny? What part do I play?" Dragh drank from his cup.

"That is a murky ripple. But I can tell you that your family and your children's children will regain what your family has lost," Azal explained.

"And what more can you tell me? Anything?" Dragh said, a little frustrated.

"No, I'm sorry. I cannot tell you more. You will find it out when the time is right." Azal put his hands out, an apology to Dragh.

"I can't tell if you are crazy or wise." Dragh eyed Azal.

"Of course. Most don't know which they are until the end," Azal laughed, looking back.

"Who do you speak to Azal?" Dragh cocked his head.

"I speak with those who came before me, Sunborn," Azal said, getting up from the fire. "Sleep, my young friend. You have journeys ahead of you yet."

Dragh lay by the fire, his mind still rolling over Azal's words. What of them? Was he an old crazy man in the hills of the North? What was he really? All things could be explained, and nothing could be certain.

He slept as the fire died in front of him. Whisps of smoke twisted up from the fire, and Dragh swore he could see a face in the smoke as his eyes closed.

CHAPTER 19

"I t's about time he woke up." Pello nudged at Dragh with his feet.

Dragh rolled over, pushing himself up with his arms.

He felt better than he deserved to. His wounds, his head, his shoulders and back. They all felt better.

He felt almost younger than he did before he left for the North with the Second.

"What the bloody pit is going on, with you all up so early?" Dragh asked. His nose smelled the roasting meat over the fire before his eyes focused. He rubbed the sleep out of his eyes.

"We thought we'd get a jump on you, Primus," Relish said, embellishing the word with a short bow.

They sat around the cook fire outside Azal's hut. The sound of the ocean swells breaking over the rocks, the gulls crying out for food, and oil sizzling in the fire, were all mixing together, as Dragh tried to push sleep from his mind and body.

He stretched out, pushing his arms up and yawning, shaking his head at the end of it.

The cool air of the morning was biting as he yawned. He pulled the cloak he'd been sleeping under up around his neck.

"I see you're feeling better!" Dragh said to Relish.

Relish was sitting up, his face flush with colour for the first time since the camp fight.

"I know, I know, it must be the air up here. I really thought I was a goner," Relish said, grabbing his side where he'd been stabbed.

Geral and Dragh exchanged a look.

Dragh looked around the camp. "Where is he?"

They all knew who Dragh spoke of.

"He left before you woke. Told us he'd said everything he needed to say to you last night," Zeffo said to Dragh, offering him a plate of meat.

Dragh accepted the meat and began to eat. "I bet he did. That old bastard is out of his mind."

The rest of them nodded.

"I'm just saying what you all are thinking," Dragh said to them.

"Aye, best not to speak of what we don't understand. What we don't know," Geral said to them.

Dragh grunted. He knew when he was beaten. He knew when he'd said enough, having stuck his foot in his mouth many times before. He finished his meal, taking a long drink from the water skin.

"Everybody up!" Relish called, his eyes on the horizon.

Dragh stood, swiveling to face what Relish was watching.

Men of war, a line of them, were on the horizon.

"Mount up!" Dragh called to them all.

In practiced movements, not a wasted step, they all mounted their horses and pulled weapons from sheathes.

They would face whatever this was on horseback. From a position of strength. Dragh looked on at the men as they crested hill after hill.

"Zeffo, Pello, I want you on the western flank." Dragh pointed inland.

"Aye," Pello replied, kicking his mount into action. Zeffo followed.

"Geral, stick with Relish," Dragh told the big silent man.

Geral nodded. Relish began to protest, but was quickly stopped by Dragh.

Dragh pushed out, walking his horse forward, sword held at his side, away from the horse he was on.

These men, whoever they were, knew he was here. Knew his men were here. They might not be mercenaries from across the ocean, but Dragh and his men had to assume they were an enemy.

The line of men on foot spread out as they met Dragh on even ground, half a league from Azal's hut. They looked like mountain men, swathed in furs and leather, weapons on their persons.

"Is that—?" Relish asked as they watched each other.

Dragh nodded, trying to keep the surprise from his voice. "It is."

In the line of men, swaddled in furs for warmth, there were men and women of the north.

Dragh had heard of the warrior women before. Men and women fought in battles, not just their men. Accounts from the north had always spoken of it, but Dragh had not seen it before now.

A short and stout man stepped forward. His hair was a long mess.

"Where is Azal?" the man accused Dragh with a look.

"He left this morning. Who the pit are you?" Dragh asked.

"I am Teffal of the Argu tribe," the little man explained.

"What business do you have with Azal?" Dragh asked, not convinced he was being honest.

"He's my shaman. My business is my own," the little man spat back at Dragh.

Dragh considered the man and the men in front of him. He looked around, looking for any others. He checked the flanks.

"I'm not here for war, flatlander," the little man chuckled. "If I'd come to kill you all, you would never have seen us."

Dragh smirked. Spoken with confidence; he believed the little man.

"We have some meat and water." Dragh nodded back towards the small tendrils of smoke from Azal's hut. "Join us."

Teffal's eyes rose in surprise. "I've not had an offer from a flatlander before," he commented.

Dragh shrugged his shoulders. "I'm tired of death."

He swung his horse without waiting for an answer from Teffal.

He motioned for Teffal's warriors to come in, and for Geral and Relish to put down their weapons, as he returned to the fire in front of Azal's hut.

Dragh dismounted and passed his reins to Geral, who accepted them without comment.

Zeffo and Pello returned from the flanks to join them.

The Northerners sat around the fire with practiced ease. Dragh figured this meant they'd been here before, a familiar place, by how they organized themselves. They all arranged themselves around the fire, eyes on the opposite group.

The women looked fierce, more so than the men.

Dragh chuckled.

"What's funny, big man?" the slighter Teffal asked Dragh, his voice calm.

Dragh motioned around the fire with his hands. "The laws of hospitality apply, yet here we are eyeing each other prepared to kill. The tribes's law confuses me, Teffal."

Teffal didn't laugh. He looked around at his men and then to Dragh's.

"Tribal law is absolute. That you can be sure of. That does not mean that my men and I do not want revenge on you and your men for what you've done."

Dragh shook his head at the newcomer. "What do you want?"

One of the larger men who was swathed in furs made a motion to lurch forward. Teffal stopped him with a deadly look.

"I am here for Saravas. He calls on Azal to advise him." Teffal sat back.

"Advise him on what?" Pello asked.

Teffal's eyes didn't leave Dragh's. "I would muzzle my dog if I were you..." He waited.

"Dragh." Geral cautioned Dragh.

"I would muzzle him in the North. We do not take kindly to tongues that cannot be held." Teffal held Dragh's gaze.

Dragh laughed aloud. "I fear that I'd be out of place up here if that was the case."

The men and women around the fire laughed at that, raising Dragh's spirits among these cold faced Northerners.

"We prepare for war for what you've done to us, Dragh. I pray that we meet again outside the code, outside of this hospitality. I promise you that you will die," Teffal said, his voice cold.

Dragh struggled with explaining himself to Teffal. How would he explain the men of the east? "You know of the men across the ocean?" Dragh asked.

The northerners started to whisper to each other in a language Dragh did not fully understand.

Teffal was put off by the question. He raised up his hand to quiet the others chatter. "Why do you ask?"

Dragh found the men of the North's reaction interesting. What did they know? Had they been attacked recently themselves? "The blood eagle," Dragh commented, watching Teffal.

"Be careful what you say next. The law of the tribes says that I must not kill you when offered hospitality," Teffal said.

"You know what I speak of, don't you?" Dragh asked.

"I saw," Teffal said.

"And you'll know that we do not do that. The men of Landor would not debase themselves with such horror. I promise you that."

"Yet you'd kill tribesmen and women in villages along the Car Lauch," Teffal spit back.

"We did no such thing. We are men of the Second. We came here because we were convinced that you had killed our people. We were wrongly convinced that the tribes were rising up against the people of Landor."

"I've seen the horsemen, Dragh. The red and gold of Landor. They kill for pleasure. You all sicken me." Teffal spit on the ground.

"We've both been deceived, Teffal. I tell you now that the men of Landor were brought here on false pretenses. The men from the East, the ones who inflict the blood eagle, they are to blame. We did not do this. I swear to you and your men on the Gods. On Zufier Himself," Dragh pleaded.

"You speak lies through your teeth, Dragh. I was a child when I first met your kind. A couple of wayward wanderers came to our village from the mountains.

They claimed hospitality. They left us dead and dying. I lost enough to those men; I will not be tricked again." Teffal was venomous, his body tense.

Dragh watched them all, their bodies tense as if ready to spring on Dragh and his kin.

"Yarrs… he was a friend. A Praetorian in Landor—." Dragh stopped, not sure how much to reveal to this tribesman.

"We will meet you on the road, and we will spill your blood." Teffal spit on the ground as they all rose.

Dragh stood, wishing he could convince the man that he was not their enemy.

"If you must. Please consider my words, Teffal. We want peace, not war with the North."

"You should have considered that before you invaded my lands, Dragh," he said with sad eyes.

The tribe moved as one, leaving without a backward glance.

Dragh and his men stood. They watched the people of the North, tribesmen and tribeswomen both, trot their horses down the trail.

"What a strange breed. Sitting around a fire, threatening to kill us, and then walking away," Zeffo commented.

"Did you see the women?" Relish asked.

Dragh laughed. "They are fierce. Some even become Chieftain. Their histories tell that all can die by the blade, so all must wield them. Do not underestimate them."

Dragh could see his men were confused; they'd never seen such a thing.

Relish exhaled loudly. "No matter if they fight, they are all proud. Honour is everything to them."

"And we've offended their honour, my friends. We need to be ready for what comes next," Dragh said.

The group sat quietly, the fire and sea the only noise around them.

The tribes disappeared into the hills, not far from the camp.

Dragh knew that there would be a trap, that they would be waiting for them.

"We need to move quickly. They will wait for hours and then come at us with speed once we leave this place," Relish said to them all, ushering them to their horses.

Chapter 20

"Where are they?" Dragh murmured to himself.

They were aware that an attack from the Northerners could come at any time. The only respite that Dragh felt was that the men they'd encountered did not have horses.

But nothing stopped them from having horses hidden from sight.

Deceive the enemy, show him what you want him to believe. Not what is.

Nestor had taught him well enough.

"We can't be far from the next village," Zeffo cursed, cracking his neck as they held their horses in a trot.

Dragh cursed. He and his men did not know about the North, or not enough about the North. He wished he understood their culture, their customs. What was it that he had to do now? Was he going to be able to escape the coming battle?

Was Landor going to escape the coming battle? Or were they going to be dragged into a war that neither side had started?

Relish and Geral both reported seeing mounted men in the distance, to the north and west. They were being followed. Likely the men they had encountered at Azal's hut.

His uncle Nestor would be the ruin of Landor.

"They need to believe us. The bloody tribes are animals," Pello commented.

The ride was made up of the pounding of hooves on the ground. They were all tired still from the weeks they'd been running.

"They are defending themselves, their people. Would you do any different?" Zeffo scolded his brother.

Silence followed, the pounding of hooves on packed dirt, the snorting of horses the only sounds in the hills.

The tribes had never really been conquered. They had reached agreement with Kallen's father, Dragh's grandfather. That peace had been tense, hard-won after many years of battle in the mountains. The tribesmen would attack in passes and peaks. Then melt away.

It was a war that Landor could not afford to fight. The North had a long memory. The last to conquer them had been the emperor. The histories of Landor told Dragh that he took thousands of men into the mountains and rooted them out.

He set them back a thousand years. Razed their cities, killed half their population. It was a genocide.

Dragh shivered. No one had the appetite to do that now. That was an eon ago.

"I see a village ahead," Relish alerted Dragh.

"Any vessels?" Dragh asked Relish, who stood above him on a rock outcropping.

Relish focused his eyes. "I see masts."

"What else?" Dragh asked, knowing Relish's tone.

"I see smoke, Dragh. A lot of it."

"Pit," Dragh said, looking to the north.

They were between a hammer and an anvil. The men of the North would surely come. Their honour was wounded. And smoke, the smoke that Relish saw could only mean one thing: the men of the East.

"There are no good ways to do this, men, so I'm going to be honest," Dragh said, looking around the group.

"We've got killing to do, huh, Primus?" Pello asked with a grin.

Dragh grinned back. "If the men of the East are down there, they want us dead. Most of the Northerners want us dead too, blaming us for what's been done to them."

"What are we waiting for?" Zeffo asked.

Dragh laughed out loud. "If there were a choice, men, I wouldn't have anyone but you all." His eyes began to tear up. "I'll be honoured to die today, fighting by your side," he exclaimed.

They nodded back to him.

"Let's go kill our way to the first boat we can find. I want out of the North," Dragh said, clapping Pello on the back.

Dragh felt the pull of the past, worried that he was leading his men into another funnel of death. Worried that they may not survive this fight.

He swallowed the fear, putting on a brave face for his men.

He owed them that.

"A good time to spit in the face of fate, my friend," Zeffo smiled, gripping the reins of his horse in one hand, brandishing a sword in the other.

"You know how to use that thing?" Dragh jested with Zeffo.

Zeffo looked down at the horse and the reins in his hand. "I think you kick it in the ass and hold tight." He shrugged.

"That's not how you use a sword, boy!" Dragh joked, impersonating his old Primus Cello.

The squad laughed, bleeding some of the tension from the moment.

"I'll lead the charge. We ride hard to the village. I want to get to that dock as fast as possible. The dock gets us a boat, the boat gets us to Landor."

"Let's ride. I have a night with Anne and the Beak all lined up," Relish said.

Dragh chuckled. "You dirty little toad."

He spurred his horse towards the village. His blood pumped, his hearing sharpened, and his eyesight focused, as he balanced in the saddle.

Battle brought a clarity to Dragh that he felt no time else.

Life was simple: he needed to get to a boat. He'd kill any who got in his way. A boat meant his men were safe, that they had a chance to save Landor from a war that would destroy them.

Dragh could see the village in front of them, leagues away. Smoke rose, dark and inky towards the sky. He could see fires in the village, some roofs engulfed in a blaze that was still building. He knew that meant the men of the east.

To the west, he saw horsemen, wearing red and gold. They were milling about the village outskirts. A large pile was ablaze in a clearing.

Two men had dismounted. They were abusing someone on the ground, a weapon of some sort rose and fell. Dragh could smell the sickly-sweet smell of death on the wind as he rode. He was beginning to become all too familiar with it.

He tried not to gag.

Dragh could see the villager that the men were beating get up from the ground as the enemy moved to face them.

Dragh was enraged; they were killing innocents.

"Dragh?" Geral shouted above the wind.

Dragh looked back.

Geral pointed towards the village, away from the newly discovered horsemen.

Dragh shook his head and turned back towards the enemy.

"We kill them all!" Dragh shouted to his men, putting pressure on his horse's flank with his knee, changing direction to the west as the first of the enemy noticed them.

"DEATHH!" Relish screamed, pushing his mount to match Dragh's stride.

"DEATHHH!!" the rest of them howled, their fear and anger washing away as they screamed at their enemy.

The enemy had time to form a loose line as they charged across the hills, moving north, towards them.

All Dragh could hear was the roaring of his own beating heart, the ragged breaths he took, and his mount snorting as he pushed her hard.

And then they were on them.

Dragh angled himself at the last minute, pushing with his outside leg on his horse's flank. He leaned hard away from a spear's thrust, sending a sword stroke across his body, through the belly of the man he faced.

As his sword went through, Dragh's horse stumbled, hit in the rear, spinning them both. Dragh clung with his thighs as the horse righted itself.

A blade whispered above his head as he swayed with the horse.

He was being attacked from his blind side. He pushed to the right, into the stroke, not away from it. Lessons from Car-Laugh.

He whipped his elbow around, letting go of his reins and trusting his horse.

He hit the chin of the helmed horsemen, snapping the man's head back.

Dragh blocked a sword stroke at the same time, dragging his blade along the sword and down to the hilt. The man punched at Dragh, hitting his ribs.

Dragh grunted in pain, letting the pain feed his rage. He pulled his dagger from his belt and pushed their swords up and above their heads. He pushed his horse with pressure from his outer thigh to fill the gap between him and the enemy.

He felt his leg squeezed between the horses. The man grabbed at Dragh's hand, seeing what he was trying to do.

Dragh head butted the man. Dragh was close enough to smell the ale on his breath.

As the enemy reeled, Dragh stabbed his dagger forward and felt it cut flesh. The man screamed as Dragh opened up his belly. Hot blood poured over Dragh's hand.

Dragh pulled the dagger back, his head still ringing from the head butt that he doled out.

The man dropped his guard, his sword falling down as he tried to stop his insides from spilling out. Dragh pulled his sword back and jabbed it out towards the man's neck, skewering the man.

The man fell from his horse, gurgling.

Dragh looked around at the battle. Most of his men were ending their own attacks. Relish chased after horsemen who had broken away from the group.

"Relish!" Dragh called him back.

The rest of the enemy were down, and his men were still standing. "Finish it, men," Dragh said to them, dismounting.

They had learned the hard way at Argyle. Once down, the enemy could still hurt you. He moved about the battlefield, finishing the wounded. Ensuring the dead were dead.

It was sick work. But they couldn't take the chance.

Relish reined in beside him. "I had them!" he challenged Dragh.

Dragh looked up at the enraged Relish. "And if they'd turned on you?" he raised his voice so the others could hear.

"I would have handled it," Relish defended himself.

"Do your job. Search the village with Geral." Dragh motioned to the burning village behind them.

Relish looked about to challenge Dragh, but moved on, gathering Geral and going into the village.

"You should have said more," Zeffo commented.

Dragh shook his head. "I almost got him killed. He gets some slack."

Zeffo huffed but nodded.

Dragh found the villager who was being beaten as they rode down the slopes; she had been killed with a stroke of a blade across the neck. Her glassy eyes stared up at the sky.

"They enjoy it," he muttered. He rose from the body. "Search the village for any who survived this."

They moved through the smoky village, all of them with ash-covered faces. The death and destruction was senseless. Almost all were dead. Slain villagers laid across the road, inside of homes, murdered where they were found. Slashes and stab marks across them all.

All but a mother and child.

Dragh and Zeffo had found her when she burst from her home.

She screamed and cried as they struggled to calm her. She cursed them and shouted that they were murderers. That they killed the rest of the village.

"Men of the North, Dragh. They are here," he said quietly, one hand on Dragh's shoulder.

"You're sure it's the North?" Dragh asked.

"They wear furs," Relish explained.

Dragh turned back to the irate woman from the village. Her child was no more than a month old. "Listen. Your people are coming. They are almost here. We are going to leave you."

He put his hands up to show he meant no harm.

She looked around, her eyes darting between them all.

Dragh smiled, trying to calm her. He backed away, motioning Zeffo to follow. He set a water skin on the ground for her.

"We need to be gone when they get here," he said to his men as they gathered around him.

Their faces were haunted, having seen more death than any man deserved to in a lifetime. The scars were of the mind. Dragh could feel his own deepen with every horrific killing he came across.

They all grabbed their packs from their horses and left the horses standing in the village.

They ran through the village, taking the path that had already been burned. Ash was all that remained on the dock side of the village. Ash, of both people and buildings.

"Which one?" Relish asked Dragh.

Dragh looked as he ran. There were three ships that hadn't burned. Their masts still proud and true. They were moored together on the lone dock still intact, snaking out into the sea at half a league or more.

"The dragon!" Dragh called out. The dragonhead ship was already rigged and ready to be sailed. Oars poked out from either side of its belly.

The dragon boat was moored between two other boats, tied together by ropes.

They ran down the dock, their feet pounding into the lumber, echoing off the water below. It sounded as if a hundred men ran down it.

Dragh prayed that it held. He needed to get to that ship.

They leapt from the docks and onto the ship; its sides were low in the water. There was a single mast at its front.

"Zeffo, Pello, cast off the lines!" Dragh shouted. He could hear the pounding of hooves.

Zeffo and Pello went about hacking the ropes, long lines on either side of the boat that kept the boat tied up.

The Northerners were riding through the smoke. Their horses snorted and reared as they breathed in the smoke and dust.

"Push off now!" Dragh roared to the men, freeing the locked-up tiller. "I need you all on the oars!" Dragh told them, watching the Northerners ride through the village to the dock.

The four of them pulled at the oars, sitting abreast on either side of the boat.

"PULLL!" Reish called from the back, all of them straining to pull at the oars after pushing off the other vessels.

The horsemen made it to the dock as the end of the dragon boat pulled past the end of the dock.

"DraghHH!" Teffal called out in anger.

Dragh felt his shoulder lock up as the rushing water pulled the boat to the side. He focused on the rudder, trying to steer the boat between the other boats, two boats moored on either side of the one they were on.

He could see the tide was coming into the small cove they were in. He hoped they could push the boat out with only four men. He counted ten seats on the boat, plus the rudder he held.

Could four men do the work of eleven?

"We need to get out of the cove," he called to Zeffo, Pello, Relish, and Geral.

The men didn't answer, straining at the oars as they fought the ocean.

"Heave!" Relish called, repeating the call as they pulled the oar from the water and then back in.

Dragh watched the men on the dock. He wondered if they would take to the ocean after them.

Teffal stared out at Dragh, naked anger on his face.

He hoped they would take care of the woman and child they found. One of their own. He hoped she would tell them that they'd cared for her, saved her from certain death from the men of the East.

If not, he'd made an enemy for life. He knew that.

The North was waking, and the tribes wanted blood.

"This was their boat, wasn't it? The men of the East." Relish asked, joining Dragh at the rudder of the boat.

Dragh looked around at the barrels, the chests, and the seats. "Aye, I think they came on this. There is enough room at the back of the boat for some horses. The rest of the horses, they must have stolen."

"They are using the Northerners's mountain horses against the tribes?" Relish asked.

"Aye. Most cannot sail with enough horses for a cavalry," he explained, remembering why the Second only ever took Vanor's horses.

"Why are they here, Dragh?" Relish asked.

Dragh considered Relish's question. "I think Nestor brought them here. I don't know how." He rubbed his face, feeling the grit and ash still stuck to it. "He wants the North and the tribes to go to war with Landor."

"What does he gain from that, from killing his own Legion?" Relish asked, confused.

"He gains power in Landor. He is a general. In times of war, the generals are the most powerful forces in a nation. They are more popular, more powerful, than the very kings they serve."

Dragh sipped at a ladle from a water barrel, keeping one hand on the tiller of the boat.

"He intends to challenge my father, Relish. A general's power is fleeting, it is fast. Not like a king's power that burns slow."

"But he's a Sunborn, your father's brother."

Dragh gave him a humorless smile. "I know, but he's not a king. My guess is that he wants to be. He wants power for himself."

"The Council would never accept that, would they?" Relish sipped water.

Dragh looked to the coast, keeping the boat close to the shore. "I don't know. They are a curious bunch, Relish, more interested in power and religion than guiding the nations right now."

They lapsed into silence, Dragh thinking on what Relish had asked. Were the Council involved? The men of the Council were nothing but men. Men were corruptible. He knew that. His own uncle had betrayed him and his father. Why not the Council?

They were a group of men charged with leading the kings of the nations. But were they happy with that? Were they happy with that, or did they want more?

Dragh and his men sat at the back of the boat as the sun crested the ocean sky. The rays of the sun beat through the fog to light up the sky, a beautiful pink and red mixed with orange and yellow. Dragh sat with a hand on the rudder. The boat rocked back and forth rhythmically with the lapping of waves on the bow.

"I imagine that this is why sailors set foot on a boat and never leave it," Relish said to Dragh.

Dragh nodded. "But for the storms, the sea is a beautiful place, isn't it."

"You been out in a storm?" Relish asked, eating some of the salt beef they found in the boat's stores.

They had not eaten much since Nestor betrayed the Second. They had full bellies, access to good water, and a place to sleep. A small set of skins covered the middle of the boat, giving them a dry place to sleep.

Dragh had lowered the anchor in a small protected cove, not wanting to risk navigating the ocean during the night. They did not have the skill.

"Remember when we split for Argyle?" Dragh asked Relish.

"Aye, I remember," Relish replied.

"Well, we ended up sailing down the coast, back before you were in Cello's squad. They took us by boat, those Ralarians. We hit a squall. The sailors were excited, told me they wanted to test out their new boat. It was a newly acquired boat, I'm sure," Dragh commented on the Ralarians' method of getting new boats.

The Second used the Ralarians in their sea forces. But they knew that the Ralarians were also pirates. They stole and pillaged the high seas.

"What was it like?" Relish asked.

"It was unlike anything I've felt, Relish. The ocean heaved and swelled like a bucking horse. But unlike a horse, the heaving lasted for hours. The Ralarians were like little sea rats, scampering over the decks, hauling on lines, pulling in and letting go of the sail when they needed to. I've never seen the like. Not one of them wore proper shoes. All of them wild, like the sea."

Relish chuckled. "Pirates, eh?"

"They are good people when they want to be," Dragh commented.

They lapsed into silence. The only sound was the lapping of waves on the boat and, seconds later, the shore. The gulls were still bobbing up and down in the water. The land was still.

Dragh basked in the heat of the sun's new rays. He leaned his head back and took a deep breath of fresh air. It tasted of salt and sunshine.

Dragh opened his eyes back up. "We need to move early this morning, my friend. We are a day's sail away from Landor, from my father."

"I'll wake the rest of them," Relish replied.

Relish had fallen into second-in-command easily after he'd recovered.

Hemmelle's presence was missed, a hole in their ranks, a hole in Dragh's life. He missed him, his conversation, and his presence.

He wondered how Hemmelle fared. Their run-in with the Northerners, Teffal and his men, had not given him a comforting feeling that all was well. He worried that he sent Hemmelle to his death. Or something worse.

He shuddered. The North was not known as a kind place. The tribes had a long memory, and they treated outsiders with a certain venom.

"Ready when you are, Primus!" Geral called from the anchor line.

"Haul it in!" Dragh called back, his hand back on the rudder.

He felt at home on the boat after the last couple of days. It felt comfortable, his hand on the tiller of the rudder, steering the vessel.

The boat was a sluggish thing, responding after some time.

He felt the pull of the wind in the back of the boat as the front sail was released from the top of the mast. The large sail unfurled a huge dragon head, matching the dragon head that led the boat. Geral, Relish, Zeffo, and Pello all took turns at different positions as they navigated the ocean. One would head the boat, ensuring that they didn't hit anything.

Dragh was unfamiliar with navigation and the depths of water. Two would man the oars. In the event they needed to stop or slow, they would dip the oars in the water. When the wind was weak, they would take turns at rowing the boat through the waters, one stroke at a time. The fourth would rest.

And the rotation would begin again.

Dragh was always at the tiller, steering the rudder as they moved through the water. The large boat smooth atop the sea.

They moved out of the protected bay they'd slept in, and the day had begun. Dragh tried to keep within a few leagues of the shore. He wanted to be able to see land, because that was the only way he knew to navigate south when the sun was hidden.

They had seen groups of men out in their fishing boats. All of them were excited to see a vessel of that size on the ocean. Some of them were excited, some terrified. Dragh had watched some boats tack or row away as fast as possible.

The dragon evoked fear. It was a symbol of the unknown. He'd seen many maps in his life. Pouring over them as a child, he knew that when the maps said "here be dragons", it was the unknown. In the deep waters it was always written as *Hic Sunt Dracones*.

"We make Landor tonight if this wind keeps!" Dragh shouted.

He knew they'd be faster the further off the coast. But there was the risk of overshooting Landor. He needed to get there fast. He suspected Nestor was already there spinning his tales to Dragh's father.

He'd have his war if Dragh didn't intervene.

"SAILS!" Geral called from the bow of the boat.

Dragh put his hand over his eyes to block out the sun, scanning the horizon.

"To the east!" Geral called out.

Dragh looked to the east at the open ocean. Three sails, the triangular shape of Ralarian design, were heading inward. The ships took a diagonal line to the land, moving to intercept Dragh where he was headed, not where he was.

They were facing Ralarians. For all Dragh knew, they were pirates, not the navy.

"We need to beat them on the seas, but we also need to be prepared to fight!" Dragh called out to his men.

"Aye, Dragh, we will dip oars if we have to," Relish responded.

Dragh knew that four men on oars, on a boat made to seat ten, would never beat a Ralarian craft.

Relish's face told Dragh that he knew it too.

It was a tense waiting game. He tried to keep the sail full for as long as he could. The wind at his back ebbed and flowed. He needed to make a choice.

Slowly, the Ralairian boats gained on them; league by league, the triangular sails pulled them together.

"Haul it down!" he called to the men.

Relish and Geral ran to the ropes that secured the sail back to the deck. The prow of the boat was abandoned. He was on his own to navigate now. They pulled at the ropes, releasing the sail. Then, they went to the sail lines and hauled the lines back up into the tow of the mast. They pulled and stowed the rope, fighting the wind the whole time.

"To oars!" he called once it was stowed. There was no need, they all knew their jobs. They didn't need to be told. His men knew what was at stake.

They sat at the rowing benches, spread on either side, and began to row long and deep strokes, moving to short and choppy as they built up speed.

They had adapted in the few days they'd been on the vessel. Their backs and arms could move the oars, but their legs gave them power. They pushed them now.

"It'll be close, men!" Dragh called, seeing the Ralarian sails moving in, gaining on them.

Dragh steered in closer to the coast, hoping that the larger vessel wouldn't hit any rocks in the shallows at the speed they were traveling. Dragh could see tanned Ralarians on the boats chasing them, scrambling to the sides of the decks with weapons.

Dragh cursed to the gods. He needed to make Landor.

"They are coming for us, men. We are not going to make it. TO ARMS, MEN OF LANDOR," Dragh roared to his men.

Dragh put the tiller down, tying it in place so they did not veer too far off course. He pulled out his sword and picked up his shield.

"TO ME!" he called out, his men already moving to the stern of the boat.

The Ralarians moved as a pack. One of the boats overtook them, another at the midship, and the last cut across the stern of Dragh's boat, so close he could hear the Ralarians shouting at each other on deck.

"We do not give up, men," Dragh told them and himself for strength.

"We've fought worse than these fish," Pello spouted.

"Come to death!" Geral shouted, uncharacteristic for him.

Dragh waited for what was next. He and the others had been boarded before. He knew that he could expect a barrage of arrows, ropes, and grappling hooks. Planks were thrown across the gunnels of the boat.

"Hooks!" Relish called out.

Dragh could see a hook arc in the air, a perfect throw from the boat between him and the land on the starboard side.

Then another, and another. Typically, Cello would have told them to cut the ropes that were thrown instead of letting them be pulled up by the enemy boats.

Dragh didn't have the men, just five of them against three ships of pirates. They would make their stand here. Otherwise, he would be guaranteeing them all a quick death.

"Be brave, men. We spit in the face of death today!" Dragh said to his men. Their ragged breath was loud in front of him.

A great creaking sound issued from their boat as it slammed into the Ralarians' boat, bouncing off its side.

Then another.

Their vessel was now sandwiched between two ships. One at the port and another at the starboard. The Ralarian boats began to slow, pulling in their sails.

At the same time, the first wave of men landed on the boat— pirates with short pants, no shirts, and more blades than Dragh had seen on a person's body. Then, more, as the planks were thrown across from boat to boat. Pirates built up on the deck, masses of them, facing Dragh and his men.

"Easy." Dragh said through gritted teeth.

Dragh ignored the churn of his guts, the panic in his heart.

This was it. He would stand against the fury of many. He would die with honor, with his squad.

"Forgive me, Lucille," Dragh said.

"At least they haven't killed us yet," Zeffo laughed.

The rest joined, and the grim humour was what they needed.

"Come on, you stinking fish!" Dragh called out. His men jeered at the insult.

The Ralarians looked ready to kill, some of them beginning the crawl forward from midship. Swords, hammers, and axes all held in hands, ready to kill. They bunched up, preparing for a surge towards Dragh and his men.

"No need for that, my friends!" a voice rang out from among the pirates.

A tall, tanned man with long, black hair braided behind his head walked forward. The group of pirates closest to Dragh and his men parted to make way for him.

Dragh watched. The man walked like royalty, his long legs eating up the deck and his body swaying with the heave of the ships as if he were on dry land.

"Come now. Put down your weapons. There is no need to spill blood on such a fine day," the tall man said, looking up at the morning sun in the sky. The pink of the sunrise still lingered.

"Of course, come and get them!" Relish said, teeth bared.

The pirate didn't waver. The smile on his face was as if they were in at the Duck's Beak having a chat about the weather.

"Let us start over. I am Georges El Alera. My friends call me El Alera. You can too. Who are you, where are you from?" the tall pirate asked.

"They are from Landor!" a skinny pirate behind the tall one said.

"What the pit?" Dragh muttered to Relish.

The skinny pirate walked up to the tall one, speaking quietly in the man's ear, gesturing at Dragh and then to Pello.

El Alera glanced from man to man, listening. The smile on his face melted away slowly. Dragh felt the tinge of familiarity at the back of his mind.

"My countryman tells me that he delivered you to the North with a great host of men from Landor. What are you doing on this boat, a boat of the eastern oceans?" El Alera asked.

Dragh knew he recognized the little man. He was one of the deck hands on the ship they had sailed on from the Landor harbour. The Ralarian pointed to Pello in the same way that he'd accused him of the murder of his friend.

"Is that all he tells you, El Alera?" Dragh asked.

El Alera forced a smile onto his face, his white teeth standing out to Dragh. "He tells me…many things. For instance, you are Dragh, and you defended your friend who my deckhand claims is a cheat and a killer."

Dragh sighed, looking around at his men, who were tense and still prepared for battle. "My men are soldiers. We are killers by profession." Dragh gestured around at the pirates. "You Ralarians. Always calling yourselves sailors. I see a pack of killers in front of me too."

El Alera considered this, his eyebrows raising in surprise. "I ask you once more. Put down your weapons."

"Guarantee me that my men will not be harmed," Dragh retorted.

"Not even the Gods give you this promise. Death is the only promise," El Alera snapped at Dragh.

Dragh could hear dripping, wetness falling to the planks of the ship. "We will not give up our arms. You will have to take them from us."

El Alera shook his head, looking behind Dragh and his men. "Now."

Dragh was confused until he felt the cold, hard bludgeon hit the back of his head.

The Ralarians had climbed the stern of the boat, silently slipping through the water until they were behind Dragh and his men.

—--

Dragh could smell salt and grease as he awoke. The lump on the back of his head throbbed; his vision was messy again, unfocused. He strained to see through the dark. The sound of lapping waves was all that told him where they were.

"Ahhhh," a groan came from somewhere near him.

Dragh turned around and could see a shaft of light. The light shaft was square and coming from what he assumed was the deck of one of the ships that had taken him and his men.

"Hey!" he called out, getting to his feet. "El Alera!" he shouted, remembering the man's name.

Dragh was surprised that he was not tied down or shackled in any way. He was free to move about.

His eyes adjusted to the dark that he was in; the figures of his men were clearer. They were held in the belly of one of the smaller, fast-moving ships. He could smell the sea and the slosh of water that was in every hold.

No one from above came down, so Dragh moved from man to man, making sure that Relish, Zeffo, Geral, and Pello were okay. They all carried headaches and bumps on the back of their heads.

"Those pirates. I'll skin them alive for this," Pello commented.

Relish got half-up from where he was seated. "You are the bloody reason we are here to begin with, Pello. Don't start that shit with us."

Pello got up. He pointed his finger at Relish. "You don't know what the fuck you're talking about. How could I be the reason we are here?" he challenged Relish.

"We all know you killed that Ralarian. If not for you being no better than the prisoner you were when you joined the Second, Dragh would have had a chance of talking us out of here." Relish pushed forward, swatting Pello's hand away.

"Easy, men, easy!" Zeffo pushed between them, trying to calm the situation down. "Dragh?"

"We don't know what they want, or why they took us. It could be that we were easy prey," Dragh tried to calm them.

"Don't take his side! What the pit, Dragh," Relish shouted.

"He knows it ain't my fault we are here, you little runt!" Pello tried to push through his brother.

Zeffo pushed Pello against the bulkhead of the ship, stopping him and Relish from fighting.

The ever-quiet Geral began to talk low, speaking first with Relish.

"What's that?" Zeffo asked over his brother's curses.

"I said, we must ask them what they know," Geral explained.

"What do you think they know, Geral?" Dragh asked, intrigued.

"They mentioned the men from the east. They must know of them, when they came, how they got here." Geral looked at each of them in the dark hold of the ship.

"They know the ocean, they know everything that moves on it," Dragh agreed with Geral.

"So, stop your fighting. Save your energy," Geral said simply, sitting back down.

Dragh looked around. Pello and Relish had both lost the fire in their looks, their anger subsided.

"What next, Primus?" Zeffo asked, his voice calmer.

"Now," a sing-song voice with a heavy Ralarian accent spoke from the dark. "I will tell you what I know about, my good men." El Alera stood up, walking into the light.

He'd sat there, unnoticed beyond the shaft of light from above. The light had blinded Dragh. He'd assumed they were alone down here with the cargo and the bilge water.

Smart man, for a pirate.

"So, what do you know, El Alera?" Dragh asked.

El Alera whistled.

A wooden ladder was dropped down through the hatch in the deck.

"First, let us go up into the sun. You will see that we have relieved you of the burden of your weapons. That will ensure that we have time to talk like reasonable men." He smirked and then pulled himself up the wooden ladder.

They grumbled, but when they exchanged looks, it was clear that no one wanted to stay in the dirty water that swirled at their feet.

One by one they made their way up onto the deck.

Dragh was the last. He squinted in the sun, the bright rays hitting his already pounding head. He looked around the deck. The Ralarians were all at their positions. Some of them were on the rigging, some scrubbing the decks, one was at the wheel, another on the prow, and another in the crow's nest.

"Gods, I would never be able to do that," Zeffo said to Dragh, both looking up at the man in the makeshift crow's nest, an obvious addition to the boat.

"They must have stolen this vessel too," Dragh muttered to himself.

"You'll have to excuse the eavesdropping, but if you call us pirates one more time, I think I'll allow my first mate to cut out your tongue," El Alera said to Dragh.

Dragh looked up. The pirate who'd knocked him out, stolen his ship, and thrown him into a hole was now threatening him.

"I don't need a blade to kill you, El Alera," Dragh growled.

El Alera and his first mate laughed. "We know you don't. I've gathered that you are of the Second and we know what being in the Second means," he said.

Dragh watched the first mate. He barked his laugh. The man's face was covered in scars, some of them from swords, while some of them looked self-inflicted. There were bars of iron in his nose and ears. He was the stuff of nightmares.

"Aye, so watch yourself, you fish," Dragh said with as much gusto as he could muster. He swayed, his stomach turning.

"My dear, Dragh. You don't look so good," El Alera said to Dragh.

Dragh ran to the gunnels of the ship and threw up, heaving multiple times. He threw up until he got to bile. The stuff stuck to his beard.

"Here." A hand appeared with a cup.

Dragh groaned in pain as his stomach rolled.

"Take it, sip it. We all feel sick some days," El Alera said, his voice suddenly kind.

Dragh did as he was bid. Sipping on the water.

He looked out across the sea. The land was no longer visible. The boat was in the middle of the blue. Nothing but ocean.

"Where have you taken us? Dragh asked.

El Alera hopped onto the gunnel, gripping rope from the rigging and leaning back with the tack of the boat. "I have moved us to a place of negotiation," he smiled.

Dragh grinned. "It's a choice then? Agree or drown?"

"Easier to understand that you are powerless when you cannot swim to shore, my friend."

"I need to get to Landor, El Alera," Dragh said.

"First, you will explain to me why you were in a boat of the Eastern men," El Alera said, all humour gone from his face. "You do this, or I will kill you as spies."

Dragh roared his laugh, loud and long. He laughed until he felt tears on his face.

El Alera jumped from the gunnel, pulling Dragh to the edge by the hems of his coat. "You laugh, you son of a dog! They killed my family. I will kill you here and now."

"STOP!" Relish called out, pushing past the first mate.

Dragh watched as a Ralarian stepped forward from the mast he'd been working on and shoved Relish back. Zeffo, Pello, and Geral started on the first mate, grabbing for his weapons.

"Stop! No!" Dragh called to his men.

The conversation was spinning out of control. Soon the Ralarians were going to kill him, or one of his men. He knew this was deadly serious. He had to do something.

"I'm Dragh Sunborn!" he shouted to El Alera.

The men on deck stopped in their tracks.

The look of surprise on El Alera's face wiped his anger from his eyes.

The rest of the men on board had heard Dragh as he called out.

Dragh could feel all eyes on him now.

"My men protect me, please do not harm them," he begged El Alera.

El Alera was speechless. He hauled Dragh back from the edge, no longer threatening to throw him off the boat. "What did you say?" he said, confused.

Dragh took a breath, holding a hand up to Relish and his men to be calm. "I am a Sunborn, El Alera," Dragh said with more authority now.

The men around him took steps back, some of them leaning away.

El Alera smiled. "Prince Sunborn, eh?" he chuckled.

"We are survivors of the Second, you were right. We shipped out to the North to put down a rebellion of the tribes. King Saravas has gathered his tribes, and they are organized and against us." Dragh paused.

El Alera motioned for him to continue.

"It turns out that the men of the East have tricked us and Saravas both. We were led to believe that the tribes were against us, killing at the base of the Car Lauch Mountains. So, we sailed with the Second to the North, and we launched an attack on Saravas."

"And what happened to your Legion, my friend?" El Alera asked, confused. "You said you were survivors?"

Dragh wondered how much he should tell El Alera, how much he could trust him.

He looked to Relish who nodded.

"The Second has been destroyed, just as the Fifth and General Theas before it."

El Alera took a sharp breath. "You're all that is left?"

"There are a few others that chose a different path. But the Legion is gone," Dragh said, keeping some information to himself.

El Alera smirked. He knew when he was being sold a half-sack of goods. "How do I know that you are who you say you are?"

Dragh considered it. "You cannot. My face is not known, just my name."

"And what can I do with a man that might pretend to be a royal of the Sunborn family?"

"Sail me to the Landorian Port. The Praetorian can confirm it." Dragh hated to think that the Praetorians might be his salvation.

"Come with me." El Alera pointed to the captain's quarters under the stairwell that led up to the wheel and tiller.

"For what?" Dragh asked, not sure if he'd sold El Alera.

"A drink. Your Highness." El Alera gave him a mocking bow.

"Relish, you're with me." Dragh gave the command, hoping that the good will of the first mate would take his lead from El Alera.

"Cruze, it's okay." El Alera waved Relish forward and he walked to his quarters.

Dragh and Relish followed. He was one step closer to Lucille, to home.

El Alera poured them drinks, three cups with a dark spirit from a dark bottle. The captain's quarters were smaller than a broom closet in the house he had with Hemmelle. But on the open sea, any privacy was a palace.

"Drink as much as you like." El Alera left the bottle on a table and offered them seats.

Dragh sat with a grunt, his sore body happy to have the support of a chair after so many days on the open sea on the bench of the tiller.

"Will you take us to Landor now?" Relish asked.

El Alera watched Relish, his thoughts a mystery behind his eyes. "Yes." He looked to Dragh.

"Tell me what you know of the men from the East, Capitan." Dragh waited. "Please," he added, hoping that it would prod El Alera.

El Alera downed his drink and poured himself another.

"The fire of the isles," he toasted them and drank the second.

Dragh and Relish toasted, taking drinks themselves. Dragh did his best not to cough as it burned his throat going down.

"I can tell you what I know, what I've seen, and what is whispered," El Alera started.

"What is whispered?" Dragh felt a shiver creep up his neck.

El Alera leaned forward, his face grave. "It is said that there is money to be made on the open ocean, my friend. If you are willing to ferry to the North—supplies, horses, men. And not just that, a great lord has called for a war. A war to rival the nations and the Council."

"Zufier above," Relish whispered to himself.

"Who would dare?" Dragh asked aloud.

"Who destroyed the Second? Ask yourself who would want war?" El Alera asked.

"A man who wants to do battle. A man who wants something for himself," Dragh answered, lost in thought about his uncle, about what Nestor had done and how far it spread.

"When did you hear this? Where?"

"I hear things in every port, my friend, from every ship that passes in the night. I am a Ralarian, a captain of many vessels," El Area explained. "The men only want bounties. It is my job to get them. We travel the sea, from here to there." He motioned to a chart behind him.

Dragh hadn't noticed it. Seeing it for the first time, he got up from his seat and stepped closer to look at the detail on the chart.

"Where did you get this?" he asked.

"It is a chart that the Ralarians share among their own." El Alera was surprised by Dragh's response. "Don't you have these in Landor?"

"Aye, we have charts," Dragh said. "But not in this detail. Where is this?" Dragh pointed to the east, a partial continent sketched out across the ocean.

"Ahhhh, you want to know how they make their way here?" El Alera asked, getting up. "That is where many of my people go to make their fortune. Gold has been offered and accepted by many, with the stomach to traverse the great expanse."

"And this place?" Dragh asked about the scribbled inscriptions on the open ocean.

"*Hic Sunt Dracones,*" El Alera whispered. "That is where we dare not go. Where the gold of the lord has pushed many men. We know that many ships are lost there, and many good men have died there and gone down to the depths."

"Tell me everything, El Alera. For what you tell me could save the nation, not just my own, but the Ralarian Islands, too," Dragh pleaded.

El Alera gave Dragh a look, not convinced.

"What does a prince do when he takes land? Where there is independence?" Dragh asked.

"He consolidates power,"" El Alera quoted the great works that Dragh's tutors had him study.

It was Dragh's turn to be surprised. He recovered as quickly as El Alera. There was more to this man that met the eye.

"Indeed, he does. And what do you think will happen to your islands after Landor is taken? After men of the East control the ports of Argyle?"

"They will come for us. This I know." El Alera sat heavily. "Sit, and let me tell you what I hear. I will tell you of the rich lord who calls for a fleet. He came with his cane, even on the ropes that joined our vessels."

Dragh blinked hard, sitting to listen.

Questions grew in his mind.

CHAPTER 21

"You think he's telling the truth?" Relish asked.

Their ship made good time, moving with the wind and taking back towards Landor. Dragh was surprised how close they were to the shore. Dragh had lost sight of land, the water seeming to go on forever.

"I don't suspect he has any reason to lie, Relish," Dragh told him.

"Who is this lord they talk about? Do you think it's Nestor?"

Dragh looked out at the Landor Harbour in the distance. "I think it could be," he said slowly.

He had his doubts. The way El Alera spoke of the man did not match Dragh's uncle. Nestor was a force of nature, a large man who stood out in a crowd. Not the tall and skinny schemer that the captain had described.

Relish clucked his tongue. "We knew he did this. Didn't we?"

"Aye, we did," Dragh agreed. "We need to go quietly into the city, Relish. Tell the men to wear their cloaks and hoods up. I need to speak with the captain."

Relish gave him a quick nod.

Dragh walked to El Alera, who was now at the stern of the ship. "I need you to come to the palace, Captain," Dragh addressed him by his title purposefully.

"I will go with you and your men when we make landings at the docks," El Alera agreed with Dragh.

"No, I need you to come later. We will depart the ship first, you follow after," Dragh said.

"What are you not telling me, Dragh Sunborn?" El Alera gave Dragh a hard look; something was amiss.

"I'm not telling you for your own good, El Alera. Trust me." Dragh asked him.

El Alera stared at Dragh, his eyes narrowing.

"As you wish, prince." El Alera gave him a mock bow.

Dragh smiled. The captain was a funny man, his humour dark, like Dragh's. "Bend the knee."

"You'll need to invade my islands before that happens, my friend."

"Keep at this and I just might convince my father that we should use your navy against you," Dragh laughed.

El Alera laughed aloud. "I will depart after I deal with the merchants on your docks, Sunborn."

Dragh stopped laughing, forgetting about the merchant's customs that inspected every vessel coming and going from the port. He'd never dealt with them, being in the Second Legion. They never inspected when the men were on the ships.

"Can I... avoid these customs men?" Dragh asked El Alera.

He knew that an inspection could be a problem. What if Nestor had men on the docks?

A wicked smile crossed El Alera's face. "Now you need the pirate, how convenient."

Dragh waited, hoping El Alera could help him. "To save Landor, I need you to do this for me. I will look the other way, Captain. Just this once."

El Alera shook his head slowly. "I knew you were trouble. What are you dragging me and my men into?" He paused. "Get down below, tell Cruze that we need to get a shipment ashore without being seen. He will know what to do."

Relief swept over him.

"Thank you, El Alera. All will be explained if I make it to the palace," Dragh said.

"If?" El Alera asked.

"Indeed, my friend." Dragh clapped El Alera on the back, moving to tell his men what was happening.

—-

Dragh was curled up in a sack, his body surrounded by beans. He tried to breathe as little as possible. His body tossed and jostled as he was unloaded from the ship.

He could hear the men grunting with strain as they unloaded the "beans" on a small jetty before hitting the main dock of the Landor Harbour.

The waterfront was sprawling. The small port became busy in the last wars, a staging place for soldiers and merchants alike. They had a guild for iron work, a guild for woodwork, boat builders, cloth merchants, and more.

The warehouses at the main docks would rival the palace in size, let alone worth.

Dragh had heard his father complain in the past that the merchants could hold their own war with any nation. They had gold, blacksmiths and weapons. Rumors had it that the merchants had enough gold to raise armies many times over.

The old king kept the merchants in check with one thing they were not immune to: greed.

The king looked the other way when he knew that there was a little money pocketed. A little pushed to the side which did not see taxes or import fees.

That greed was what protected Dragh and his men now.

They were being pushed off the boat before they went through the regular inspections.

First Mate Cruze had made some story up, but Dragh knew that avoiding taxes and customs men was what sailors did on a regular basis.

The Ralarians were pirates, thieves on the ocean. But they also seemed to live by their word.

Cruze had taken great pleasure in stuffing them into sacks and crates, ready to be pushed off the deck of the ship at the first set of docks in the harbour.

Cruze had explained that he could get away with offloading a little cargo in the daylight. But never people. It would be known.

The men handling them knew that they were handling human cargo but said nothing.

Dragh wondered if the Raliarians had done this before. And how many people had been snuck into the city. He had promised that he'd look the other way for El Alera. That was the deal.

Dragh saw light through the cloth as he was carried across the dock. He could hear the creaking of the boards, the grunts of the men carrying them.

The light went out, indicating he'd been taken inside. He couldn't see anything now, he was immersed in darkness.

He gritted his teeth as he was thrown to the floor.

He tried not to, but let out an "ooof" as the wind was knocked out of him. He breathed through the cloth that he'd tied to his face to stop the beans from choking him to death.

He felt the release of pressure as someone cut open the sack of beans he'd been crammed into.

"Kiever below," he heard from beside him. Another sack was cut open, and Pello spilled out. "These pirates better not show their faces again. They kicked me in the face when they pushed me off the boat."

Dragh tried not to laugh. He was lucky they didn't stab him when he was put in the sack.

The only thing that kept him alive was Dragh's bargain with the captain.

"Do you think we can make it to the palace?" Relish asked.

They were all out. The dock workers disappeared out of the warehouse as soon as their job of freeing Dragh and his men was complete.

They were inside, no windows spilling in light, but Dragh's eyes slowly adjusted as he counted his men. They had all made it in.

The wooden floors of the warehouse were thick, but Dragh could still hear the sea below them.

"We need to move quietly, and we need to move quickly. Nestor's men will kill us if they see us," Dragh said, his voice low.

"I hope it's Vanor," Zeffo whispered.

"Tie that up. We are not here for revenge. We are here first for Landor," Dragh snapped at Zeffo.

The men were angry; he could feel it.

"The blood you are owed will be spilled after the palace. I promise you that," Dragh pledged.

His killers looked on with vicious smiles. The whites of their teeth bright in the low light.

Dragh felt the rush of the hunt; he was setting out to finish what Nestor started. And the "lord" that El Alera had told him of.

"We are north of the palace and east of it," Dragh told them, knowing which dock they'd been dropped off on. "We need to move quickly. No one runs, and no one pulls their blades unless they need to."

"With our luck, we might make it out the door before we need a knife," Relish commented, looking around the warehouse they'd been smuggled into. It was packed with sacks of food, equipment, cloth, barrels, and more.

Dragh was surprised by the cleanliness of the warehouse. The floor was spotless.

Dragh pushed out of the rear door of the warehouse and onto the streets of Landor quietly, looking up and down the street before motioning for his men to join him.

The solid cobblestone ground made his legs feel unsteady after so long at sea. He braced himself against the wall as his men filled out of the warehouse door.

The sun was high in the sky, its bright rays making him squint; his eyes had to readjust.

"Move, now," he told them.

They moved quickly through the streets, walking with their hoods up, a slow pack of men moving with purpose.

Dragh watched each corner. Merchants and working men moved throughout the city conducting business at shops and stores.

Dragh and his men took a roundabout route to the palace. He knew all of the ways in and out of the palace from his days of youth.

He passed the entrance to the Street of Roses. He paused, thinking of Lucille.

"We don't have time," Relish pushed him on.

Dragh knew he was right, but his heart tugged at him to stop, to see Lucille. He knew Relish was right. He had his duty to Landor.

Dragh bowed his head, breathing deeply and exhaling loudly.

"Let's go," Dragh said.

They turned a couple of corners towards the Duck's Beak, the smell of ale heavy in the air.

Dragh stopped dead in his tracks. Vanor and ten of his cavalry squad sat outside on the open tables, their feet up in the air. Their leather cavalry boots with hobnails through the soles muddy atop the tables.

"Oh, pit," Zeffo murmured.

Dragh was stopped mid-stride. His face drained of colour as Vanor locked eyes with him.

Relish edged back, his hand going to his sword.

Vanor's face turned to a sneer as recognition dawned on his pocked face. "I see a whole raft of dead men," he said. It echoed across the empty stone street.

His squad got up around him, their hands going to their swords.

Dragh watched as they all pulled cavalry swords. The long, curved blades glinted in the sunlight.

"Remember men, we must make the palace," Dragh said, pulling his own blade. It was shorter and thicker, a heavier swing for a grunt in a foot squad.

"You sure about this, Primus?" Geral asked.

"Remember what I said about waiting for revenge?" Dragh asked them.

"Yeah, you said we'd have to wait," Zeffo replied.

"These traitors die now," Dragh said, bellowing his war cry as he launched himself at Vanor and his men.

Dragh brought his sword up to the high guard above his head, launching forward and into the fray. He could see that he'd surprised Vanor and his men. The fools were not ready for their fury. He swung hard for the first man who'd stepped in front of Vanor. His blade was half way up as tried to defend himself from Dragh's swing.

Dragh's blade, the heavier of the two, carried the cavalry man's blade down, letting Dragh's blade slice into the man's shoulder.

The man screamed, dropping to his knees as the blade cleaved his shoulder open.

Dragh felt the moment before he saw it: a woosh of air as a knife cut his face.

Dragh grabbed his face, then threw up his blade to defend against the swing of the blade that came after the distraction.

"You're supposed to be dead, you rat!" Vanor shouted at him.

Dragh felt the rush of blood as his heart kicked into overdrive. He swung his fist and was satisfied with the connection to Vanor's midriff.

Venor coughed and doubled over. Dragh's punch left him breathless.

Dragh stood up straight. The rest of his men were dispatching their opponents; Geral was killing his third, driving his sword through the man's belly with a savage twist to keep the wound open.

"You traitors, you're the rat, Venor. You deserve the death you get. You'll be in the mud." Dragh spit on the ground.

Venor lunged, his sword stabbing towards Dragh's stomach.

Dragh anticipated the feint. Venor's sword rose up as Dragh batted the tip of the cavalry sword away, spinning off of the man's lunge.

Dragh let Venor's own momentum be the death of him. He followed through the spin, hacking off Venor's head with a vicious twist backwards.

Venor's head dropped from his body, thumping to the ground moments before his body crumpled.

Dragh leaned down to the body, breathing hard from the fight. He wiped the blood off his sword.

"Let's hope the rest are not close," Relish commented on the forty other men of Venor's squad.

"We need to move, we need to get to the palace," Dragh said.

Relish led the way, picking up the pace. The dying light from the sun crested the buildings around them.

They ran now, all stealth forgotten about as they closed in on the palace.

Dragh made it to the palace doors without being spotted again or without having to kill anyone else.

"Hold!" one of the guards called out as they hit the long street that ran through the middle of Landor and straight to the palace doors.

"Dammed Praetorian," Dragh commented.

They piled up behind Dragh as he stopped. Two Praetorians guarded the door.

"What's your business?" the guard said, eyeing the rest of the martial men that had come with Dragh.

"You can't bring your weapons into the palace!" he said to them all.

"I'm Dragh Sunborn, I'll bring whatever the pit I want into the palace!" Dragh roared, pushing past the guard.

Out of the corner of his eye, he saw the Praetorian reach for his sword.

As he reached for his sword, the second Praetorian lunged, snapping a punch that connected with his partner's temple.

The Praetorian saluted Dragh. His partner lay on the ground.

"Sorry, sir. It won't happen again," the guard said in a phlegmy voice.

Recognition flashed through Dragh's mind. "Thank you, Pars," he said with a quick nod.

They pushed through the doors, throwing them open in a rush to get to his father.

Dragh and his men ran through the courtyard of the palace, pushing past politicians, guards, and servants. Many of them outrightly shocked to see Dragh's face.

He was sure that he made a wild sight. His face was surely covered in his own and Venor's blood.

All of their clothes were travel-worn, covered in blood and death. He could smell himself and his men.

Dragh paused his mad dash for a moment, gathering his breath outside the massive wooden doors that protected the throne room.

His father would be here with his court.

He hoped that El Alera had been admitted, knowing that the sailor had enough information to gain access.

Dragh looked around at his men, all heaving chests from the effort they exerted. They had made it, his father had to know what was really happening in the North.

"Ready, men of Landor," Dragh said.

"Hic Sunt Dracones," Relish said with a laugh from the rest of the men.

Dragh pushed the doors open.

CHAPTER 22

"We have to go back—."

Dragh walked through the doors and into the large throne room.

Nestor stood in the middle of the throne room, stopped in the middle of recounting his tale.

The room was covered in tapestries from his house. They depicted the many battles and victories of Landor and the Sunborn family.

Around the room were many seats and benches, full of men and women of the court. Some of them were politicians, some of them men and ladies-in-waiting. There were Generals of the other Legions, members of the court of Landor and of course, the merchants.

On the throne, in all his glorious dress of the Sunborn, was his father, King Kallen.

Beside him his mother Queen Sherris.

Dragh watched all faces turn to him as he and his men marched towards Nestor in the middle of the throne room.

The fat priest from the Council, Malek, stood in the center of the crowd.

Dragh watched the looks on his father's and uncle's faces.

Both were unhappy with the interruption of the court. Surprised.

Then, his father's face turned to a smile, one that he'd reserved for large accomplishments in life.

He'd seen his father smile like that three times in his life. It stopped Dragh in his tracks.

"Dragh?" his father's voice faltered.

"Aye, Father, I'm alive and well." Dragh paused, looking around the room for the reaction of those seeing him.

"How?" The cold question came from Ellis, to the right of his mother on the dais of the throne room.

Dragh watched the men in the court, Ellis, and the other sycophants. They all glared at Dragh, the ugly stain on the house of the Sunborn.

"No... not yet," Relish whispered. "Wait for the right time."

It was time to take control and go on the attack. Dragh had been running for his life for long enough.

"After we were attacked, we made our way back to our decimated Legion. Then, after being captured and chased through the North, we made it here with the help of some Ralarians."

Dragh paused, finding El Alera in the crowd.

He waved El Alera forward.

"After our Ralarian allies helped us at sea, we learned of a plot to take the crown of Landor," Dragh said, making sure to say it loud enough for the crowd to hear.

El Alera had made his way forward to Dragh's side, bowing to the king.

"What is the—."

Nestor began to protest, but was quickly cut off by Kallen. "You've had days to explain, Nestor... It seems the Second is lost."

Dragh looked to his uncle. The man's face was turning red, his eyes darting back and forth. It appeared he was spinning a tale of the Second's survival.

"Thank you, Father," Dragh said, acknowledging his father in public. Something he hadn't done in many years.

Dragh swallowed, his mouth dry. The Landor court was intent, watching his every move. He could see them leaning forward in their seats, standing men pressing inward.

"Go on," Kallen commanded, gripping his throne's armrests with white knuckles.

"We were waylaid by men from the East. The Second was decimated, with the exception of some cavalry, who I've just dispatched on my way here," Dragh continued.

"Traitor! You see! He killed men of the Second!" Nestor shouted, interrupting Dragh.

Some of the crowd shouted in support of Nestor.

Dragh faltered.

He hadn't expected to have to defend his action to the real traitor in the room. What was he going to do, call Nestor the traitor?

Kallen looked on, his mother as well. Waiting.

Dragh took a breath. He'd not survived the Pit in the North to stop now.

"How did you survive the death of my Legion?" Dragh turned on Nestor, his eyes narrowing on the traitor.

Nestor opened his mouth, then closed it.

His face turned a deeper shade of red, his eyes bulging with anger. "The Second was MY Legion, you little stain!" he shouted.

Dragh smiled.

"What do you mean, General?" Kallen asked quietly.

All strained to hear him. The king was never quiet unless he was upset.

All who knew him knew that when he asked a question you strained to hear, he was forcing himself to calm.

"I mean, that it is my Legion. A slip of the tongue is all," Nestor tried to brush off his slip to the king.

"What do you mean it WAS your Legion?" Kallen repeated the phrase that Nestor had used.

Dragh caught Ellis's face twitch from the corner of his eye. The slight man was inching away from the throne.

"I didn't mean it, I'm telling you, your son is out of control. You need to arrest him for what he's done. You know he's killed before!" Nestor said, putting his hands up in defense.

"No, Nestor. I'll hear Dragh finish his...tale of exploits." Kallen looked to Dragh and nodded, his brows furrowed.

"Thank you." Dragh nodded to his father. "When we were in the forest, we ran into the men that killed our Second. They were in the Gallen Forest, on the path to the south. They feasted. Drank and ate and were celebrating their victory over our Legion." Dragh felt tears on his cheeks.

The salty tears mixed with drying blood, filling Dragh's nose with the coppery smell of battle once more.

"They killed our men, they nailed them to the fort, and burned it to the ground. These men caused the North to rise up, kill villages, and display elders in blood eagles." Dragh paused, letting the accusations sink in. Letting the court of Landor think about what he was saying.

"We found them on the path. And with them was Vanor and his squad." Dragh paused, looking around the court and then at his uncle. "And General Nestor. Celebrating his victory."

There were gasps as Dragh finished his story. His father went rigid, his back straight in his throne, his hands still gripping the armrests with white knuckles.

"Liar!" Nestor shouted above the din of the whispering crowd. "You're a liar!"

"Take your hand off your sword. NOW." King Kallen's voice boomed across the room, driving it to silence.

Praetorian moved forward, from behind the king and through the crowd behind Dragh and the rest of Landor's court.

The fat priest, Malek, stepped forward with his hand up to placate the king. "Let us not resort to violence, the Gods—."

Kallen stood and walked down his dais to Nestor.

His Praetorians slunk behind him. Not the guards of the doors, but real predators, moving with death in their shadows.

"EVERYONE OUT!" Kallen called to the room.

He stared at Malek with hate in his eyes.

The room emptied. At first slowly, then in a tide of rushing men and women.

Nestor stood, watching the court empty, his plans failing as Dragh dragged him back into the mud, telling the truth of his crimes to Landor's ruler.

El Alera was going to leave, but Dragh gripped his arm to steady him. "I need you here."

"My king, perhaps we should…" Ellis started to suggest.

"ENOUGH!" Kallen raged at Ellis, his temper lost.

He took a stride towards Ellis and raised a hand pointing at the man who was halfway out of the door. "OUT, ELLIS!"

Ellis put his cane and hands up in apology, groveling to Kallen, before exiting the room.

El Alera watched him go, shifting on his feet.

Tap, tap, tap. Ellis's cane sounded as he walked across the marble floor.

"Speak," Kallen barked at Nestor, turning back to his brother, glaring at him from the steps of the throne.

"I… I…He's lying to you, my liege," Nestor sputtered.

"Enough, Nestor. Did you really think I would side with you? My own son witnessed it. You think I'd ignore the signs?"

Nestor was unable to speak, his mouth moved, but no words came out. His face turned white.

"Who did you work with?" Kallen asked.

Nestor pursed his lips, choosing not to speak. Not to answer his brother's questions.

Dragh watched on, pride swelling in his chest at his father's trust in him.

Kallen shot forward, gripping Nestor by his collar. "I am the one who cut the rope. I saved your life."

Kallen pulled down Nestor's high collar, revealing scars around his neck.

The scene froze Dragh. What was his father talking about?

"You STOLE the crown from me, you bastard!" Nestor spit out.

"You stole it from yourself. I should have let you hang for what you did. The mercy of being my blood is the only thing that kept you alive." Kallen nodded down to the scars around Nestor's neck.

Dragh had never seen the scars. His uncle's dress uniform was always above the collar.

He'd seen men's necks after having been hung at the end of a noose. Nestor's crimes must have been horrific for Nestor to have been hanged for them.

A prince, a prince in line for the throne, at that. Hanged.

Dragh watched in disbelief.

What had his uncle done to be hanged?

"Father," Dragh said, moving towards the king.

Praetorians moved forward quickly, grabbing Nestor's arms and twisting them behind the man's back to restrain him.

"It ends now," Kallen said, sadness in his eyes.

"We must speak, Father, our allies have something you must hear," Dragh said.

"Not now, Dragh." Kallen waved him off.

"I need you to hear this, Father. Trust me," Dragh said, trying to pull his father away from Nestor.

El Alera moved to Dragh's side. "King Kallen, I am El Alera, a captain of the Ralarian Islands. My fleet was lucky enough to run into Dragh. He was... convincing in his need to get here."

Kallen looked El Alera over with a suspicious eye. "What is it? Speak."

El Alera nodded.

"It concerns the ocean passage from the East. It may not be closed. That may not be all that comes."

"What?" Kallen asked, looking back at Nestor.

Nestor broke from the Praetorians, pulling a dagger from his belt and lunging for Kallen.

Kallen pulled his sword, a falchion-style blade as he spun away from Nestor.

Dragh watched the sword, his family heirloom. Dawnbringer. It was the blade of the Sunborn house.

Nestor lunged. The dagger went through Kallen's robe, cutting his side.

Before the Praetorian or Dragh could act, Kallen had impaled his brother. His sword came up, and Nestor's momentum carried his body onto the blade.

Dragh could see a tear in his father's eyes as he held his brother close, his sword embedded in Nestor's body.

"I saved your life, brother. I loved you." Kallen moved back, kicking Nestor off his sword, pulling it out with the great sucking sound of an open wound.

Nestor grunted, hanging onto life as his body crumpled to his knees.

"And you betrayed me," Kallen said solemnly, raising his sword and bringing it down on Nestor's neck.

Dragh watched his uncle's body spasm, his head rolling away from his body as it hit the stone floor. His blood spread out on the quarried stones from the Car Lauch Mountains.

The only sound now was his uncle's lifeblood spilling from his headless body. The same blood dripping from the tip of Dawnbringer.

His father stood with his shoulders slumped. Tears rolled down his cheeks.

The Praetorians stood at attention, swords in their hands, many looking into the corners of the room, to the door for more threats.

"Dragh. Come to my study, bring the sailor," Kallen said, walking away and out of the throne room. Dawnbringer was still held ready in his hand.

El Alera was rooted to the spot, not sure what to do, much like Dragh.

Dragh nodded to the Praetorians who, as Dragh and El Alera began to leave the throne room by the main exit, began to remove the body.

One man picked up his uncle's head by the hair. Blood still oozed from it.

"Put it out on a stake," Dragh growled.

The Praetorian looked to his superior, not sure what to do with Dragh's command.

"Praetorian!" Dragh snapped.

The Praetorian looked back at Dragh, put off by the king's son giving orders. But Dragh had learned in the mountains of Cal-Launch that the man who takes command is in command.

"Get it out of here. I never want to see that traitor again." Dragh felt wrath in his blood as he turned and walked out with El Alera.

"You are a hard man. Remind me not to cross you," El Alera said without jest.

Dragh felt the betrayal of Nestor then. A knife in his heart. He could hear the dragging sound his uncle's body made as he and El Alera walked towards his father's study. He didn't look back.

His uncle, who had helped raise him, betrayed Dragh and his father.

Dragh shook his head and wiped at the tears.

"He killed my brothers. Thousands of them. He will rot in the Pit for the rest of time for his betrayal," Dragh shrugged.

He felt empty again—the sadness of his loss at odds with his anger.

CHAPTER 23

"And you are certain that it was him?" Kallen looked at Dragh.

Dragh stood across from his father and El Alera. The room was cold with the rage that rolled off Kallen. The room was adjacent to the throne room, a study that his father worked in when he wanted to be alone. It was built of stone with a simple wooden desk and fireplace.

Scrolls littered the room, in shelves, on the desk, and on the side table in front of the cold empty fireplace.

There were only two chairs. Kallen sat with El Alera.

Dragh stood and watched, waited.

El Alera told Kallen of the threat from the East. The offer of the lord to ferry men to the shores of not just the North, but Landor and beyond.

Kallen took it all in without question.

El Alera explained how this lord had walked across the deck, tapping a cane with a sword in it with each step.

El Alera and Dragh shared a look. Dragh nodded to the Ralarian.

"Nestor would never have moved alone. He wouldn't have had the power of the full army on his side. The generals were as shocked as you," Dragh said, adding to El Alera's story.

"My own brother." Kallen leaned back in the chair behind his desk, eyes flicking between the two men.

A single lantern lit the room on Kallen's desk. The light from the candle within was low, giving the room a sense of darkness that made Dragh's skin crawl.

Dragh nodded.

His father still had the blood of his own brother on his clothes. His hand and arm were covered with a spray of reddish, flaking blood.

"El Alera. Landor owes you a debt. I owe you a debt," Kallen said.

El Alera bowed. "Thank you, King."

"Leave us now, El Alera. Call on me or my family when you are in need." Kallen waved El Alera away.

El Alera stood from the chair, exchanged a nod with Dragh, and then turned to leave.

Praetorians opened the door at El Alera's knock, then closed it as he left.

"Praetorian!" Kallen shouted.

The door opened. One of the Praetorians walked in and bowed.

"Bring me Ellis. Now," Kallen said.

Dragh shivered at the ice in his father's voice. He was used to being on the receiving end of his anger. Now to watch it from the other side was an oddity.

The Praetorian didn't speak, simply nodded and marched off in his red and gold armor. The clanging of armour rang in the hall as the door was closed again.

"We are going to do this now?" Dragh asked, surprised by his father's choice.

Kallen motioned for Dragh to sit in front of the desk.

"A rat will jump off a ship in the middle of the ocean when it sees fire," Kallen sighed. "This rat needs to have its head cut from its body. It will poison the crew if we let it scuttle around."

Dragh nodded, understanding that letting Ellis live, letting him get away with this a minute longer, could not be stood for.

A knock from the door came, soft in the stone room.

"Enter," Kallen said.

The doors creaked, opening on their old hinges.

Ellis presented himself, a look of relief on his face when he saw Dragh and Kallen.

"My king, thank the Gods that you are alright," Ellis said, his cane tapping with each step on the stone floors.

Tap, tap, tap.

Dragh sat up in his chair, his eyes finding Ellis's.

Ellis's stared at Dragh, trying to dig into his mind, to understand what Dragh had to do with this meeting.

"Ellis, I've had some disturbing news today," Kallen said, watching the unspoken exchange between Ellis and his son.

The Praetorian that was sent for Ellis stepped into the room, behind Ellis.

Ellis looked over his shoulder at the Praetorian as if he were a bad stench that sullied Ellis's nose.

The Praetorian did not move.

"Of course, my lord, I'm so sorry about your brother," Ellis said, looking back to the king.

Dragh scoffed. 'sycophant," he muttered.

Ellis looked up with a sharp look, hate in his eyes for Dragh. "We should talk about the readiness of the army, my king," he said, looking back to Kallen.

"Why would we do that, Ellis?" Kallen asked.

Ellis looked between them again. "We need to defend ourselves from the East and then the tribes."

"Why would we need to defend ourselves from the tribes, Ellis"?" Dragh asked. "Is that what you really wanted when you brought over men from the East?"

"What?" Ellis asked Kallen, ignoring Dragh's question.

"Enough," Kallen said, deadly quiet.

Ellis began to protest, but was cut short by Kallen standing up and throwing his glass into the empty fireplace.

Dragh stood, watching a tick begin on Ellis's face. His eyes scrunched up, and his shoulders bunched.

"We know what you've done, Ellis," Kallen said.

Ellis started to protest, then stopped. Letting his shoulders relax.

Kallen walked from behind the desk to stand in front of Ellis, his fierce gaze boring into the slight man.

Dragh watched as Ellis's face turned from a groveling weak politician to a commanding presence in the room.

"Fine, have it your way, Kallen."

"I knew you were always playing the angles, but this?" Kallen asked Ellis, his hand on the hilt of Dawnbringer.

Dragh took a step forward to stand beside his father.

Ellis looked at them both, his eyes narrowing the way a snake looks at a mouse, ready to pounce.

"Nestor, he always wanted what you had. I saw the opportunity, and I had the money," he chuckled. "It was your money that brought your ruin to these shores."

Dragh was surprised—the change in the man, the full admittance for what he'd done. He hadn't expected this.

Ellis had always been a politician. Now, he was different, as if this had always been lurking beneath.

His true self.

"Why?" Dragh asked.

Ellis shrugged. "Weak men are easy to manipulate. If Nestor had done his job and killed you, little princeling, I would now be with my fleet and army." Ellis pointed to Kallen with his cane. "And you, you've been selling us out to the Council. They move here with their men of *religion* and you let them. They command the Skellen Pass. And you let them. They order you around like they are the kings of Landor. And you let them."

"And you think you can do better?" Kallen laughed.

"Of course I can do better," Ellis said.

Kallen laughed again.

Ellis's face turned, again, to one of anger. His eyes narrowed, his mouth a firm line.

Dragh could feel the tension in the room again.

"The long game requires patience that you do not understand, boy," Kallen said to Ellis, his voice tired, a teacher to an unruly pupil. "You think in weeks and years. I think in generations. I do not explain to you the strategy that this kingship takes because you wouldn't understand it."

"I came from NOTHING to this court. I think I can grasp simple strategy, Kallen," Ellis spit out.

"I raised you up from nothing. And this is what I get, more betrayal." Kallen shook his head.

"It's over, Ellis," Dragh said, finishing his father's statement.

"It's not over. *Your* reign is over, Kallen!" Ellis raised his voice.

The Praetorian stepped forward, moving towards Ellis.

Dragh could feel the ebb of coming violence. Tension before the strike.

"You'll never see it happen, you stain." Kallen turned his back to Ellis.

Ellis drew his cane sword, moving his feet to a sword fighting position. Something Dragh had not seen before. The fool was something more than he'd pretended.

Another surprise.

The Praetorian drew his sword.

Dragh laughed out loud.

"What?" Ellis snarled at Dragh.

"I learned another thing from the Ralarians, *my lord*." Dragh looked Ellis in the eyes. "How to knock someone out from behind."

Ellis spun, leading with his sword, but it was too late.

The Praetorian who had moved behind him swung a trudgen, a long wooden bat with an iron center to give it mass.

Ellis's head thumped when he hit the ground. Unconscious.

"He hangs in the morning. Throw him in the dungeon," Kallen commanded the Praetorian.

Another Praetorian entered the room, helping the first. They moved to disarm Ellis, dragging his body from the room.

The second of the night. This one was living.

"Father." Dragh wanted to reach out to his father but was unsure of what to do.

Kallen turned and put his hand on Dragh's shoulder. "We have things that need to be done, Dragh. I need you in the North again."

Dragh nodded. "Before I go, I need to see her."

Kallen sighed. "Be fast. Landor is in danger if we do not root out the evil that Ellis has brought with him to the North already. If they are successful in turning the tribes against us, it will ruin Landor."

Chapter 24

Dragh walked the Street of Roses, the familiar scent gone from the coming winter months. The cold grew in Landor as the seasons changed, and the plants and wildlife began to bed down.

Lamps were lit on either side of the street, giving a glow to it as the sun was descending to the west.

"Hurry up. We want to catch her before she goes to sleep. You know that waking her is like waking the dead."

Dragh stopped on the street, watching for a moment as Zeffo and Pello emerged from a shop's door halfway down the street.

In the quiet, their voices carried far.

Dragh started forward, then thought better of it, watching the pair continue down the street with the bag of sweets.

Darkness swallowed them up as they moved past the last lamp.

He smiled to himself. His men needed to be without him for a time, to go home and remember why they fought, what they were fighting for.

What he asked of them next would test all of them.

Dragh's nerves were worse than when he'd run to the palace to stop his uncle. He could feel his heart pounding in his chest. His hands were sweaty.

He'd given his men the rest of the night to make their peace with Landor.

They were not here for long.

Dragh had his own business to take care of.

Something he'd been thinking about for many months. He stood in front of Lucille's house, the beautiful facade evident even in the dark.

He paused, not sure what he'd say to her, even now. Especially after all the time that had passed.

She might even think him dead. He remembered the message he'd asked his men to deliver when he thought he'd be dead in the North, shuddering.

"Are you going to knock?" a voice came from a window above him.

Dragh smiled, joy creeping into him.

"Let me in, Lucille, we need to talk!" he said to her as she leaned out of the window.

She came to the door; her servants had gone to bed.

Her cheeks were rosy red. Her belly was half as wide as her. Dragh looked at her and smiled.

"I'm sorry, Lucille." Dragh began, tears in his eyes.

"Dragh," she said with tenderness. She pulled him into a hug.

Dragh collapsed into her arms, burying his face in her shoulder as he sobbed.

They moved into the house together as Dragh held her close. He could scarcely believe that he was here, that she was in his arms.

He couldn't keep his eyes off her belly. Their child.

Dragh found himself in her room, sitting across from her. His cheeks ached from smiling, his face wet with tears.

Dragh sat and stared at Lucille in her comfortable chair beside her fireplace. The large house disappeared when he sat with her. The world itself didn't exist in those moments. Just her.

Dragh flexed his hands and looked down, watching the scars pop out on his white skin, showing the battles he'd survived.

He looked at the baby bump.

"What if I can't change? What if all these hands know is death?" Dragh whispered.

Lucille shed a tear, a sad smile on her face.

"I'm a killer. How can these hands support life when all they do is take it?" Dragh slumped in the chair, defeated.

Lucille got up and sat on the arm of his chair. She stroked Dragh's hair, letting him lean into her side. "We will raise this child, Dragh. Both of us."

She put her hands over his, letting her fingers slip in between his scarred and cut-up hands. His hands of war.

Hers were beautiful, smooth.

"I will give him Landor, Lucille. I am not what my father wants, but this boy, our boy, he can be the man I wish I were," Dragh said to her, looking up into her eyes.

"You will be his shield, and I will be his mother," Lucille replied.

Dragh smiled.

"What will you do now, Dragh?" she asked.

"I must go to the North again. I need to make sure that the tribes, that Chieftain Saravas, knows we did not start this war."

"You go for peace?" Lucille asked, hopeful.

"I do, my love. I do it for both of you," he said, his hand on her bump. "I promise, I will return to you both."

Lucille smiled and held him close, his head on her heart.

Dragh listened, convinced he could hear the faint heartbeat of his child mixed with hers.

Chapter 25

"Sit down, boy. You need the rest," Kallen said to Dragh from a chair at the study's fireplace.

Since Dragh was last in it, Kallen had added a chair to his study. The once dark and cold study had been warmed by a fire in the stone fireplace. A pair of chairs was now arranged in front of the fireplace.

Dragh poured himself a drink from the small table between the chairs and rubbed at his neck.

The execution of Ellis had been quick. When he'd returned to the palace, the deed was already done.

The fire was hot and quiet.

Kallen sank into a large cushioned chair, his feet up, a drink in his hand.

Dragh sat, waiting for his father. He could tell something was bothering him.

"You know, when they hanged my brother, I did nothing at first. The trial, the accusations, all of it rocked my mother and father. They didn't want to admit that their first son was a monster. That he was a criminal. A—murderer."

Kallen sipped his drink.

Dragh did the same. The strong spirits warmed his belly.

Kallen stared into the fire. His eyes glassy and far away. "I didn't want to admit that I knew what he was. That he loved the thrill of killing."

"When did you know?" Dragh asked, fearful of his own dangerous love of war.

He loved the thrill of combat, the excitement of battle. The nervous energy of a charge towards the enemy.

Dragh smelled the spirits; they smelled of smoke. He swirled the liquid around the glass, taking another drink.

"I knew when I saw him kill our hunt lead, the dog boy. The boy was out with his spear, and we were hunting boars in the forest. The dog boy was beating at the bushes. His dogs were out corralling the boars. Nestor speared him through the chest. He didn't think I saw it. But I did." Kallen's words were lightly slurred.

His father had drunk much of the spirits before Dragh received his summons at Lucille's.

"I'm sorry, Father," Dragh said.

"For what, boy?" Kallen asked, his voice sharp.

"I know he was your brother. I know he was your family. I'm sorry for what he forced you to do," Dragh said.

"He's forcing me to invade, Dragh. We cannot have the tribes revolt. It would end us. I have to deal with the Easterners."

"Father, I told you, I've sent Hemmelle. He will calm the tribes. He will ensure that Saravas knows we didn't do this."

Kallen sighed. "I wish it was enough. Son, you'll learn the blade is what these people understand. The tribes, they know nothing but strength. We must show ours. They value honour too greatly to turn a blind eye to this."

"Does it not end with Ellis's death? With Nestor's death?" Dragh asked.

Kallen shook his head, looking over to Dragh. "No. It ends when we root out the darkness that they brought to our shores."

"Invading the North, even to deal with the Easterners, will force a war by the tribes. You'll be facing more war! They will react, as they must to any invading force," Dragh argued.

"I know, son. Nestor may very well get what he wanted," Kallen chuckled darkly.

"Let me go!" Dragh said to his father. "Let me go north before the army. Let me go to Saravas and the Tribal Council. I will speak with them, try to repair the honor that they believe is damaged."

Dragh swallowed, watching his father think. He had to convince him. To help save Landor.

"They will believe a Sunborn. A prince."

Kallen looked at Dragh across the top of his glass and sipped at it. "Are you agreeing to come back to the line?"

Dragh knew he was asking if Dragh would lead, if he would take over from his father.

"No, Father. I am not built for it." Dragh looked at his scarred hands. "I am a man of war. I will make my son the leader that you wish for. Give me the Legion, let me rebuild one out of the ashes of the Second, Father."

Kallen watched, his eyes now calculating. "What would you call it? The Second must die for what Nestor did."

"I would call it the Dragon Legion. It would be the sword of Landor."

Dragh felt the nerves again, the dread in his stomach that he'd felt so many times in front of his father. Waiting for judgment from his father.

Hoping for his love or acceptance.

"*Hic Sunt Dracones,*" Kallen said in a murmur. "I will think about it, Dragh."

Dragh felt relief. That was all that he could hope for from his father.

"Give me a month. If I'm not back, tell Mother... tell her that I did this for the Sunborn."

Dragh began to leave his fathers" room, trying not to let the emotion overwhelm him.

"Son," his father barked.

Dragh turned, bracing for anger. "Father?"

"Come back to us," Kallen said. His voice was distant again.

Dragh took a breath. "I will. For you, for my child."

Chapter 26

"I've never seen so many!" Relish said to Geral, Pello, and Zeffo, walking ahead of Dragh.

Dragh looked around. The men of Landor and the armies were here. Not just one Legion, but three. The king planned for war. His job was to hope for the best, but to plan for the worst. The First, who called themselves the Spears, the Seventh, who called themselves the Eagles, and the Tenth, who called themselves the Crows.

All pennants were flying from their flagships, snapping in the wind.

His father had called all of the Legions home. All of the men to Landor's capitol. They were coming now, preparing the ships of Landor's fleet for the journey north. They would repeat the landing of the Second, but this time, they would be there as defenders of the North, not invaders.

The Landor Harbor was full of ships; masts and sails filled the horizon as Dragh and his men walked the docks to their ship.

He'd told his squad of their plans the night before, letting them make their peace in Landor. They had little time to get to the North and find Saravas, the Chieftain.

He'd spent the night with Lucille.

Dragh closed his eyes, letting the salt smell wash over him on the breeze. He felt the warmth of the sun, the kiss of her rays on his face.

He may not return to Landor. He knew that.

"Dragh. It's time," Relish said, putting his hand on Dragh's shoulder.

Dragh shook his head. "Let's go."

Three Legions were to sail. The others called back, but not yet in the capitol, were to guard the homeland. Kallen would disperse them through the nation, pushing many to the North and the foothills of Car Lauch.

"My Lord," a legate from the Tenth Legion gave Dragh a salute as they entered the guarded section of the docks.

"Sunborn!" another called out, saluting.

"What is this?" Dragh asked Relish and the men.

Geral chuckled. "They know you, and they know of your deeds now. The legend grows."

"The legend?" Dragh asked, confused.

"You unmasked a plot to take your family's line. You escaped the men of the East," Relish added.

"They think of you like the generals of old, of the empire," Zeffo said, taking a bite out of an apple and mumbling through a full mouth.

Dragh laughed. The generals of the empire were great men, men who came up with the strategies of war that were still studied today.

The nations had been broken, tribal, and disjointed. The generals were the group of men that had raised the first emperor up. The group broke the tribes and united them. They had been warriors and prophets.

Dragh was secretly proud to be compared to them. He could see the eyes of the soldiers and sailors moving over him. Many nodded, greeting him as they walked the docks.

There was a time when he used to be sneered at. The men of the Second were used to the hatred, the comments from the other legions. Now they nodded and gave the respect of fellow soldiers. Pride swelled in his chest now.

"Out at the end of the third dock, I can see our old ship's head," Pello said to the group, walking ahead of them.

"My Prince!" A voice came from the crow's nest of one of the Ralarian vessels as they approached it.

"El Alera! Come down, Captain," Dragh called up, shading his eyes from the sun.

El Alera spun down a rigging line, his movements nimble despite his tall frame. The captain hung tight to the rigging of his ship, *the Ralaria*, as he quickly spun down to the deck of his ship.

Relish, Geral, Zeffo, and Pello flanked Dragh. They were all dressed for battle, packed for a journey to the North.

El Alera vaulted the rails of *the Ralaria* and landed on the docks, presenting himself to Dragh with a bow.

"I come to you with another favour to ask, El Alera," Dragh said, clasping his hand as the captain offered to shake his.

El Alera took in the men flanking him, then looked back to his men and boats.

"Take your dragon boat, my friend." He gestured to the smaller boat that had been towed behind his three larger vessels.

The dragon boat.

Dragh laughed, as did Relish and the rest of the men. "I spent far too long at the tiller of that little thing to want to get back in it."

"It's better than most of the boats of the Landorian Navy," El Alera jested.

"Half of them are made up of your kin, and I wouldn't expect anything less," Dragh shot back.

"May be, but we only give you the worst of them," El Alera laughed aloud.

"We need you to make the North again, as far up as you can take us," Dragh said, his voice serious.

"Why? Where are you trying to go, my friend?" El Alera asked, curious.

"I need to make it to the Tribal Council. To Saravas," Dragh said.

El Alera looked to Relish. "How was your lady of the Duck's Beak?"

Relish blushed.

Zeffo, Pello, and Geral laughed aloud, making Relish blush harder.

"We need to go. It's our only hope to stop a war," Dragh pleaded.

El Alera sighed.

"You go to your death. I do not take you up that far, it would weigh on my soul," El Alera said, his hand over his heart.

"Take me, or the death of thousands will be on both of us," Dragh explained. "Nestor and Ellis started this war. To end it, I need to get to the far North. I need to get to Saravas and satisfy his honour, beg him if I have to."

El Alera considered Dragh, then looked to Relish. "This man is crazy. What do you say?"

Relish grinned. "I say he's crazy. But he is right. Saravas will come for us, the tribes will come for us. And they will not stop for generations. There is no give in them. All they know is honor, it is their way."

"Yes, I have heard this, it is why I would not transport men of the East. I knew this would bring a blood debt on my people. The Ralarian Islands would be in the minds of their grandchildren, and theirs." El Alera shook his head. "Get on. We leave as soon as the supplies are restocked."

"The legal ones?" Dragh asked, pointing to the spirits loaded under the cover of canvas.

"You looked the other way, my friend. For this, we will give you some to keep you warm. The North is cold, even in the summer. The tribes, worse."

Relish and the rest of them loaded onto the ship. The sailors did not make a comment, knowing that the captain had made a deal.

They all listened without seeming to listen. Dragh admired their skill, appearing not paying attention to what was being said. He'd never mastered it.

They all glared at Pello. Some things were not to be forgiven, no matter the cause.

Dragh shook his head. "Don't let him die, El Alera."

The captain watched his men on deck standing beside Dragh.

"He has my protection. On the sea, that is all that counts."

—--

Dragh wrapped his cloak around his shoulders and over his head.

The cold air had him seeing his own breath, clouds in the sky, as he breathed out. Relish and he stood at the prow of the boat, having done some light sword work to keep their muscles warm and supple.

Relish passed Dragh a water skin.

"What chances do you give us?" Relish asked, watching the dark shore of the north.

They had sailed for two days now, and they were far up the coast of the tribe's lands. Past the Car Lauch Mountains.

Dragh passed back the water swig and offered Relish some salt beef. They both chewed on pieces.

The Ralarians had provided them with supplies and rations far surpassing any food the Second had on their last journey.

Cruze, the first mate, had laughed when Dragh pointed it out, commenting that perhaps that's why they were so weak.

Dragh shrugged. "Hemmelle, if he made it, may have bought us some time. Some respite. I do not know if we have a chance, if he did not make it."

"What happens to us if he failed?"

"You know what happens, Relish. The tribes, they will do what they do once the laws of hospitality are done. You heard Teffal. He and his men were ready to kill us," Dragh said.

Relish clapped Dragh on the shoulder. "This place will not be our death, that I know."

"How?" Dragh asked, confused.

"Old Azel, he told me my death would be defending the line of the Sunborn."

"Shit, you're finished then, once the old man has spoken," Dragh said in jest.

Relish did not laugh, clearly bothered by the matter. "It smacks of truth. When he told me, I don't know. I felt like it was right. Like he was right."

"I know... He felt like a man out of time, or of time," Dragh said, remembering the feeling that Azel left him with.

"What of the men of the East?" Relish asked, changing the subject.

"Father is going to be sending three Legions north. We left a month before them."

"And if the tribes do not agree with us, do not believe us?" Relish asked.

"If they kill me, an heir to Landor, the armies will go to war with them. To the last man. If the tribes want to fight, Father understands that there is only total victory. The tribal people will not accept anything less than total destruction."

Relish whistled and spit off the prow.

The wind off the land was cold on their faces. The sweat they'd worked up was cooling their skin and bodies. Dragh could feel it in his bones.

"Generations at war. That's what my destiny is," Relish broke the silence after a time.

"I know, that's how I feel. I am a sword and a shield. I'd prefer the latter," Dragh agreed.

"We are what we are, brother," Relish said, his hand on Dragh's shoulder.

Relish watched the land as it passed the ship.

"I just hope Hemmelle made it," Relish exclaimed.

"Me too, Relish, me too," Dragh said, imagining all of the things the tribes would do to him.

Chapter 27

"I would say that I will be there for you when you are done, Dragh Sunborn, but I do not know that you will be alive to leave this place," El Alera chuckled. "You also owe me three favors, my friend."

They were disembarking *the Ralaria*, set as close to the shore as the cutter would go.

El Alera and Dragh were at the rail; Dragh's men had pushed off.

"I only owe you two," Dragh protested.

"The other thing. The thing you asked for..." El Alera looked over his shoulder to a squabble on his boat.

"I must go, the men, they do not like being in this land... It is... Let us say, we want to be back to the ocean. She calls to us."

"Remember, El Alera, make sure it burns," Dragh said.

El Alera's face was dark for a moment. "I understand. Are you sure?"

Dragh nodded. "I return with my father, victorious, or I will not return."

El Alera pulled Dragh in as he stuck his hand out. "Survive, my friend."

Dragh gave one last nod to the crew that had seen them safely to Landor and then back to the North. He pushed up and over the side of the boat. Hand over hand down the rope ladder, fighting the twist of the rope with each step.

The water was biting cold. Small flakes of snow began to fall around him. He waded to shore with his men, then onto the beach.

The crescent moon beach was empty of life. Sand and rock led to a forest and scrub further up the shore. The green was turning here; leaves were yellowing and turning with the new cold temperatures as the season changed.

"Haul it in," Dragh said to his men, dropping his pack.

Relish, Geral, Zeffo, and Pello were already holding the rope that the Ralarians had given them.

Dragh watched as the boat was cut loose from the tie lines of *the Ralaria*.

"Heave!" Relish called, pulling on the rope.

Dragh watched for a moment as the dragon boat that had been hauled behind them moved on the waves.

"Dragh! We need a hand!." Relish called out, pulling on the rope.

The boat was moving towards them now, a couple of lengths away.

Dragh shook his head. "Stop."

They stopped pulling, looking over at Dragh.

"The Pit are you talking about?" Zeffo asked.

Dragh pointed out to sea.

Three fire arrows arced in the sky. They burned bright yellow, and orange flames tailed them.

"NO!" Relish and Pello both shouted.

The arrows, hanging high in the sky, turned downward, thudding into the deck of the dragon boat with the sound of a hammer hitting an anvil.

The blaze took her quick.

Relish and the rest of the men fell to their knees.

The flames licked the floorboards first, then up the masts, and then they consumed the sails stowed on the mast rails. The flames, a clean white smoke, a beacon to the Gods, shot into the sky.

"NOO!" Pello shouted again, rising up from his knees and pointing at Dragh.

"We survive, or we die. There is no escaping this fate, men," Dragh said to them. The smell of the burning ship reached them on shore.

Dragh could smell the hardwood smoke. It reminded him of the fire in his father's study and the spirits they drank.

"Why?" Relish said, shaking his head.

Dragh looked around at his men.

They looked at the burning boat as the fire consumed it. Their eyes reflected the burning boat.

"There is only one path for us. Forward. We save Hemmelle, we convince the Council of Chieftains that it was not Landor that did this to the North. That is our only hope at surviving."

Zeffo spit on the ground. "We could have escaped! It took us weeks to escape last time!"

Dragh nodded. "And if we'd slunk away in the middle of the night, we'd be killing the men, women, and children of Landor. The North would rise up and descend on us like a plague. This place, the North, it has more power than you can imagine. They are just too fractured to wield it. But if we let them believe that it was Landor, if these menaces from the East keep killing with our red and gold, they will come for us. Believe me."

Pello gripped his brother's shoulder.

Zeffo halfheartedly pushed his brother away.

"How far?" Geral asked.

Dragh smiled. "A week or two. Could be more."

"Let us begin," Geral said, hoisting his pack.

Dragh did the same, patting Geral on the shoulder as he walked by.

Flakes of snow were falling and melting on the ground. The cold wind blew down across the Car Lauch and through the hills.

Dragh pulled up his coat around his neck.

Winter was coming.

CHAPTER 28

"**D**own!" Relish cried out as they crested the hill.

Dragh and the rest of the men dropped to the ground, just behind Relish. The ground was hard and unforgiving as they dropped.

"Ooof," Zeffo exclaimed.

Dragh didn't look back, knowing that the sudden change in seasons had made the going hard. They'd had fires every night in the last week to keep warm enough to sleep.

They were close to the spires; Dragh could see them in the distance. They had travelled for leagues and leagues. They'd come across three villages, all of them empty. Two of them were burned, with only husks of buildings left.

Snow and rain followed them each day, replacing the fog of the previous season.

Cloaks were worn day and night. Dragh and his men slept close to the fires.

Two massive spires rose on either side of a large valley, far north of the Gallas Forest. The spires were jagged, sheared off at the top, two sheer faces, a gap between them. A door into the world of the far North.

Dragh inched forward, crawling on his belly with his forearms and legs.

"Cavalry of red and gold!" Relish whispered, pointing to the west.

Dragh focused on the west, a rolling landscape where he could just see the rise and fall of men on horses. The glint of colours far enough away that Dragh had to trust Relish.

"Landor will not be here for at least two weeks. It's the East," Dragh grunted.

"Watch," Relish said, excitement in his voice.

Dragh stained to see. "What is it?"

Rising out of a valley to the south, a mass of tribesmen flew into the flank of the men of the East.

Dragh could hear the clash from where they lay.

Geral, Zeffo, and Pello had made their way up to the lip of the hill.

"Zuffier above. I didn't know they had that many," Pello commented.

"Must be three squads of horse."

Dragh counted as best he could.

"They've leveled the men of the East. Gods," Relish said.

Dragh watched. None of the men of the East were still on their horses. The pass of the tribes horsemen had been absolute, cutting down the men of the East with one pass.

"They are turning," Relish said.

"Pit," Zeffo took the words from Dragh's mouth.

Dragh looked at Relish. "You knew?"

Relish nodded. "They are coming for us."

"How long have they been out there?" Dragh asked Relish.

Relish thought on it, quiet, before responding to Dragh. "I haven't been able to see them, but I've felt them. They were close to us. They know we are here."

As the horsemen thundered east, Dragh made the decision.

"Everyone, get up," he said, trying to keep the nerves from his voice.

His bowels were liquid. This was it. He had a chance to make peace with the tribes, and this was the first step. The men of the tribes were on their way. He wasn't going to face them with arms. He knew then that if he did, they would answer arms with death.

"No one raises their weapons," Dragh said.

"What the Pit are you talking about?" Pello said, both eyebrows raised.

"If we look like a threat, they will level us. I will give them no reason. Remember why we are here. We are here for Hemmelle and Landor. If you die now, you'll help neither."

Grumbles went through the group, but they kept their hands off their weapons as they got up off the ground.

They tightened around Dragh, as if to protect him.

The thunderous sound of more than one hundred horses became a wave as they cantered towards the group.

The horses and men rose and fell out of each hill and valley like water over the land. The column of horse was so long that while its middle was in a valley, its front and rear were visible on opposing rises.

They moved as one, like men who'd grown up on horseback.

Dragh stood tall for his men. He could see Relish's and Zeffo's shoulders shake.

The last time they'd faced a heavy horse charge, they'd lost almost their entire squad.

The horses charged up the hill towards them, the earth shaking under Dragh's feet. Dragh took a deep breath, the crisp air smelling of pine.

He could almost smell the leather of the saddles, the lather of the horses, and the sweat of the warriors astride the horses as the tribes bore down on Dragh's men.

Dragh fought to keep from leaping away from the horses coming at them.

At the very last moment, the horses split to either side of Dragh and his men.

Dragh gritted his teeth, knowing he could be facing death again.

The horses moved past them. There was wind on Dragh's face as the enemy thundered past his squad, horse after horse. Then, as the last of them came, the two columns of horses turned outward at the bottom of the hill. Both pushed back up to the Landorians.

A wall of horses reined in, facing Dragh and his friends.

Spears were leveled at them, ready to strike.

Dragh went still, praying his friends had the sense to not provoke the Tribes,

"I told you last time we met that I'd kill you if I saw you again." A tall tribesman dismounted from his horse, tossing his reins to his neighbor.

"Teffal, I come with a message of peace from the king," Dragh said, finding his voice.

Dragh put his hands up, looking around at his men, and then stepped forward out of the scrum of them.

"I'm not interested in your silver tongue, boy," Teffal said, stepping to Dragh with his hand on his sword hilt.

"We've been betrayed. I beg you, please hear me." Dragh kept his hands at his back.

"I don't doubt your bravery, just your honesty," Teffal said, spitting on the ground. "Only a fool would return to this land without reason. Speak quickly before I have my men kill you and rid this place of more Landorians."

Dragh took a breath. "Thank you, Teffal."

The horses behind Teffal neighed and pawed at the ground, kicking back grass and dirt from the frozen earth. Their breath was hot, steam issuing as they snorted in the cool air. Steam rose off their rumps.

"The men you just killed. You know they are not Landorians, don't you?" Dragh asked.

Teffal stiffened. "Your Hemmelle. He made such claims. Why do they wear your colors if they are not your people?"

Dragh tried to suppress his relief at hearing Hemmelle's name.

"My uncle, the General of the Second, betrayed us. I was not honest with you before. I am Dragh Sunborn."

Teffal and his people all reacted to the name. They all knew what that meant.

Spears pointed at Dragh, raised, not all the way, but some.

Dragh knew it was something different to kill a prince. It weighed differently than any ruffian. He could see understanding dawn on Teffal's face.

"I am here because those men were hired by my uncle to sow dissent between the tribes and Landor. They were meant to work the tribes up into attacking Landor. And to force Landor to commit her armies to the North. To destroy us both."

"They have done their job. Your Second's grave is not far from the Gallas Forest," Teffal spit back.

"And you don't think it odd that the tribes didn't have to kill the Second? That they were killed without your help?" Dragh fixed Teffal with a look of anger.

Teffal narrowed his eyes at Dragh.

Dragh could tell he was getting to Teffal.

"I need to speak with your King Saravas, and the Council of Chieftains."

"Outsiders are not welcome at the Council of Chieftains."

"Saravas leads your people?" Dragh asked.

"He is the shield of the tribes. The Chieftain of the Argu."

"Take me to him, please. If you do not, our people will destroy each other," Dragh pleaded.

Teffal paced in front of Dragh, his hands behind his back. "I will take you to the Spires. You can come as prisoners or not at all. I make no promises about Saravas. He will see you, or he will not."

"Pit's sake," Relish said.

Teffal stopped and looked at Relish. "It's this or die, little man."

"Are we at war, Teffal?" Dragh asked, thinking of how he and his men might be treated. He knew of the atrocities that the tribes could commit.

The Tribes were known to do horrible things to their enemies. Striking fear into the armies of Landor even. Dragh and his men knew what could face them.

Teffal said nothing, simply waiting for Dragh to decide.

Dragh held up his hands again. "We need to stop this war, Teffal. We will go."

Dragh looked back and nodded to his men.

He prayed to the Gods that he was making the right decision.

Chapter 29

"Zufier above," Relish swore.

Dragh, Geral, Zeffo, Pello, and Relish crested the last rise to the Valley of the Spires. The majesty of the place struck them as its full view came into focus for them. The two peaks on either side were monuments, and vast and terrible-looking spires reached up and into the sky. Up close, Dragh couldn't see their peaks; they rose high into the sky through the cloud cover. Beyond the spires Dragh could see a great river, raging with rapids and the spray of white waters.

The inside of the spires looked to be clean-cut faces, but the closer Dragh got, the more detail Dragh could see. They were smooth but fractured, and fissures were spiderwebbed up and down either side. The rough rock was granite, like the mountains of the Car Lauch.

Inside the two spires was a stone circle. Large pillars of stone were all placed about in a circle, with a large lower stone in the exact center.

"What is this place?" Zeffo said, awe in his voice.

"This is the Valley of the Gods, to you, the Spires," one of Teffal's tribeswomen said, pushing Zeffo forward with the flank of his horse.

"The Tribes believe the Gods touched down here. That when Zufier and his kin shot down from the heavens, they cleaved this mountain in half, creating the spires," Dragh said, low and to his men.

The tribeswoman who had pushed Zeffo said nothing, but didn't lash out at Dragh.

The Argu were around them, travelling in a long column. Dragh and his men were kept in the middle of the column of the Argu.

The occasional hit with the flank of a horse and the butt of a spear was endured by his men without complaint.

Different Tribes were arrayed all around the valley. Ringed all around the place, large tents were set up. The sigils of the tribes on banners flew over the largest tents.

"Gods, there must be a hundred tribes," Pello commented.

Dragh said nothing, not wanting to give away his knowledge, or lack thereof, in front of the Argu.

They moved forward down the lip of the valley. Dragh could smell wafting smoke and fat burning in the cookfires below. There seemed to be more people than would fit into Landor. A massive group of tribes all mashed together.

This was something he'd never thought he'd see. The tribes were so fractious. He'd been taught that there was no common ground between them. Too much hate, too much history. He'd seen their fights before. To the death in most cases.

The column stopped just outside of the first camp overlooking the whole valley.

Teffal trotted back, reining in to a stop in front of his prisoners. Teffal hopped off his horse, dismounting with a dance-like grace.

"You'll be here for the night. You will camp with the Argu. My people. You will be watched, so do not try anything."

"Saravas must have some power, to bring these people together," Dragh commented to Teffal. He looked up at the mounted man.

Teffal nodded to Dragh. "He does."

Women, children, and warriors had begun to notice Dragh, exclaiming and pointing at the men of Landor.

"I thought a gathering of the tribes would be for a war, Teffal. Why all the women and children?" Dragh asked.

Teffal sighed, as if annoyed by an annoying question from a child. "We do not gather the tribes without their families. Why would you decide on the fate of the tribes without family? It will affect all of them."

"What about the womenfolk to fight?" Relish asked.

Teffal laughed. "You Landorians, you fight only with men? So simple of you." Teffal motioned around at the Argu. "My people fight for the Tribes. All of them. The Tribes are not just men, but the women and children too. Our women know that to defend the Tribes is to defend the future. Their future and ours. Do they deserve any less a chance?"

Relish said nothing in return to Teffal, looking around at the warriors in the camp.

Dragh looked around, amazed at the people. So many of them, all of them wearing the distinct patterns of their tribes. Many of them mingled with other tribes. "How do you stop the blood feuds?"

Teffal looked back to Dragh. "It is a sacred place. All tribes know this."

"But how do you enforce the laws on such a large group? They could settle their blood feuds and their anger so quickly." Dragh was confused.

"They would not dare. This place is sacred to the Gods. Not just us. To break the peace would mean to be an outcast from your tribe. No one would," Teffal explained further.

"What of the stone in the center of the ring?" Relish asked, glancing at the people around him with unease.

Teffal's face darkened. "The shaman tells us that there was once darkness in the North. That we did things to appease the Gods when they were angry with us. Many generations ago, the ground was drenched in blood."

Dragh watched Teffal, obviously uncomfortable with the subject. He waved Relish off from asking any more questions.

"Do not stray too far from the camp. To the other tribes," Teffal said, starting to walk away.

"Why not walk the valley?" Pello asked from behind them.

Teffal turned, annoyance on his face. "Because the laws of our people do not apply to you."

"Are we not under the protection of your king and you?" Pello challenged.

Teffal raised his eyebrow. "There are tribesmen that might slip a blade between your ribs and let you bleed out."

"That's the same as killing us," Pello said.

"Then pray that you listen well," Teffal said, vaulting to his horse and kicking it into action.

Most of the Argu rode off with Teffal, leaving Dragh and his men with their guard.

Five men dismounted around them, ushering them into the war camp of the Argo.

The smells of the tribe's cooking fires and the roasting meat wafted over the camp. The Argu lived sparsely, few tents and fewer fires.

Dragh moved with their guard, noting the large man who the Argu all deferred to.

"You'll stay here," the big man said, his long-braided hair reaching past his chest.

They reached a single tent with a small fire burning outside of it.

One log was rolled up on its side in front of the fire.

The tent flap moved, a sparse face emerging.

"About time," Hemmelle said, smiling to Dragh and the Landorians.

Chapter 30

"Watch the big one," Hemmelle said to Dragh as they walked.

The minders of the Argu would let them walk the outer rim of the valley, keeping Dragh and Hemmelle well back from the other tribes. The big one had a large scar on his face, down the side, beside his eye.

Dragh had taken to walking the rim with Hemmelle.

"Truly, they listened to you?" Dragh asked his friend.

"I've told you, yes. The Argu listened. The big one, he was always there. But never Saravas. He has not come. They wait for him and for the rest of the tribes before the Council of Chieftains meet." Hemmelle stopped, catching his breath.

"How bad was it?" Dragh asked.

Hemmelle looked over, his face tight with emotion. He pulled his cloak tighter around his shoulder.

"Sorry. We don't have to talk about it." Dragh looked down at the ground. He felt the emotions welling up inside of him at what he'd asked his friend to do.

Hemmelle walked on, wheezing as he went.

Dragh noticed an improvement in Hemmelle's stamina, just from the walking they'd done over the last few days. He worried about his friend, soaked in the guilt of what he'd asked him to risk.

The tribes had beaten him, starved him. They didn't believe his story.

But they'd listened.

And then the Argu found him. He'd been taken here and kept ever since.

"You need to understand, the Argu, they are not the enemy that you think."

"Didn't they do this to you?" Dragh asked.

"The Ambi, they dress in green, down below the Galas Forest. They found me— they were not kind." Hemmelle paused again, motioning to turn back towards the Argu's camp.

Dragh watched the minders. Two followed them, a man and a woman. The man had a large scar across his eye, the woman deferred to him, looking to him with each move the two Landorians made.

He nodded to them both as they passed them.

The minders nodded back.

"The Argu, they took me from the Ambi. They fed me, listened to my tale," Hemmelle explained.

They walked, slowly. Their breath billowing like fog in the cold crisp air.

Dragh watched children play in the valley. Gathering in groups and playing war with each other. The boys and girls both fought, ran, and played together. Bloody noses, hits to the head, tumbles and falls. Nothing slowed the kids down. They played, fought, and had fun.

Laughter was all around them.

Dragh was amazed at their numbers. The Tribes were a larger nation than even Landor. If they would work together, fight together, they could take the nations for their own.

"But they listened to you? They believed you?" Dragh asked. They'd walked the rim of the valley daily. He knew it well now.

"Aye, they listened. I know not if the tribes will." Hemmelle looked back at the minders. Then, in a lower voice, he nodded to the people in the valley. "They are a mob. A mob of men and women who follow their chieftains. Chieftains are like priests, what they say goes."

A group of tribesmen and tribeswomen were making their way up the rim, arguing as they went. Dragh saw them and then went back to his walking with Hemmelle.

He wanted to speak with them, but he knew the minders would not allow it.

Dragh nodded, and the uncertainty of their future clouded his mind. He clasped his hands behind his back. "They won't let me speak with the chieftains yet. They are waiting for something. They ignore me when I ask questions."

Hemmlle chuckled, his laugh full of phlegm.

Dragh focused on his friend, trying to ignore the noise from the group coming up the rim from the tribes.

Dragh cringed. His friend sounded like he'd endured more time on the mountain. The Ambi had taken their hate out on him.

"HOLD!" the shout came from behind them.

Dragh reached for his sword but came up empty.

He looked around, knowing the sound a warrior made when danger was afoot.

Two from the group of tribesmen and tribeswomen had broken off and lunged at Hemmelle and Dragh.

Dragh could see the glint of a weapon in their hands.

He cursed the Gods, knowing that if he were armed, he could protect himself. Protect Hemmelle.

Dragh shoved his frail friend away as the tribesmen came at them.

He could see the glint of murder in their eyes as they came at Dragh.

Hemmelle fell to the ground as Dragh pushed forward, ever pushing into the danger, into the swing to shorten the blow.

He knew that this was it. His time was now.

The tribesmen shouted in another language.

Dragh bowled into the first man, trying to push him to the ground. He hooked his leg in the other man's and pushed forward.

He caught the two tribesmen surprised and with his forward momentum, Dragh shot his foot behind the tribesman's legs and carried them to the ground.

Dragh shouted in pain; a searing sharp pain lanced through his arm.

He grappled with the man he fell on, trying to grab his arms to stop the blade from doing any more damage.

The man struggled, shouting at him as they rolled on the ground.

"Dragh!" he heard Hemmelle's warning.

Before he could look up, strong hands gripped Dragh and yanked him up.

Dragh found himself on the ground, thrown from on top of the tribesmen.

He bounded back up, looking for his enemy.

In front of him were the two minders, swords out, pointing at the two attackers.

The one Dragh had tackled was still on the ground. The other was standing, his dagger dropped, held at sword point by the bigger Argu minder.

The big man nodded to the tribeswoman. "The debt must be paid."

The woman nodded, her mouth a tight line.

"Hold out your hand," the woman said.

Dragh said nothing, watching.

They'd warned Dragh and his men not to mingle with the tribes. What happened when the tribes mingled with them?

"HOLD IT OUT!" she shouted.

The man on the ground held out his hand, dropping his dagger.

Dragh could see his blood on the blade.

The group from the tribes was watching now from a distance. They were far enough away that they could claim not to be involved, but close enough to hear what was being said.

"Tell your Chieftain that the men of Landor are under the Argu's protection."

The man on the ground nodded. His face white with fear.

"And for spilling their blood," the Argu tribeswoman said, low, but loud enough for the crowd to hear.

The woman took up her sword in both hands and swung down with force.

The man on the ground screamed, the blade slicing clean through his arm.

His hand dropped to the ground, blood spurting from the stump.

The other attacker lunged forward but was put down with a punch to his cheek with the minder's off hand.

Dragh watched it all with confusion. The Argu were hurting their own.

Did they really value their honor this much? Enough to kill their own, perhaps?

The second attacker gathered up his friend who'd passed out from shock, wrapping the stump where their hand was cut off with a cloth.

The Argu minders watched it all, letting it happen.

The Argu who'd cut the arm of the attacker glared at Dragh. His scar glinted white against his flushed face.

"Why'd you do that?" Dragh asked.

She looked at Dragh with anger written on her face. "Because you are here, I spilled my brethren's blood."

"Why?"

The tribeswoman shook her head. "Honour demands blood. We Argu pay it."

The big Argu that had stood by, watching the event, stepped forward and nodded to the tribeswoman. "It's okay Genne."

Dragh looked around. Two more men from the Argu had run from where they watched, swords at the ready.

They watched as the attacking tribespeople retreated.

The men watched the bigger Argu, waiting for his words.

"Saravas," Dragh pulled his hand from his arm. Blood coated it.

The big minder who'd defended them stepped forward. His sword still in hand.

"The Laretti. They will not bother us again," he said.

Dragh looked back at the group of tribespeople retreating down the rim with their injured.

"It does not bode well for an alliance," Dragh said, searching Saravas's face.

Saravas said nothing, turning, and walking back towards the Argu camp.

Chapter 31

"You bring no army, no warriors with you?" Saravas motioned for Dragh to sit at a fire pit away from his men. The coals glowed red.

Dragh looked at his men behind him, they sat, wrapped in cloaks, watching Dragh and Saravas.

"This is my Legion," he paused. "My Dragon Legion."

The sun was setting across the rim of the Valley of the Gods, casting shadow between the pillars. The wind was cold on Dragh's face.

"What of your people? If the chieftains agree to Landor's terms, do you have enough to go to war?" Dragh pushed the big man.

"There are many more tribes, but these are the largest. For every one of us there are a dozen more in the North. All of them are proud of their heritage. All strong," Saravas said.

Men were on either side of the Chieftain, the Argu protecting their leader.

Dragh nodded. "My father always feared the North. He said it was the graveyard of empires."

"Our histories tell us that we've never been defeated." Saravas nudged at the fire.

The new wood ignited in the blaze, throwing yellow and white light out where there had only been glowing red and orange.

"You've been invaded," Dragh said.

"Aye, but we are still here. Free. Where are the men that invaded? Where are the empires?" Sarvas gave Dragh a mocking grin.

"Gone," Dragh admitted.

"We think of the future, unlike your kind. We think in generations, my friend. And we will never lose," Saravas said, rubbing his hands together.

Dragh nodded. "When will I speak to them?"

Saravas rubbed at his chin. "Soon."

"My father, he will come. You know that?" Dragh asked.

Saravas nodded. "And we will decide the fate of the North then."

Dragh shook his head. "How can you waste so much time? Zufier above. We need to move now."

Saravas held his hand up as his Argu crept closer to the fire. Their hands on their hilts. "Dragh. You are our guest. You have rights, but only from us. I will defend you, but do not insult my people or my ways."

Dragh took a breath to collect himself. "Aye."

Saravas dipped his head. "I will give you and your men a token of trust. And in this, you will have to trust me. The Council of the Chieftains will meet. And you will have your time."

"If I live that long," Dragh said, rubbing at his arm where the dagger had sliced into him. He could feel the tender wound. It was wrapped up, but still fresh from the day.

"This will go a long way, but don't betray my trust or I will feed you to the Larretti."

Dragh nodded.

Sarvas motioned a man forward from his side.

"Here is your sword and dagger. We give them to you in faith that you will not use them against the tribes." Saravas nodded to his man who handed Dragh his weapons.

Dragh slung the belt around his waist; the familiar weight of his weapons gave him a comfort he didn't realize he'd missed.

"The tribes will honor the same?" Dragh asked.

Saravas gave away nothing, his face a stone slab. "The Council of the Chieftains will decide. We are the sword."

Dragh wanted to push Saravas for more information, but the man turned and walked away.

Dragh watched as all but two of the Argu melted into the darkness of the night.

CHAPTER 32

"Welcome, Prince of Landor. Dragh Sunborn," Azal said to the mostly silent group of men and women of the Tribes.

Dragh looked around at the regal-looking men and women, the obvious chieftains. Members of their courts stayed with their chieftains in tight groups, no more than five with each leader.

Whispers began, and an advisor leaned forward to speak into their chieftain's ears.

"He comes to speak with us about the menace that we face. To sue for peace!" Saravas said to the tribes around him, speaking from the centre of the ring beside Azal.

Dragh had not met with Saravas again. It had been back to the angry minders like Teffal and Genne. The Argu had confined Dragh and his men to the camp after the attempt on their lives.

The circle of stone was lit with torches, throwing light into each nook and cranny of the circle.

Whispers grew louder until Saravas called for silence.

"You are the menace! You and your people!" The chieftain of the Leretti shouted.

Dragh nodded to the man; his hostility naked for the Landorians.

Dragh knew that not all wounds healed. Nothing he could say would help. This he knew from the animosity that the Leretti would have for Landor. The Leretti suffered under their reign of the tribes.

The Argu men were the sword and shields of the tribes. They surrounded the large stone circle, on its perimeter, guarding the gathering. All were dressed in furs, with weapons in hand.

The stone circle was filled with men from all of the tribes.

"Yarrs would not stand for this treatment of a guest. He has the rights of hospitality, Venatos! He spoke for Dragh before his death at the hand of the East. He was a man of honor. Do not insult his memory with your actions." Azal said.

Dragh felt tears tugging at his face as Azal spoke kind words for the empty seat where Yarrs should have been seated.

The tribes all spoke kind words of the old man.

As Azal spoke to the Leretti, he spoke of Chieftain Venatos and his son Karn. The chieftain glared at Dragh.

The son, Karn looked on impassively. His well-muscled frame spoke of violence to Dragh.

Saravas sat close to the center; the large scar across his eyes and his hawkish features gave him a foreboding look in the torchlight.

"Thank you, Azal. We bow to your wisdom and we ask the Gods for their guidance." Saravas made a sign of thanks and then one for the Gods.

The rest of the chieftains thanked Azal and repeated the movement of thanking the Gods. When it got to Dragh, Azal murmured something and waved them on.

"Why is the flatlander here?" Venatos asked.

Saravas looked at Venatos. "Keep your tongue until it is your turn to speak, Venatos, or I'll have one of my Argu see you out."

The eldest son, Karn, stepped forward in response to the threat.

The circle was silent with the anticipated violence; all of them knew of war and could smell the impending conflict.

"I invited him here, Venatos. He is under the protection of the Argu," Saravas spoke to the Council.

That seemed to calm most of them, nodding their approval to Saravas. Venatos glared at Saravas for a moment before pushing his son back to his side.

"Now, to business," Saravas said to the men gathered for the meeting. He nodded to Teffal.

Teffal cleared his throat. "The men of the Argu can report that there are men massing in the south, coming from the ocean. There is also a contingent of men in the interior. They ride their horses through the territories, killing and razing our villages to the ground."

"That's my…" Dragh started, before Azal jammed his staff into Dragh's side.

"The Landorian would like to apologize to the Council," Azal said.

Dragh coughed, trying to catch his breath. He took the hint. He was not meant to speak until he was called on.

"As I was saying, we are beset through the south. A mass of Landorians were killed in an armed camp after they invaded the North some months ago. We have reports from the survivors that they were attacked by men from the East." Teffal said to the crowd.

"Men from the East?" Venatos said, scorn dripping from his voice.

Venatos looked around the circle in the moonlight, making eye contact with those around him. His face mocked Teffal.

Dragh was straining to say something, like he used to as a child in his father's court.

"I have a report from a survivor that the raiders were from the East. The Landorians were not responsible," Teffal explained.

Murmurs erupted from around the circle; men were angry with what was being said.

Dragh could feel tension in the tribes.

"Lies!" called a man from the Belge. Neighbours of the Leretti.

Venatos smiled at Dragh.

The circle erupted into chaos again, voices overlapping until Dragh could not understand anything being said.

"ENOUGH!" Saravas shouted over them all, standing at the altar.

All quieted to hear Saravas. Teffal stepped up beside Saravas, a look of anger on his face.

"My men have reported to you. There are strange men in the North. Not just Landorians. Their entire Second Legion was killed." Saravas stopped and looked around. "Unless one of you would like to claim the kill, then you will shut up and listen."

None challenged Saravas as he started to pace back and forth.

Dragh could see a look of hate in some of the eyes around the circle.

"I have seen the damage done. I know that the Landorians invaded us. They invaded us because they thought we were a threat. They know our strength and they know that we would fight them to the last man or woman."

Some quiet agreement came from Saravas's supporters.

Dragh could see the divide in the meeting. Men looked to Saravas, and others to Venatos, for their lead.

The only among them impartial were the shaman. Some strange men like Azal. Quiet, looking around and through the men in the circle.

"I have seen the blood eagle. The mark of their people," Saravas said.

No one spoke. They all stiffened. Knowing what had happened to Yarrs.

Azal spoke, his voice claiming respect. The rest of the Council was quiet. "You all know me. I am Azal. Not of a tribe, but of the tribes. I speak for the shaman. I speak for the past and the future."

Azal moved to the center of the circle. "You know the spires from our stories. Our Gods touched down here. Two of them are encased in stone on either side of the valley. The spires and the valley gave birth to us."

Azal ran his hand over the altar stone, stained brown with blood. "I spilled blood here for the Gods," he said, looking up. "I spilled blood here for the tribes to the Gods. For that I was cursed with life." Azal chuckled then. "I was cursed with life, so listen to me now. I have seen what will be. We are in peril. We face many enemies. The East has sent men. I know their blood magic's scent. The Sunborns have also sent Legions. They react with might because that is all they have known since the time of the empire.

"I have seen the men of the horse roll over this land, sowing it with blood. I ask you all, give your swords to Saravas. We must fight the East *with* the men of Landor. Else we will be crushed by them, and generations of our people will fight them, until neither stand."

Azal stood in the circle now, pleading with the men of the tribes. The chieftains looked on.

"The blood of my people demands BLOOD!" Venatos shouted at them, stepping forward. "I care not for your tales, Argu. Landor has spilled my people's blood, and my honor will be satisfied!"

Saravas sighed, his anger fraying his voice around the edges. "Then fight the men of the East, they did this."

"No, *he* did this, and his people." Venatos pointed at Dragh. "I claim him as my blood right. My honor demands that he pay in blood."

"Then you will fight him for the honor of his blood. Man to man," Azal said to Venatos.

Dragh looked at Azal and Saravas. Then back to Venatos. "We did not do this, Venatos. I am of the Second, my people were killed by the men of the East, just as yours were."

"Your people have been killing mine for generations. You think because you tell some tale that I will put aside what you've done? Pah." Venatos spit on the ground.

Dragh shook his head. "We offer you freedom, freedom from Landor. Independence!"

Venatos's face turned red in the moonlight. "We are free."

Dragh bit back a retort. "My father, he offers you an alliance, a peace between our people and a freedom from the crown of Landor. I am here because if we let them, these people from the East, they will destroy us all from the inside."

Murmurs told Dragh he was winning some of the tribes over. He gazed around the circle.

"The Argu are for the peace," Saravas spoke up.

Dragh noded to him. "Thank you, Chieftain."

"Stop speaking, flatlander," Venatos said to Dragh. "My champion Karn will fight in my stead." Venatos put his hand on the large man's shoulder.

Dragh looked at Azal and Saravas.

"The laws of our tribes allow for combat in blood feuds," Saravas said by way of explanation, his voice on edge with Venatos's upset of the council's meeting.

"I'll fight the spawn to shut the old man up. But he commits his sword to fight with Landor if I win," Dragh said, his voice icy, meeting Venatos's gaze across the circle of stone.

"This must be settled now," Azal said to Saravas.

Saravas gave a tight nod to Azal and then one to Dragh. "Kill him. We need the Belge. They will only follow if the Leretti and Venatos fight."

Dragh felt the twisting in his stomach, the usual nerves before a battle. "I'll make it quick."

—-

The Council of the Chieftains moved quickly to form a battle circle around the two men, a mass of flesh serving as their boundaries in the fight to come. They moved in silence, a seriousness that Dragh had only seen in the lines of battle.

This was a solemn affair under the moon.

Dragh was surprised at the speed of it. Teffal and Saravas were with him; not his men. He wished Hemmelle or Relish were with him. "Need to piss," he said to them.

"Then you are alive and ready for battle," Saravas said, smiling.

Dragh laughed. "I guess it doesn't matter if you are from the tribes, we all speak the language of death."

Dragh removed his weapon belt and cloak, pulling at his sword.

Teffal handed Dragh his sword pommel. "Take my blade, Dragh."

Dragh let his blade go and accepted the offer. Sharing a look with the Argu. Teffal still hated Dragh, but there was a respect in his face Dragh had not seen before.

"And my dagger. Her name is Drago," Saravas said to Dragh, handing him a large knife with a wicked curve on its tip. The blade was heavy, with a large leather handle. "She's a dragon's tooth from the forges of my people in the spires."

Dragh held the dagger in his off hand, thanking Saravas.

"Don't stop moving. Karn will attack like a bear, do not let him corner you," Teffal said of Dragh's opponent.

Dragh went to the quiet place, his mind emptying of the men in front of him as he walked to the edge of the circle marked by bodies. He stared across the circle to Karn, the massive man of the Leretti tribe.

Karn stared at him, his chest bare, his only clothing a loincloth. He held a battle axe in two hands. The head was double-bladed and curved on both sides. Karn's body was covered in scars, his chest marked out with tribal scars, signifying his ascension into manhood.

Dragh breathed in and out, letting the nerves spread through his body. He rolled out his shoulders. He worked through scales of the sword, flashing his blade up and down, high guard, mid guard, and low guards.

Karn swung his axe back and forth. He watched Dragh with cold eyes.

Dragh remembered Hemmelle's advice to him, an axe wielder himself. "Don't ever let the blade trap you."

"A blood feud will end with DEATH!" Azal decreed, standing in the centre of the circle.

Dragh thought he saw a glint in Azal's eyes.

"Are you ready?" Azal looked to Dragh and then to Karn. Both nodded. "Begin." Azal moved back to join the press of bodies that formed the circle.

Karn bellowed his war cry, raising his axe above his head as he barreled towards Dragh.

Dragh knew the move would come; he'd faced many axe wielders in his life. He was still standing; they were below the earth now.

Dragh rolled to the side as the first blow of the axe tried to fall on him. The momentum of Karn took him past where Dragh stood, allowing Dragh to stab Drago into the man's side. Not deep, but deep enough that he drew blood.

The giant bellowed in rage and swung back at Dragh, who had both his dagger and sword in his hands.

Dragh raised his blades up in a cross and took the axe swing, deflecting it to the side.

"*Move with the power, do not get in its way,*" Hemmelle's voice came to him.

Dragh poked his sword forward at Karn, the blade deflected by the haft of the axe.

Dragh moved again, always bouncing on the balls of his feet. "Come on, big man," Dragh goaded the tribesman as they circled each other.

Karn came at him with speed, his axe coming from below. Dragh barely caught it with his sword coming down out of high guard.

The clash of weapons was the only sound in the circle. All was quiet in the pressing darkness.

Dragh saw his breath as he panted from the action.

Karn slammed his forehead into Dragh's as he stepped forward.

Dragh reeled back; the blow had him seeing stars. Karn did not let up, he came again, swinging his axe for Dragh's head.

Dragh ducked, just in time.

He could feel the blade cut through some of his hair. Dragh drove up with all his might, driving the top of his head into Karn's chin.

He felt the connection, and Karn's mouth snapped shut with an audible click.

Dragh steadied himself, wiping some blood from his eyes that had run down from a cut across his forehead. He grunted, spitting a wad of blood out, and shook his head.

Dragh lashed out with his sword at Karn's torso, but the big man pushed Dragh backward, into the crowd of men, who pushed Dragh forward again.

The big man threw himself into battle with rage now, swinging wildly and trying to kill Dragh quickly.

Dragh could feel the man's awesome strength, each blow chipping away at Dragh's defense.

Dragh realized his mistake: he was giving ground, giving Karn the advantage. Dragh struck back, trying to land blows, trying to change the tide of the battle.

The first cut landed on Karn's bare hand, at the top of the haft of his axe.

Dragh followed up with another to Karn's arm and then his leg.

Karn circled warily now. Dragh and Karn circled each other, both breathing ragged, blood on their bodies glinting black in the moonlight.

Dragh knew he had to end it; he'd not survive longer than the larger and stronger axe man. He knew there was only one way. To win the fight, he had to be willing to die.

Dragh dropped his sword and lunged forward as Karn threw down a prodigious blow from above.

The axe haft struck Dragh in the head as he drove Drago into Karn's heart through his breast.

They both fell to the ground.

A roar came from the crowd around them.

Dragh felt darkness creeping over his mind as he rolled onto his back.

"You've won, Sunborn." Teffal appeared before Dragh as he blinked the darkness away.

"Water?" Dragh asked as Teffal helped him up. His hair was matted with blood and sweat. His body ached with the cuts that Karn had scored on his body.

The chieftains surrounded Dragh, many clapping him on the back, their faces serious.

Teffal and Saravas helped him to a chair, letting him drink.

There was a moment of silence as Venatos knelt beside his champion's body, his son, saying a prayer and looking up at Dragh.

Dragh could feel the hate emanating from the man's look as he turned and stormed out of the circle. Men and women of the Leretti followed behind the Chieftain.

Dragh poured the water over his face, shaking the extra water free. "What now?" he asked them.

"The blood feud is done in the eyes of the tribes. The chieftains agree that it was a good fight. You need not worry about the Leretti while we are here at the Spires," Saravas said.

"And when I'm not at the Spires?" Dragh asked.

"He's a vindictive man, Dragh. He will strike out at you because you've killed one of his sons," Teffal shrugged.

"Perfect, I can always use another enemy." Dragh closed his eyes and leaned back.

"I will have the army of the tribes, Dragh, if your father will honor the deal. Freedom from Landor. We will march within a day." Saravas gripped Dragh's shoulder.

"You have my word, Saravas," Dragh said, gulping more water.

CHAPTER 33

"My people know war, Dragh," Saravas said with pride.

Dragh watched the army of the tribes snake out along the long column of men, women, and children. The mass of people moved with efficiency, as if they were a professional army. Dragh sat with Teffal and Saravas atop a cliff jutting out of the earth, on the lip of the Valley of the Spires. "I've not seen better. They move as one."

"They understand the need to be swift. I told the chieftains of your father's Legions and the men of the East. They have agreed to crush the East with you," Saravas explained.

Dragh struggled after his fight. His mind scrambled from the blows he'd taken. Teffal had gotten him back to his men in the camp of the Argu. There, he'd filled them in on what Dragh had done.

None were surprised. Dragh was a killer among killers.

"My father should be south of the Gallas Forest. You've sent riders?" Dragh asked.

"Indeed, four of them. If your father is out there, and he doesn't have my men killed, I will get your message to him."

Dragh thanked Saravas. He'd given a scribe a message to carry south, making sure to let the scribe know that he needed to be precise.

His father would only respond to a message from Dragh himself. He'd assume all others were false.

"We must move with them. We cannot move as two entities. This enemy is smart, they would kill us off separately and win the day," Dragh said to Teffal and Saravas.

The two tribesmen nodded. Men who preferred actions to words.

Dragh admired them.

They had talked strategy into the day after a night of meeting with the chieftains. It had been a long day, but they'd gotten the tribes moving the next day, breaking camp and moving south.

The Leretti moved reluctantly, but Teffal did not believe they'd stay with the tribes.

Chapter 34

"Teffal told me they made contact with the Easterners," Relish commented.

Hemmelle, Relish, and the Landorians sat around a campfire among the tribes. The Argu were off protecting the tribes on the move.

The night was dark, the fires and torches around them lighting the camp. Darkness crept in between the spaces of the fires. The crags and valleys sparkled like a night sky full of stars.

"How many?" Hemmelle grunted, all of them tired after a long day of marching. One of many in the last week.

"He said the East broke contact, chased the Argu but then held off, fearing the Argu offered a feint," Relish said.

"Smart. They fight like the hordes of the west. Those horsemen do the same, pulling you in by showing weakness, then surprising you with a secondary force," Dragh said "I learned of the battles between the council's nations and the horde. They are the reason that we have the Skellen Pass."

"Tricky," Hemmlle said, with some spirit in his voice.

"We'd do the same if we thought it would work, my friend. An army that does not change its tactics will be an army that loses a nation," Dragh said.

"Listen to the scholar," Zeffo said.

"He's a genius, he should really be leading the rabble," Hemmelle said back.

Relish chuckled. "We should convene the Council of Chieftains again. They should know about this."

"Traitors," Dragh muttered, smiling at the jokes at his expense. "Men, I wanted to say thank you, for all that you've done over the last year. It's been more than anyone could ask for. I tell you that I love you all," Dragh said to them.

"We know, little one," Pello said, clapping Dragh on the back.

"For you, we'd march through the Pit, Dragh," Relish said, his voice grave.

"And we'd gut Kiever himself," Hemmelle said in agreement, raising his cup. They all raised their cups.

"And I for you, men," Dragh said, getting choked up.

CHAPTER 35

"Come with me, Dragh."

Dragh awoke looking at the night sky and Saravas looming over him.

He'd fallen asleep after the night with his men. They had talked about their families, the war, and what they thought the men of the East might do in the coming days.

"Saravas, what is it?" Dragh asked.

"Come quickly, I need you to see this," Saravas said, pulling him up and leading him towards a set of waiting horses.

Dragh shook the sleep from his body, rubbing it from his eyes.

Darkness pushed in on them; he could hardly see the whites of the horse's eyes.

Dragh followed Saravas to Teffal and mounted one of the horses Teffal held. The full moon was high in the sky, illuminating the earth like a second sun.

"What's happened, Saravas?" Dragh asked as they kicked their horses into motion.

Saravas said nothing, pushing his horse into a gallop.

Dragh had no choice but to follow, the cold wind whipping into his face. He fought back tears at the cold air.

They headed south. There were hills and craigs as far as the eye could see.

Dragh knew this land north of the Gallas Forest as the land they'd lost the Second in. Dragh could still smell the smoke of the day in his nose. He could still feel the tears in his eyes. The anger was there; it lingered, ready to ignite into flames of rage.

They slowed, Saravas letting Dragh catch up to him after many leagues.

"We went to the fort. The king has sent his men to treat with us," Saravas said to Dragh.

Dragh said nothing.

What would his father do? He knew that Dragh was there to find peace. He knew that the tribes were a powerful enemy, but a powerful ally too. Who would he send? One of the generals? General Artoro, General Marcus ?

He knew these men. The Generals of Landor had been at his father's court for many years, before Dragh's eventual outcast from the Eighth, and his time in the Second.

His father would have wanted him to learn from these men.

So Dragh ran; he ran from the crown, and he ran from responsibility.

Now he was responsible for bringing the tribes together with the men of Landor. How time had changed him.

They trotted through the night, joining a large group of the Argu closer to the Gallas Forest.

They moved through the patrols of the night without protest. Saravas sometimes stopping for reports and then galloping back to them as they moved.

Dragh didn't know the area as well as Saravas and his men, but he'd been here once before, hunted and hurting. He remembered enough. They were close.

The old fort was a skeleton on the plains of the North. Its remains were a reminder of itself. A hulking shell of what once was.

Even in the low light of the dawn, the burnt-out camp looked like an unnatural scar on the landscape as Dragh moved through the woods surrounding the camp.

It was quiet, as if death was still in this place. There was no sound but the movement of their horses through the thick foliage.

Dragh shook his head, bad memories flooding him. A man nailed to the wall. The charred smell of burning flesh. There was no smoke in the air, but Dragh could still smell the ash and the burned wood.

Saravas signaled two of the Argu to stop as they spotted the camp.

They exited the ring of woods around the camp.

As they rode into the husk of a camp, they slowed to a walk, all of them alert and wary of an attack.

A night attack was something they all knew that the men of the East would do.

Dragh dismounted and handed his reigns to one of the tribesmen. The surly man gave him a curt nod back. Old hostilities were a hard thing to forget.

Three hooded figures were walking along the inside perimeter of the old walls. Most of them burnt so completely that all you could see of them was ash at the top of the mound of earth. The large piles of earth thrown up were the only real defense against any line of sight.

"Ho, men of Landor," called Teffal.

The hooded figures moved towards them.

Dragh recognized the colour of Landor, red and gold. He thought they had the look of Praetorians, jittery and always scanning. He braced himself. The Praetorians were a hard bunch, and they hated the tribesmen.

The first man threw his hood back.

"Father?" Dragh asked.

Kallen's face, a match of Dragh's, was smooth in the moonlight. None of the marks of his age upon him. "Son, I knew you'd be here."

"King Kallen," Saravas greeted the king of Landor.

"What do I call you? Saravas, Chief?" Kallen asked.

Teffal shifted, his hand on his sword. The edge in Kallen's voice gave him pause.

"You can call me Saravas, king," Saravas said, defusing the situation.

Kallen smiled then, some of his frustration bleeding out of his voice. "You can call me King."

Saravas laughed, the formalities over with.

"Why here, Father? In this place?" Dragh asked about the meeting.

The other two men removed their hoods, two Praetorians who Dragh didn't know.

"I came here to see, Dragh. I needed to. My men died here. I sent them to their death. I wanted to feel the anger and the hate. To be ready for what's to come," Kallen explained.

Dragh was surprised by his father's honesty in front of the tribesmen.

War was the great equalizer. All men were stripped back to their base.

"I am sorry, King Kallen," Saravas said with sincerity. "I know the feeling of loss. We all do in the North."

"Will you put aside our differences and fight with me against this menace from the East?"

"Your son fought to defend Landor's honor. The chieftains accepted the terms. If you will hold to them." Saravas motioned to Dragh.

Kallen eyed his son with a curious look. Then looking back to Saravas, Kallen nodded. "I am pleased to hear it. The tribes will have their freedom. I swear it on the Sunborn name."

Dragh held back a laugh. His father, ever a politician, he thought.

"The chieftains have decided we will fight with Landor," Saravas committed.

"I wish for a lasting peace, Saravas. The tribes would grow stronger with Landor as her ally," Kallen said. "One king to another."

Saravas nodded his thanks to Kallen for the compliment. "Fighting gives us, in the tribes, a measure of a man. We will talk when we feast over the corpses of these invaders."

"I will send my general, Marcus, north. He will coordinate with you and your chieftains for the battle plans."

Kallen paused, looking to his Praetorians. "I would like to speak with my son now."

Kallen shook Saravas's hand and they parted ways.

"Come with me, son," Kallen said to Dragh.

Dragh walked with his father. The masses of ash round the burnt-out camp brought back dread and sadness in Dragh that he'd not expected.

He looked around, seeing the camp as it was before his squad had gone out on patrol.

He thought of his squad, of Legate Jaze. Or even Cello. The old primus had tried to be a leader, he hadn't deserved the death he received.

"I can't help but think that I should have known. I should have seen the contempt in both of them," Kallen said, surprising Dragh.

Dragh considered his father, his typical icy demeanor dropped.

"I was thinking about the same, Father. How couldn't I see it? I should have known on that first day on the sea."

"We will have our revenge," Kallen said, his voice thick with regret.

Dragh walked with him, pausing at things he recognized, the things that had surrounded him in his time with the Second on campaign. A pot for cooking. Stones laid out for small fires, where he and his men had gathered.

"I am proud that you made primus, son. I always knew you would be more than you thought of yourself," Kallen said, gripping Dragh's shoulder for a moment.

"It didn't feel like I earned it, Father," Dragh said, remembering how he'd made primus and Cello had been demoted.

"I had reports of the attack by both Jaze and... my brother," Kallen said. "They both gave accounts of you taking control at the gates of the camp. They both commended you for your action."

"You know I found Yarrs," Dragh said, remembering the old man.

"You did? I always knew he'd wanted to return to his people," Kallen said with a small smile on his lips.

"He'd become a chieftain of his village. One of the Council of the Chieftains." Dragh said.

"He was always smarter than a Praetorian should be," Kallen chuckled. "What happened to that old bastard?"

Dragh paused. Remembering the blood, the smell of innards. "They... they killed him in their quest for war."

Kallen's face flickered with darkness. He said nothing. They continued to walk the perimeter of the camp, now halfway around it. Their men were in the center of camp, talking quietly and watching the pair.

"I came here to see it with my own eyes," Kallen said by way of explanation. "I need you to remember that for when I'm gone, Dragh."

Dragh said nothing, not wanting to argue with his father.

"I know that your son will lead Landor when I die. I accept that you will not take the crown." Kallen stopped and turned to Dragh. "I accept it, Dragh. I ask that you be the sword of the nation, the shield."

Dragh paused, not sure what to say to his father. He'd been fighting him for so long that his father's acceptance surprised him.

"You will show him the way. You will show him that a man must never command men to their death without a cause worthy of spending their lives. You will know that blood cannot be shed without thought on some petty thing."

Kallen waved his hand around at the camp.

"I did this."

Dragh protested but was stopped by his father's hand.

"I am the king. No matter what happens, it is my responsibility."

Dragh looked at his father in a new light. "How? It's too much to bear."

Kallen nodded. "And you will bear it for your son until he is ready. You will be his shield and his sword until he is a man."

Dragh looked down at his hands, the scars standing out among the grime and dirt. He flexed them, balling them into the fists he'd used to kill, over and over again. He shook his head. "I'm nothing but a killer. All I know is death. How can I?"

Kallen watched his son, narrowing his eyes. "My son. We look to the Gods for answers, but they are right in front of us." Kallen held out his own hands.

Dragh looked at them. They were scarred like Dragh's own, white livid scars on the back, some of them over his wrists and forearm.

"We are all killers. The world makes us into what we hate most." Kallen paused, taking in a breath. "What matters is what is in here." Kallen put his hand on Dragh's chest.

"It doesn't change what I've done," Dragh said, remembering all the horrible things he'd done with his life that burned him with shame.

"I... regret more than I will ever be able to tell you, son." Kallen wiped his sleeve across his eyes. "What matters is that we be the men that we want our children to be in this world. That we do not kill with hate, but only to defend the very things that we love."

Dragh cleared his throat. "I... don't know how."

"You are my son, Dragh. I haven't been there to show you. I promise you, from now on, I will be. We are the line of Sunborn. And we will make our ancestors proud. We go to defend our nation, our people, against this evil."

Dragh took a moment to collect himself. His fears of the future and the fear he wouldn't be a good father out in the open made him raw.

"Some hands are bloody. Mine will not wash clean," Kallen said, looking down at his hands. Kallen gripped Dragh by his shoulders. "What makes a man is his actions, my son. Forgiveness is what we all strive for. I ask for yours now, son."

Dragh nodded to his father, choked up at the truth between them now.

"Thank you, Father," Dragh mumbled, his voice breaking.

Kallen gave his son a real smile, his teeth showing, his cheeks rosy. "Together."

"Together," Dragh said to his father.

They kept walking, not talking for a time. The group of men they'd brought loomed closer to them as they walked.

"You brought the tribes here. You killed that old bastard's champion to bring them here. You did what was needed," Kallen said.

Dragh wondered at Kallens's source of information. What spies he must have, to know of the fight between him and Karn.

"Let us talk to our brethren and see if we can bring an end to this madness," Kallen said, pulling Dragh into a hug.

Dragh wrapped his hands around his father, tears coming unbid to his eyes.

"Survive this, Dragh. I need you," Kallen said.

Dragh let the tears stream down his face. "You too, Father."

The two made their way back to the tribesmen and guards. Dragh wiped at his face, unashamed at the tears he cried now, unashamed for the first time in many years.

"Saravas!" called Kallen, his voice commanding.

Dragh nodded to Teffal, and the tribesman nodded back.

"King, what have you and your son decided?" Saravas asked.

"The men of the East know where you are, where you march to." Kallen put his hands behind his back, pacing between them. "They also know of my Legion's landing. They move now to the west, trying to encircle and flank you."

Saravas and Teffal shared a look. One that Dragh understood after so long with the men.

"What are you truly saying?" Saravas asked.

Kallen paused, looking Saravas up and down. "I'm here to tell you, one man to another. You have a traitor amongst your tribes."

"Lies!" Teffal said aloud.

"We captured a man moving south at speed, ahead of your own messengers, Saravas," Kallen said, looking at Teffal after his outburst.

Saravas cursed, looking to Teffal and then to his other Argu. "I knew it was a risk. We brought your son into the council, and he killed one of the Leretti. It was bound to cause a rift between the tribes."

Dragh understood, this was the price of the blood feud. Betrayal.

Saravas locked eyes with Dragh and nodded. "The Leretti will be gone by the time we return to the tribes."

"You must find him, kill him. He will tell them everything!" Dragh said, suddenly understanding what Venatos could do to their armies, to the war.

"I cannot," Saravas said simply.

"What kind of king are you?" Kallen asked, failing to hide the distaste in his voice.

"You flatlanders," Teffal scoffed.

Saravas held up his hand to quiet Teffal. "I am not a king, Kallen." He stared down at Kallen. "I am a Chieftain of the Argu. Do you know what that means?"

It was Kallen's turn to look confused.

"It means that my family, my son, daughter, and wife, are all dead. Their blood covered my very hands," Saravas said. "I was charged with leading the Argu, a tribe of outcasts. A tribe of men and women with nothing. We serve the tribes, we defend them."

Kallen looked on with a softer face, his disdain gone.

"I am a chief of war for the tribes. I will not hunt one of them down while the defense of all tribes hangs in the balance. Let these men come. They will find nothing but cold steel. Not some children playing at war. I will KILL THEM ALL," Saravas said, his nostrils flaring, his eyes wild.

"I understand," Kallen said, bowing slightly to the man in respect.

Dragh watched the two men of power face each other, a force of will that made Dragh feel small and weak.

Kallen and Saravas were both powerful in different ways. Kallen's power rolled off him, a king with the bearing of power. Saravas's power was a quiet power, one that leaked from him, his actions; his words had weight, meaning.

Dragh knew he was watching two forces that would destroy each other if they could not reach agreement today.

"I ask that you take my son. He will be my general in this war," Kallen said to Saravas.

Dragh's mouth opened. He tried to say something but was faced with a quiet smile from his father.

"We will take him. His council will be valued in the times ahead of us," Saravas said to Kallen.

"Dragh, you remember the tales of the empire, the tales of when they faced the horde?"

Dragh smiled at his father. "We will be ready. Where?"

Kallen looked at Dragh, excited at the prospect of battle in his face. "Be ready at the Farrin Gap."

"Aye, Father," Dragh said, giving his father a salute, his fist against his chest.

"Fight well, King," Saravas said goodbye, turning and walking from the meeting.

Dragh met his father's gaze one more time. A kindred spirit now. They nodded to each other.

Chapter 36

"What do you think we are? Barbarians?" Teffal asked Relish.

Relish and Zeffo roared with laughter as Teffal and Genne watched them. The two Argu trading skeptical looks.

Dragh chewed on a leg of mutton from the mountains as his men and the Argu talked around their camp fire.

They ate and drank even before battle, a feast for the ages across the tribes. Dragh could hear merriment and celebration from the fires around them, happiness and boasting, whoops and shouts from young men in contests of strength and games of the mind.

Dragh felt at ease amongst the tribes now, his former prejudice gone.

Saravas laughed with them, shaking his head at the argument that Genne and Teffal were having with the Landorians.

"Well then, tell us about it," Relish said, "if it's in your histories, too?"

"What? Tell you the histories? Then there will be no proof that you know!" Genne said, swigging from his ale horn.

"Come on!" Hemmelle groaned. "Dragh, what do you think?" the big man asked, his eyes cheerful and drunk.

"I think that you should be drinking water, my friend," Dragh said. Happy that his men were ready for the battle tomorrow.

They had made it back to the tribes easily. Saravas sent out scouts to ensure that their betrayal by the Leretti would not have them killed on the path to the Farrin Gap.

He and Dragh had discussed the battle plan for the Farrin Gap. They both shared history there; men of the empire and men of the tribes had fought at Farrin. Dragh had read in his studies that it was the beginning of a treaty that had lasted hundreds of years.

Until it was broken by the blood feud from a murdered shaman in the flatlands. The tribes had revolted, and many died.

"I think it's time, Argu. We need our strength for the morning," Saravas said to them, the moon high in the sky.

Genne snorted, swigging at her horn of ale.

Teffal laughed with Hemmelle and the others.

Dragh and Saravas had spoken to the Council of Chieftains, explaining the plan.

They had only asked if the Landorians could be convincing enough. Dragh had assured them that his father could play the part that was needed. He knew his father, and he would ensure there was no escape for the men from the East. They'd be dead to the last man.

The trap had been planned, now it was for the bait.

"Hemmelle." Dragh asked him to stay behind as the rest of the warriors departed with their usual grumbles.

They sat together, the fire still roaring with wood. Dragh poked at it with a long stick, his poker. He pushed and prodded at the coals and at the logs, turning them over, sending up embers like fireflies into the night sky.

The dark sky was ink black, stars shining brightly.

"You feel it?" Hemmelle asked.

Dragh grunted his response.

"I do too, we are not ready for tomorrow. The tribes, they are furious fighters. But they are not the Legions of Landor, are they?" Hemmelle replied.

"They are not, and they do not have the strength that we do," Dragh said.

"I've seen them, Dragh. They mass, they shout, and—" Hemmelle paused.

In the Farrin Gap, they would be facing a charging army. A mass of men and horse flesh. It would not do to face them with weakness.

"They will break," Hemmelle said simply.

"We must hold them. Are you with me, Hemmelle?" Dragh asked. "I know what I've asked of you. It's not fair, but I need you."

"To the Pit, Dragh," Hemmelle said. "I'd follow you to the Pit if you asked me."

"We will be their strength tomorrow. The Argu and us," Dragh said, thankful for his friend.

—--

Dragh and Saravas sat on their horses overlooking the large gap between the mountains and a large canyon in the east. The canyon stretched on for leagues.

The mountains west of the Gallas Forest were of the Car Lauch Mountains range. Angry and jagged, with a biting wind howling off of them.

Dragh took a drink of his water skin and passed it to Saravas, who accepted it with thanks.

"My father's men will be moving quickly. We need to ensure that we cannot be seen before they are committed," Dragh said.

Saravas peered out over the Pass. "It has enough gullies and hills that from horseback we can be sure we are not seen. A line of at least seventy-five men wide can cover it at the narrowest point."

"Is the work complete?" Dragh asked, looking out at where they would position the front line.

"The Argu that we sent out worked all night in the cover of darkness. Did you send word to your father?" Saravas asked.

"I did." Dragh paused. "My men and I want to be in the centre of the line with the Argu."

Saravas shook his head. "No, you'll be on the right flank with the Belge, as we discussed with the chieftains."

"You know they can hold the flank. I'm worried about the rest of them."

"You need not worry about the tribes, Dragh. We are a people made for war," Saravas said, dismissing Dragh's concerns.

"Look at me, Saravas," Dragh said quietly.

Saravas looked off into the distance of the gap. He slowly turned to Dragh, defiance in his eyes.

"I am a man of war, like you," Dragh stated, his voice even. "You and I know that while these men and women of the Tribes are built for the North, they do not have the experience of an army of soldiers. The Laretti have left us, that coward Venatos gave us up as fast as he could."

"It makes no difference. The Tribes will stand," Saravas said.

"I need you to understand that the Argu are going to be the backbone, and we will be with you there."

Saravas took some time, looking into Dragh's eyes, before giving him a nod. "It will be so."

Dragh sighed. "We will beat them together, I promise you."

The two men sat in an uneasy silence. Saravas was in his own world, preparing for the coming battle, the weight of his men, his tribe, and his people on his shoulders.

Dragh sat on his horse and thought of his father, the Legions that he sent. He thought of Lucille and his child. They'd be born now, a boy or girl, he did not know.

No messengers could make their way to Dragh in this war. He was with the tribes.

"Zufier, please let me see her." Dragh looked up into the sky. Communing with the Gods.

A horn sounded in the distance, echoing off the peaks and through the gap. Another took up the note. Two long blasts.

"They are coming," Saravas said to Dragh.

"Let us meet them with cold steel," Dragh said.

"General." Saravas nodded, pushing his mount back to the line of the tribesmen.

Dragh followed after a moment, emptying his mind for the battle to come. He would sow death today.

————

"How's the shoulder?" Dragh asked, watching Hemmelle swing his axe back and forth in front of his body.

Hemmelle grinned, swinging his axe fast enough to make the blades sing.

Men and women around him took a step back, their eyes narrowed in concern.

"How's the head?" Hemmelle fired back as Dragh let his mount be led away from them.

Dragh laughed at the comment, his nerves firing with the upcoming battle. He could hear the commotion from the other end of the Farrin Gap, shouts and the clash of steel. His father's first force of men would be running towards them now.

"The fox will chase the hare, if it smells the blood," Dragh said. His tutors had explained the feint to him. Pulling the enemy into the gap, a false weakness.

"You and your tutors," Hemmelle laughed aloud, garnishing some looks from the Argu as they firmed up the middle of the tribal army.

Savaras was in front of the army, facing the thousands of warriors with Dragh and his men.

The sun shone down on him, its rays burning through the clouds of the North.

The grass had begun to push up from the earth, giving it a glow of green, the colour of life across the Farrin Gap.

Dragh smiled. Hemmelle, Relish, Geral, Zeffo, and Pello were at his side. "Ready, men of Landor?"

"We are ready to die for Landor," the men said, dark chuckles from them all.

It was time for vengeance. These men of the East would know death soon.

Saravas held up his sword, the blade glimmering in the sunlight high above them in the blue sky. The murmuring, banging on their hardened leather breastplates, shouts for bravery, all stopped, standing stark still at Saravas's call for quiet.

"My brothers and sisters!" Saravas bellowed.

Dragh was surprised at the hard looking warriors of the tribes. Men and women both stood in their army. Such as it was.

"Ambi, Belge, Bevoni all standing with the Argu," Saravas called them all out, one at a time.

The tribes answered his call, excitement thick in the air. Th cries for blood were deafening.

"We are here to avenge the death of our people." Saravas pointed to the Farrin Gap rising on either side of them. They were in a slight depression, half-way up the north side so that they wouldn't be facing a charging army on horseback downhill.

"We fight with the Landorians, the flatlanders! Who will show them how we fight?" he asked loudly, a challenge in his voice.

A roar came from the Argu, then the Belge on the right flank.

Saravas shook his head. "They can't hear you in Landor! I SAID, WHO WILL SHOW THEM HOW WE FIGHT?" Saravas roared at the tribes.

Dragh felt the earth shake with the bellowing answer that the tribes let loose at Saravas. Their eyes were alive with bloodlust. Dragh knew at that moment the tribes were a tide of war, not like a Legion, but a wave from the ocean that would crash over their enemy.

He shuddered.

"BLOOD AND HONOUR!" Saravas cried out.

"BLOOD AND HONOURRRRR!" the tribes screamed back, the noise rolling across the mountains and down the pass.

"Pit be damned, I'd turn around if I were from the East," Hemmelle muttered so that only Dragh could hear him.

Saravas walked back to take his place beside Teffal, between Dragh and Hemmelle. "Fight well, flatlanders." He saluted them in their way.

"Kill them all," Dragh growled, his mind in the battle.

The Landorians, real ones, crested the rise in front of the Landorians and the collection of tribes moments later. Dust rose behind the enemy squads, their horses lathered with foam and spittle. Dragh could see the eyes of the riders and horses.

The Landorians looked as though they were shocked to see the tribes, so many of them in one place, an army in front of them.

The horsemen bunched. A couple of flags marked the outer boundaries of the archers' firing lines. The Landorians squeezed their squads between them, just five horses across, pushing in to form a tight line.

"Thank the Gods," Relish and Hemmelle both said as the Landorians crossed the outer boundary.

Dragh was relieved when they turned a lazy arc to the right flank of the tribe's army. Saravas and Dragh had asked his father to send a full squad of cavalry. He hoped they'd been enough bait to pull the brunt of the enemy in.

"They should be following. Wait for it!" Dragh said, his sword in his hands, his palms sweating. He felt the ache of his bladder; the nerves running through his body were on fire.

"Men of Landor!" Dragh shouted. The sound of the hooves was loud, and the earth was shaking again.

"Archers, prepare!" Saravas called out again. The command was repeated back to the units of archers arrayed slightly uphill of the main body of the army.

Dragh felt the anticipation of the army, the mass of tribesmen. They tensed as the first of the false Landorians, the men from the East, charged over the crest of the hill chasing the real Landorians.

Dragh had to give them credit. He could see the ripple of surprise in the body of the horsemen. Not one of them stopped, but a simple change in tactics was called, shouted in a language that Dragh himself didn't understand. They slowed slightly and then charged, spurring their horses down the crest.

Horse upon horse followed, squads of them.

Dragh held his breath, not letting himself hold onto hope that the enemy might fall into their trap, the one that had the tribe digging all night. The enemy horsemen pushed their mounts to a canter, narrowing their line of horses to twenty across.

"READY!" Dragh shouted at the same time as Saravas.

Archers pulled back on bowstrings.

The enemy horsemen on either side of the middle five pitched forward as they hit the boundary of the archers' flags.

"FIRE!" Saravas shouted. The call echoed in the valley as the swish of fletching whistled in the air.

The screams of horses and men, bloodcurdling pain, was loud, echoing in the valley.

Dragh cringed. Death was here, and her hunger would be sated this day.

The center of the line that made it through was assailed with arrows, falling and reaping death from the sky. The archers knew they need not fire on either side of the center—those men fell into the large trench filled with spikes. The Tribes had dug on either side of the center channel for their armies to cross.

The lines of horsemen behind the charging line pushed more men into the trenches, filling the trenches up; men and horses both died.

Between the flight of the arrows, more and more horsemen poured through the gap. They quickly stopped, bottlenecked. Arrows flew fast through the air, bringing death.

The enemy pushed their way through by numbers. More and more horsemen had made it safely through the gauntlet. They massed and charged at the tribesmen.

Dragh gripped his sword, ready for battle. His knife, Drago, was in his other hand. Dragh was always moving forward, never defending.

Arrows flew still, up and then down. Many fell, but many continued on.

The arrows slowed, thousands having been spent already.

"SPEARS!" called Dragh.

The Tribes moved forward with spears, throwing them as the horsemen came within striking distance. Many fell, but there were more and more coming.

"HOLD THE LINE!" Saravas called out. The horsemen were bearing down on them.

Dragh screamed out a guttural war cry, and the men all around him did the same as the two front lines clashed.

Dragh felt the blow of the sword on his own held in the high guard. The blow made his legs weak. He felt the pain radiate down his arm.

The next horseman behind the first rode directly at Dragh. He rolled forward, his sword held up as he dove to the left of the horse. He felt his sword bite the legs of the horse as he'd dove under the swing of the rider's sword.

As he continued up, he heard the horse crash into the ground. The horse screamed, the rider too.

Dragh kept moving, always forward. The dagger was in his belt now— he needed both hands to defend as he was attacked.

"FORWARD, MEN!" Dragh called, not waiting to see if he was being followed.

He ran towards the carnage, the screams, and the blood.

Dragh struck out, parrying swords and dodging the bodies of horses as the Easterners came at him. Men on foot, unhorsed in their ditches, made their way through to the lines of the tribes. Dragh fought them, killing and cutting.

He lost track of the men he fought; the mechanics of what he was doing took over his body.

Dragh caught sight of Hemmelle on his right, the large battle axe hewing a path of death behind. He could see Relish on his left, bloodsoaked, but battling through a gash on his forehead.

Horns sounded in the distance. Dragh paused. There was a lull in the battle.

Hemmelle and Relish, both heaving clean air into their lungs, came to his side.

"There are too many," Relish said, looking at the mass of horsemen on the other side of the trenches.

Thousands still.

Dragh looked around. He and the men with him had fought their way to the gap in the archers' forward markers.

Some of the tribe had fought with them, but most of them were still engaged in fighting the Easterners who had made it through the defenses.

"More of them up there," Hemmelle said through gritted teeth.

Dragh looked back up the hill. They were on the upward slope of the opposite hill they'd started on. The Farrin Gap was high on the sides, hemming them in.

"Where are you, Father?" Dragh asked aloud.

"He should have been here already, Dragh," Geral said, defeated.

"We have more killing to do than the men of Landor," Dragh said to them, trying to keep hope alive, if not for a short amount of time.

"Aye. We do," a voice came from behind them.

They turned around, ready for another fight, as the men of the East massed at the top of the hill in front of them.

Saravas, Genne, Teffal, and what appeared to be the remaining Argu had made their way forward to them.

Saravas limped from a wound on his right leg.

Genne's left arm was hanging limp at her side, her brown hair splashed with blood. The rest of the Argu limped or clung to injured limbs.

Dragh smiled through the gore that splattered his face.

"If my father lives, he will pin them," Dragh said. His own concerns burned hot in him, but he wanted to project calm on these men and women who were about to die.

"If this is the end, I'm happy to have fought with you, flatlanders," Teffal grunted.

They laughed, turning to the massing men of the East.

Those without horses were preparing a charge from the top of the hill, connecting themselves in whatever legions and squads they had organized themselves in.

"They fight like dog shit, but there are many of them," Saravas said. "Blood and Honour, my friends."

Dragh scoffed. "More of theirs than ours I hope."

"Make ready, here they come," Saravas said as the men of the East began their descent to meet them.

Dragh felt the men around him bunch up, a tension that was all too familiar to him. He let his mind empty, the wounds, the fatigue. He let it all go; he knew that it did him no good to hold onto it. He closed his eyes and let out a breath.

"Hic Sunt Dracones." Dragh said.

The men of the East came on, running on foot and riding on horse downhill now, quicker and quicker.

The line braced.

Dragh could feel the vibration in the ground as they advanced.

Dragh dropped his sword into a low guard. Fighting men uphill was different; it meant certain death. The first man to reach him swung hard downward.

Dragh sidestepped and drove his sword through the man's face, killing him and throwing him backward into his own ranks.

Dragh threw his shoulder into the next man to challenge him, knocking him over.

Dragh then drove his sword through the enemy's chest and into his heart.

Then he was in the crush of battle.

The two lines were pushing inward, the men in the middle being crushed between them.

Dragh could feel it, men pushing on both sides, but Dragh's side was losing ground. He pushed and pushed, but could make no difference.

He was bound up between the Argu and whatever other tribes had made it forward, and the enemy. Dragh couldn't swing down, and he couldn't move forward. He shouted and drove his legs and knees into the enemy, trying to hurt them, trying to survive.

A blade thrust forward, cutting his cheek. He reared back from the sharp pain. Dragh couldn't get his sword down from about his shoulders. The crush of bodies didn't allow the space. Instead, he opened his palm, letting the blade drop down, and changed his grip so that the blade was faced downward.

Dragh stabbed out with the blade, skewering the eye of the man in the second line in front of him.

The enemy he was pressed up against took an arrow in the eye, screaming into Dragh's ear.

Dragh cringed, closing his eyes. His breath became ragged. He could hardly breathe in the space he was trapped in.

He began to think he'd be suffocated. He prayed to the Gods. He wanted to make it home. This was no way to die.

He began to heave for air. The crush. The bodies. He couldn't move, couldn't think. His mind began to fog.

Tears rolled down his face.

This was how it was going to end.

Not with glory, not with rage or honour. He was going to be crushed in the fight between the tribes and the men of the East. The men that his uncle Nestor and Ellis had brought to these shores to sow unrest in Landor and the North.

He'd done his best.

—

A loud horn sounded, echoing off the mountains and the Farrin Gap.

"Dragh! It's Landor!" Hemmelle wheezed, out of breath.

Dragh opened his eyes, the will to live lighting within him. He gasped, pushing himself up, kicking and shouting to get his body to move upward. He climbed on the shoulders of men around him until his torso was released from the crush.

He sucked sweet fresh air.

He pulled Hemmelle, the man closest to him, up so that he could breathe. They hacked at the living around them, in front of them. The battle was a dirty, crushing front of death. Bodies on both sides held up, dead. Blood and shit oozed from them.

Dragh and Hemmelle were unable to drop to the ground because of the pressure on both sides.

"There they are!" Dragh said, pointing up the hill to the rest of the Landorian army that had followed their cavalry feint.

"Thank the Gods. I didn't know if I'd make it," Hemmelle said.

It started as a ripple moving backward. The enemy responded, turning their rearguard to face the new threat.

Dragh and Hemmelle dropped down back into the front ranks as the pressure was relieved. The enemy backed off, and the tribes pulled back.

The space, the length of a couple of horses, opened up between the armies.

Dragh eyed their enemy with wariness. His body was heavy, weary.

The men of the East stared back with hate in their eyes. The wounded from both sides writhed and screamed on the ground between the armies.

Screams pierced the air between the armies.

"Men of Landor!" Dragh called out. The horns of his father's army called out over the hollow they battled in.

"BLOOD AND HONOUR!" screamed Saravas, his voice carrying out the war cries of the enemy.

"BLOOD AND HONOUR!" the army behind Dragh roared, their screams giving them anger and energy to move forward, staving off the exhaustion of the fighting they'd already done.

Dragh ran at the enemy, screaming as he did. The roar of two armies clashing boomed from above where his father had attacked the rear of the army.

Dragh swung at the first man he met, driving the sword into the man's neck from above. The spurt of blood from the man's neck squirted into Dragh's eyes, blinding him for a moment. He wiped at his face, clearing his eyes just in time to see an axe driving towards his face.

He ducked and rolled into the man's legs, crashing the man to the ground with him. He clamoured with the big man, the axe between them.

Dragh wrestled with the blood and guts that coated his arms and hands after rolling on the ground.

Dragh saw stars as someone kicked his head.

Dragh was flipped on his back by the big man. Dragh fought on, trying to stave off the darkness he felt at the edge of his vision.

If he passed out, he would die.

Dragh let the axe fall, keeping one hand in front of his neck. He could smell the bastard's breath as he tried to choke the life from Dragh, pressing down on top of him.

Dragh slipped his arm down, his hand wrapping around his gifted knife, Drago.

He pulled Drago from its sheath and jammed it into the man's guts, pulling up and driving the blade towards the man's lungs and heart.

The Easterner on top of him wheezed as Dragh felt the hot mass of guts and blood fall out of the man's body and onto Dragh. He rolled the man over, pulling the axe from the dead man's hands.

Dragh was up. Drago left in the man's guts, the battle axe in his hands.

He screamed. Death was all around him, the pain in his head raging.

He threw his axe into the closest man, and shot by him.

He choked a man to death with his bare hands and then moved to the next.

He killed, and blood and death followed him, a mess, a blur.

Dragh couldn't tell what was happening in the battle. All he knew was that he had to survive. He had to make it to the other side. To his father.

"Dragh!" the call bellowed from his side.

Dragh looked around. His instinct, more than his thoughts, propelled him back just in time to miss the sword and horseman who barreled towards him.

Dragh ducked and slashed, the horseman gone into the mist of battle.

"Dragh!" the call came again. In the confusion, Dragh could only hack his way toward the voice.

Men came at him, one at a time. The real battle line had moved up the hill, towards the Landorians.

Dragh made it to Hemmelle, who, under a horse, called for Dragh.

Dragh felt relief as he pulled his friend free of the death trap he was in. Hemmelle had bodies on either side of him, half-covered by the horse.

He sat his friend up, looking around.

"Where is Relish, the rest of them?" Dragh asked, trying to get his bearings.

"I don't know." Hemmelle winced, his leg broken, twisted in an odd direction.

The calls of Landorian horns made Dragh look up beyond the horse and to the upper battle lines. "They are charging. The Landorian Cavalry are going to break them."

Hemmelle tried to twist back and look, but he cried out in pain, looking down at his legs.

Dragh looked back at his friend. Hemmelle's color was gray and there was sweat on his brow. "You need help."

Hemmelle winced. "Go, finish this." He tried to push Dragh off of him.

"No, my friend. I won't leave you again," Dragh said, knowing what had happened the last time he left his friend.

The battle was all but done, the cavalry sweeping through the back ranks of the men of the East.

"I thought they had us in the crush." Hemmelle let the tears roll down his cheeks.

"So did I. So did I, Hemmelle," Dragh said, handing his friend a water skin he'd found lying on a nearby body.

CHAPTER 37

Dragh sat with Azal and Saravas outside the king's tent. A bright fire burned with roasting food atop it not far from the tent.

"Benefits of being king." Saravas laughed, sharing a look with Dragh.

Smoke wafted to Dragh and Saravas, the sweet smell of beef with spice and oil topping it. The sizzle of drippings from the fire mixed with the sound of crackling logs.

They stared into the fire, tiredness pulling them all down, except for Azal, who seemed sprier than either Dragh or Saravas.

"I told you, the Gods have plans for you, young Sunborn. Dying was never an option," Azal said with some smugness.

"I—" Dragh began.

"Don't bother, lad." Saravas laughed. "I've been arguing with the old shaman my whole life. He is annoyingly right."

Dragh shook his head. "How come you couldn't convince Teffal I was not the enemy before he chased me out of the North?" Dragh accused Azal.

"How did I know that he would hate you so?" Azal said, raising his eyebrow.

Dragh stared at Azal, not sure if he was kidding. "Is he going to make it?" he asked.

Saravas drew a sharp breath. "With the help of Azal's Gods, he may yet."

Dragh nodded, his thoughts with Teffal. He'd taken a blade through the chest and into one of his lungs defending Saravas.

"We are all connected. You are not done yet," Azal said, getting up from the fire.

"Where do you go?" Saravas asked.

"I go to help the tribes. There are more who need my help, beyond your selfish needs," Azal snapped at Saravas.

Saravas put his hands up, letting Azal push past him and towards the cries of the wounded.

It had been half a day since the battle, and the wounded were beyond count.

"He's ready for you," a guard called to Dragh, giving a slight bow.

Dragh chuckled, pushing up from his seat. The Praetorian, they harbored grudges for life.

Dragh looked at Saravas's bandaged leg. "Come with me, my friend. We have much to discuss about our future."

Saravas looked surprised, rising with a slight limp from his leg, and followed Dragh to the tent.

The tent was set up for war, with a map table in the middle of the generals and Kallen at its head. There were chairs set up around the table, but none sat.

Light pushed inward through the heavy fabric of the tent. The floor was planned wood, worn from use.

"Son," Kallen called, dismissing his generals.

Dragh nodded to the generals: Artoro, Marcus, Gregus, Crassu, and Xenoph. Proud generals and Landorians, they all met Dragh's eyes with a respect that he was not used to.

The men filed out of the tent, some limping from the battle, all proud in their newly cleaned armor.

"Son, Saravas." Kallen motioned them to sit on chairs and the like strewn about the tent.

They sat while Kallen poured them both cups of ale.

Dragh watched his father with confusion—the king serving them ale instead of his servants.

A rare occurrence, one he'd not seen before. Looking around the tent, Dragh noticed that there were no servants and no one else in the tent. Another oddity.

"I owe you both a debt." Kallen raised his glass to them both, taking a seat across from them.

Dragh and Saravas remained seated, drinking a warm mead of honey from the south. Dragh drank greedily.

"To the Sunborns, the Tribes thank you." Saravas returned the toast to Kallen.

Kallen smiled and nodded.

Dragh could see the sunken eyes and weary lines of his face.

This battle had been hard. It had taken life from his father.

Dragh had met with him briefly after the battle; his father spoke of the remaining men of the East. A contingent had broken through Landor's left flank, skirting the gap's outer limit and back down to the south. He'd sent an entire legion after them.

"We are in your debt for what the tribes have done, Saravas. You may call on me for anything that you like," Kallen said to the tribesman.

"I am not in control of the tribes, and I cannot speak for all of the chieftains," Sarvas said simply.

"All of the chieftains did not do this for Landor, for peace. You did," Kallen explained. "The tribes have their freedom from Landor. We will not interfere with the North."

Dragh smiled. His father was ever blunt.

"Well, there is the matter of the Leretti and Venatos," Saravas said.

Kallen looked at Dragh, then back to Saravas.

"You believe he was the one that betrayed us to the East?" Kallen asked the chieftain.

"I do. He and his men were gone when we returned from the Gallas Forest. It cannot be a coincidence. They have a deep hatred for Landor. After Dragh killed his son at the spires... Well, let's say that he has ample reason."

Kallen smirked. "It seems we have a mutual enemy. What do you propose?"

"I ask that you join me and the Argu in righting the wrong that was done to both of our people," Saravas said.

Dragh scoffed. Both of them spoke about killing casually. Dragh was ignored as the men talked details of what they would do.

Dragh was surprised to find the two men getting along well. Both of them were blunt and ruthless.

Dragh thought about Lucille and his child. How was she? Was the child healthy?

"Dragh?" His father shook Dragh's shoulder.

Dragh looked over to Saravas, but found the chair empty. He blinked.

"Back with me, I see," Kallen said, taking Saravas's chair in his stead.

"Where is Saravas?" Dragh asked.

"He's gone to rouse the Argu. We march in the morning to deal with the Leretti."

"I see you'll be doling out the king's justice," Dragh laughed. "Two enemies in one trip, that's impressive."

"The smith keeps the iron red. The smith strikes as many times as he can while the iron is hot," Kallen said, amused by his son.

"And what of me?" Dragh asked.

Kallen smiled and handed Dragh a folded piece of parchment. His face was split by a smile that Dragh did not remember his father possessed.

Dragh took the paper, confused at what it could contain that would spark such excitement. He read it, his lips forming a smile as he took in the words.

"Harin, she named him Harin!" He looked to his father, who wore the same smile as Dragh.

They stood and embraced, tears rolling down their faces.

"He will be a fine lad. A strong name!" His father squeezed Dragh's shoulders.

"I need to go." Dragh said. "But you need..."

"Nonsense, son. I will deal with the Leretti. You need to make it to Landor. Our future is on the Street of Roses," Kallen said to Dragh.

"You're certain?" Dragh asked.

Warmth filled his fathers face.

"I command you, General Dragh. Return to Landor. Take up our future prince and form your Legion. I will need both of you once this business is done in the North."

Dragh felt pride swell in him. A general by his father's hand.

"I know what I will name it, Father," Dragh said. "The Dragon Legion."

Chapter 38

Azal sat on the cliffs of Vannor; a fire blazed behind him, of driftwood and herbs. He breathed in the smoke as it pulled itself out to sea.

Visions of light and streaking stars in the sky filled his mind.

He threw his head back and started to chant.

Deep into the night, he chanted. The moon rose high in the sky, and the fire behind him burnt down to the embers of a once great blaze.

Azal saw the old man seated before him with more clarity than he should have. The lines around the old man were sharp, darkness forming into shape. The man's white hair was bright, glowing in the moonlight it reflected.

"It has been some time, my young friend," the old man said, his voice the crashing of waves on the cliffs.

Azal looked over the old man and laughed. "You never change, you cantankerous old bastard," Azal muttered.

The old man looked at Azal with a scolding look of a father to a rude son, but said nothing.

"I see fire. I see men and women, children and horses burning on a great plain now." Azal rubbed his face. "What have I done?"

The old man watched Azal, a thoughtful look on his face. "Do you doubt the fates, my old friend? Do you think that we would lead you astray?"

Azal looked at the old man, narrowing his eyes. "I see what the Sunborn will do. I see that he will be the destroyer of nations. The blood of the innocent will drench the earth by the time he fulfills his destiny." Azal paused. "What have we done?"

The old man nodded along, agreeing with Azal. "Everything that we've done, there is reason, purpose. A push and a pull to keep you on the paths that were laid generations before either of us were on this earth. You think of things as right and wrong. I've told you for generations now, there is more to it than that. There is no right and wrong; there is only the path and what is."

Azal shook his head. "It is wrong that one such as Dragh can be the cause of so much death. And yet I saved him. Am I not to blame for what he does?"

"No, Azal. He is the cause of his own destruction. He is the one to blame. Not you. He is important. Would you trade the tribes for his life?"

Azal considered the old man, knowing that he had the power to make it so. The old man's words were slippery things, full of promise and death.

"No."

"For the tribes to survive, Dragh must live. You've seen what comes of his will. His line, the Sunborn, is how your people live." the old man watched Azal.

"We do what must be done. The people of the plains will curse me, as the blood of their women and children soak the earth beneath our feet." Azal sighed.

"And the world will continue. The tribes will flourish until the times of the empire return," the old man said.

CHAPTER 39

El Alera waved to Dragh from the bow of the boat. His smile was bright against his sun-tanned skin.

"Prince! You bless us with your presence on our humble ship." El Alera waved his hands in welcome as Dragh pulled himself up and over the rail of the Ralarians' ship.

Dragh's father had sent word to El Alera to meet Dragh after the battle had been won. He had left Hemmelle, Relish, Geral, Zeffo, and Pello to start recruiting for their Legion.

The dregs, Dragh told them. Just like the Second, Dragh would make a legion of his own. He promoted all of his men to Legates before he left.

Dragh looked out on the sea; masts stuck up like the trees of the forest.

"I see that you've added to your fleet." Dragh pointed to the seven ships that had grown from three.

"Of course I did. You know what I do when I'm not transporting royals?" El Alera asked.

"What's that?" Dragh asked. He swayed with the rolling of the ship's deck, the waves low but powerful.

"We're pirates," El Alera said with a wicked grin on his face.

Dragh laughed with El Alera.

"Get me home, El Alera, I have business," Dragh said, clapping his friend on the shoulder.

"I hear that you have a squealing business to deal with," El Alera said, a glint in his eyes.

Dragh laughed. The spies that the Ralarians had in Landor were indeed good, if El Alera knew of Dragh's new child.

"Let us have a drink then," Dragh said.

El Alera led Dragh to the captain's cabin and offered him a seat.

The captain handed Dragh a cup of wine and sipped on his own.

They spoke of the past and of the future, the weaving and waning of the ship forgotten in their many cups of wine.

"It's funny. When Ellis tried to recruit us, he mentioned a priest, some man of the cloth. He'd said the priest would curse me if I rejected their offer," El Alera said.

Dragh's blood ran cold.

A priest, the Council. He had to tell his father. Their war in the North was over. Another was to begin in the south, in Landor. A war of shadows and politics.

EPILOGUE

"General!" the call rang out, a greeting and warning to the men standing at attention.

Dragh walked the walls of the camp that the Dragon Legion had built a month before. He saluted back to the men on the wall, peering into the dawn's mist.

The battlefield before him was a mess of dead men, horses and spent arrows. The injured, the ones that the Dragon Legion and the Third Legion of Landor could not rescue, had stopped crying out hours ago.

Between him and the enemy, broken homes and burnt-out buildings were all but rubble, smoking after Dragh had set them ablaze weeks ago.

He could still smell the burning after weeks of battle and blood.

All of them haunted Dragh. His sleep plagued by the men he could not save.

Across the battlefield was a fortress. One that his father, Kallen, the King of Landor, had commanded Dragh to take.

The city of Ghent had been a holdout, a thorn in the side of Landor's peace for many years. The city spoke out of one side of their mouth, but the Council's hand was a play.

The Council whispered in the darkness, egging on Ghent to train her mercenaries to kill the men and women of Landor in secret, in darkness.

The last attack had been the killing of an entire village on the borders of Landor. Hundreds of villagers were burned alive as the village was set ablaze.

Dragh had been in the throne room when the survivors had told their tale. They escaped by hiding under their dead neighbor's bodies.

Dragh's men had tracked the killings back to Ghent's walls.

Ghent had refuted the accusations.

Dragh and his father knew that they did not mean well to Landor. To the Sunborns.

He could see the dead men who he'd spent the last weeks with. Men who had trusted him to take them from Landor and deliver them to victory.

Dragh cursed.

All generals knew that death followed the Legions like a lover, hands gripping them as they marched. Waiting for an arrow or sword stroke that would deliver them into her embrace.

Dragh's hands gripped the rough-cut lumber of the camp. He felt the sharp splinters poke into his hands. He ignored the pain.

He had to end this conflict. Protect Landor and his men.

He nodded to himself.

It was time.

Dragh turned on his heel, walking from the walls to the ladder, descending and storming off to his command tent.

His guard opened the flap of his tent as he rushed in.

"Men," he acknowledged the men standing in the tent.

Relish, Hemmelle, Geral, Zeffo, and Pello stood around the maps table. They were Legates in his Dragon Legion. Their primus stood behind them, quiet and at attention.

All saluted him.

They waited for Dragh to speak, watching him.

"Raise the Dragon banner. All will die on this field of war now," Dragh said, slamming his dagger, Drago, into the map table.

All watched on, saying nothing.

Dragh met their gazes. He needed them to know that they would not be abandoned in the mud, left for dead. They were his men. And he would take his revenge on this enemy.

"They must understand that to wake the Dragon Legion is to invite death." Dragh raised his arm, pulling at his sleeve.

The blood-red dragon tattoo crept out from underneath his shirt. The dragon's body curled around his arm and down onto his hand, where the dragon ended in a snarling mouth.

All nodded.

"*Hic Sunt Dracones!*" Dragh said aloud.

The men around him raised their arms, bloodlust in their eyes.

"*HIC SUNT DRACONES!*"

ACKNOWLEDGMENTS

First, to my wife. Without your support I wouldn't be the person and the author I am today. Thank you for everything.

To my daughter, you are my legacy.

Bruce, thank you for your support, the encouragement. To the day in Hampton, NB many moons ago, when I told you that I wanted to be a writer; that I wanted tell stories and put pen to paper. You never laughed, you never discouraged. Without you, this wouldn't exist.

To Writers Together Halifax. Without you and your crit I would not have been able to tell this story. Thank you for making me a better writer. Joe, Wendy, RJ, Jason, Kevin. Now, with love and kindness, do it better!

To The Break Ins. In no particular order, strangers that have become friends: Josh, Scott, Kaden, Calum, Adrian, Rob, Louise, Sam, Bryan, Andrew, Nick, Jonathan, Nicholas, Zac and Francisca. Thank you for the push, the support and the community. Without you, this book wouldn't be out in the wild.

To my friends and family. Joan for reading the endless drafts. Dave for reading all of them, even the bad ones! Jason, for the cheap movie nights and talking stories and characters with me for so many years. Stefano, for the first writing challenge I ever did. That book will never see the light of day! Thank you for the kind words, the support and the feedback.

To my editors, Kelley Tai and Nathan Hall. Thank you both for helping me shape this story into what it is today.

To you, the reader. Thank you for picking up a new author. An aspiring author. Without your trust, the sails would have no wind. Thank you for letting me tell stories and for reading them! If you have the time, please leave a comment on a post, a review on Amazon, Goodreads or other platforms. Those things are our lifeblood.

And finally, to my Grandfather. Everett Ethen Hill. You never got the chance to read this, so this one is for you. I hope you are kicked back in your lazy boy, enjoying your study in the sky. I love you Pup.

About the Author

Isaac Hill is a self published fantasy and fiction Author from Nova Scotia, Canada. Isaac's current project is his Sunborn Series, a generational story of the Sunborn Empire. Isaac enjoys spending time with his wife and daughter in the great outdoors, reading a wide variety of stories and scribbling his own thoughts down in his spare time.

Isaac's hobbies are wide and varied. He's built a boat, owns a fully functioning blacksmiths forge, made his own traditional bows and raced on downhill skiing. Now, he collects books, typewriters and tells stories of his own. Inspired by David Gemmell, Pierce Brown and Anthony Ryan, he tells stories of heroes, of deeds echoing through generations.

You can find Isaac at:

www.isaachillauthor.com

Instagram: @isaachillauthor

X/Twitter: @isaachillauthor